The
Painter's
Apprentice

The Painter's Apprentice

Charlotte Betts

piatkus

PIATKUS

First published in Great Britain in 2012 by Piatkus

A CIP catalogue record for this book
is available from the British Library.

ISBN 978-0-7499-5822-0

Typeset in Caslon by M Rules
Printed and bound in Great Britain by
Clays Ltd, St Ives plc

Papers used by Piatkus are from well-managed forests
and other responsible sources.

MIX
Paper from
responsible sources
FSC® C104740

To Simon

The Coronation of James II

April 1685

The night air was chilled and the trumpets and the kettledrums echoed the pounding in James's head. The barge rocked a little under his feet as an anticipatory drum roll made him look up. His stomach gurgled and fizzed with gas and elation; he wondered if he should have refused the second serving of duckling. The richness of the delicious dishes, over fourteen hundred of them, at his coronation banquet in Westminster Hall that day had been enough to tempt anyone into gluttony.

Then the first fireworks burst from the platform of barges like a crack of thunder and a dazzling array of coloured stars exploded into the black dome of the night sky, dropping gobbets of white fire on to the Thames below. A gigantic blazing sun made up of firecrackers hung over the river and a myriad of water cannon shot flumes forty feet into the air, while explosive charges crackled and popped all around.

As the crowd on the banks of the Thames roared in delight, James's heart swelled in exultation. *Listen to them!* The populace loved him. His brother, Charles, had always been too afraid to stand up and declare his faith, haunted by memories of their father's execution, but now he, James II, would tear down the walls of Anglican domination just as if they were the walls of Jericho. This was *his* time. Now he had the power to bring the True Faith back to the people.

Chapter 1

November 1687

Darkness had already fallen when shouts and then the sound of a whistle blown three times made Beth's head jerk up from her easel. Her paintbrush slid from her hand and fell unheeded to the floor. Instantly alert, she reached for her own silver whistle, which always hung around her neck. Noises in the night were not unusual in a lunatic asylum but generally the disturbance came from within the walls, not from the outside.

Several sets of footsteps raced along the gallery, and in the courtyard below, Orpheus began to bark as furiously as if the Devil himself had knocked at the gate. Beth pushed open the casement and hung shivering over the sill to peer into the frosty night.

The servants had run outside with lamps and were shouting and milling around in the flickering light. The commotion was too great for anyone to hear her when she called down to them so she hurried to investigate.

In the stone-flagged hall, the front door was wide open to the night air; a small group of anxious inmates huddled together, while

Beth's mother and her youngest brother, John, attempted to reassure them. Orpheus still raged outside, his barks reverberating around the courtyard louder than a peal of bells in a belfry.

When Beth caught sight of her father's black-clad figure striding purposefully across the hall she ran after him down the front steps into the courtyard.

'Orpheus!' William Ambrose caught hold of the wolfhound's collar and pulled his huge grey head around to face him. The dog's teeth were bared in a vicious snarl, his muzzle spittle-frothed. William snapped his fingers. 'Quiet, sir! Your job is done!' Orpheus gave a throaty growl and William raised a warning finger. 'Beth, take control of this hell-hound, while I find out what is happening.'

'Yes, Father.' Beth hooked her fingers through the dog's studded collar and tickled his ears until he quietened.

Emmanuel and Joseph had a man pinned between them, his face pushed between the bars of the great iron gates. The prisoner fought furiously but he was no match for the sheer bulk and strength of the two black men.

'Let him go!' William's voice rang out above the grunts and shouts of the struggling man.

'We found him climbing over the gate,' said Emmanuel, the whites of his eyes gleaming in the lamplight. Emmanuel looked at Joseph and winked. Slowly they lowered the intruder, chuckling as they held him so that his feet hung just above the ground.

'Down, I said!'

William held up the lantern to study the trespasser, who straightened his travelling cape, adjusted the lace at his cuffs and turned to face them.

The light illuminated a young man's features, currently arranged in a scowl.

'Well, sir, what have you to say for yourself?' A frosty cloud of William's breath hung in the air between them.

Beth didn't envy the intruder. It had been a while since Father had spoken to her in that way and she sincerely hoped it would never happen again.

'Forgive me, sir.' The voice was that of an educated man but he didn't sound at all as if he was seeking an apology. Bending over, he picked up his wide-brimmed hat, now severely trampled, dusted it off, tweaked the feather back into shape and replaced it upon his head. 'I lost my way. The cart dropped me off in the village and some mischievous child thought it amusing to direct me to the wrong road. By the time I'd found someone to point me to Merryfields it was dark.'

Beth was astounded at how unruffled he sounded. He certainly didn't behave like a common thief.

'I rang the bell,' the young man continued, as he stamped clods of mud off his high boots, 'but no one answered. Since the gate was locked and the hour so late, I took the liberty of climbing over the top, intending to knock on the door.'

William frowned. 'And the purpose of your visit?'

'I have a letter for Mistress Susannah Ambrose.'

'My wife.'

'Then you must be Dr William Ambrose?'

'Indeed. And the content of this letter?'

The young man tilted up his chin. 'I prefer to speak directly to Mistress Ambrose.'

Beth saw how the visitor, only a little older than herself she judged, met Father's stare and couldn't decide if he was fearless or simply arrogant.

William grunted. 'You had better come inside before we all catch a chill.'

Joseph, his steward's keys jangling at his waist, held the lamp up high and spoke to the servants. 'Back to your duties, everyone.'

Orpheus growled again. Beth pulled on his collar and patted his wiry head.

William led the way up the steps into the hall.

Shivering, Beth closed and bolted the massive oak door behind them.

'Susannah, my dear,' said William, 'this young man brings you a letter.'

Beth's mother, her pretty face anxious, let go of Poor Joan, who had been weeping on her shoulder, and came forward. 'A letter? But what was all the shouting about?'

'The servants merely became overexcited when they thought our visitor was an intruder.'

'Well, for goodness' sake!' Exasperation showed in Susannah's green eyes. 'What a fuss about nothing!'

'Let me present . . .' William turned to the visitor, with an enquiring look.

The young man took off his battered hat, exposing a fine head of wavy chestnut hair, and bowed low to Susannah.

She gasped, her face turning as white as bone. 'But . . . ? It can't be! Tom? Oh, Tom, is it you?'

Then, almost before her husband could catch her, she fainted.

Supper was about to be served in the great hall. A fire crackled and danced in the stone chimneypiece; high up amongst the beams the vaulted ceiling, painted cerulean blue, was studded with embossed stars of gold. Antlers of ancient stags adorned the walls, a relic of the time when Merryfields had been a rich man's hunting lodge. A group of chattering people clustered around a long table, lit by candelabras and gleaming with polished pewter plate. The air was rich with the scent of woodsmoke and chicken soup.

Beth and her parents, brothers Kit and John and her sister, Cecily, filed in to take their places at the top table on the dais under the minstrels' gallery. The visitor, whose name it transpired wasn't Tom at all, but Noah Leyton, accompanied them.

William nodded at a portly man dressed in a shabby crimson

velvet coat and an extravagantly curled wig topped by a golden crown. 'Your Royal Highness, will you honour us by saying grace?'

The man bowed, cleared his throat and raised an imperious hand. 'Pray silence!'

Beth squinted at Noah through half closed lashes, stifling a laugh at his expression of amazement.

After the grace there was a scraping of chairs and the hubbub of conversation began again. Peg and Emmanuel's daughter, Sara, bustled between the tables serving the soup and bringing more bread and baskets of russet apples.

'His Royal Highness?' whispered Noah, leaning closer to William. 'Who is your illustrious guest?'

'An honorary title,' said William. 'He was born Clarence Smith but imagines himself to be Henry VIII. It's a perfectly harmless fancy but his family are unable to live with his notions.'

'So you eat with the inmates?' asked Noah, looking with raised eyebrows at the handful of people sitting at the long refectory table.

Susannah smiled. 'It's important for our *guests'* wellbeing that they feel they are a part of our happy family. A regular daily routine is helpful in guiding them back to health and happiness.'

'I had thought that *guests* in a lunatic asylum ... '

Susannah put a gentle hand on Noah's arm. 'We never call Merryfields a lunatic asylum. It is merely a place where those of a melancholic disposition can come in times of sorrow to rest and mend their spirits in good country air.'

'I h-h-help them to plant their g-g-gardens,' stuttered John.

'We have embroidery, singing and drawing groups, too,' added Beth, smiling at John, who so rarely spoke except within the bounds of his family.

Noah studied the guests, who were bent over their soup bowls. 'They certainly seem to be enjoying their supper,' he said.

'Some have helped to grow the food we eat,' said William. 'Digging and planting leave little time for melancholy.'

'It's almost disappointing that this is so far removed from how I had imagined a place such as Bedlam,' said Noah. 'I can see I must forget any notion of dining out on tales of how I broke *into* a lunatic asylum.'

Susannah froze in the act of spooning soup into her mouth and Beth glanced at her father, but William only frowned and said, 'Indeed you must.'

Beth passed Noah the bread. The hunting-green of his well-fitting coat perfectly complemented the burnished chestnut of his hair. She couldn't help noticing that his eyes were a warm shade of amber and wondered, if she were painting his portrait, how she would achieve the little flecks of gold that gleamed in his irises. 'Have you quite recovered from your unfortunate reception?' she asked.

'Perfectly! Although I can't say the same for my hat.' His lips twitched in amusement. 'And I trust you are none the worse from the shock of my arrival, Aunt Susannah?'

'You have the same lean figure as my dear brother, Tom. It must be thirty-five years since he left us but then I saw you standing there and I thought, just for a moment, that I was seeing a ghost. It's hard to imagine him as a grown man with children of his own.'

'Your hair is even redder than Beth's,' said Kit, tweaking one of his sister's copper-gold curls.

Beth glanced down the table at her siblings. All had hair as dark as their father's. 'Mama and I are the odd ones out in this family,' she said. But, of course, although William had been the only father she had ever known, his cousin, her birth father, had been fair.

'You'd feel at home in Virginia,' said Noah. 'I have three sisters and all are as red-headed as the Old Queen.'

Beth glanced at Noah from under her eyelashes. He carried with him an air of restrained energy, as clean and fresh as the scent of the air on a spring morning in the smoky hall.

'But why have you come to England?' demanded Cecily.

Noah looked down at the table. 'I fear I have been a great disappointment to my father.'

'Surely not!' Cecily looked up at him with limpid green eyes. 'How could you *possibly* be a disappointment to him?'

William gave her a sharp stare and she lowered her eyelashes.

'He has worked very hard to make his tobacco plantation so successful. He had every expectation of passing it on to me, his only son, in the hope that I would continue to fulfil his dreams and make the name of Leyton mean something in the world.'

Kit gazed intently at Noah. 'And your interests do not lie with the plantation?'

Noah shook his head. 'But I shall always be grateful that the good living Father makes from it gave me the opportunity for the education I received.'

'Where do your interests lie?' asked William.

'I am an architect.'

'An architect!' said Beth, her curiosity aroused.

Noah's face lit up. 'And I have such plans! I am come to London to learn from some of the great masters of the art. There is a great deal to see now the city has been so nearly rebuilt since the Great Fire. I shall return to Virginia and build fine houses and public buildings. *That* is how I will make the name of Leyton well known.'

'But will these fine buildings be enough to soothe your father's sadness? It would be a hard thing for a son not to carry forward his father's ambitions.' William glanced at Kit, who bit his lip and looked away.

'Perhaps not at once,' said Noah. 'Oh! I quite forgot!' He took out a letter from inside his coat, which he proffered to Susannah. 'Father asked me to give you this.'

Susannah took it with eager fingers. 'It's been more than a year since I had news from him.' She opened the letter and angled it towards the candlelight to read it.

'Noah, you will be able to stay for a few days, won't you?' said Cecily. 'There's *so* much to talk about!'

Susannah, still bent over her letter, drew in her breath and Beth glanced at her curiously.

'Do stay!' said Kit.

Noah glanced at William, who inclined his head. 'Then I would be delighted to accept your invitation.'

'Yes, of course you must stay,' said Susannah, tucking the letter away in her bodice and giving Noah a bright smile.

Beth wasn't sure but she thought she saw the gleam of tears in her mother's green eyes.

Chapter 2

The following morning Beth eased herself out of bed, careful not to allow in a draught of freezing air under the sheet, which would disturb her sister. Father rarely allowed fires in the bedrooms any more, except in the case of sickness. Cecily still slept, her mass of black hair tumbled on the pillow; Beth was determined to escape without being followed.

Shivering violently in the penetrating cold, she slipped on a clean chemise and hurriedly stepped into her favourite blue petticoat with the embroidered hem. Cecily stirred as Beth lifted the lid of the chest to take out her bodice and skirt. Holding her breath, she waited until Cecily sighed and burrowed back into her nest of blankets.

Beth laced her bodice and slipped the chain of her silver whistle over her head. She twisted up her hair, securing it with a tortoiseshell comb. Shoes in hand, she made her escape.

Gales of laughter were coming from her brothers' bedchamber as she pushed the door open. Kit and John, still in their nightshirts, were propped up against the pillows while Noah, fully dressed, lounged on the end of the bed.

'I see you are already awake and in bad company, Noah,' said Beth.

John wiped tears of laughter off his face. 'N-N-Noah was telling us about his voyage to England. One of the s-s-sailors had a parrot and he'd trained it to say all m-m-manner of things.'

'Most of them unfit for a lady's ears, I'm sorry to say,' said Noah with a warning glance.

'How long was the journey from Virginia?' asked Beth, settling herself on to the other corner of the bed.

'Six weeks. I didn't enjoy the first week very much but after that I found my sea legs. I travelled with an acquaintance, Harry de Montford, whose father is a landowner near Jamestown and he always had a merry tale to tell or some mischief to get up to. Then there were other passengers who would play a game of cards with us. And, of course, I had the care of the trees to keep me busy.'

'Trees?' asked Beth.

'The roots had to be kept damp in sacking and the leaves misted with fresh water every day. It was a constant difficulty to guard the barrel of water to prevent the sailors helping themselves. Fresh water was always in short supply on the ship.'

'But why did you bring t-t-trees to England?' asked John, his weather-beaten face puzzled. 'We have p-p-plenty of trees here.'

'Our clergyman charged me with bringing specimens native to Virginia, but unknown in England, safely into the care of Henry Compton, your Bishop of London.'

'For the gardens at Fulham Palace?' said Beth. 'The Bishop has a great collection of exotic trees and plants, I believe.'

'Indeed he has. The Bishop has been of great help to me,' said Noah. 'He was pleased with my tender care of his specimens; in return he furnished me with letters of introduction and invited me to reside in Fulham Palace. I've had the good fortune to secure the opportunity of working with Sir Christopher Wren on the construction of several churches which are being rebuilt in the city.'

'But you intend to return to Virginia?'

'Next autumn.'

Kit sighed. 'I would so like to travel to the New World. I'm tired of living in a village and tired of Merryfields.'

'How c-c-can you say that!' said John.

'Do you really wish to travel, Kit?' asked Noah, giving his cousin a searching look.

Kit shrugged. 'Father will never allow it. I am to be a doctor and in due course take his place here at Merryfields.'

John's stomach let out a growl of hunger and everyone laughed.

'Time for you lazy boys to rise from your bed!' said Beth, pulling the pillow away from behind him. 'And I shall take Noah to find some breakfast.'

Beth led Noah along the gallery, stopping to show him the solar with the minstrels' gallery overlooking the great hall.

'These old houses are full of fascination for me,' he said, running his hands over the carved oak balustrading while he peered down at the great hall below. 'We have nothing as old as this in Virginia.'

'When we were children, Kit and I used to peep down from the gallery at the grown-ups eating their dinner. Phoebe, our nurse, used to scold us back to the nursery but Mama and Father never really minded.' Beth took Noah's arm and turned him to look at the paintings that lined the panelled gallery walls. 'What do you think of these?'

Noah studied them in more detail. 'Magnificent!' he said. 'Dutch?'

'Yes. And no.' Beth smiled. 'They were painted by a Dutchman here in England. Take a closer look.' She paused beside the portrait of an elegant woman dressed in green damask, standing with her face turned to catch the light of a window.

Noah's face broke into a smile. 'Why, it's Aunt Susannah!'

13

'And if you look at the painted view out of the window you'll see that it's the garden at Merryfields.'

He leaned closer to study the delicate brushwork of the lace on Susannah's gown. 'Who is the artist?'

'Johannes van de Vyver. Would you like to meet him?'

'Most certainly!'

'Come with me, then.'

Further along the gallery Beth opened a door. She watched Noah's face, hoping that he would like her most favourite place in all of Merryfields.

Three tall windows with diamond-paned glass flooded the room with light, even on such a grey and misty day. The walls, ceiling and beams were whitewashed to reflect light to every corner and the air was heavy with linseed oil and turpentine. A paint-stained work table was cluttered with earthenware pots of brushes, a half-stretched canvas, a wine-red grinding slab of speckled porphyry and neatly folded cleaning rags. One wall was covered with marvellously lifelike botanical paintings and larger canvases of landscapes and interiors in the Dutch fashion were propped up against the walls.

A great bear of a man, untidily dressed and with ragged blond hair, stood before an extravagantly large canvas on an easel by the window. He had an ancient piece of sacking tied around his waist, encrusted with multicoloured daubs of paint. The tip of his tongue protruded through his lips as he worked.

Noah moved forward but Beth caught him by his sleeve and put her fingers to her lips.

After a moment the painter sighed and wiped his brush on his apron, adding a new rose madder stripe.

'Johannes?' whispered Beth.

The big man started. 'Ach, Beth! I tell you before not to creep up on me!' He pulled a piece of muslin carefully over the canvas, hiding it from view.

'Forgive me, Johannes, but I wanted to introduce you to Noah, lately come from Virginia. He is an architect.'

Johannes offered his hand, noticed that it was smeared with ultra-marine paint and wiped it on his breeches. 'Everyone was talking about you at supper last night.' His English was good, although he spoke with a Dutch accent.

Noah bowed. 'I've been admiring your work displayed along the gallery, sir. I, too, like to draw but I recognise real skill when I see it.'

Johannes shook his head. 'My efforts are never enough.'

'Johannes is as hard a taskmaster to himself as he is to others,' said Beth, smiling fondly at him.

'May I see?' Noah moved towards the canvas but the artist folded his sturdy arms and blocked the way.

'No one sees my work until it is finished!' He glanced at Beth with a half-smile. 'Except for Beth, if she has worked hard.'

Noah glanced around the studio, taking in a still life set up on a side table with a lute, a glass decanter and a Delft fruit bowl of apples all carefully arranged on a richly patterned Persian carpet. He noticed a smaller, uncovered canvas rested on another easel and stepped up to take a closer look.

Beth watched his face intently while he studied the watercolour painting. It depicted a deep mauve hellebore, the petals delicately veined in purple with lime green stamens to the centre. A drop of dew shimmered on the stem as if stirred by the draught from the window.

'This is beautiful!' he said, reaching out to stroke the velvety petals before drawing his hand back. 'It's so lifelike it makes me want to touch it.'

Beth let out a small sigh. 'It's mine.'

'Johannes painted it for you?'

Johannes gave a shout of laughter. 'My pupil still has much to learn but this little daub doesn't disgrace her too badly.' He pulled Beth to his broad chest and hugged her. 'Perhaps I'll make a painter of you yet, my little chicken!'

15

'This is your work?' Noah asked Beth, his eyebrows raised.

Beth nodded and felt her cheeks warm. 'I've been Johannes's pupil for nearly four years now.'

'It's a pity she isn't a boy or I'd have taken her on as an apprentice,' said Johannes, dropping a kiss on to the top of her head as he released her. 'As it is, she'll probably waste my efforts by marrying and having a houseful of babies.'

'I expect you're right,' said Noah. He smiled kindly at Beth. 'Still, many women with artistic tendencies do enjoy dabbling with their paints again when the children are grown.' He turned away from Beth's hellebore to study one of Johannes' landscapes.

Rage boiled up in Beth's breast. 'I do not *dabble* with my paints. And I'll not waste the skills that I have by taking a husband and spending the rest of my life waiting upon his whims,' she retorted.

Noah glanced back at her. 'Really? I'll wager you'll change your mind within a year or two.'

'I will not!'

Johannes put his great hand on her shoulder but she shook it off.

'Don't glare at me!' said Noah, a gleam of amusement in his eyes. 'I see your red hair makes you quite as fiery-tempered as my sisters. I had no intention of upsetting you but, you must agree, it is the way of the world for a woman to marry and have children?'

'Because that is the way it has always been doesn't necessarily make it right!'

'Beth, Beth! Calm yourself,' said Johannes. 'It doesn't matter what other people think. You will continue to make the best work you can and let nothing prevent you. Your paintings will speak for themselves.'

'Please, let us not argue since it is plain to see that you do have a considerable gift,' said Noah.

Appeased by his response, Beth shrugged. 'Do you need me to prepare any more paints for you, Johannes?'

'Go and enjoy yourself and I'll see you later.' Johannes picked up his paintbrush again.

16

'Shall we go, Noah? We have disturbed Johannes enough,' she said.

The artist lifted a hand to them and turned back to his canvas.

'Your Johannes has a great deal of talent,' said Noah once they had left, 'and, plainly, he cares a great deal for you. How lucky that you have such an excellent teacher.'

'Isn't it? One of my earliest memories is of seeing the sunshine playing on the coloured water in the glass bottles on the apothecary windowsill and standing on a stool trying to catch the magic of the reflections on a piece of paper. As a small child I always had a stick of charcoal and a sketchbook in my hand.'

'I did too! But my father never understood why drawing interested me so.'

'Neither did mine. I was fortunate to have Johannes to encourage me. After he arrived here I used to creep into the studio and watch him at work. Seeing one of his paintings grow from a simple outline to something that appeared very real and beautiful seemed like magic to me. I became consumed with the desire to learn how he made it happen. One morning when I thought he was still abed, he caught me mixing up some of his pigments and applying them to one of my sketches.'

'And so he began to teach you?'

Beth laughed and shook her head. 'I dropped the palette in fright when I heard his roar of fury and I've never had such a scolding before or since! Then he picked up my sketch and looked at it. He didn't say a word about it but made me clear up the mess and set me to grinding pigments for him. After a month of this he showed me how to look at a still life; to see how the colours changed with the light and how the shadows fell. Eventually he let me sit beside him and draw my own still life. I learned never to disturb him with idle chatter and, in time, a whole new way of looking at the world.' She dropped her intent gaze from Noah's face and her cheeks flushed. 'But most of all, Johannes made me feel as if what I was doing was

17

important. As if I was unique and special and my developing talent really mattered. Can you understand that?'

'It's true,' said Noah thoughtfully, 'that if you feel passion for something it alters your perspective. I cannot look at any building without seeing what I can learn from it or how I could improve upon it and enrich the lives of those who will live in it.' He smiled at her. 'We are alike in our passion, I think.'

They set off along the gallery again.

'Johannes is working hard on a seascape now,' said Beth, 'and I'm hoping he'll make good progress before he becomes unwell again.'

'Unwell?'

'Perhaps I didn't say? Johannes is one of our long-term guests.'

'A guest?' Noah caught hold of her arm. 'You mean he ...'

'Yes.'

'But is it safe for you to spend so much time with him?'

'Johannes never hurts anyone but himself. Sometimes he becomes very sad and self-critical. I have known him to weep for days and once he dragged all his paintings outside and set fire to them.'

'What a terrible waste!'

'Father says his humours are out of balance,' said Beth. 'But I blame the Catholics.'

Noah smiled. 'The Catholics are blamed for a lot of things here in England. What did they do to Johannes that was so terrible?'

'It's not amusing, Noah! Nine years ago the French murdered his brothers in the Battle of Cassel. They killed more than *eight thousand* of the Dutch and Johannes has never forgiven himself for being the only one of his brothers to survive.'

Noah looked grave. 'I can see how a man might be stricken with guilt, even though it wasn't his fault.'

'And then, to make it all worse, a French soldier ravished his wife.' Beth sighed, remembering all the times Johannes had broken down as he relived those terrible events. 'Later, Annelies and the babe she carried both died of her injuries. He hates the French, and therefore all Catholics, with a passion.' She lifted her chin and clenched her fists. 'And so do I, for what they did to him.'

'But your Johannes seems well now?'

'Yes, he is.'

Downstairs, the kitchen was busy. On either side of a cauldron, sizzling on the fire, sat a black woman with her hair tied up in a colourful turban and a stout, elderly maid, each plucking a chicken. A large tabby cat patted at the cloud of feathers drifting to the floor. Peg, her fair hair already escaping from her cap, was making pastry at the table and her daughter, Sara, a pretty girl with skin neither as black as her father's nor as pale as her mother's, worked at the table peeling a mountain of carrots and potatoes.

'Are we too early for breakfast, Peg?' asked Beth.

'The fire in the hall hasn't taken yet. It's warmer here.'

'Do you mind eating in the kitchen, Noah?'

'Not at all, if we won't be in the way?'

'Always room at my table, sir,' said Peg, a smile on her freckled face.

Sara cut bread for them and brought cheese, ale and cold meat.

'I think you have already met Emmanuel, Sara's father, in the courtyard last night?'

'I certainly did,' said Noah, smiling at Sara, who dimpled and curtsyed.

'Emmanuel has been with the family since he was a boy. And this is Phoebe and Jennet who are plucking chickens for our dinner. Phoebe was our nurse and Jennet has been with our family for ever.'

'Jennet?' said Noah. 'My father talks about a Jennet who used to make delicious little sugar cakes for him.'

A smile broke across Jennet's broad pock-marked face. 'You're the dead spit of Master Tom!' she said.

'He remembers that you were kind to him after his mother died.'

The door to the garden opened and a young man soberly dressed in a dark brown coat came in with a swirl of wind.

'Close that door, Joseph!' said Phoebe. 'You're bringing in the cold.'

'Yes, Mammy,' said Joseph. He winked at Sara, who blushed, and then he gave Noah a wide smile, his teeth very white in his nut-brown face. 'Good morning, sir.'

'Joseph is our steward,' said Beth. 'I believe you also met him last night, Noah?'

'Indeed.' Noah nodded his head curtly but was then unable to resist responding to Joseph's infectious smile.

Once the servants had turned back to their tasks, Noah said in an undertone, 'That must be the Joseph my father mentioned to me? Your birth father's son?'

'He told you about that?' said Beth, her cheeks flushing.

'He thought I should know, as I was coming to England, in case I unwittingly said anything to cause your family embarrassment.'

'My birth father, Henry Savage,' said Beth, her colour still high, 'was Father's cousin. He grew up with Phoebe on his family's plantation and they fell in love. Joseph was born some five years before Henry married Mama. After Henry died, Father was determined that his cousin's child would have an education.'

'He has a great sense of responsibility.'

'Indeed he has. But when Mama first told me about Joseph some years ago it upset me a great deal.'

'These things happen in the best of houses.'

'I know but I thought . . . ' She bit her lip. 'I thought it meant that Father, William that is, didn't really love me as I'd always believed but was simply doing his Christian duty by me in the same way that he took on the responsibility for Joseph.'

'*Is* there a difference in the way he treats you and your siblings?'

'He's too much of a gentleman for that. But it's what he feels in his heart that matters to me. And I've never been able to find the answer to that question. In any case, Johannes arrived at Merryfields at the time I was so very unhappy and he cares for me now as if I were the daughter he never had.' She was suddenly conscious that she'd voiced aloud to a near-stranger the doubts about Father that still troubled her. Mortified, she stood up. 'Let me show you the rest of Merryfields.'

'I'd like that.'

Beth took Noah to the library first. She took down a collection of Donne's poetry and showed it to him. 'This was one of Grandfather Cornelius's books,' she said. 'Father saved them from Grandfather's apothecary shop just before it burned down in the Great Fire.'

Noah took the book and reverently ran his finger over it, smoothing the blackened corner of the calfskin cover. 'It's strange to touch a book that once upon a time my grandfather held in his own hand.'

Beth replaced the book carefully on the shelf. 'Shall we go and see the rest?'

She led him into the garden courtyard and from there to the summer and winter parlours where the guests were able to paint or work on their embroidery; they poked their noses into William's study, the rear hall leading to the kitchen offices and the laundry room, game larder and still room.

'What's in here?' asked Noah. He stood on tiptoe and squinted through a peephole in a heavy door at the dark end of the passage.

'Oh! Nothing.' Beth repressed a shiver. 'It's just an empty room.'

But Noah had already turned the big key in the lock.

The room was empty of furniture, about seven feet square, the walls padded and lined with leather. A set of manacles were chained to the wall. A small barred window set high up on the walls allowed a little light to penetrate.

'A cell?' asked Noah.

As a child the cell had given Beth nightmares. Even now, after all these years, the skin on her neck crawled when she came near to it. It was bad enough that Noah knew the shameful secret of Joseph's birth but now he was insisting on poking his nose into the restraining room.

'Beth? What's the matter?'

'I hate this place. When I was five or six my uncle Joshua, he's only a year older than I, locked me in here. It wasn't until suppertime that his brother Samuel came to find me.'

'What a horrid trick!'

'Father thrashed him for it.'

'I should think so, the little devil! And do you use this room often now?'

'Sometimes we have guests who need to be restrained for their own good,' she said. 'Occasionally someone becomes overwrought and is a danger to himself or to others. It's rare because we don't take guests who are violent and we have far fewer guests now than we used to. Of course, that brings problems of its own. Father cannot bear to turn away any guest whose family stop sending his upkeep.'

'I see.'

'It wasn't always so. As a child I remember that the dormitories were full of guests at Merryfields, all of whom paid well. But over time Father has lost his London connections and there isn't the same supply of people wishing to come and stay here to recover their spirits.' Beth sighed. 'I shouldn't talk of such things.'

Noah looked as if he was about to speak but then simply said, 'Shall we move on?'

They walked back across the courtyard and Beth opened another door. She stood in the entrance for a moment, inhaling the familiar scent of the apothecary, a heady mix of lavender and sulphur, camphor, beeswax and turpentine. Bunches of dried herbs hung from the beams and light slanting through the casement illuminated a row of potion-filled bottles, making them as colourful as a church window.

Susannah stood before a large table, an apron tied around her slim waist as she ground dried parsley roots in a great pestle and mortar. She glanced up and flashed a brief smile. Beth noticed that she was unusually pale.

'Good morning!' said Susannah. 'I hope you slept well, Noah?'

'Very well, thank you. It's so quiet here in the country after London.'

He looked around, unashamedly staring at the walls lined with gallypots and neatly labelled wooden drawers, the set of balance scales and the glass dome of leeches on the counter and the stuffed crocodile hanging from the ceiling. 'Oh!' he said, his face breaking into a smile. 'My father told me about the crocodile!'

'Sadly, it isn't the same one that Tom knew,' said Susannah. 'That burned in the Great Fire. William searched high and low for a replacement because he said I would never feel like a real apothecary without one. But this pestle and mortar was your grandfather's.'

'I do wish my father could see all this!' Noah reached up to pinch a bunch of dried rosemary suspended from the ceiling, sniffing the clean, resinous scent upon his fingers.

'Oh, what have you done?' exclaimed Beth. She took Noah's hand and pulled back the lace from his wrist, exposing a purple bruise.

Noah gave a wry smile. 'Emmanuel doesn't know his own strength. He and Joseph lifted me clear of the ground when they found me climbing over the gates last night.'

Susannah took an earthenware pot off a shelf. 'Try this,' she said. 'Comfrey and neat's-foot oil with elder. It's good for bruises.'

He sniffed at the pot. 'Thank you,' he said, rubbing a little of the salve on to his wrist.

'Mama, Johannes needs some more linseed oil and pigments. Shall I help myself?'

Susannah hesitated. 'Some of the gallypots are empty. You may need to wait until we can buy more supplies.'

'But ...' Suddenly Beth remembered that the supplier had said he wouldn't deliver more goods until his account had been settled.

'Aunt Susannah,' said Noah, 'I wondered if you've had time to consider my father's letter?'

'Of course,' she said. 'The contents kept me awake for half the night.'

'I suspected they might.'

Beth raised an enquiring eyebrow at her mother.

Susannah pushed away the pestle and mortar and wearily smoothed back a loose strand of hair. 'I almost wish you'd never come to see us, Noah.'

'Mama!' Beth was shocked to hear her mother speak in such a way to a guest.

'It's all right, Beth,' said Noah. 'I perfectly understand Aunt Susannah's meaning.'

'Tom's letter asks if one of your brothers would like to go to Virginia. Since Noah doesn't wish to step into his father's shoes, Tom thought one of my sons might do so instead.'

'Kit or John go to Virginia?' Beth faltered. 'But they can't! We'd never see them again.'

'Hence my sleepless night,' said Susannah. She sighed. 'But have I the right to deny them such an opportunity?

Beth was lost for words. The thought of one of her brothers sailing away to Virginia and never setting eyes on him again was too painful to imagine. 'Why, it would be as if they were dead to us!'

Susannah's chin trembled. Too moved to speak, she bent over the pestle and mortar again, grinding the parsley roots vigorously, as if to obliterate her unhappy thoughts.

'Beth, it's not for me to bring any pressure to bear on either of your brothers,' said Noah. 'I am merely the messenger.'

'But you cannot deny that it would assuage your own guilt at forsaking your father's dreams!'

A muscle flickered in Noah's jaw and he reddened. 'No, I cannot deny it.'

There was a sudden pounding of footsteps along the corridor and

Cecily, Kit and John tumbled through the doorway, breathless with laughter.

'There you are, Beth!' said Kit. 'We've been looking all over for you.'

'How could you be so mean,' pouted Cecily. 'You knew I wanted to come with you when you showed Noah around Merryfields.' She gave Noah a beatific smile.

'Beth didn't want to watch you m-m-mooning over Noah,' teased John.

Beth looked at her siblings and her heart ached with love for them. It would be unbearable if any one of them left Merryfields. She turned to Noah. 'Mama is right,' she said, her voice breaking. 'I wish you'd never come!' She saw John's eyes widen with astonishment as she pushed past Cecily and ran from the room.

Chapter 3

The only sounds to be heard in the studio were the creaking of Johannes's shoes as he shifted his weight from one foot to the other in front of his easel and the faint cawing of the rooks outside as they wheeled through a pale sky above the frosted elms.

Beth touched the vellum twice with the tip of the brush as lightly as a butterfly settling on a leaf. Slowly, she let out her breath and studied her watercolour through half-closed eyes. Should she add a few more tiny brush strokes to the sprig of holly? Perhaps the leaves needed a little more shadow to make the glistening frost appear to sparkle more brightly in contrast? She dipped the brush into the paint again, wiping surplus pigment against the rim of the pot. Brush poised, she leaned forward.

'Stop!' A large hand appeared over her shoulder and grasped her wrist. 'Think very carefully!'

Beth turned her head. 'You startled me, Johannes!'

'How many times must I tell you to consider each brush stroke before you make it? When will you learn to listen to me?' He snatched the brush from her fingers and threw it on to the table.

'I *was* thinking!'

'An apprentice does not argue with her master!'

She took one look at his broad face, grey with fatigue, and knew there was no point in discussing the matter. Standing up, she stretched the stiffness out of her shoulders. Watery light filtered through the stone-mullioned windows into the rapidly darkening studio. Outside in the garden, frost tipped the clipped yews with silver and a blush of rose pink along the horizon warmed the pearly sky.

'The light is fading,' she said. 'I'd no idea I'd been sitting here for so long.'

Johannes stood beside her, his expression pensive. 'Time passes quickly when the muse takes you.'

Covertly, she studied his face. 'Did the day go well for you?' she asked.

He let out a deep sigh. 'Well enough. It is finished.'

'Johannes, that's wonderful!' She had respected his desire to keep this work hidden from her until he was happy with it but it had been hard to resist lifting a corner of the muslin to take a peep. 'May I see it now?'

The oil painting, worked on an oversized canvas, was propped up on the easel. Johannes turned it to face the room and waited, watching her face.

The painting depicted an exuberant seascape of military vessels, trading ships, rowing boats and yachts jostling for position in the mouth of the river, their sails billowing. Bright sunlight cast strong shadows and the brisk wind stirred the surface of the water into choppy waves. The decks of the ships were crowded with sailors and passengers, some waving and some climbing up the masts. Beth could smell the salt of the sea in the air and hear the sailors shouting as the sails snapped back and forth in the wind.

'It's magnificent,' she said quietly.

'I think so,' he said, with no trace of conceit in his voice, 'but I will study it tomorrow in the daylight.'

'You should rest now.'

He nodded. 'And your watercolour, that is finished too. A good artist judges when it is well to stop.'

'Yes, Master.'

A smile flitted across Johannes's face. Beth turned to look at his canvas again. 'This is the most ambitious painting you have undertaken and it lifts your talent to a higher plane, Johannes.'

'Neither of us knows yet of what we are capable. We must always strive to do better.' Briefly, he touched her shoulder before turning to the door. As he lifted the latch he looked back at her. 'Your holly watercolour . . .'

'Yes?'

'It looks so real that if I touch its spiny leaves I might draw blood. For one so young you show much promise.'

The latch clicked behind him and Beth stared at the closed door. A slow smile spread over her face.

Later, after she'd cleaned the brushes and covered the paints, she made her way downstairs. Orpheus appeared from nowhere and padded along beside her.

Preparations were being made for supper. Poor Joan and old Nelly Byrne sat together at the big kitchen table, peeling turnips and potatoes. Peg, misted in a cloud of steam, stirred a vast copper vat of hambones.

'What's for supper?' asked Beth.

'Same as yesterday.' Peg peered into the depths of the cauldron. 'I'll have to add extra turnips to the soup again. I've already used these bones twice and there's no flavour left in them.'

'Can't we get some new bones?'

'The butcher won't let me have anything else until we settle his bill.'

Beth didn't answer. The financial situation was worse than she thought if the butcher begrudged them a few bones.

Orpheus peered down into the cauldron, his nose twitching.

'Shall I fetch some herbs from the garden?' asked Beth.

'You can try,' said Peg, pushing Orpheus away, 'but there's hardly anything at this time of year. Your mother's stripped the rosemary bush almost bare for cough medicine. Take the dratted dog away, will you? I daren't turn my back or he'll have his nose in the soup.'

Removing herself and Orpheus from the kitchen, Beth went to find Kit, who was in the library with his head in his hands, books spread out in front of him.

'Am I interrupting?' whispered Beth. He looked up at her and she was taken aback by the bleakness of the expression in his hazel eyes.

'I'm glad of an interruption,' he said. 'I promised Father I'd study this afternoon but the words dance on the page so that I can't read them.'

Beth picked up one of the books. William Harvey's *Essay on the Motion of the Heart and the Blood*. 'Isn't this interesting?'

'Not noticeably.' Kit sighed. 'It's bad enough that I have to read about scrofulous diseases and study drawings of dissected bodies and aborted babies but once I arrive at Oxford I'll be expected to take all the exams in Latin. What is the point of learning in a language different to our own that is used in no country one can visit?'

'Latin has always been used for medical matters.'

'But the common man doesn't speak in Latin!'

'You must have Latin if you're to be a doctor.'

'And there's the problem.'

Kit rubbed his eyes with his fists and Beth was reminded of him when he was a little boy struggling with his letters. 'Perhaps I could test you on your Latin vocabulary?'

'You always kissed the grazes on my knees when I fell over, didn't you, Beth? But I have to do this myself.'

29

Beth replaced the book on the table, afraid to ask the question. 'Don't you want to be a doctor, then?'

'What does it matter what I want?' asked Kit, his voice bitter. 'Father has always told me I shall be a doctor. You know he expects me to take his place at Merryfields when he's gone. I've tried to be a dutiful son. God knows, I love Father and Mother with every ounce of my being. That's what makes it so hard; I can't bear to disappoint them. But Merryfields is their dream, not mine.'

The earth seemed to shift slightly under Beth's feet. It had always been understood that Kit would join the medical profession. 'But . . . if you don't become a doctor, what will you do?'

'I've spent hours thinking about that. It's not that I have a pressing desire to do anything else in particular but I *know* I don't want to be a doctor. I can't bear the sight, or smell, of blood. Of course, Father promises me I'll grow out of that, once I've seen a few amputations.' Kit swallowed, his face taking on a peculiar greenish tinge.

Beth paced over to the fireplace and vigorously raked the embers with the poker. 'This is Noah's fault, isn't it? If he'd never come to visit us you'd have gone on being perfectly happy.'

'I haven't been happy for a long while. Noah makes me feel like a coward for not owning up to Father before. Oh, I've tried! But he always turns the conversation as if he knows what I'm attempting to say. Noah at least had the courage to stand up for what he believes.'

'Kit, please don't leave us!' Suddenly afraid, Beth caught hold of his hand.

'Little chance of me going to Virginia, is there? I could never find the funds for my passage. Father's struggling hard enough already to make ends meet to keep Merryfields going.'

A knot under Beth's breastbone, a knot that she'd barely realised was there, loosened in relief. Momentarily, she was thankful for their impoverished state.

'Beth, don't you ever have *any* desire to visit the outside world?'

Kit asked. 'Sometimes I feel as much a prisoner behind these walls as any of the guests.'

'Why would I want to leave? I love it here! There is my painting and Johannes, the gardens and the servants and guests, who are almost family anyway. Merryfields is a whole world of its own.'

'But there's a whole *new* world outside these walls.' Wild-eyed, Kit paced across the floor. 'I'm suffocating here. I don't care where I go, Virginia, Babylon or, or . . .' he floundered, 'or Billingsgate, but I *have* to leave Merryfields.'

Beth stared at him, a hollow feeling in the pit of her stomach. 'I'd no idea you were so miserable.'

'Why should you, when you walk around in a glow of self-satisfied happiness, spending every minute possible closeted away with Johannes? You *know* what you want to do with your life.' He went to the window and stared out at the gardens, bounded by the high brick wall. 'I'll have to face Father,' he said. 'He'll be angry but even that is better than spending the rest of my life in a lunatic asylum.'

'I hate to see you so miserable.'

Kit gave his sister a tight little smile. 'I can't put it off any longer. I must speak to him. If I haven't reappeared in an hour or two you'd better come and save me.'

Sometime later, Beth passed the half open door to William's study and heard raised voices from within.

'Even if I had the money, which I do not, I wouldn't give it to you so that you could sail off on a hare-brained scheme to Virginia. You know nothing about growing tobacco . . .'

'But I could *learn*, Father!'

'You will *learn* how to be a doctor at Oxford.'

'You must have realised by now that I will make a poor doctor. I don't *like* sick people.'

'Don't be ridiculous! The sick are the same as you or I.'

31

'But they bleed and purge and sweat. I can't stand it; it makes me ill. And I'm frightened when one of the guests starts rocking or weeping or banging his head against the wall. I lie awake at night with my heart pounding if I hear a disturbance, terrified you'll call me to help. I may not know what I want to do but I do know this. *I will not stay trapped behind the walls of Merryfields with a pack of lunatics!*'

The study door flung back, nearly knocking Beth off her feet, and Kit sprinted out, slamming the front door behind him.

Shocked, Beth looked into the study to see her father at his desk with his head in his hands. She went in and sat down before him.

William looked up, his face creased with worry. 'I don't know what to do for the best. All these years your mother and I have spent in making Merryfields a model for the care of the melancholic will be wasted if Kit doesn't take my place.'

Beth experienced a tiny stab of jealousy, wondering if her own absence would cause William as much distress as Kit's. 'Perhaps you need another doctor to come and work with you?' she said. 'One who will share your ideals for Merryfields?'

'It isn't as simple as that.'

'Why not?'

William frowned. 'It's no concern of yours. Young women need not trouble themselves ...'

'Not my concern? Of course it is! Whatever happens at Merryfields concerns me, even if I am only a woman.'

'Sometimes you are as hot-headed as your mother.' He sighed. 'I'm too worn down with it all to argue with you. The income Merryfields produces is barely enough to support us. Certainly I cannot pay a decent wage to employ another doctor.' William pulled the ledger towards him and opened it, running his finger down the page. 'You wouldn't believe the price of coal. Then there are the servants' wages and the housekeeping bill. So many mouths to feed!'

'Mama says you have too many charity cases.'

William shrugged. 'She's right. But take Clarence Smith and Old Silas, for example. Their families gave up paying our fees years ago but if I send them home, they will either march them off to Bedlam or put them out in the streets to fend for themselves. They'd be dead within a few weeks!'

'What can we do?'

'I wish I knew. But if things don't change I shall have to sell Merryfields.'

A cold finger of apprehension ran down her spine as the absolute misery in his voice brought home to her the very real threat to them all.

Chapter 4

Beth was in the studio working up a sweat as she vigorously pounded some lumps of ochre pigment into a powder. She didn't hear the door open and started when she saw Noah.

He smiled at her, his brown eyes sparkling. She caught her breath, suddenly conscious of her stained old work skirt. Lifting her fingers to her lips, she glanced at Johannes who was absorbed in sketching a still life set up on the table. She untied her apron, slipping quietly from the room.

'I came to bring you these,' said Noah, handing her a box of candied quinces, 'by way of an apology. It was not my intention to cause you distress on my last visit.'

Reluctantly Beth took the peace offering from him. 'Unfortunately, sweetmeats, however delicious, do not compensate for the loss of my brother.'

The hopeful smile on Noah's face disappeared.

'And, as I pointed out at the time, the invitation you delivered was not without self-interest.'

'Perhaps not. But have *you* the right to decide what is fitting for Kit? If you persuade him to stay for your own selfish reasons, you may be doing him a great disservice.'

'How dare you!'

'I dare because it is true. Perhaps you should think about that, Beth?'

Then, a low keening sound made them turn to look along the gallery. The noise came from behind half-closed window drapes and Beth hurried towards them. She pulled aside the curtain and exposed a young woman curled up on the window seat with her head in her hands and her pale hair loose around her shoulders. 'Joan, what is it?'

Joan lifted her swollen face, drowned in tears. 'They took my baby! Did you know they took my baby?'

'Who would do such a terrible thing?' asked Noah.

Beth shook her head at him slightly. 'It won't make you feel any better to sit here weeping, Joan.'

Joan shook her head. 'It *is* a terrible thing,' she said, turning to Noah. 'They took my baby and put another child in his place. An evil vicious creature that screams and screams all night and all day.' She leaned forward and whispered, 'The Devil's child.'

Beth opened Noah's box of candied fruit and offered it to Joan. 'Would you like one of these?'

Slowly Joan took one of the sweetmeats. She touched it to the tip of her tongue and her eyes opened wide. 'Sweet,' she said.

'Peg is making apple pies in the kitchen,' said Beth.

'With sugar on the top?'

'Peg's apple pies always have sugar on the top.' Beth held out her hand.

Joan uncurled herself from the window seat. 'And will you ask the doctor to speak to my husband again and ask him where he hid our baby?'

'I will.'

'A little piece of apple pie will make me strong again, won't it?'

'Peg's apple pies are well-known for their strengthening properties.'

They trooped downstairs and before long Peg had set Joan to peeling apples at the kitchen table.

'I'll see you at suppertime, Joan,' said Beth.

'Poor Joan has a very sweet tooth,' she said to Noah as they left the kitchen, 'and I use it shamelessly to guide her into a happier disposition.'

'It is a great kindness to her. She would not be so well used in another place of detainment.'

'That was always Father's ambition: to make Merryfields a safe haven for the troubled.' She stopped by the window. 'It's such a lovely sunny day.' She sighed. 'I don't want hard words between us.'

'And I haven't come halfway around the world for us to quarrel.'

'Shall we take a turn in the garden?'

Noah reached for her hand. 'Truce?'

They wrapped themselves in cloaks from the boot room and went outside. In spite of the November sunshine the cold wind made Beth's eyes water and Noah's nose turn pink. Woodsmoke drifted on the air.

'What did happen to Joan's baby?' asked Noah as they ambled along the neatly raked gravel paths. Rooks circled above the leafless elms, cawing raucously all the while.

'Nothing. Sometimes women have strange fits and ideas after they have a baby. In Joan's case she woke up screaming two days after she gave birth and accused her husband and his mother of stealing her baby and putting another in its place. They were quite unable to persuade her that she was mistaken. The child is nearly a year old now.'

'Will she ever recover?'

'I don't know. In these cases it usually takes some time. Sadly, it's not uncommon for a new mother's spirits to sink so low.'

'But you treat her with compassion.'

'What else can we do? Sometimes we find the lengthening summer days can be helpful in this type of melancholy. And a diet rich in ginger and other warming spices can rebalance the humours.'

Noah paused and turned back to look at Merryfields, the bricks blazing russet in the sunshine. Tall chimneys twisted up towards the sky and the diamond-paned windows reflected back the orange light of the sun.

'It would make a wonderful painting, wouldn't it?' said Beth. 'Perhaps one day I shall attempt it.'

Noah took a small sketchbook from inside his coat and began to draw. 'I shall build houses at least as beautiful as this one,' he said, his eyes glowing with fervour.

Beth raised her eyebrows at his lack of modesty. 'Part of the charm of Merryfields is the mellowness that has grown with the passing of time. Can a new house ever compare with that?'

'I believe so. Virginia is growing fast and there is the opportunity to shape its future with handsome buildings, which will last for generations. I want to take my grandchildren by the hand and show them the mark I will leave behind on the world. What could be a better epitaph?'

'Mine will be my paintings.' Beth peered over Noah's shoulder to look at his deft sketch of the twisted chimneys. She sighed. 'I can't begin to imagine why anyone would want to leave Merryfields but Kit feels differently.'

Noah turned abruptly towards her. 'So he might come to Virginia, after all?'

Beth shook her head. 'We don't have the funds for the passage. But Kit will leave Merryfields and find work elsewhere. That letter you brought has been the catalyst for his decision to leave us. And now Father has retreated to his study and Mama weeps silently all day.'

Noah closed his sketchbook with a snap. 'I am truly sorry to hear that but it is most unjust of you to blame me. And you should know that my father has arranged for funds to be available to Kit for his passage to Virginia, should he decide that is what he wants to do.'

Beth folded her arms across her chest, steadying herself as if an abyss had opened at her feet. She had almost become used to the idea of Kit making his own way in the world somewhere other than Merryfields but now there was a real and frightening possibility of him going to Virginia after all.

'Don't look so heartbroken, Beth.' Noah touched her gently on the shoulder. 'My father is a wealthy man and he would treat Kit as if he were his own son.'

'Virginia is so very far away!' she said, pulling her cloak more tightly around her and shivering with a chill that didn't come entirely from the biting wind, 'but I do want him to be happy.'

After Noah had gone to find Kit, Beth returned to the solace of the studio. Johannes glanced up at her from his easel and smiled before concentrating upon his work once more.

Beth sighed. Each time she saw Noah he brought disquiet into her life. Wherever would it end? In an attempt to soothe her ruffled thoughts, she busied herself with routine tasks. Carefully, she squeezed a little verdigris paint out of the pig's bladder on to Johannes's palette, between the massicot yellow and the malachite green. The cheerful clarity of the colours made her think of daffodils growing in lush new grass in the spring. She glanced out of the window. Autumn was nearly over and the coming long, dark winter must be endured before the spring bulbs pushed up through the earth again. Sighing, she pressed an air bubble out of the pig's bladder and twisted a piece of thread around it to keep it airtight.

Downstairs, Orpheus began to bark and then there were footsteps crunching across the gravel and the sound of the door knocker.

Johannes dropped his paintbrush on the table. 'Ach! So much noise to disturb us!'

'I'll go and see what's happening.' Beth slipped out of the room and trotted downstairs to the hall.

Susannah had arrived before her, untying her apron while she opened the front door.

Beth restrained Orpheus by his collar.

Two young men, both blond, blue-eyed and almost impossible to tell apart, stood in the doorway, smiling widely.

'Josh! Sam!' Beth found herself swung off her feet and soundly kissed on both cheeks. 'It's months since you came to see us. Have you come to stay?'

'Just for tonight,' said Sam.

'And we've brought Mother.' Josh's eyes were alight with mischief.

'Arabella is here?' asked Susannah, hurriedly straightening her cap.

'Indeed I am,' said a voice from the doorway. 'And I'll thank you to send a servant down to my boat at once to fetch my trunk before one of your lunatics runs off with it.'

Beth caught sight of the quickly suppressed horror on her mother's face and her own heart sank as her step-grandmother, Lady Arabella, swept into the hallway. Expensively and fashionably dressed, she was only a year or two older than Susannah.

Unsmiling, Lady Arabella undid the buttons of her fur-trimmed travelling cape and held it out, waiting, until Susannah took it from her. Smoothing down the heavy silk of her skirts, she shivered theatrically. 'No servants to open the door to me? And am I to be offered refreshments or must I continue to stand in this draughty hall? I am surprised to see that you still haven't lit the fire, Susannah, even though the afternoon is advancing.'

Susannah rallied and pinned a smile of welcome on her face. 'What a surprise to see you, Arabella!'

There was no answering smile in Lady Arabella's ice blue eyes. 'Against my better judgement, the twins persuaded me to break the journey here. Beth, is that paint on your hands?'

Beth let go of Orpheus's collar and reluctantly came forward to make her curtsy. 'Yes, Lady Arabella.' She never had been able to call her 'Grandmother'. 'I was in the studio when you arrived.'

Lady Arabella's delicate little nose twitched. 'You smell unpleasantly of turpentine. Perhaps it wouldn't be too much to ask for you to wash before you join us?'

Orpheus sniffed at the lace on the hem of Lady Arabella's skirt and she kicked him away with the toe of her fine calfskin shoe.

'Shall we go into the little parlour?' said Susannah. 'I can light the fire in a trice.'

'Joshua, Samuel, you shall escort me.' Lady Arabella, one of her twin sons on each arm, set off along the corridor.

Samuel turned back to wink at Beth over his shoulder.

Susannah hung back. 'Beth, will you ask Peg to bring refreshments? And tell Sara to air the bed in the best bedroom.' She raised her eyes heavenwards. 'A visitation from her ladyship is the last thing we need.'

Beth hurried to the kitchen where she found Kit and Noah hunched over the table in earnest discussion while they ate slabs of bread and cheese.

Jennet stood at the sink, scrubbing the pans with coarse sand. Peg and Sara were peeling turnips.

'The twins are here,' Beth announced. 'And Lady Arabella is with them.'

Jennet dropped the pan with a clatter and Peg looked up with an expression of dismay in her grey eyes. 'Oh Lord!' she said.

'Sara, Mama said can you air the best bedroom? Sam and Josh will have the blue room, as usual. And Peg, will you take refreshments to the little parlour?'

'Oh Lord!' said Peg again. 'Lady Arabella would have to come on the day I can only offer stale cake.' She sniffed. 'Still, I've better things to do than wait on a papist's whims and fancies.'

'Hush, Peg!'

'When her ladyship is being her most difficult,' said Jennet, 'I always remind myself she only comes from Shoreditch, like me, and I suppose she isn't enough of a papist to do any real harm.'

'Noah, will you let me introduce you to Josh and Sam?' said Beth.

Noah frowned. 'Father and Aunt Susannah's younger brothers?'

Beth smiled. 'It's strange, isn't it? They are only a little older than me so I always think of them as cousins rather than uncles since they spent so much time at Merryfields when they were growing up. It suited Lady Arabella to have them off her hands.'

'And Lady Arabella must be the disagreeable woman that Grandfather Cornelius married?'

'She's so full of airs and graces. The only one of us who admires her is Cecily, rather more for the extravagances of her wardrobe than for her disposition, I'm sorry to say.'

'She's an appalling woman and no grandmother of mine,' said Kit with feeling. 'Especially since she married Sir George Vernon a couple of years ago. He's secretary to James Cecil, Earl of Salisbury, Gentleman of the Bedchamber to King James and a known papist. Would you *believe* that Lady Arabella converted to Catholicism to hook him in?'

'Mama always did say that she turned with the prevailing wind,' said Beth. 'And you can be absolutely sure she'll mention that her husband has a place at Court within the first twenty minutes of conversation.'

'Sir George is her fourth husband,' Kit said, 'and the first three are dead. I can't help wondering how long poor Sir George will last.'

Noah raised his eyebrows. 'She sounds terrifying.'

Beth held out her hands to inspect the verdigris paint ingrained around her nails. 'I've been told to wash before I grace her ladyship with my presence.'

Twenty minutes later Beth entered the little parlour to find Lady Arabella holding court.

'There you are, at last!' she said. 'I hear Noah is an architect and I've been telling him about the renovations I wish to make to our country house in Windsor. A larger and more draughty old property would be hard to find anywhere but Sir George is uncommonly fond of the place. And I suppose it is very convenient when the Court is at Windsor.'

Beth tried to keep a straight face but was nearly undone when she saw Kit give Noah a sharp nudge in the ribs. 'And is the King currently at Windsor?' she asked.

'Whitehall.' Lady Arabella smiled fondly at the twins, sitting one on each side of her. 'Sir George has whispered a word in the right quarters and Joshua and Samuel have also been found a place at Court.'

Cecily, sitting on a footrest at Lady Arabella's feet, gasped and clasped her hands to her breast. 'Court!' She turned to the twins, her eyes wide. 'You'll see the King!'

'They are to present themselves next week,' said Lady Arabella, a self-satisfied little smile upon her painted lips.

'How very interesting,' murmured Susannah, offering her a slice of cake. 'My father would have been proud of them.'

'Your father?' Lady Arabella looked momentarily confused. 'Cornelius? What does he have to do with it?' She took a nibble of her cake and wrinkled her nose in disgust.

'Cornelius was the twins' father, after all!'

Arabella pursed her lips. 'It will do Joshua and Samuel no good at all for it to be known that they began their lives above a lowly apothecary shop. We've come a long way since then and I have no wish to be reminded of those dreadful times.'

Beth saw the warning glint in her mother's green eyes and hastily changed the subject. 'And to what do we owe the honour of your visit, Lady Arabella?'

'We left Windsor late and there was a question as to whether we would arrive back at Chelsea before dark. Joshua suggested we break the journey here because he fancied to ask if you and your sister would care to accompany us to a concert.'

'At Stationer's Hall,' said Joshua, 'near Ludgate, in the city. It's St Cecilia's day tomorrow and Dryden has written an ode which has been set to music by Draghi. And there will be refreshments after the festival of music.'

Cecily jumped to her feet and snatched up her mother's hands. 'Oh, Mama, do say we can go?'

Beth felt a tingle of excitement run down her back. She'd not been to London since she was a child.

Her mother turned to her. 'Beth?'

'I should enjoy it very much.' Even if it meant spending time in Lady Arabella's company.

'Then I see no reason why you shouldn't go.'

'Thank you, thank you, Grandmother!' Cecily impulsively ran to Lady Arabella and kissed her powdered cheek.

Arabella looked surprised but gratified. 'I'd prefer you to address me as "Lady Arabella", Cecily, unless we are alone with the family. "Grandmother" makes me sound like Methuselah's wife. We shall return to my house in Chelsea by boat and change there before continuing our journey in Sir George's new carriage.' She turned to Noah. 'Perhaps you would care to join us? It would afford us further opportunities to discuss the renovations I intend to carry out at Windsor.'

Noah bowed. 'I should be delighted.'

'That's settled then. I will go to my bedchamber to rest now. Cecily, my dear, will you show me the way? And Susannah, I do not care to take my supper with the inmates.' She shuddered. 'No, I shall have it in here on a table by the fire and very much hope that I shall not be obliged to endure any more of that dreadfully stale cake.'

Chapter 5

The party of concert-goers travelled in Sir George's fine, velvet-lined carriage, bowling along from Chelsea at a cracking pace. The iron-shod wheels thundered along the rutted road, spitting out stones and clods of mud at any unfortunate passers-by. The coachman and his boy wore smart blue liveries while the horses, matched greys, had their manes and tails tied up with sky-blue ribbons.

Beth, queasy from the motion and pressed tightly between Noah and Cecily, wondered how any traveller could endure a journey of several days.

Cecily, barely able to contain her excitement, bounced up and down and exclaimed in delight as she peered out of the windows at each new spectacle they passed.

'The country mouse comes to town!' said Joshua, reclining back in his seat next to his mother and affecting world-weary boredom. As usual, the twins were dressed identically. Today they were elegant in ochre brocade waistcoats worn under topaz coats with brass buttons.

Cecily took no notice of him. 'Is that Westminster Abbey? It's so large our own church of St Botolph would fit inside it a hundred times! This is my first visit to London, you know,' she said to Noah.

'So you said, at least a dozen times.' Noah smiled at her in amusement.

Lady Arabella sighed. 'I'll thank you to stop treading on my new shoes, Cecily. I had thought your mother might have taught you manners more befitting to a young lady.'

'I beg your pardon, Grandmother.'

'I do hope you aren't going to disgrace me this afternoon?'

Cecily remained chastened for at least three minutes until Joshua pointed out Whitehall Palace and she squealed in delight as she stood up to press her nose to the window.

'Sit down, Cecily!' said Beth. 'The coach is swaying enough without you making us seasick with your hopping up and down.' She pressed a lavender-scented handkerchief to her lips and sucked on a piece of candied ginger, hoping desperately that they would soon reach their destination.

Cecily managed to sit still while they progressed past Charing Cross and then along the Strand.

'We're coming up to Fleet Street very soon,' said Noah, 'where Grandfather Cornelius had his apothecary shop.'

Lady Arabella sniffed and her lips tightened into a thin line.

The carriage began to slow its pace since there was a great deal more traffic now: drays and horsemen, carts and costermongers.

Beth leaned forward to look outside, wondering where the apothecary shop had been. Except for one half-timbered building, all the houses and shops were newly built of brick and stone. 'What a shame almost all the buildings burned in the Great Fire,' she said. 'I should have loved to see the old apothecary shop.'

'It was a mean little place with a narrow front,' said Lady Arabella. 'And I'll thank you not to mention it to any of my acquaintances this afternoon.'

'Don't your fine friends know you came originally from Shoreditch?' enquired Beth pointedly.

Lady Arabella gave her a hard stare. 'Unfortunately, as you grow older you become more and more like your mother, Beth.'

The carriage became caught up in the press of traffic and finally jerked to a standstill behind a bottleneck of hackney coaches and a fishmonger's cart.

Samuel pulled down the window glass.

Instantly their ears were assailed by the sound of angry shouting and the high-pitched squealing of pigs. Somewhere a dog barked itself into a frenzy and the hoarse, repetitive call of a knife-grinder carried over the whole appalling cacophony.

Beth put her hands over her ears; she had never heard such a racket.

'Welcome to the city!' said Noah.

Samuel slammed the window shut but not before the carriage was filled with the eye-watering odour of pig dung, stale fish and a swirl of sulphurous sea-coal smoke. 'The pigs being driven to market are causing the delay,' he said. 'They've upset a fruit stall and the swineherd is quarrelling with the greengrocer.'

'I told you we should have come by the river, Mother,' said Joshua. 'The streets are always hideously congested.'

'And ruin my new shoes with mud from the public stairs at Paul's Wharf?' his mother replied.

'Sir Christopher Wren told me that several architects drew up plans for a new city of London after the Great Fire,' said Noah, 'with fine, wide streets, which would have solved these continual obstructions. What a pity nobody listened to their suggestions.'

Outside, the squealing of the pigs reached a climax and the swineherd bellowed at the top of his voice while he used his stick to prod his charges in the right direction.

All at once the coach was rocked violently from side to side as the horses reared up, whinnying in terror as the pigs hurtled past.

Lady Arabella let out a scream and snatched for the hanging strap.

At last some semblance of order was restored and the carriage jolted forward over the cobbles again, resuming its swaying progress towards Ludgate Hill.

There was a long queue of carriages outside Stationer's Hall and the coachman had difficulty in finding a convenient place to stop. Finally he pulled up a little distance away, much to his mistress's disgust.

'I didn't arrive in Sir George's new carriage for no one to see it,' said Lady Arabella as the coachman handed her down. 'Noah, you may take my arm.'

The street was crammed with a chattering crowd, all richly dressed. Beth thought she has never seen so much lace and silk and was startled to see the number of ladies who painted their faces unnaturally white and whose lips were as improbably red as a cherry. She felt very plain in her best Sunday dress; like a dove amongst richly feathered peacocks. Cecily was uncharacteristically quiet as, wide-eyed, she took it all in.

For herself, Beth was simply relieved to be standing on steady ground again.

'This is very grand,' she whispered to Cecily as they entered Stationer's Hall. The ornately embellished ceiling was at least twice the height of the great hall at Merryfields. The entrance screen was heavily carved and the walls oak-panelled, while tall windows allowed the last of the November afternoon light to penetrate.

The milling mass greeted each other with loud exclamations of delight as they postured and preened to their friends and acquaintances. The noise level meant that everyone had to shout and the air was thick with perfume, pomades and perspiration.

On the other side of the hall Beth noticed a young woman with blonde hair waving frantically at Arabella and trying to force her way past an exceedingly stout man in a green velvet coat. 'I think that lady is trying to attract your attention,' she said to Lady Arabella.

'Oh, it's Harriet! Joshua, Samuel, fetch your sister to me, will you?'

The twins shouldered their way through the crowd and pushed the fat man aside to allow Harriet through. He blinked when he saw the two indistinguishable young men and stared after them with his mouth open.

Joshua winked at him, then caught Samuel and Noah by the elbows and led them off.

Harriet, fine boned but with an unfortunately sharp little nose, went straight to Lady Arabella and kissed her perfunctorily on the cheek, completely ignoring Beth and Cecily. 'Mama, I have the most exciting piece of news for you!' Her eyes gleamed like a cat with a particularly tasty piece of fish. 'Do tell me you haven't heard yet because I am determined you shall hear it from my lips first of all.'

'What news is that, my dearest?'

'Well,' Harriet lowered her voice. 'I was speaking with the Duchess of Norfolk just now and she has it on the highest author-ity . . .'

'Do tell!'

'The Queen is expecting a happy event!' Harriet, her face posi-tively glowing with self-importance, wasn't disappointed in her mother's reaction.

'Never!' Lady Arabella's eyes widened. 'After all this time!'

'Incredible, isn't it? She went to take the waters at Bath this autumn and, of course, the King made a pilgrimage to Holywell. It seems to have done the trick.'

Lady Arabella shook her head in delighted disbelief. 'Who would have thought it? Just wait until I tell Sir George. What marvellous news! If the King has a son this could make a very great deal of dif-ference to our fortunes.'

'Mama, I must go. I can see my husband looking for me and I

48

cannot endure one of his black moods if I am away from his side for too long.' Harriet kissed her mother again and pushed her way through the throng towards an elderly man of small stature who was watching her with a scowl on his face.

'How very rude!' whispered Cecily to Beth.

'Not many people in this country will be as pleased as Lady Arabella,' said Beth

'What do you mean?'

'Cecily! You've heard Mama and Father talk about how the King wants to turn us all into papists.'

'Would it really matter?'

'Of course it would! Look at the religious massacres in France. King Louis has no parliament and does whatever he wants. If King James follows suit Catholics would hold all the important positions here and the Protestants would be persecuted. Imagine if Merryfields was confiscated and given to a papist.'

Cecily's eyes opened wide in horror but then the Master of Ceremonies called for order and the milling crowd was persuaded to find their seats in order for the concert to begin.

Noah and the twins reappeared, together with a darkly handsome companion lavishly dressed in a velvet coat the colour of ripe plums and decorated with gold lace.

Noah introduced them to his friend, Harry de Montford, who bowed low and kissed Beth's and Cecily's hands.

'How very delightful to make the acquaintance of two such charming young ladies,' he said.

The intensity of his gaze made Beth tongue-tied but she was saved from embarrassment as it was time to sit for the performance.

Cecily nudged Beth in the ribs. 'I like the look of Noah's friend,' she whispered. 'Have you ever *seen* a man so fine-looking?'

Beth frowned at her. 'Shh! The concert's beginning.'

The choir and the musicians filed into the hall and on to the dais. There was a momentary hush, someone coughed and scraped a chair across the floor and, finally, it was quiet. Then the liquid notes of a flute broke the silence, soon joined by the other instruments.

As the music flowed and swelled around her, Beth's thoughts kept returning to the implications of Harriet's news. If what she'd said was true and the Queen was pregnant, it could affect every person in the land. A son born to Roman Catholic Mary of Modena would take precedence over Anglican Princess Mary, the current heir. In that case there would be no restraining the King in his mission to convert every one of his subjects to Catholicism. And who knew what atrocities would take place if the King's zeal overcame his moderation?

A clear soprano voice as pure as spring water broke into Beth's reverie, soaring up to the roof and filling the hall with sweetness. Cecily's hand crept into Beth's and she turned to smile tremulously at her as the final notes drew to a close.

After a moment's silence tumultuous applause and the thunder of stamping feet reverberated around the concert hall. A buzz of conversation broke out as the audience stood up and moved towards the refreshments.

Lady Arabella waved her fingers at a dozen people and then abandoned her charges when she flitted away to gossip to an imposing dowager in puce silk, whose face was adorned with black patches cut in the shapes of a moon and stars.

Noah came to lead Beth and Cecily through the throng towards Harry de Montford. 'I believe I mentioned that I travelled to England in Harry's company?' he said.

Cecily fluttered her eyelashes. 'How very exciting that must have been, Mr de Montford.'

'For me or for Noah?' asked Harry. He raised one black winged eyebrow, a wicked gleam in his eye. 'Noah was indisposed for the beginning of the journey and spent the rest of it watering his precious trees. Still, I managed to win a few games of cards with some of the other passengers; enough to pay for my passage, at least.'

'How very clever of you!' said Cecily, looking up at him from beneath her eyelashes.

'Wasn't it?'

Beth thought that his voice was as smooth as the honey syrup her mother made but with an aftertaste of something dangerous; nightshade perhaps? 'And are you enjoying your visit to London, Mr de Montford?' she asked.

'Certainly I am, Miss Ambrose. There are some very lovely sights to see.' He looked her up and down with admiring eyes and then glanced at Cecily. 'Very lovely, indeed!'

Discomfited, Beth felt her cheeks become warm.

'Take no notice of Harry,' said Noah. 'He can't resist a pretty lady.'

Beth was saved from further awkwardness when Samuel brought her a glass of burnt wine. 'Did you enjoy the music?' he asked.

She gasped as a man pushing through the throng jogged her elbow, causing her to spill her drink. As she mopped at the stain on her skirt, Samuel began to chat to Noah and she couldn't help overhearing the loud conversation of a group of men a few feet away.

'The Queen's priests have predicted it will be a boy.'

'Papist babble!'

'Well, they have at least a fifty per cent chance of being right.' The speaker began to honk with laughter, his jowls shaking in mirth.

One of the party, a dour-faced man in a grey wig, said, 'You'll be laughing on the other side of your face, Farnham, if there is a papist prince. When all the high-ranking positions go to the Roman Catholics you'll lose your place, like as not. And you, Mannington,' he turned to a plump man stuffed into a blue brocade coat, 'how will you feel if Mannington Hall is confiscated and given to some trumped up papist who has caught the King's attention?'

The man recoiled. 'That would never happen!'

'Wouldn't it? Remember all the confiscations during the civil war?'

Then Beth noticed Cecily walking away on Harry de Montford's arm and she heard no more of the conversation. The way Harry de

Montford looked at Cecily made Beth uneasy; she began to push her way through the crowd to follow them. Noah, however, reached Cecily first and firmly led her back to her sister.

Darkness was falling outside and the candles were being lit. Gradually, people began to leave and soon Lady Arabella joined them, her eyes glittering with suppressed excitement as she simmered with the latest scandals.

It was time to go. The coachman was sent for and they went out into the night. The street was bustling as ladies kissed their friends and climbed into their carriages while knots of men stood in the street exchanging loud goodbyes.

An orange-seller caught Beth's arm and thrust an orange into her face. 'Oranges! Lovely oranges!' she shrilled. On an impulse Beth rummaged in her pocket and found a few coins to exchange for one of the fruit. She would give it to Johannes as a gift.

Link boys lit the way to where their coachman waited for them and Noah handed the ladies into the carriage.

The twins lingered in the street, laughing and chatting to their acquaintances until Lady Arabella called sharply to them.

Full of good cheer and burnt wine, they climbed into the carriage, rocking it about on its straps and slamming the door too hard.

The coachman cracked his whip and they rolled away.

'Well!' said Lady Arabella. 'What excellent news! There were some who decried me when I married Sir George since he is Catholic.' She narrowed her eyes and gave a small self-satisfied smile. 'But I reasoned that since the King is a Catholic, too, it could only be a matter of time before the old religion would be in the ascendant again. And so it has proved. I live in the sure and certain hope that once the King's son is born there will be considerable scope for advancement for Sir George.'

But what would that mean for the rest of us, wondered Beth.

Chapter 6

In the morning Beth drew back the heavy damask bed curtains to find that a fire had already been lit in their bedchamber and warm water and Castile soap laid out for them.

A little while later she came down the imposing staircase to find Noah in the hall, sketching the carving on the wall panelling.

'I like to keep a reminder of interesting details,' he said, 'for when I'm designing a new building.' He lowered his voice. 'Some of the detailing in this house is a little fulsome, in my opinion. I prefer more restraint.'

'May I see your sketchbook?' asked Beth, curious.

Noah handed it to her and she turned the pages carefully, interested in the variety of sketches: some vivid and quickly executed in charcoal and others worked in more precise detail in pen and ink. She felt a strange sense of relief that his work showed a high level of competence. It would have disappointed her if his drawings had been clumsy and unskilled. She returned it to him with a smile. 'There is a vivacity about your sketches that is very pleasing,' she said.

'Praise indeed, from one as skilled as yourself.'

A door closed upstairs. Lady Arabella came down, fetchingly dressed in a ruffled dressing gown and embroidered slippers. Her blonde hair had been curled and her face carefully painted.

'I will take my breakfast downstairs today,' she said. 'The twins are still asleep.'

'Joshua certainly will have a thick head after the considerable quantity of wine he drank last night,' whispered Noah as Cecily came, yawning, down the stairs to join them.

In the dining room, where a fire crackled merrily in the elaborately carved marble fireplace, two maids brought them coffee and warm bread.

'I should like a house as beautiful as this when I'm married,' sighed Cecily as she smoothed her fingers over the crisp linen tablecloth.

'Sir George's family home in Windsor is so damp and draughty that I insisted on a new house as our main residence,' said Lady Arabella. 'I do like everything to be comfortable.'

'This house is so warm!' exclaimed Cecily. 'Merryfields is always bitterly cold in the winter.'

'Housekeeping never was one of your mother's strong points,' said Lady Arabella.

Beth bit her lip to prevent herself making a sharp retort.

The dining room door opened quietly and Sir George joined them at the breakfast table. Tall and lean, his pink cheeks were freshly shaven and the buckles on his shoes as carefully polished as his manners. Lady Arabella kept up a flow of bright chatter and he watched her through heavy-lidded eyes as she made known her views and expectations following the previous day's gossip.

'My dear,' he said, 'it is unwise to anticipate too much at this time. The Queen has been disappointed on many occasions.'

'But you must see,' said Lady Arabella, pushing away her untouched plate of bread, 'this is *exactly* the time you need to be seeking out every opportunity of bringing yourself to the King's notice? Once the prince is born the King will have the confidence to seek out the Roman Catholics around him and elevate them.'

'I fail to see ...'

'Must I spell it out to you? You must be *there*, Sir George! Wherever the King turns, you will be at hand to flatter and support him.'

'Quite the little politician, aren't you, my dear?' He drained his coffee cup and stood up. 'I have business to attend to but I shall be home for supper.'

'Then we shall continue our conversation later.'

Sir George smiled sardonically. 'No doubt.' He bowed to Noah and the door closed softly behind him.

Lady Arabella sighed. 'He doesn't seem to realise the richness of the opportunities which await us. Ah well, I shall bring him round in time.' She turned to Noah. 'Meanwhile, I'd like to hear your suggestions for improving our house in Windsor. Something absolutely has to be done about the kitchens; I cannot go on with the smell of burning pig fat clinging to the curtains in my boudoir. And then there's the front façade; it's simply not grand enough.'

Noah raised an enquiring eyebrow. 'Especially if you expect to be entertaining a great deal more than at present?'

'I knew you'd understand!'

After breakfast Beth and Cecily took their leave of Lady Arabella, thanking her prettily for the invitation to the concert, and Noah accompanied them along the lane to the public stairs. Beth took a deep breath of fresh air, relieved to have escaped from Lady Arabella's testing company. 'You may have found yourself a commission to redesign Sir George's house, Noah.'

'So it would seem. Assuming, of course, that Sir George is happy to indulge his wife's whims and that I have time to visit Windsor. Sir Christopher Wren keeps me very busy.'

'I know that he's been responsible for much of the rebuilding of the city.'

'Sometimes I wish I had been born twenty years earlier. What an incredible time that would have been, to be an architect immediately after the Great Fire, with the opportunity to leave your mark upon such a prominent city! But there is still work to be done on many of the churches.'

'Is that what occupies your time?'

'St James Garlickhythe is my special concern. The church itself has been rebuilt already. It's a beautiful building with ceilings some forty feet high and so filled with natural light that the people call it "Wren's Lantern". I'm working on drawings for the new steeple.' Noah's eyes shone with enthusiasm and he lengthened his stride as he described the church. 'It's to be a grand affair with ascending tiers set upon columns, all built in white stone.'

Cecily, tagging along behind, ran to catch them up. 'Tell me more about London, Noah.'

'The theatres are most entertaining. Once I saw King James and his party.'

'How thrilling!'

'He's not much liked in the city. The Bishop of London, a truly estimable man in my opinion, fell foul of him and is suffering for it.'

Beth frowned. 'What could a bishop do to displease the King?'

'One of the clergy spoke out against the King's Catholic leanings and the King demanded that the Bishop dismiss him. But he refused.' Noah laughed. 'Still, since he's been suspended, he's had more time for gardening, which pleases him greatly. Gardening is his passion as much as architecture is mine.'

Noah hailed a boat and made sure that the boatman erected the canopy, since the sky was grey and full of rain.

'Come and see us soon,' said Cecily as the boatman pulled away upstream.

'I will.' They waved at him until he was out of sight.

'And Grandmother has all new furniture and fires in *every* room, even the bedchambers,' said Cecily.

Beth caught her mother's eye and returned her wry smile. Still in their travelling cloaks, they sat at one end of the great hall warming their toes by a meagre fire.

'And I had a glass of burnt wine and it made my head spin and the music and the singing were so beautiful that it made me cry,' continued Cecily.

'You c-c-cry at anything!' said John, leaning against the fireplace picking lumps of mud off his boots and tossing them into the flames.

'You're jealous, John because you weren't invited.'

'I wouldn't have g-g-gone if you'd paid me.'

'It was a marvellous concert,' said Beth, ignoring her siblings' squabble.

'And how was Arabella?' asked Susannah.

Beth made a face. 'You know how she is. And we met her daughter, Harriet.'

'I knew Harriet very well, once upon a time. She was an ungovernable child.'

'She was so rude, Mama,' pouted Cecily. 'She ignored us completely while she told Grandmother the latest gossip. And she's married to an ugly old man and it serves her right!'

'Harriet did have some interesting news, though,' said Beth. 'The Queen is to have a child. Her priests are predicting a prince.'

Susannah shivered a little and moved her chair closer to the fire. 'She's just as likely to have a girl. And that would save a great deal of trouble.'

Later, Beth pushed open the studio door. 'I'm back,' she said.

Johannes glanced up from the table where he was arranging a pewter candlestick and a delftware bowl filled with apples against a carefully draped backdrop of a Persian carpet. His brow was furrowed and his lips tightly compressed. 'Tell me, what is it that is wrong with this, Beth?'

She looked at the arrangement carefully for a while. The richly intricate pattern of the silk carpet seemed curiously bland against the other objects. She said, 'There is something lacklustre about the colour . . .'

Suddenly she had the answer. She took from her pocket the orange she had bought for him and placed it in the fruit bowl. 'There! Isn't it beautiful? The ultramarine in the carpet makes the colour of the orange sing by its contrast. And see how the fruit reflects like gold on the metal of the candlestick!'

Johannes studied the composition, walking around it to see it from different angles. 'I think, perhaps, you have it, Beth.' He twitched the Persian carpet so that the silken folds lay in a different direction, leading the eye up to the orange and then on to the top of the candle. He muttered to himself and moved one of the apples a fraction, then snatched up a taper from the mantelpiece and thrust it into the glowing embers. Shielding the flame with his hand, he lit the candle. 'There! What do you think now?'

'Perfect!' Beth watched him closely, letting out her breath in a small sigh as his face relaxed. He selected a piece of fine charcoal and rubbed it to a point on the rough sacking of his apron, then pulled his easel a little closer and began to draw.

She watched him for a while, his skilful and economical strokes creating a delicate outline on the canvas. Reaching for the burnt sienna, she scooped a little of the ground pigment into a small bowl and dripped in some linseed oil and turpentine. She mixed it together until it was the consistency of thin cream, pressing it hard against the side of the bowl to check for any lumps. When the mixture was ready she put it on the table next to Johannes, together with a fine squirrel hair brush, ready for the under-painting.

Now that Johannes was settled, Beth was able to concentrate on her own work. She ground small quantities of pigments and mixed them with water in an array of mussel shells, the colours of the different paints clear and beautiful against the pearlescent linings. Earlier she had collected a handful of leaves from the garden in a variety of glorious autumn shades from russet to gold; she spent a happy few hours drawing and then painting them in watercolour.

At last she rinsed her brush and glanced up at the window. Darkness was falling. Johannes's head was still bent over his easel, his homely face illuminated by the single wavering candle in the gathering gloom.

'Johannes? The light is going.'

He eased back, stretching his arms out in front of him. 'I know. The shadows are changing.'

'You look tired. Why don't you rest until supper?'

He was silent for a moment. 'I cannot sleep. When I close my eyes I have terrible dreams.'

Beth's heart sank. 'The same nightmare again?'

'I can never forget what happened to my wife and that I was not there to help her when those soldiers ...' He sat back down and eased back, stretching his arms out in front of him. 'I am not a violent man but I dream of finding those French soldiers and hacking them to pieces, laughing all the while with the pleasure of it as they scream. I want them to suffer as Annelies suffered.' He looked up at her with unfocused eyes. 'How much I want that.'

Alarmed, Beth remained silent. She ached with compassion for him. Would he always have to endure such agonising memories?

He stood up abruptly and enveloped her in a sudden fierce hug. 'Don't look so sad, my little chicken! Take no notice of old Johannes. You know I suffer from melancholy spells.'

She slid her arms around his broad waist. 'I wish with all my heart that I could help you to find peace as you have helped me, Johannes.'

'No more than you and your family helped me in my hour of

need. Besides, it's plain to me, whatever you may think, that Dr Ambrose dotes on *all* his children.'

'Perhaps. But I still wish I could help you to be happy.'

Johannes sighed. 'Maybe tomorrow all will be well again.'

That evening at supper, Beth's own melancholy seemed to be reflected in other members of the family. Kit kept his head down, refusing to engage in conversation and chewing his bread and cheese as if it were made of ashes. Susannah, too, was very quiet.

'Shall I fetch a headache powder for you, Mama?' Beth asked.

Susannah shook her head, continuing to crumble a piece of bread she didn't eat.

After supper, William called the family into the parlour. His expression was sombre.

'I've called you together to tell you that Kit is leaving us to go to Virginia.'

Before she could stop herself, Beth had let out a cry of distress.

Cecily shrieked and burst into a storm of sobs, throwing herself into her mother's arms.

'How *c-c-could* you leave Merryfields, Kit?' asked John, his expression full of hurt bewilderment.

'I *have* to take this opportunity. If I don't, I'll spend the rest of my life wondering. Surely you can see that?' His face was wretched.

There was a hubbub of questions and tears but at the end of it Beth was resigned to letting Kit go. She no longer had any doubt in her mind that he would never be happy to remain at home and it was fruitless to attempt to persuade him. She went to sleep that night wishing with all her heart that Noah had never come to Merryfields.

Chapter 7

Two days later, supper was being served when a visitor arrived. Emmanuel opened the gates to allow a powerful grey stallion to clatter into the courtyard and then Joseph came to whisper in William's ear.

William wiped his fingers on his napkin and stood up. 'Susannah, my dear, will you come with me, please?'

'W-w-what do you think has happened, Beth?' asked John.

Beth shook her head, still too dejected at the thought of losing Kit to speculate.

William and Susannah were closeted in the parlour with the stranger for some time before Sara was sent for to take in a jug of claret.

Considerably later on, Susannah emerged, her face a little flushed. 'It's too late for our visitor to return home tonight. Beth, will you speak to Peg and have the best bedchamber prepared? Oh, and ask Emmanuel to set the fire straight away.'

'Who is it who has come to visit?' asked Cecily, round eyed with questions.

'I can't say at present.' Susannah looked around her distractedly. 'Oversee the servants, will you, Beth? Oh, and see old Nelly Byrne to bed. I don't want her wandering around in her nightshift tonight.'

'Of course, Mama.'

'Well!' said Cecily, after her mother had left. 'Whoever can it be?'

But the visitor remained behind closed doors with William and Susannah until everyone had gone to bed.

Early the following morning, Beth was surprised to find the studio deserted. Perhaps Johannes had managed to sleep after all. She picked up one of her previous day's sketches of an oak leaf and took it to the window to study it more carefully. Fading from yellow to buff, it was spotted with black mould; not a pretty painting but a faithful representation. A sudden draught whisked the paper from her fingers and sent it spiralling to the floor. When she bent to pick it up she caught her breath as a sturdy pair of men's boots strode into her line of vision.

'Allow me!' The voice was deep and authoritative. A middle-aged man with bushy eyebrows and his own greying brown hair falling to his shoulders stood before her.

Beth took the proffered painting from his outstretched hand, her fingers trembling a little.

'Forgive me if I startled you. Henry Compton, at your service.' He smiled, the skin around his eyes crinkling in his weather-beaten face.

Beth curtsyed. 'Beth Ambrose, sir.'

'I came to visit Dr Ambrose last night and our talks were more prolonged than I had expected.'

'Dr Ambrose is my father.'

'It seems we are both early risers. I thought I'd take a look at the garden before the rest of the household awakes but my attention was caught by the magnificent seascape in the gallery. The artist has a great deal of talent.'

'He is one of our guests. His name is Johannes van de Vyver.'

Henry Compton's gaze took in the other canvases before it fell on Beth's botanical paintings displayed on the wall opposite the window. 'The seascape is magnificent, of course, but these are more to my own taste. Johannes van de Vyver is proficient in such different styles.'

'Oh no, those are my paintings. Johannes is my painting master.'

With a sharply enquiring glance as if to check the truth of her statement, Compton moved to her hellebore and the foxglove more closely. 'He has trained you well. I congratulate you.'

'Thank you.'

'I have a notion to look at your excellent garden before the whole world arises,' said Compton. He went to look down to the garden. 'There is something haunting about a garden touched with frost, don't you think?'

Beth stood beside him, studying the scene below. Silvery mist wreathed amongst the topiary peacocks, spheres and pyramids, all painted with glistening hoar frost in the opalescent early morning light. 'My younger brother, John, says that winter is the true test of a garden. In warmth and sunshine, full of the sweet scent of roses and honeysuckle, it's hard for a garden *not* to be lovely. But in the winter you can see a garden's bones. That's why he pays such attention to trimming the yew and the box trees, so that they make shapes pleasing to the eye even when there are no flowers.'

'He is wise for one so young. I should like to meet him.'

'Then I will accompany you to the garden. We are sure to find John in the potting shed.'

'I should like that very much, Miss Ambrose.'

Johannes was back in his accustomed place at the easel and only glanced up at Beth with a smile as she slipped into the studio later on.

Several hours later her stomach rumbled with hunger. She'd been so absorbed that she'd forgotten to go down for dinner. The fire had died down, too and the studio was cold. She hesitated to interrupt Johannes, still bent over his easel, so she cleaned her brushes and went in search of a crust of bread and cheese.

Along the gallery she heard a repeated banging coming from the open door of the best bedchamber and found Sara beating the bed hangings and Jennet wielding her besom behind the linen press.

'Isn't it the wrong time of the year to be spring-cleaning?' Beth asked.

'Your ma's given the order to ready this bedchamber for an important visitor,' said Jennet.

'Who is this important visitor?'

'The King himself, I shouldn't wonder, if all the fuss is anything to go by,' said Jennet, vigorously sweeping the dust into a pile. 'It seems she's too good to sleep in the women's dormitory with the other guests. And we're to make ready the little parlour for her private sitting room.'

Beth trotted downstairs to find the kitchen was as hectic as a hive and full of the delicious aroma of roasting meat. Peg was shrouded in a cloud of flour making a pastry coffin ready for a vast pile of rabbit meat, pigs' kidneys and carrots to be baked inside, while Phoebe pounded sugar and Emmanuel riddled the grate and poured coal on the fire. A leg of mutton seethed and spat in the cauldron and the gears of the spit clanked as a haunch of venison turned over the crackling flames.

'Peg, wherever did all these supplies come from?' asked Beth, helping herself to a fresh-baked roll. 'I thought the butcher wouldn't give us any more credit?'

'The bill's been settled by last night's visitor. Joseph handed me a purse of gold this morning and told me not to stint on meals fit for a banquet.'

'I don't understand!'

'Me neither.' Peg's mouth was set in a thin line. 'You'd better ask your ma. I just do as I'm told. Been working here for nigh on twenty-two years but it's not my business it seems.'

Beth left Peg to her grumblings and went off to search for her mother.

Susannah, as usual, was in the apothecary, straining lavender flowers steeped in sweet almond oil through muslin into a jar.

Beth dipped the tip of her finger into the oil and sniffed the pungent perfume. 'The scent of this takes me straight back to summer,' she said.

'I thought I'd put a little bottle in the guest room. Lavender is so helpful for headaches.'

'And does our expected guest have headaches?'

'Don't we all, at difficult times? She also has a chronic defluxion of the eyes so I'll distil some eyebright into a soothing eyewash for her.'

'Why all the secrecy? Who's coming?'

Susannah pressed the lavender heads with the back of a spoon to squeeze out the last of the oil. 'I have been asked to be discreet about our guest. She is an important lady who needs a short while to escape from the pressures of the world. In the past year she has suffered a stillbirth and the death of two children from the smallpox. In addition there are other ... pressures and her state of mind is fragile.'

'Poor soul!' said Beth. 'Shall I write the labels for the lavender oil?'

Susannah took a pen and ink from a drawer and placed it on the counter. 'I believe you met our visitor who arrived last night?'

'I did. He admired my paintings and then we went to walk in the garden.'

'He came to Merryfields to see if it was a suitable place for this lady.'

Carefully, Beth wrote *Oil of Lavender* in her neatest writing and couldn't resist adding a tiny drawing of a bunch of lavender.

'He was most interested in what we do here. He also thought that you would be an admirable companion for her during her stay. A young lady of compassion and good sense is how he described you. As our expected guest is only a few months older than you, it should not be too onerous a duty.'

'Who is she?'

'A titled lady who wishes to remain anonymous. She will be known as Mistress Anne Morley while she is with us. The visitor who came last night is the Bishop of London. She used to be the Bishop's pupil and he has remained her confidant and adviser.'

'Noah's bishop? But he didn't seem like a bishop at all! I thought he must be a farmer.'

'How should a bishop be?'

'Not someone whose eyes sparkle in such a merry way or who likes dirtying his hands in the garden or who rides on a horse rather than in a carriage.'

Susannah laughed. 'He used to be in the army so he's of a practical nature but all those things don't prevent him from being a clergyman.'

'No, I suppose not. I know that Noah likes him.'

'It was Noah who told the Bishop about Merryfields. We must thank him for that since the fee for accommodating Mistress Morley will make a significant improvement in our circumstances.'

'I see.' Beth wiped the pen clean and stoppered the ink. In that, at least, Noah had brought them good fortune.

Chapter 8

December 1687

Beth and Susannah were in the great hall making a final inspection of the tables, carefully laid for dinner. Sara had polished the pewter with lemon juice and horsetail until it gleamed and Poor Joan had shown a surprising aptitude for folding the starched napkins into intricate crowns. Beth had arranged garlands of holly, yew and ivy running down the length of the tables.

'It all looks very fine,' said Susannah with a satisfied sigh. 'I was worried it wouldn't be what our new guest is used to but I don't think she can find fault here. I'd better poke my nose into the kitchen and then all we have to do is wait.'

The kitchen table was laden with fine white manchet bread, fragrant apple and quince pies all sparkling with sugar, the coffin of mixed meats decorated with pastry birds with real pheasant's feathers for their tails and two monstrous pike on a dish, while the venison, the lamb and a spiced beef stew kept warm by the fire.

Jennet was almost lost behind the stack of pots and pans she was scrubbing, Peg was mashing a dish of carrots and Sara was chopping herbs, while Phoebe arranged half a dozen golden-roasted chickens on a platter, watched closely by the tabby cat.

'It is only one new guest arriving, isn't it,' asked Beth, her mouth watering. 'We could feed the five thousand with all of this.'

'I tell you, my feet are as swollen as two pigs' bladders,' said Peg. 'We've been at it since before dawn and there's still supper to make ready for later.'

'What a feast!' said Susannah. 'Get down, Tabitha!' She gently pushed the cat off the table as she jumped up to investigate, 'Well done, all of you. You've done Merryfields proud.'

The garden door flew open and Joseph burst into the kitchen. 'They're here! We can see the barge coming upstream.'

'Beth, call your father,' said Susannah. 'I'll hurry on ahead.'

William, wearing his best wig, was in his study but left his desk as soon as Beth told him that the expected guest was in sight. The barge was tying up at the landing stage by the time they arrived. There was only just time for the family to line up before Henry Compton handed the new guest on to dry land. He indicated to William that he should come forward.

The lady, heavily veiled, was wrapped in a claret velvet cloak trimmed with fur but Beth could see little of her, except to ascertain that she was of middling height and solidly built.

'Mistress Morley, may I introduce Dr Ambrose?' said Bishop Compton.

William gave a deep bow. 'At your service, madam. My family and I will do all in our power to make your stay at Merryfields a pleasant one.'

She inclined her head and murmured a reply.

The Bishop introduced Mistress Morley to all the family one by one. They made their bows and curtsies, then he led the way back to the house. The new guest's liveried manservant and a lady's maid followed.

Once inside, Susannah suggested that she accompany Mistress Morley and her maid to her bedchamber, where she might care to wash her hands before dinner.

'What Mama means is that she's going to show her the p-p-private closet with the close stool,' whispered John to Cecily.

'Shh!' Beth nudged her brother in the chest. 'She'll hear you!'

'Why all the secrecy?' asked Kit.

'Surely she'll take off her veil before dinner?' said Cecily.

'You never know, she may have a face covered in fur and start howling at the f-f-full moon!' John tipped his head back and made as if to demonstrate.

'John!' William's voice was frosty. 'Perhaps you'd better go and wash your own hands or our guest will think you are nothing more than a common gardener's boy.'

'But I *am* a gardener!'

William's lips twitched slightly. 'Nevertheless, I don't wish to see hands at the dinner table with enough dirt under the fingernails in which to grow potatoes. Off you go! And all of you, please treat our guest with the respect she deserves.'

Mistress Morley did remove her veil before dinner. Beth was relieved to see that she had a pleasant, if rather sallow countenance, lightly pockmarked and with a broad forehead and a long nose. Her eyes appeared to trouble her because she blinked a great deal.

At dinner the manservant stationed himself behind her chair and the guests stared at her with curiosity but, since she appeared so ordinary, soon turned back to concentrate on their exceptionally fine dinner.

After saying grace, Bishop Compton kept up an easy flow of conversation.

William carved Mistress Morley a choice piece of venison, while Susannah talked to her of the many agreeable diversions she might find at Merryfields. 'And Beth will remain close at hand, should there be anything you require.'

Mistress Morley inclined her head and then turned to Beth. She blinked as if it took a special effort to concentrate. 'I understand you paint pretty flower pictures.' Her voice was low, with a slight French accent.

'I'd be happy to show them to you, if you wish?'

Mistress Morley nodded but turned her attention to the feast without engaging in further conversation. In spite of the downward droop to her mouth, she ate a good dinner.

'I must return to Fulham before darkness falls,' said Bishop Compton, 'I'll call on you next week and see how you do, Mistress Morley.'

'I'll accompany you to the landing stage,' William said to the Bishop. 'And Beth, my dear, will you look after our guest?'

'I shall be glad to, Father.'

Bishop Compton kissed the visitor's hand and took his leave of Susannah before saying to Beth, 'I am very content knowing that you will befriend Mistress Morley.'

Mistress Morley watched the Bishop leave, her plump chin trembling a little.

The others at the table dispersed to follow their various pursuits, leaving Beth to entertain the new guest.

'Shall I take you on a tour of Merryfields, Mistress Morley?'

Anne Morley bit her lip. 'Perhaps later.'

'Or would you like to retire to your bedchamber to rest a little?'

A shake of the head.

Beth gave her a friendly smile, wondering how she was going to manage time spent in the other woman's company if she rarely spoke. 'We have prepared a private sitting room for you. Of course, you are welcome to mingle with the other guests if you prefer but Bishop Compton thought you would like to be secluded.'

'I should like to sit quietly for a while.'

Groaning to herself, Beth kept up a flow of bright but unanswered conversation while they walked to the little parlour. The manservant followed at a discreet distance.

'Here we are!' Beth said. She opened the door to a pretty room lined with oak panelling and a cheerful blaze dancing in the grate. A cushioned seat built beneath the window overlooked the knot garden. Mistress Morley looked around her. 'It will do very well.'

Beth stood awkwardly in the doorway. 'Is there something I can bring you? We have a good library or perhaps you would like to play a hand of cards?'

'No, thank you.' Mistress Morley sat down in front of the fire and folded her hands in her lap.

'Shall I leave you or—'

'No!' Mistress Morley looked up quickly, her expression anxious. 'Don't go!'

'Of course I'll stay, if you wish it.' Beth sat down on the edge of the other chair. This was going to be much harder than she had expected.

The silence stretched into minutes while Beth struggled to find something to say.

'My mother has put some lavender oil in your bedchamber for you,' she said at last, in some desperation. 'It's made to her own recipe and is very good for headaches if you suffer in that way.'

'Yes, she told me.' Mistress Morley pulled a handkerchief from her pocket and dabbed at her eyes.

'I'm chattering too much. I can see that you're unhappy and I don't know what to say to help.'

'No one can help.'

Beth chose her words carefully. 'We have had a great number of guests here at Merryfields over the years. Almost all of them, in time, do recover their spirits.'

'It is true that I have been in low spirits lately.' Her voice quavered and her hands restlessly pleated the handkerchief on her lap.

'Would it help to talk about your troubles?'

Mistress Morley shrugged. 'Nothing can change how things are.'

'I know that you have suffered terrible losses,' prompted Beth. 'Do you have children?'

Beth shook her head.

'Then you cannot know how sharp is the pain I carry in my heart. Mary and Sophia were everything to me. And I lost all the others even before they took their first breaths.'

'Every child is irreplaceable but perhaps, in time, another little one would help to assuage your grief?'

'If I am ever able to give birth to another baby. I begin to doubt myself.' She broke off, her face twisting in anguish and great tears rolling in fat drops down her cheeks.

'Oh, please don't cry, I didn't mean to distress you!' Beth leaned forward to clasp the poor girl's hands.

Anne Morley collapsed into racking sobs.

Helplessly, Beth rocked her against her shoulder.

When at last the storm of weeping subsided Beth stroked the dark hair off Mistress Morley's forehead and proffered her handkerchief.

'Forgive me,' the guest sniffed.

'There is nothing to forgive. You have a great deal to be sad about. Tell me about your husband. Is he a comfort to you?'

'George?' Mistress Morley's lips hovered on the brink of a smile. 'George is a kind husband and has never blamed me for not providing him with an heir.'

'I should think not, indeed!'

'My older sister, Mary, has lost one child and still waits in hope. Our mother lost many babies, too, and I sometimes wonder if these difficulties run in families.'

'You're still young and there is plenty of time yet.'

'Perhaps.' She sighed.

'Tomorrow we will walk in the garden,' said Beth firmly. It would do no good to let Mistress Morley sit about moping. 'Or perhaps into the village. The fresh air will put some colour into your cheeks.'

Mistress Morley glanced out of the window. 'My sister and I lived not far from here when we were children.'

'Where was that?'

'Oh,' she waved her hand vaguely in the air. 'Not far. I lived with my grandmother in France for a while and then came back to England. We had a governess, who had children also.'

'And your father?'

'We didn't see much of him.'

'So you must be close to your sister?'

'She lives in The Hague now and I do not see her as often as I would wish.'

'The Netherlands?' Beth realised that she hadn't seen Johannes for several hours, with all that had happened, and wondered briefly if his mood was still low.

'I have no mother, God rest her soul. After my babies died I wanted to go to my sister for comfort but my father wouldn't grant me permission. He doesn't allow me to write to her, either. He intercepts my letters.'

Beth frowned, puzzled. What kind of father would be so cruel? And surely Mistress Morley's husband would have had something to say on the matter? 'Why did your sister go to The Hague?'

'She married our cousin and that is where he lives.'

'My painting master, Johannes van de Vyver, comes from Holland. Sadly, he is subject to fits of melancholy but when he is well he is full of good humour.'

Mistress Morley sighed. 'There is much trouble in the world.'

'You must try not to think of it while you are at Merryfields,' said Beth, exasperated. 'Perhaps you can imagine your stay here as an island of shelter in your grief? A time to rest and be far away from all your troubles so that you may deal with them more easily when you return.'

'You are very kind. We shall be friends, I believe.' Mistress Morley sighed again and managed a wavering smile. 'And since we are to be friends you shall call me Anne and I will call you Beth. But now let us talk of happier things. Tell me, have you always lived here?'

'Always. I love Merryfields more than any other place on God's earth.'

'And you have the good fortune to have your family around you.'

'For the time being. My brother, Kit, intends to go to Virginia next month. It grieves us all. My father had always hoped that Kit would follow in his footsteps and take his place here at Merryfields.'

A shadow passed over Anne's face. 'Fathers sometimes will force their own ideals upon their children. I know mine does. We have so many differences of opinion. He is a papist.'

Beth raised her eyebrows.

'He will never cease in his efforts to convert me.' Anne stood up abruptly, her handkerchief falling unnoticed to the floor. 'He refuses to see that the Church of England is, without all doubt, the only true Church.'

Beth frowned. 'He is a papist but you are not? A child usually follows her parents in matters of this kind.'

'My stepmother is a Roman Catholic and when my father converted to Catholicism, my uncle insisted that I be brought up as an Anglican. He put me in the care of Bishop Compton.'

'I am surprised that your father allowed your uncle to make such a decision.'

Anne hesitated a moment. 'My uncle is dead now but he was a man of considerable influence.'

They sat in silence again until, in desperation, Beth said, 'Father always says that if you are miserable the best thing is to keep busy. 'Come on, we shall go to the kitchen.' Ignoring Anne's startled expression, she took her hand and pulled her from the room.

The servants were putting away the last pots and pans after dinner.

'Peg,' said Beth, 'Mistress Morley and I are going to make some jumbals, if we won't be in your way?'

'You carry on. I intend to put my feet up until it's time to prepare supper.'

Beth took a small book down from a shelf and opened it. 'This is my Grandmother Elizabeth's recipe book,' she said. 'And this is her recipe for jumbals.'

Anne read the recipe. 'Shall I grind the sugar, while you wash the salt from the butter?'

Beth handed her an apron and fetched the ingredients from the larder. She watched in surprise as Anne carefully weighed the sugar and set to with a will to pound the lumps out with the pestle and mortar.

Anne cut off a small piece from the cone of sugar and popped it into her mouth. 'I love all sweet things,' she said with a small smile, 'but I have a terrible weakness for sugar plums.'

Beth reflected that perhaps Anne and Poor Joan were not so very different in seeking consolation for their troubles.

'I must confess,' said Beth later on as she bit into one of the still-warm jumbals, 'I thought you were too fine a lady to turn your hand to baking but these are delicious.'

'My governess taught me, along with her own daughters, to be useful in the kitchen,' said Anne. 'However many servants you have, you never know when you may need a housewife's skills.'

'In that case, shall we help Phoebe peel the potatoes?'

Anne looked nonplussed as she glanced at the potato mountain waiting on the table but then rolled up her sleeves and set to work. She glanced up at Beth as she wielded the knife and was overtaken by an unexplained fit of the giggles.

Chapter 9

Beth suppressed a yawn. The parson was well known in the village for the length of his sermons and it wasn't unusual, especially during warm weather, for a cacophony of snores to reverberate around the church. This Sunday, however, the church was so cold that you could see the vapour of the parson's breath rising like hellfire from his mouth as he extolled the virtues of piety and sobriety.

Anne, sitting beside Beth and warmly wrapped in her fur-lined cloak, seemed not to feel the cold but drank in every one of the parson's words, never taking her eyes off him. Since she didn't own a fur-lined cloak, Beth was sincerely hoping that Anne, a great deal more devout than herself, wouldn't want her to go to evensong as well as morning service.

Beth was beginning to find Anne's company a little claustrophobic. It wasn't that she was difficult, only that she desired Beth's presence at all times. Beth was itching to go back to her painting but, on the occasion she had taken Anne into the studio with her, it had proved impossible to concentrate on her work while her guest chattered and exclaimed in delight. Besides, it made Johannes irritable.

'When will you return to your studies?' he'd asked fretfully that morning. 'I need you to tidy the work table and clean the brushes properly. 'I can never find anything since you've abandoned me.'

She'd promised to come to the studio early every day before Anne had risen from her bed and that had placated him for the time being.

At last the seemingly interminable sermon ended. The congregation roused itself from its torpor and rustled and coughed in preparation for the next hymn. There was a slight disturbance at the back of the church and Cecily, sitting on Beth's other side, poked her in the ribs and nodded her head meaningfully.

Beth turned just in time to see Noah and Harry de Montford slip into a pew at the back.

Noah and Harry were waiting for them as they left the church. Noah made a deep bow to Anne, who fixed him with her gaze and shook her head a little. 'How do you do, Mr Leyton,' she said, proffering her hand.

'I see you have already made Mistress Morley's acquaintance,' said Susannah. 'What a pleasant surprise to see you today, Noah.'

'Mistress Morley? Why yes, indeed. We have met several times at Fulham Palace since we both know the Bishop of London,' said Noah. 'May I introduce Mr de Montford? He accompanied me on the journey to England from Virginia. And Harry, you already know Miss Ambrose and her sister Cecily.'

Cecily simpered and preened so, that Beth felt obliged to tread sharply on her toe.

'Ow!' Cecily glowered angrily at her sister.

'Forgive me, Cecily,' she said, smiling sweetly, 'but Mama and Father are waiting for us and we should set off home. Noah, you and Mr de Montford will stay for dinner, won't you?'

'How kind! Harry is travelling to visit friends later this afternoon but I wondered if I might invite myself to stay tonight as I have business at Richmond Palace in the morning? Sir Christopher Wren has been asked to update the royal nursery and he has sent me to make a preliminary survey.'

Anne drew in her breath and clutched at her cloak. 'So, the King intends his papist brat to be brought up there once it arrives, does he?'

Beth's eyes widened at the harsh tone of Anne's voice but Noah merely said, 'Why, I believe so.'

'The local people will not like the thought of a possible Catholic prince being brought up on their doorstep,' said Beth. '*I* don't like it and if Johannes should hear about it, after all he's been through at the hands of the papists ...'

Noah spread his hands wide. 'There may be no prince. And my only interest in the royal nursery is not the child within it but the considerable renovations required to the building. I expect to gain some valuable architectural experience.'

Ill at ease, Beth glanced at Anne, whose lips were set into a tight line but then the squire and his wife, Mistress Fanshawe, came to shake their hands and make Mistress Morley and Mr de Montford's acquaintance and she put the matter out of her mind.

'And you won't forget to come to the ball at Fanshawe Manor the day after tomorrow?' said the squire, rubbing his hands together in a vain attempt to keep warm.

'How could we possibly forget?' said Cecily. 'Nothing *ever* happens in the country and the ball is the most exciting event. Mama is making me a new dress.'

'I'm sure you will look delightful, Miss Cecily. And perhaps Mistress Morley and Mr Leyton and Mr de Montford would care to join us? The more the merrier, I say!'

They said their goodbyes and Harry de Montford took Cecily's arm on the walk back to Merryfields. Beth was too preoccupied with watching his flattery reduce Cecily to speechless giggles to listen to any other conversation.

There was a welcoming fire in the great hall and, shivering, Anne and Beth reached out their hands to the flames. They were soon joined by Harry and Noah with Cecily following close behind.

'Mr de Montford has promised to play cards with us after dinner,' said Cecily.

'You want to watch out for him,' warned Noah. '*Somehow* or other very few people ever beat Harry at cards.'

Harry de Montford raised one eyebrow and his dark eyes gleamed. 'Are you accusing me of cheating, Noah?'

'Of *course* he isn't!' said Cecily.

'Perhaps I sometimes encourage Fortune to smile my way,' said Harry, 'but I would never cheat a beautiful lady such as yourself.'

Then the servants carried in a roast sucking pig surrounded by glazed apples, followed by a succession of pies and other delicious dishes and everyone sat down to enjoy them.

'Isn't it lucky that we are having such a rich feast since Mistress Morley is here,' whispered Cecily to Beth. 'I should have been mortified if we'd only been able to offer Mr de Montford turnip soup.'

After dinner the young people retired to the solar where they played cribbage and other card games but after a while, Cecily threw down her hand of cards. 'Noah was right,' she pouted. 'No one can beat you, Mr de Montford. I propose we play something different. I know, blind man's buff!'

Kit produced a large handkerchief which Beth tied around Harry's eyes before she spun him three times.

John and Noah darted at Harry, prodding him on the shoulder while he moved with his hands outstretched as the others formed a circle around him. Harry lunged forward and caught at John's coat but it slipped through his fingers.

Cecily squealed in glee and Harry turned towards her. 'Aha! I am coming to catch you, Miss Cecily!'

Cecily squealed again, dodging his grasping hands, and Harry caught hold of Anne.

'Who have we here?' drawled Harry, as he pulled her towards him. 'Oh, not Miss Cecily, I believe.' He leaned closer and sniffed. 'Lavender, if I'm not mistaken.' Anne stood, frozen, while he ran his fingers over her cheeks. 'Miss Ambrose!' declared Harry triumphantly.

Everyone laughed.

'Wrong!' called out Kit as Harry pulled off his blindfold.

Beth took the blindfold and whispered to Anne, 'You don't have to play if you prefer not to.'

Anne shook her head. 'No. I want to.'

Beth spun her three times and pushed her gently into the circle.

Anne reached out blindly and brushed against Noah but he was too quick for her. John boldly touched her on the arm; she caught her breath and whirled around. A moment or two later, giggling as the others taunted her and then dodged away, she snatched hold of Kit's arm. 'I have you!' She ran her hands over his hair. 'It's John,' she said. 'Or perhaps ... ' She fumbled at the buttons on Kit's coat. 'No, it's Kit.' She pulled off her blindfold, her eyes sparkling. 'I can tell because I noticed earlier that you have a button missing.'

Beth watched Anne with amazement as she joined in the silly game and then, at the end of it, sank on to a chair, breathless with laughter.

'It makes me happy to see you laugh, Anne,' said Beth as they watched Noah and John set up the draughts board.

'I remembered what you said about imagining Merryfields as an island shelter in my sea of grief and this afternoon I have put aside my sadness. It is strange how that foolish game has put me in cheerful spirits again.'

Beth squeezed Anne's hand. 'There is something magical in the air of Merryfields, I believe.'

Shortly afterwards Harry took his leave to visit his friends and Cecily moped by the fire for the rest of the afternoon.

Joseph came to light the candles as the evening began to draw in. Since Anne was engaged in trouncing John in a game of draughts, Beth took the opportunity to slip away, intending to see if Johannes was still working in the studio. Treading softly along the gallery a movement of the air made her candle flicker and she turned, gasping as she spilled wax over her fingers.

'Here, let me take that!' Noah appeared out of the gloom and took the candlestick from her while she peeled the hot wax off her fingers. He took her hand in his and examined it. 'Are you burned?'

'Only a little.'

'I came to find you. I wanted to ask ... ' He stopped and looked uncertain for a moment. 'How much do you know about Mistress Morley?'

'She has been unwell and suffered a sad loss.'

'How do you like her?' His voice was curious.

'At first it was a duty to be her companion but the more I come to know her, the more I like her.' Beth smiled. 'However, it's irksome to be her companion for almost all my waking hours; not because of any defect in her character but simply because I need time to paint. Anne has had a difficult life, I think. Her father sounds most unsympathetic, always interfering in her household, even to the extent of choosing her servants.'

Noah nodded. 'In many ways you're right that she has had a difficult life. In others she has led a life of supreme privilege.'

'In what way?'

Noah rubbed a finger against his nose. 'Clearly she doesn't want you to know who she is but ... '

William came briskly along the gallery, holding aloft a guttering candle.

'What do you mean?' asked Beth.

'Ah, there you are, Noah!' said William. 'I've been looking for you. I wanted to show you some books in our library, which may be of interest to you. Excuse us, if you will, Beth.' William, tucked his arm firmly through Noah's as he led him away.

Noah glanced back over his shoulder and Beth thought she caught a hint of relief in his face.

Chapter 10

A couple of days later, Cecily woke early for once.

'What is it?' groaned Beth as Cecily leaped out of bed and wrenched back the curtains to let in the light. She rubbed the sleep from her eyes.

'I wanted to look at my new dress again.' Cecily picked up the armful of ivory taffeta and lace which was draped over the coffer and held it against herself. Twirling around as if she was dancing, she curtsied low to Beth. 'What do you think?'

'You look as lovely as you did each of the twenty-two occasions you asked me the same question yesterday.'

'I really, really wanted scarlet silk because it would look wonderful with my black hair but Mama wouldn't let me.'

'I should think not indeed! Entirely unsuitable for your first grown-up ball.'

'Perhaps I could have scarlet ribbons in my hair?'

Beth relented. 'Maybe one but don't be surprised if Father makes you remove it.'

'I'll tie it into my curls just before we arrive and he'll never notice. And what are you going to wear, Beth?'

'I have the green silk that used to be Mama's.'

'Mmm.' Cecily looked doubtful. 'The colour always suited you but it is rather old fashioned.'

'I don't give a fig for that!'

'Well, I do. I could spend my whole life going to balls and soirées and the theatre. One day I'll go to London again and drive around in a golden coach and people will say, "There goes the beautiful Mistress Ambrose!"'

'You want to be careful what you wish for! Think of your reputation.'

'Beth, do you always have to be so ... so *sensible*?'

After breakfast, Beth went to the little parlour where Anne's manservant, Forsyth, was stationed outside. He bowed and opened the door for her.

Anne drooped on the window seat; Beth's heart sank as she noticed that her eyes were red and swollen.

'Anne? Have you been weeping again?'

Anne's fingers twisted endlessly at the handkerchief in her lap. She took a deep, shuddering breath. 'I dreamed last night of my two little girls playing with their kittens in the sunshine. I gathered them up on to my knee and could feel their silky hair against my face. And then I woke up and remembered that I'll never hold them in my arms again.'

Beth took Anne's hands. 'It is a hard thing to bear but I promise you that time will lessen your sorrow.'

'Why is it so difficult for me to have a child?' Anne sobbed. 'Is God punishing me? I have made every effort to walk in God's ways, to follow His true doctrines in a church that is pious and sincere. My closest friend, Mistress Freeman, is to have yet another child next month and I try,' she swallowed another sob, 'and I do try to be happy for her but it breaks my heart.'

Beth clasped Anne's hands. 'Father often says you must simply keep putting one foot in front of the other until one day you will find the sun is shining again. If you keep healthy and cheerful, maybe the next baby will stay well.'

Anne's chin quivered but she mastered her emotions and squeezed Beth's hand. 'Each month I count the days, hoping and praying to the good Lord that my courses will not come.'

'You must try not to dwell on it. Time enough for unhappiness if what you fear comes to pass.'

Anne took a deep breath. 'I count myself fortunate to have you for a friend. You are my friend, aren't you?'

Beth smiled. 'Of course. And I want to see you in happy spirits again. Yesterday it was wonderful to see you laugh while we played those silly games.'

'There is the ball tonight. But I'm not sure if . . . '

'Do come, Anne! I'm sure it won't be as smart as the balls you are used to but it's the pinnacle of all the social events here. Why, Cecily is almost bursting with delight and can talk of nothing else but her new dress.'

'I used to like to dance. What will you wear?'

'Mama has given me her green silk with the gold underskirt that she wore when she was young.'

Anne looked at her curiously. 'Don't you have ball dresses of your own?'

Beth shook her head.

'But you cannot wear a dress that is decades old. Come with me at once!'

Anne led Beth away upstairs. 'My maid will dress your hair and powder your face and make you fit for the smartest ball.' She pushed open the door to her bedchamber and began to pull dresses out of her travelling trunk.

Anne's maid, a middle-aged woman dressed all in black with a sour expression to match, came forward to restrain her. 'Madam, please sit down and tell me what you are looking for.'

'The pink silk ... No, perhaps not with strawberry blonde hair. I want to lend Miss Ambrose a dress for the ball tonight, Edith. The blue watered silk?'

Edith took hold of Beth's arm and turned her around, looking her up and down until Beth turned hot with embarrassment.

'Well?' said Anne.

Edith began to rummage in the trunk. 'This one.' She pulled out a froth of aqua silk which she held up against Beth.

'It's not really a ball dress,' said Anne doubtfully.

'Madam, we are in the *country*. She is young and does not need anything too formal.'

'Yes. Of course.' Anne smiled. 'And that colour is perfect for you, Beth. Go on, put it on!'

Beth fingered the silky fabric, marvelling at the quantities of fine lace and the seed pearls sewn all over the puffed and gathered sleeves.

'Undress!' commanded Edith.

Beth began to tug behind her back at the laces of her bodice but Edith deftly untied them herself. Before she knew it, Beth stood shivering in only her chemise.

Edith held out the damask underskirt and shook it impatiently.

After Beth stepped into it the overskirt was wrapped around her, buttoned at the waist and pinned back to show the embroidered satin lining. The maid loosened the ties at the neck of Beth's chemise, exposing a great deal more naked skin than she was used to showing to the world. She opened her mouth to protest but closed it again at the fierce look she received. Then came the low-necked body, with a stiffly boned busk and gossamer thin sleeves gathered on to the armholes. Edith pulled tightly on the laces and Beth felt her breasts being pushed up so high that if she dropped her chin it would rest in the valley between them.

'I can't breathe!' she protested. She wriggled her fingers under the point of the busk, which extended downwards from her waist as far as her honour.

'It's the latest fashion,' said Anne. 'The shape elongates the silhouette. Most elegant.'

'It is necessary to suffer in the pursuit of beauty,' said Edith.

'You'll become used to it,' said Anne. 'Just remember not to bend forwards.' She turned to the maid. 'What do you think?'

Edith studied Beth, tweaking the skirt into shape and pulling at the neckline to expose even more of Beth's breasts. 'She will do. But we must dress her hair. Bring her to me this evening.' Without more ado she swiftly unlaced the body and Beth could breathe again.

That evening the women assembled in the hall and waited as Anne Morley's coach was brought from the stables. The womenfolk were to travel to the ball in the coach, while the men walked behind with Joseph carrying a lamp to light their way.

Beth, self-conscious in her borrowed finery, stood up very straight, unable to slouch even if she had wanted to, since the murderously hard busk prevented it. Her hair had been dressed in a complicated and sophisticated style with artless curls draped over one, very nearly bare, shoulder. She had caught her breath when she'd seen herself in the mirror in Anne's bedchamber. A beautiful stranger looked back at her. When she had taken a few careful steps the yards of fine blue-green silk embellished with seed pearls whispered around her ankles as if she were floating on a cushion of air.

Anne, resplendent in butter-yellow satin, had smiled and offered her a fan and shown her how to flirt behind it. 'You will have all the young gentlemen clamouring after you!' she said.

Beth wasn't sure how she felt about that but there *was* something special about wearing such fine clothes.

Cecily's eyes widened when she saw her sister. 'Beth! You look like a princess.' She pouted. 'And I thought I was going to be the prettiest tonight.'

'You look beautiful and much older than sixteen.'

Mollified, Cecily smoothed her skirts. 'I'm going to tie red ribbons in my hair once we're in the coach,' she whispered.

'I thought it was always the ladies who kept the gentlemen waiting,' said Susannah to Mistress Morley.

With a clattering of shoes Kit, John and Noah jostled their way down the stairs, all dressed in their Sunday best and full of self-conscious good humour.

'Well, don't we all look fancy?' said Noah, elegantly dressed in bronze-coloured velvet that matched his eyes.

'You look splendid,' said Beth, thinking how handsome he was.

'I m-m-may not have the most m-m-modish coat but I have scraped the mud from under my fingernails,' said John, laughing as he held out his hands for inspection.

Kit adjusted the lace at his cuffs and buttoned and unbuttoned the indigo jacquard coat he'd borrowed from his father for the occasion. 'I'm not used to dressing up,' he said.

Noah clapped him on the arm. 'You look very fine and I can see you'll be setting my sisters' hearts aflutter when you arrive in Jamestown, Kit. I've written to them and told them to expect you so they'll be in a flurry of visits to the dressmakers, all competing for your attention upon your arrival.' He turned to Beth and took her hand. 'But none of them could possibly outshine you,' he said quietly. 'You look radiant tonight.'

Beth flushed at his compliment before realising she was holding his hand for far too long to be polite. Flustered, she murmured something inconsequential and turned away.

William, austere in black, took Susannah's arm. 'You look as lovely as ever, my dear,' he said, his face softening into one of his rare but dazzling smiles.

Cecily, jiggling about in excitement, called out, 'Time to go!'

After a deal of careful manoeuvring, the ladies climbed into the coach with their skirts arranged to crease as little as possible.

Fanshawe Manor had never looked better. The carriage drive was lined with flaming torches and crowded with coaches. Servants in new livery took the guests' cloaks. The hall was lit by a thousand candles and decorated with garlands of greenery entwined with swathes of white silk. A small group of musicians played to amuse the guests while they waited to be announced.

'It's as bright as day!' said Cecily, her jaw dropping at the magnificence of it all. 'I've never seen anything so wondrous.'

'Imagine the bill for the candles!' whispered Susannah. 'Why, there are enough to light Merryfields for ten years.'

William took Cecily's arm and turned her to face him. 'I see a scarlet ribbon has appeared in your hair on the journey here.'

Cecily's cheeks flushed to match the offending ribbon.

'And it looks delightful,' continued William. 'I am blessed with my womenfolk; you paint a vision of loveliness.'

Squealing with delight, Cecily stood on tiptoe to kiss his cheek. 'I wonder if Harry de Montford is here yet,' she said, glancing around the crowd.

They all moved on into the ballroom to chat with old friends and acquaintances.

'I hope I won't make too many mistakes with the dancing,' whispered Cecily. 'John and I read Playford's *Plain and Easy Rules for the Dancing of Country Dances* from cover to cover and practised all the steps but we only had Emmanuel to play the tunes on his whistle and I'm not at all confident that I shall remember them.'

'It's simple when you hear the music,' said Anne.

'Have you been to a great number of balls?' asked Beth.

Anne smiled. 'Never any as fine as this.'

Cecily gripped Beth's arm. 'There's Harry! And he's coming to see us!'

Harry de Montford, extremely modish in a light-blue coat embellished with a great deal of silver lace and fancy buttons, bowed low to the ladies making Cecily giggle. He kissed her hand and she fluttered her eyelashes shamelessly at him until Susannah gently pulled her away.

Then the dance music began and before long the young people's feet had started to tap. It didn't take much persuasion from the caller to encourage them on to the floor and after walking them through the steps, the music speeded up and the dancing began in earnest.

Kit bowed to Anne and offered her his arm. 'Mistress Morley, may I hope that you will be my partner in this dance?'

'I should be delighted,' she said.

Harry came to ask Beth to partner him. His eyes glittered like jet and his direct gaze discomfited her. 'Tonight you shine brighter than the stars,' he said, his gaze lazily roaming over her décolletage.

She took a step back. 'Why, Mr de Montford, you surprise me. I didn't imagine you had anything of the poet in you.'

'You need to know me better, then. And that would be my very great pleasure, believe me,' he added in a whisper. He laughed and took her hand. 'What fine company I'm keeping these days! A dinner fit for the King in the great hall at Merryfields a few days ago and now an elegant ball in an imposing country seat. But I suppose that to you this is nothing out of the ordinary?'

'The balls at Fanshawe Manor are renowned in the vicinity.'

'Then, may I have the honour?'

She nodded and allowed herself to be led on to the dance floor.

An hour and a half later, the fiddlers finished 'Cuckolds All in a Row' with a flourish. The flautist wiped his forehead with his handkerchief. The drummer picked up his drum, improvised from a Roundhead's old helmet, which had occasioned great amusement from the guests, and the musicians retired to enjoy a jug of ale.

Beth, out of breath from the last dance, surreptitiously eased the point of her busk, which was digging into her. She wondered if there would be a bruise. But that was for tomorrow and tonight she was having a mighty fine time.

'What fun!' said Noah, who had been her final partner in the last dance. 'And Mistress Morley appears to be enjoying herself, doesn't she?'

Beth glanced across the hall to see Anne, flushed and laughing with Harry de Montford. 'I'm glad to see she has put aside her sadness for tonight,' she said. 'I saw Kit whirling her around so fast in the last dance that she became giddy.' They watched Anne for a moment as she fluttered her fan teasingly at Harry. 'Noah, I've been meaning to ask you what it was that you started to say about Anne not wanting me to know who she is?'

'Did I?' Noah's eyes were guileless. The music started again.

'Please tell me about Anne Morley,' she urged, as he took her hand and bowed.

'Don't talk to me now!' said Noah, looking at his feet with an expression of comical dismay. 'I'm having the devil's own job keeping time. I'm always half a beat behind everyone else.'

'Bend your knees and try to glide. And don't look so anxious. Now jump up on your toes and smile.'

'Both at the same time?'

But before she could laugh at his worried expression she was on her way again and taking Kit's hand.

It was well after midnight when Beth and Cecily followed Anne and Susannah into the coach.

'Wasn't it wonderful!' breathed Cecily.

'A delightful evening,' smiled Anne. 'It's a long time since I've enjoyed myself as much. I believe I danced with every man in the county between the ages of sixteen and sixty!'

'I can hardly bear for it to end,' sighed Cecily. 'Did you see me dancing with Harry de Montford? Didn't we make a fine couple? Mama, can *we* have a ball?'

Susannah laughed. 'I'd like to see King Henry partnering Poor Joan in a gavotte.'

Cecily pouted. 'I hadn't thought of that. No one would want to come to a ball held in a lunatic asyl—'

Susannah held up her hand. 'Shush, Cecily! You know we never say that.'

'There's no doubt that tomorrow will seem a great deal less exciting than today,' said Beth. 'I shall have to hand back my borrowed finery and put on my paint-stained work clothes again. But tonight I felt like a princess, thanks to you.' She reached out for Anne's hand.

'You must keep the gown,' said Anne. 'It suits you far better than me and I have others.'

'Oh, but I couldn't . . . '

'Of course you can! It's little enough recompense for your kindness.'

Beth hesitated. 'Then, thank you. I shall treasure it. I'm not sure when I will find another opportunity to wear such a fine gown again but when I do, I will think of you.'

Cecily, her head nodding in time with the coach's motion, gave a small snore.

Chapter 11

Cecily was still fast asleep when Beth awoke the following morning. The first thing she saw was her beautiful dress carefully draped over the clothes press, waiting to be stored away. She lay quietly for a while, reliving the previous night. The memory of Harry de Montford's breath on her cheek and the way his eyes had followed the curves of her body agitated her again. Squirming under the sheet at the uncomfortable recollection, she heartily wished she'd been able to think of a witty set down to put him in his place. Then she smiled as she recalled Noah's comically anxious expression as he attempted to follow the dance steps.

The house was quiet. Perhaps Anne would be sleeping late and it would be possible to steal a little time in the studio. Beth slipped out of bed and dressed. Shoes in her hand, she padded along the gallery until she reached Anne's bedchamber. Forsyth, dozing on a pallet outside the door, hastily sat up and rubbed the sleep from his eyes.

'Is Mistress Morley awake?' whispered Beth.

'Not for a good while, yet, I imagine. She said she would break-fast in bed this morning.'

Beth spent a satisfactory hour in the studio. She found notes and coloured sketches of some woodbine that she had worked on earlier in the year and decided to develop them into a painting. There was a lack of variety in the garden during the winter months and she hummed to herself as the sketches brought back memories of the abundance and glorious perfumes of the garden in summer.

At last, the growling of her stomach forced her to leave the studio to seek out breakfast.

Noah was already sitting at the kitchen table. 'Are we the only ones out of our beds?' asked Beth.

'Kit is snoring so loudly that I quite gave up on any idea of rising late,' said Noah.

'Noah, I've been trying to ask you about Anne but every time I raise the subject you slide off somewhere. Why is her identity such a secret?'

He tore his chunk of bread into small pieces and began to arrange them in a pyramid. He sighed. 'I should never have said anything.'

'But you did, so tell me!' She reached out to imprison his hand.

He looked up at her and their eyes met.

Beth held his gaze; for a moment, time stood still. The everyday kitchen sounds of clattering pans and the chopping of vegetables faded away and all she was aware of was the warmth of his hand and of his amber eyes fixed upon her.

He glanced over his shoulder at Sara busy riddling the fire, then said in hushed tones, 'I suppose a *king* might have the right to select his daughter's servants?'

'A king?' She froze.

'Yes. King James.'

'But if King James is her father . . .' The enormity of what he was saying made her trail off in confusion.

'Exactly!' said Noah with a smile of insufferable smugness, 'Anne

Morley is Her Royal Highness, Princess Anne of Denmark, second in line to the throne.'

'Beth glared at her mother. 'Well?'

'Of course we knew,' said Susannah, 'but we were asked not to make it known, at the Princess's request.'

'But you could have told *me*!' stormed Beth.

'We could hardly go against a royal command, could we?'

'How in the name of heaven am I going to face her now?'

Susannah raised Beth's hand to her lips. 'In exactly the same way as you did before. Anne is an ordinary woman born into an extraordinary family and leading an extraordinary life. She feels pain and distress just as you or I do and on occasion the pressures of life at Court are very great. Now, I saw Sara collect her breakfast tray a while ago and I expect she is waiting for you.'

Beth pictured the sadness in Anne's round face and blushed as she remembered how she had held her in her arms while she sobbed. She wouldn't have dreamed of taking such a liberty with a royal personage if she'd known her identity. But it was true what Mama said: Anne, in many ways, was an ordinary woman just like herself.

Forsyth stood outside the little parlour.

'Is Mistress Morley ready to receive me,' Beth asked. Her heart thudded like a drum under her bodice.

'Indeed she is, madam.' Forsyth opened the door with a flourish and Beth took a deep breath and went in.

Anne, sitting by the window working on her embroidery, looked up with a smile. 'How are you this morning?'

Beth opened her mouth to speak, found her tongue stuck to the roof of her mouth and sank to the floor in an unsteady curtsy, completely at a loss for words in the presence of royalty.

Anne's smile faded and she let the embroidery fall to her lap. 'You know, don't you? Who told you? Your mother?'

Beth shook her head.

'Then I suppose it must have been Noah Leyton?'

Beth nodded, her gaze fixed on Anne's blue embroidered slippers.

'Please rise. We are not at Court and I don't wish you to behave as if we were.'

'He didn't want to tell me, Your Highness,' stammered Beth, 'but I made him.'

'This is exactly why I didn't want you to know who I am. Look at you, shaking with fright! Am I a different person from yesterday?' Anne's eyes glistened with sudden tears. 'I have been so free from restraint here at Merryfields, playing games and dancing like a carefree young girl again. It has been very comfortable knowing that you were my friend and that you liked me for myself and not because of my station in life. *Please*, don't let matters change.'

Hesitating a little, Beth said, 'I cannot pretend that who you are makes no difference.'

'But here in this room it need not! Can you imagine how often I have to contend with fawning courtiers who try to befriend me for their own ends? All I want is to be liked for myself. Is that too much to ask?'

'No, of course not.' Beth breathed out slowly. Anne *was* just the same as before; it was only her own new-found knowledge that was different. 'You must know that I *do* like you for yourself. And besides,' said Beth, 'I am not, nor ever likely to be, a courtier and there is nothing I want from you. Everything I desire in life is here for me at Merryfields.'

Anne gave her a wry smile. 'If you have rarely left Merryfields you cannot know what else in life you may desire.'

'I've been to Richmond village many times and recently I went to London.'

'I see.' Anne's mouth twitched. 'Then you are more worldly wise than I realised. Well, let us be friends and while I am here we will forget everything outside these walls.' She held out her hand.

Slowly, Beth came forward and took it. 'There is one thing,' she said. 'I made you peel all those potatoes.'

'Ah, yes. The potatoes!'

'Noah said that might be a beheading offence.'

The Princess gave a shout of laughter. 'I shall have to speak to Mr Leyton about that.'

Bishop Compton arrived by boat that afternoon. He came straight away to the little parlour, striding in and bringing with him the breezy scent of the outdoors clinging to his travelling cloak.

He greeted Anne with affection. 'You have the suspicion of a bloom in your cheeks again,' he said. 'I do believe the country air has refreshed you, just as I hoped it would.'

'That and the kindness of the new friends I have made here.' Anne smiled at Beth. 'Though Beth has wormed my secret out of Mr Leyton.'

Beth flushed as the Bishop raised an eyebrow at her. 'Of course, I will be discreet.'

'I would have expected nothing else.' Bishop Compton turned back to Anne. 'Since Miss Ambrose is privy to your secret, I can tell you that the King is asking for you. He sent to Fulham Palace for me and I said you were staying with friends in the country. He expects you to return to Whitehall.'

Anne turned to look out of the window. 'I am surprised he troubles himself at all about me. I suspect he wishes to keep me close at hand only so that he can continue in his attempts to persuade me into popish practices.' She glanced at Beth. 'I do not wish to leave and will stay another day.'

'The King fears your closeness to your sister and her husband. The Prince of Orange poses a very real threat to the King's ambitions. He

97

is not only the King's nephew but is married to the King's heir and is staunchly Protestant. Your father will not rest until the country is become Roman Catholic again.'

'But the people do not want it!' Anne appealed to Beth. 'Would your friends and neighbours be content if we had papists in all the most important positions in the government? How would they feel if they were forced to follow Rome and were not free to worship in our Church of England?'

Beth glanced at Bishop Compton and he nodded encouragingly. 'I may live cloistered here at Merryfields,' she ventured, 'but I do know that there is a great deal of distrust of the papists. Father says that it isn't so much the fear that people wouldn't be allowed to worship in their own way but more that the King might follow the ways of his cousin in France,' said Beth. 'King Louis ignores his government and the army is large and powerful.'

'My father, God forgive him, has turned to Rome,' said Anne. 'His wife is Catholic and if the child she carries is a son, he will become the heir and England will become Roman Catholic again.' She stood up clutching at the front of her bodice, her voice high and quick. 'We *must* act to prevent such a tragedy!'

'Anne!' Bishop Compton spoke sharply. 'Compose yourself.' I have brought a letter for you from your husband.' He reached inside his coat and withdrew a folded paper sealed with red wax.

'With your permission, I shall leave you for a while,' said Beth. 'Perhaps you will send Forsyth should you wish me to attend you?'

Anne simply nodded as she eagerly scanned her husband's letter.

Bishop Compton turned his warm smile upon Beth. 'I wish to speak to your father. Will you accompany me, Miss Ambrose?'

William glanced up when Beth knocked on the door. 'Good morning, Your Grace. How do you find Mistress Morley?'

'Much improved. She has found a sympathetic friend in your daughter, I believe. I have been hearing about the ball you attended and I do believe the Princess has had as much enjoyment from that simple country affair as any glittering occasion at Court has ever brought her.'

'Oh, I assure you,' said William with a gleam of amusement in his eye, 'the ball at Fanshawe Manor was no simple affair. Dear me, no! It was the very height of sophistication in these parts and will be talked about for years.'

The Bishop laughed and clapped William on the shoulder. 'The King is asking for his daughter. She is reluctant to leave your care and I wondered if I might stay here tonight before we return to Whitehall tomorrow?

'Of course,' said William.

'I shall be sorry to see her leave,' said Beth.

'Miss Ambrose, there is something I wanted to ask you,' the Bishop went on. 'I have seen your botanical paintings and it is plain that you have a passion for flowers. In the spring, I wondered if you would like to visit my gardens at Fulham Palace? I have a great quantity of unusual specimens, which I believe may interest you.'

'Nothing would please me more!'

'Very good. Your mother may care to accompany you to see the medicinal herbs we grow.'

Beth felt excitement bubbling up inside her. 'Oh Father, do please say that we may go!'

William smiled. 'How could I refuse?'

Anne was very quiet that afternoon, spending a great deal of time staring into the flickering flames of the little parlour fire.

Beth, fretting at the inactivity, mourned time wasted when she could be painting.

'I'm not good company, am I?' said Anne. 'Merryfields has given me an opportunity to step outside the difficulties of my own life for a while but it is time for me to return to my duties.'

'Will your husband be waiting for you?'

Anne smiled. 'I hope that I have some good news for him. I may be carrying another child. It's a little early to be sure but I am holding my breath as each day passes.'

Beth's heart swelled with joy and fear for her friend. 'I shall pray for you.' After so many stillbirths and miscarriages, she hoped desperately that Anne would be able to carry this child to term.

After dinner the following day, Clarence Smith came to shake the Bishop by the hand. 'Still being troubled by the damned papists?' he asked.

Henry Compton's lips twitched. 'Fair to middling.'

'Shame I'm too involved here with affairs of state to return to Whitehall, but I'll leave it in your capable hands to deal with the problem element, as you see fit. Never forget that the Church of England is the one true faith!'

'I assure you, sire, that I will do all in my power to make sure it remains so.'

The Bishop bowed and backed away from Clarence's presence. His eyes were dancing with mirth as he glanced at William.

Anne turned to Beth. 'I will take a final look in the room where we have spent such happy times together.'

In the little parlour, Anne closed the door firmly against Forsyth. 'I shall miss this retreat and you, too, my dear friend. Your kindness and common sense have done much to lift me out of my despair.'

'I hope so much that you will find your life less difficult now. And especially that what you most wish for comes to pass.'

A radiant smile illuminated Anne's sallow face. 'I live in hope that it is God's will.' She twisted one of her rings off her finger and held it out. 'I want you to have this.'

Beth gasped and took a step back. 'It's far too valuable for me to accept!'

'What you have done for me is beyond price. Besides, it matches your lovely blue eyes. Please, wear it for me?'

Hesitantly, Beth took the ring. Moved by Anne's sentiment, Beth found herself blinking away tears. 'Then I shall be honoured.' She slid the ring on to her finger. It was a little loose but the sapphires blazed with icy fire.

'You see, I knew it would suit you! Oh, and I have asked Edith to leave you some of my gowns. I have too many and I'm sure you will make use of them.' Anne sighed as she gave a last glance around the little parlour.

In the hall Anne's maid held out a fur-lined cloak, which she wrapped tenderly about her mistress's shoulders.

At the landing stage Anne said her goodbyes, thanking William and Susannah, but when she came to Beth she kissed her cheek and whispered in her ear, 'I will always carry a little of Merryfields in my heart.'

The Bishop handed her into the barge where her maid set a hot brick by her feet and a blanket over her knees.

Beth blinked hard, already feeling the loss of her new friend and sadly aware that she would never meet her again.

The boatman cast off and the barge slid away.

Anne raised a hand in farewell then turned her face towards the city.

Chapter 12

William received word from Noah that Kit's passage had been booked for the following week and retreated to his study, barely to be seen except at mealtimes. Susannah hardly spoke at all and set to work preparing salves and cough mixtures for Kit to take with him.

On hearing that Kit was to leave Merryfields, Johannes cajoled all the guests and the family into sitting for him; he made lightning sketches of them all, binding them into a portfolio for Kit to take with him.

'Now he will never forget us,' said Johannes, reducing Beth to tears.

Noah arrived a week later.

Beth's heart sank into her shoes, dreading the following day when he would take Kit away.

'I'll return to Merryfields after Kit has set sail,' said Noah, as they went into the great hall for their dinner. 'Your father has invited me to stay here while I'm working on the renovations at Richmond Palace.'

'*Must* you work on the nursery for the King's expected papist heir?' She heard the sharp tone in her voice and her earlier reservations about him returned.

'Beth, this is a marvellous opportunity for me to gain experience in an important project with Sir Christopher Wren.'

'Still, I shouldn't talk about it, if I were you. Papists aren't much liked around here.'

Noah sighed. 'My involvement has nothing to do with supporting Catholicism, which I abhor.'

'Nevertheless, others may not understand that.'

Kit saved Beth from making any more pointed comments by monopolising Noah's attention at the dinner table, cross-questioning him about Virginia, the tobacco plantation, what he should take with him and conditions aboard ship. 'And Phoebe has made me an extra warm shirt since she says you never know what kind of winters there will be in Virginia,' he said.

'You can buy shirts in Jamestown, you know,' said Noah. 'You may be surprised how refined the colony is. Ladies dress in silk and play the virginals, just as in London. Virginia certainly isn't the primitive place it was for the first settlers.'

'I'm not sure if that doesn't make it less exciting,' said Kit, looking disappointed.

'Less exciting but a deal more comfortable, I assure you. Mind you, the Indians can still cause trouble.'

Beth pushed aside her mutton stew. All the talk of Virginia had made her lose her appetite.

During the afternoon the twins arrived.

'We wanted to see Kit before he goes,' said Samuel. 'We're going to accompany him to the docks tomorrow to see him off.'

'Give him a send-off from the Old Country he'll never forget,' added Joshua with a wicked smile.

A momentary pang of jealousy that Noah and the twins would be on the quayside to wave goodbye to Kit made Beth purse her lips.

But Kit had begged his family not to be there because it would be too upsetting for them all.

'You look as sick as a cat, Beth,' said Joshua. 'Missing Kit already?'

She nodded, unable to speak.

'Tell you what,' said Samuel, giving her a hug, 'after he's gone, why don't you come up to Chelsea and stay with us for a while? We'll see a play or somesuch to cheer you up.'

Beth sighed. 'I'm not sure how Lady Arabella would feel about that. She's never liked me.'

'Mother never likes anyone unless they can be useful to her,' laughed Joshua. 'But I can sweet talk her. And after all, we spent half our childhood here at Merryfields.'

Later, Susannah sat by the fire with her embroidery on her knee but Beth saw that she had eyes only for Kit as he laughed and joshed with the twins while they played a noisy game of cards.

William stirred the logs into a brisk blaze with the poker and then stared blindly into the flames, his head turned towards the sound of Kit's voice.

Beth sat with Cecily and John, ostensibly playing spillikins, but she, too, was drinking in every last moment of Kit's presence, engraving the curve of his cheek and the boyish lines of his lean figure on to her memory.

'Beth!' Cecily shook her arm. 'You're not paying attention!'

'Sorry.' Beth studied the pile of spillikins, but made her move too hastily and several rolled off the edge of the table.

'Careless!' crowed John.

Beth turned her attention back to Kit. He was laughing at something Noah had said, his hand of cards laid against his chest. Then, almost as if he felt his sister's gaze boring into him, he turned to look over his shoulder at her until their eyes met across the room. His smile faltered and faded.

Her heart nearly breaking, Beth called out through a mist of tears, 'Keep your eye on your cards, Kit, or you'll let those rascals beat you!'

For a long moment Kit held her gaze before returning to his game.

Beth swallowed and clenched her fists so that her nails bit into her palms, determined not to spoil this last evening with a fit of weeping.

The clock on the chimney piece chimed.

William sighed. 'It's late. It's time to say our prayers together for the last time.'

The morning of Kit's departure dawned clear and bright.

Heavy-hearted, Beth dressed in a gown of fine green wool that Anne had given to her and came down the stairs with Orpheus at her heels. Kit's trunk was waiting in the hall; her stomach churned at the visible reminder of his coming departure. The lid was open so she peeped inside.

Mama had presented him with a well-stocked apothecary box and the warm shirt lovingly sewn by Phoebe was carefully folded beside it. His father's gift of a specially bound book of Donne's poetry rested on top. Johannes's little folder of sketches was in the pocket. Tucked inside was her own painting of a full-blown pink rose, her mother's highly scented Apothecary's rose, which she hoped would remind him of the pure beauty of the garden at Merryfields in summer.

She slumped down on the bottom step with her head in her hands. A tear rolled off her chin and she rubbed at the dark stain it made on her skirt. Orpheus whined and lifted his paw heavily on to her knee, gazing up at her with soulful brown eyes. 'You'll miss Kit, too, won't you?' she said, fondling his wiry head.

Orpheus pricked up his ears, his tail swishing across the stone floor.

Footsteps sprinted along the gallery and Kit and Noah raced each other down the stairs, two at a time.

Beth wiped her eyes. It would never do for one of Kit's last memories to be of her sad face.

'You're up early!' said Noah.

'I couldn't sleep.'

'Nor I,' confessed her brother with a wry smile.

'This is harder than I could ever have imagined,' he said, his expression utterly miserable. 'I thought I wanted to leave Merryfields but . . .'

'Don't go, then!' Beth's spirits soared. 'It's not too late!'

Kit's chin quivered. 'But, can't you see? I *have* to find out about the world. I love you all so much but I'll go mad if I remain confined here.'

Her last hope flickered and died.

'If you really aren't happy you can always return,' said Noah.

'Perhaps.' Kit stared down at his hands. 'But if I don't make a success of it, what then? I must see this through but I'm not sure I can bear to say my goodbyes.' He drew a shuddering breath. 'Perhaps I should just slip away?'

Noah gripped him by the arm. 'You're too much of a man to do that! Smile and say your goodbyes but don't linger.'

Kit squared his shoulders. 'You're right, of course.'

Joseph appeared from the domestic quarters. 'Emmanuel has the boat ready, Kit,' he said. 'And Samuel and Joshua are already aboard.'

Kit nodded. He took a deep breath and made a visible effort to smile. 'I'll miss you. What fun we had as children, running wild in the garden, eh?'

'I'll not forget it.'

'And Joseph, isn't it about time you made an honest woman of Sara? Perhaps I may hear news of your marriage before too long?'

Joseph shuffled his feet, a rosy flush staining his brown cheeks.

'Mustn't keep the tide waiting,' said William, white-faced.

Servants and guests, many of whom had known Kit since he was a little boy, lined up along the landing stage, shivering in the watery sunshine, to say goodbye.

Kit, with his parents and siblings behind him, made his way slowly past them, exchanging a few words with each one.

Clarence Smith touched him on the shoulder as if bestowing a knighthood. 'Go out into the world and make us proud of you, my boy.'

Peg tucked the remains of the beef pie, neatly wrapped in a clean cloth, into his pocket. 'Can't bear the thought of you going hungry in a savage land,' she said.

Noah, laughter in his eyes, whispered to Beth, 'That pie will certainly be full of savage maggots by the time it reaches Virginia!'

Beth attempted a smile but then Cecily began to keen and faint and she had to support her while Susannah waved sal volatile under her nose.

John, rather red in the face from the effort of not crying, hugged his brother. 'Here,' he said, holding out a small packet. 'S-s-some of my favourite seeds for you. Grow an English garden for me in V-V-Virginia.'

'I will,' said Kit. 'A little piece of Merryfields in the midst of the New World.'

Cecily collapsed against him, sobbing as if her heart would break, while Beth wondered how she contrived to weep and wail to such an extent without her eyes turning bloodshot.

Then it was Beth's turn and she hugged Kit tightly, breathing in the scent of his dark hair. Pictures of him as a newborn with his eyes screwed shut against the light and then as a sturdy toddler clinging to her hand in the garden and of him laughing self-consciously in his first long trousers flashed through her mind. Now she would never see him as his shoulders broadened and he grew into a man. Tears prickled and burned at the back of her throat but she blinked them away and forced her quivering lips to smile. 'When I'm falling asleep at night I'll imagine you sitting beside me in the fork of the old plum tree,' she whispered.

'Just like when we were children and getting up to mischief.' Kit smiled a crooked smile.

Slowly, Beth let go of his hand, curling her fingers over her palm to retain the warmth of her brother's last touch.

At the end of the landing stage, Joshua jumped into the boat, rocking the boat so dangerously that Samuel had to clutch the sides for fear of falling out.

Joshua hooted in derision and splashed a fistful of river at him, while Orpheus went into a paroxysm of barking, his tail thrashing.

'*Hurry up*, Kit, or there won't be time to raise a tankard of ale to you in the Crown before you board!'

Unsmiling, William grasped his son by his upper arms and stared into his face as if fixing it in his memory. 'I'm proud of you, Kit, for being brave and honest enough to face up to me, like a man. Your mother and I will think of you every day and live in expectation of your happiness and success.' Then his face crumpled and he gathered Kit to his chest and buried his face in his dark hair.

'Kit!' bellowed Joshua. 'Come *on*! We'll miss the tide.'

Susannah encircled her husband and her son in her arms, their heads touching.

Beth watched them, an unwelcome ache in her breast at not being included. Cecily clung to her arm, sobbing convulsively.

'It's time to go,' said Susannah after a few moments. She kissed Kit's cheek, smiled through her tears and released him. 'Don't forget to write! We'll all be waiting to hear about this wonderful new life of yours.'

Kit swallowed, his eyes very bright. 'I will,' he said. He climbed into the boat, accompanied by rousing cheers from the twins.

Cecily shrieked and buried her face in her mother's neck, while Susannah, suddenly looking ten years older, never took her eyes off Kit.

Beth, too, fixed her gaze on her brother as he perched himself on top of his trunk. She burned the picture he made into her memory, taking in the blue-black shine of his hair in the pale sun and the faint shadow of stubble on his chin. She studied the chiselled line of his jaw, his finely winged eyebrows and the set of his shoulders with as much care as if she were drawing his portrait. Lost in thought, she jumped when Noah spoke to her.

'He'll be all right, you know,' he said. 'I truly believe he is going to a life that will make him happy.' His brow was furrowed and his eyes anxious as he studied her.

'Don't let the twins get him too drunk before he boards the ship.'

'I won't. And I will return tomorrow.' Noah's warm cheek brushed against hers before he, too, clambered into the boat.

Emmanuel cast off to cries of 'Farewell, God keep you!'

John reached out to Beth, his fingers rough and callused from gardening. 'You still have one b-b-brother at Merryfields,' he said.

Beth lifted his hand to her cheek. 'And I thank God for you, John.'

Emmanuel pulled hard on the oars, stirring up the olive green water to release its brackish scent. The *clunk* of the oars in the rowlocks echoed back to them over the water and the boat spun away into the centre of the river.

The twins waved and cheered.

Anxious not to miss a moment of her last sight of him, Beth stared unblinkingly at Kit's dark head and pale face as he looked back over his shoulder, a hand raised in farewell. John and Beth stood arm in arm beside their silent mother and father, watching the boat grow smaller and smaller, accompanied by the diminishing wails of Cecily's weeping.

Chapter 13

On Christmas morning Beth awoke to see grey fog and drizzle running down the window. The damp mist permeated the house, creeping in through the casements and causing the fires to smoke and the guests to huddle together, coughing.

Almost all the inhabitants of Merryfields braved the weather to walk to the church for the morning service, enduring the usual curious glances of the congregation. Nelly Byrne took off her shoes to show the squire her red Christmas stockings and Poor Joan wept unrestrainedly at the thought of the baby Jesus lying cold in a manger.

The parson gave a rousing sermon against the ills of popish practices, which set heads nodding in agreement, Johannes said Amen loudly enough for the congregation to turn and look at him. The parson ended the service with a call for peace and goodwill to all men.

Back at Merryfields, William, John and Noah dragged in the yule log and worked the bellows to fan the flame until the sodden wood stopped steaming and there was a cheerful blaze.

Susannah and Beth decorated the table with garlands of ivy and sprigs of berried holly and lit a week's supply of candles to dispel the gloom.

The centrepiece of the dinner was a great baron of beef sent as a Christmas gift by Princess Anne, surrounded by several roast fowl and buttered root vegetables.

Afterwards, Joseph and Emmanuel carried in a vast plum pudding with great ceremony, while Peg watched with a smile on her face and her hands on her hips, ready to spoon it into bowls. If there was more flour and suet and fewer raisins that usual in the pudding, no one seemed to notice. Spiced ale simmered on the fire, filling the great hall with the warm and comforting aroma of cinnamon, cloves and orange. The guests enjoyed their festive dinner but, for the family, nothing could make up for the empty place at the table where Kit usually sat.

Noah presented gifts to all the family and boxes of sweetmeats for the guests.

Beth unwrapped the roll of paper that he gave her, all tied up with a red ribbon and a sprig of mistletoe. She spread out the paper on the table and saw that it was a carefully worked pen and ink drawing of a church.

'I thought you might like this,' Noah said. 'It's St James Garlickhythe. I made a copy of my working drawing to show you how I've designed the new steeple.' His brown eyes were slightly anxious as Beth remained silent.

'This is the church that you say people call Wren's Lantern,' she said at last.

Noah smiled. 'You remembered! The steeple is to be in white Portland stone and it will dazzle in the sunlight so that people cannot help but look at it.'

'It's so beautiful, Noah.' She studied the intricate ascending tiers all set upon columns, reaching up for the heavens. 'Your line work is extremely fine.'

111

He grinned. 'I had to work on it by candlelight after the day's work was finished and was fearful that I'd make a mistake, especially as I know your own artistic standards are so high.'

'So that's what you've been doing every evening!' she said. 'I thought you were avoiding me after I spoke sharply to you about your work on the royal nursery.'

'Not at all.'

'So how are the works progressing at Richmond?' asked Beth.

'I've finished the survey. It was no easy task as the palace fell into disrepair under the Commonwealth. Once I've drawn up the plans they can be presented to the King.' He pursed his lips. 'I can tell by your expression that you still disapprove of my involvement.'

'I'm afraid I do.'

He sighed. 'It's not my intention but I appear to have displeased you ever since I arrived, haven't I? First because I didn't understand how dedicated you are to your painting, and then because I carried the letter which resulted in Kit leaving Merryfields and now because I'm drawing up plans for the royal nursery.'

'Your arrival at Merryfields was like a stone dropped from a great height into a millpond,' said Beth. 'And the ripples have spread far and wide.' She looked again at the carefully made drawing. 'But I shall treasure this.'

He gave her an uncertain smile.

'And I have something for you.' She handed him a small parcel.

Noah unwrapped the present and his face lit up when he found an apple-wood box to hold his pens and drawing instruments. Beth had painted the lid with an image of Merryfields surrounded by a garland of entwined honeysuckle and roses.

'I've never painted Merryfields before,' she said, 'but I've combined your love of architecture with my love for botanical art in this painting in the hope that you won't forget us when you return to Virginia.' She had spent many hours painting the box, in an attempt to relieve her guilt for her previous coolness towards him.

He ran his finger over the silky-smooth lid of the box. 'I'll never forget you,' he said, leaning forward to kiss her cheek, 'and I'll treasure this box always.'

She smelt the slight smokiness of the fire in his hair and the clean, comforting, male scent of his skin.

'I miss my own family today,' he said quietly.

'What will they be doing now?'

'Father will be bringing in the yule log and Mother and my sisters, Maryanne, Abigail and Kate will be busy in the kitchen.' He smiled. 'Mother will insist on giving the servants a day's holiday. The whole house will smell of baking and egg-nog and cinnamon. There will be candles in the windows and in the afternoon our good neighbours, the Sharpes, will visit with their daughters Hannah and Amy.' He stared into the fire, lost in thought.

'Your poor father will be outnumbered by all the womenfolk,' said Beth. She glanced at Kit's empty chair. 'I wonder what Kit is doing now? Imagine having only ship's biscuits for your Christmas dinner!'

'I expect they will be washed down with a swig of rum and there are sure to be other passengers who will sing a round of Christmas carols with him.'

'And by next Christmas you will be back at home.'

Noah reached for Beth's hand. 'And then I'll be missing you. I mean I'll be missing all of you.'

Johannes brought mugs of hot spiced ale and sat beside them. He picked up Noah's drawing to study it closely. 'You are a careful draughtsman, Noah.'

'That is praise indeed, coming from Johannes.' Beth smiled.

Johannes ran a hand through his thick blond hair. 'Am I such a hard taskmaster?'

'Oh yes!' said Beth. 'But I wouldn't have it any other way. You have made me delve deep inside myself to find out what I am capable of.'

He gripped her wrist with his big hand. 'And you must never forget that you are always capable of more!'

They sat in companionable silence for a while, watching John roasting chestnuts, while Cecily danced about blowing on her fingers as she peeled off the hot skins.

Clarence Smith stood up in front of the fireplace and began to sing 'I Saw Three Ships Come Sailing In'.

One by one the others moved into a circle around the fire and joined in. Joseph brought out his penny whistle and Old Silas accompanied him on his fiddle as the party worked through their entire repertoire of carols.

Noah joined in the singing with his clear tenor voice. Beth smiled to herself as she noticed how his thumb unconsciously stroked the lid of the painted pen box she had made for him. She felt a surprising tenderness growing in her feelings towards him. Perhaps he wasn't as arrogant as she'd previously thought? Johannes wiped a tear from his cheek and Beth reached out to him. He drew a deep breath, hugging her to his chest.

'Ach, Beth, Christmas brings back memories of such happy times. I remember my Annelies . . .' His face twisted with emotion. 'I will return to the studio, I think. Work is the only cure for what ails me.'

Beth watched him go, her heart aching that she could not take away his pain. Sighing, she was overcome again by melancholy because Kit was no longer with them and because the following Christmastide Noah, too, would be gone.

Later, after supper had been cleared away and the family and guests had gone yawning off to bed, Susannah asked Beth to accompany her on evening rounds.

Afterwards, in the corridor, Susannah sighed. 'We always used to do the evening round together when you were little, Beth. We had so many guests then. Your father and I had such dreams for Merryfields.'

'But you have realised those dreams in every way,' said Beth, 'except for the fact that you can't bring yourselves to turn away an impoverished guest who needs you.' She yawned. 'I'm ready for bed myself. It's been a lovely Christmas, in spite of missing Kit.'

Susannah kissed her cheek. 'He will always be in our hearts, won't he?'

Beth nodded, swallowing back her sadness. 'Goodnight Mama.'

'Good night, sweetheart. Sweet dreams.'

Chapter 14

January 1688

Muttering to himself, Johannes walked twice around the studio table, his boots squeaking. Snatching up the Persian carpet, he shook it vigorously sending a cold draught and a shower of dust towards where Beth was working at her easel. Once he'd arranged the carpet on the table he paced over to the little storeroom and gathered various items into his arms, slamming the door behind him. He clattered the candlestick against the edge of the china jug and dropped an apple, which rolled across the floor. The lute slid down from its resting place against the globe and crashed to the table.

Beth sighed and put down her paintbrush. 'Is there something I can do to help, Johannes?'

'This still life does not attract the eye.'

She squinted at the arrangement: he was right. She moved the lute and rearranged the linen backdrop, then repositioned the globe, turning it slowly upon its axis until her attention was caught by Virginia. She tried to imagine what it was like in that faraway country, a place of fearsome savages who wore feathered head dresses and covered their semi-naked bodies in warpaint. Noah had mentioned the wonderful plants there, exotic ferns and great shrubs covered in blossoms so highly perfumed they made your senses swim. Momentarily she felt a powerful longing to see it for herself; to record them all.

'Perhaps some flowers?' she ventured. 'Although there is little in the garden at present.'

'Ach! I will not waste my time on a still life that does not inspire me.' With a groan of despair, he snatched up the pewter candlestick and dashed it to the floor in a flash of temper.

Gasping, Beth looked up from her own painting, her eyes wide.

He stared at her. 'Stop!' he shouted as she started to speak. 'Don't move!' He picked up a stick of charcoal and started to sketch her.

'Johannes?'

'Shh! Keep still!'

A little while later, he stepped back from the easel and studied his sketch through narrowed eyes. '*Yes*,' he breathed. He dropped the charcoal and dragged the Persian carpet off the table, sending the apple rolling to the floor again. Placing the carpet at her feet, he carefully arranged the folds of her homespun painting skirt as carefully as if it were the finest French silk damask.

He stood back to survey the scene then darted forward to hang a mirror with a decorative frame on the wall behind her. He closed one of the shutters so that the remaining light fell from the window directly on to her face. Tipping her chin up with his finger, he turned her face a fraction to the left. After a moment he nodded decisively. 'That will do.'

Standing at his easel, he selected a fine brush and dipped it in the pot of thin terracotta paint that Beth had prepared earlier for him. He was ready to start.

Beth sat as still as she could, wondering if she could continue with her own work while Johannes painted her. He soon disabused her of that notion, shouting at her when she attempted to look down at her easel. Resigned, she stared back at him, allowing her vision to go misty while she let her thoughts wander.

Noah's drawing of St James Garlickhythe was pinned up on the studio wall and she let her gaze rest on it, touched that he would take the time and trouble to reproduce it for her. She pictured for a moment the happy family scene that he had described to her of his home in Virginia and took comfort from the thought that Kit would be welcome there.

She continued to daydream until she was jolted out of her reverie by a scratching at the door. It swung open and Orpheus ambled in. He sniffed at the apple, still lying under the table, then lowered himself down on to the carpet at Beth's feet.

'Hey, dog!' Johannes waved his arms at the offending creature.

Orpheus ignored him totally, sighed heavily and closed his eyes to sleep.

Beth met Johannes's affronted glare and burst out laughing.

'Perhaps the dog adds to the composition,' he said, his lips curving in a reluctant smile.

'May I move my head and shoulders while you draw him?' asked Beth. 'I have terrible pins and needles.'

'But don't move your feet.'

Orpheus let out a deep, rumbling snore.

***

Much later, Beth twitched her fingers and stretched her arms. 'It's growing dark,' she said. 'Shall I light the lamps, Johannes?'

He nodded. 'The useful light has gone.'

'Is it going well?'

'I think so.' He ran his paint-encrusted hands through his thatch of untidy hair. 'I shall call your portrait *The Painter's Apprentice*. That will make people look at it twice!'

'Because I'm not a boy?'

'Just so.'

'I had better prove my worth as an apprentice then. Shall I mix some more paints for you?

'Don't disturb the arrangement on the table!'

'Of course not.' She collected a piece of chalk from the little store-room and carefully drew around the porphyry grinding slab to mark its position on the wooden table, before moving it to the free space at one end.

Arms crossed over his chest, Johannes stood watching her in silence as she tied a handkerchief over her mouth and nose against the poisonous dust and began to work the white lead on the grinding slab, breaking it down into a fine powder.

A little while later Beth shook out her aching wrists and carefully scraped the white powder into a jar. She wiped the slab with a cloth, rinsing it out in the basin of water, before finally untying the handkerchief from her face. Sliding the slab back into its former position, she aligned it exactly with the chalk lines.

She glanced up at Johannes to seek his approval that she had left all as he wished but saw that he sat in his chair with his eyes closed. Poor man; he was exhausted after his concentrated efforts.

A week later Beth carried a plate of bread and cheese in one hand and a lighted candle in the other. She was anxious again about Johannes. He had missed supper and his mood had deteriorated significantly over the past week. It was plain to see from the deep shadows under his eyes that he wasn't sleeping well. Taciturn and unresponsive as he was, she had failed miserably to encourage him out of his despondent mood and hoped desperately he wasn't going to slip into one of his prolonged fits of despair.

In the studio, Johannes had set candles on tall stands on either side of his easel, casting a flickering light as he bent over a large canvas, painting furiously and muttering under his breath.

Her portrait had been put aside and this new canvas was covered with sweeping lines of under-painting, some smudged and blurred and others fine and delicate. The scene depicted was a battle. Ranks of infantrymen were ranged as far as the eye could see, glimpsed through whirling smoke from fires and muskets. Beth caught her breath as she saw men fighting hand to hand, their faces twisted in expressions of hate and terror as they stepped on the bodies of the slain. A young drummer boy, mouth open in a silent scream, still beat his drum. A terrified horse reared up at the right of the canvas, its eyes rolling and teeth bared. Sickness rose in the back of Beth's throat as she looked at the blood-soaked rider, slumped sideways, his head almost severed from his body. A pregnant woman, her hair wild and her clothing half ripped from her body, lay on the ground with her torn skirts exposing bleeding thighs. Soldiers in the French colours leered at her naked breasts as they buttoned their breeches.

Shivering, Beth turned to Johannes, too shocked by the horrific scene to speak.

'The Battle of Cassel,' he said, in a voice so quiet she could barely hear him. 'I still hear the screams in my head. I smell the fear and the gunpowder and feel the dust slippery with blood beneath my feet.'

'It's a dramatic and epic canvas and the composition of the drawing is excellent,' said Beth carefully, 'but ...'

'It's not pretty enough for you?'

'That doesn't concern me. But working on this canvas, *living* it, will make you melancholy.'

'*Melancholy*? Is that how you call this, this, *agony* that I feel in my heart? I cannot sleep without bad dreams. I remember ...' He ran his fingers through his hair, leaving it sticking up in untidy points. 'Those bloody papist bastards! The memories are burned into me. But I think to myself, perhaps if I paint this terrible vision, maybe then I will forget and the dreams will stop and I may sleep again.'

'Johannes, you will make yourself ill if you don't sleep or eat. I'll ask Mama to make you a sleeping draught.'

'Sleep!' He gave a crooked smile. 'Ask her for hemlock.' He covered his eyes with his palms. 'Then I will sleep and never wake up.'

Alarm made her voice sharp. 'Don't say that, Johannes! Eat your supper and go to bed. I'll fetch you the sleeping draught now.'

He hunched his shoulders and turned his back upon her to stare at the battle scene again.

Beth felt a constriction in the pit of her stomach as she recognised that Johannes had once more started to slide down the slope into despair. She didn't think that poppy syrup was going to cure all that ailed him.

Ten minutes later she returned to the studio to find that he hadn't moved. She touched him gently on the shoulder. 'Enough, Johannes! Time for bed.' He looked up at her, his eyes dark with sorrow; her heart clenched at his pain. 'I've brought you the sleeping draught in a cup of hot milk and I promise you that tonight you will sleep like a baby.' She blew out the candles so that the harrowing canvas disappeared into the dark.

Chapter 15

Beth came yawning down to breakfast. It was still early but her sleep had been so badly disturbed by frightening dreams of Johannes's canvas of the Battle of Cassel that she'd not dared close her eyes again.

Noah was breakfasting in the great hall, a roll of drawings on the table beside him. He took one look at Beth and poured her some coffee.

Gratefully, she sipped the bitter brew, feeling the warmth of it begin to strengthen her. 'You're up early,' she said.

'I'm off to Richmond Palace to meet the Clerk of Works.'

'May I see your drawings?' she asked, interested to see Noah's work in spite of her reservations about their purpose.

He readily untied the roll of papers and spread them out. 'This is the front elevation, showing the Great Gate. We'll be restoring the battlements over the top.'

'Very fine. And this one?' Beth smoothed down the curling edges of a plan as they bent over it, heads together.

'Here is the nursery,' said Noah. 'There will be new doorways to the adjacent chambers for the wet nurse and the dry nurse. The nursery maids and scullery maids have the attics. The kitchens are here beside the storerooms, with attendant quarters for the cook and housekeeper. There will be a laundry for the baby's breech cloths and I've made provision for the King and Queen to have their own bedchambers and salon in case they wish to visit the child.' His face glowed with enthusiasm.

'All this for one baby?' asked Beth wonderingly.

Noah laughed. 'I haven't even mentioned the quarters for the rest of the retinue or the garden. And the King spares no expense. The little princeling's quarters will be finished with nothing but the very best silk hangings and wallpapers especially imported from France ...'

'Traitor!' The hoarse shout came from behind them, startling them so much that their heads banged together.

Johannes, his face suffused with scarlet, stood before them with his fists clenched and his chest heaving. 'Papist traitor!'

A sudden cold wave of apprehension gripped at Beth's vitals. 'Johannes ...' She reached out a hand towards him but he pushed it away, his bloodshot eyes focused on Noah.

Slowly, Noah stood up. 'Johannes, you misunderstand ...'

'I misunderstand nothing! You support the papist cause and laugh in my face, describing the luxury of the nursery you make for this ... this spawn of the Devil! Can you not see that the King and his priests will destroy us all?' His jaw worked with emotion and his lips were flecked with spittle.

Noah spread his hands wide. 'Truly Johannes, I do not support the papist cause. I merely ...'

'You papists killed my family!' shouted Johannes, jabbing his forefinger at Noah. 'Liar! Murderer!' He launched himself at Noah, fastening his fingers around his throat and shaking him violently like a terrier with a rat.

Noah fought to free himself but Johannes only shook him all the harder.

'Johannes! Johannes, stop!' Beth threw herself at him, but he was seized by bloodlust and deaf to her cries.

Noah's face turned purple as he scrabbled frantically to free his neck from Johannes's vice-like grip. Beth wrenched at Johannes's arm but he flung her off and she thudded against the wall. Dazed, she fumbled for her whistle, giving three shrill bursts.

Noah ceased his struggles and his eyes rolled up to show the whites as he slumped against Johannes's chest.

Terrified, Beth yanked violently at Johannes's hair. He gave a howl of pain and lashed back, smashing his elbow into her face. Moaning, she clasped her nose as shooting stars of agony exploded across her vision.

Noah, grey-faced and with his tongue protruding, had collapsed to the floor by the time Emmanuel and William arrived to prise Johannes's fingers away and force his forearms behind his back.

Johannes continued to rage, twisting and fighting in Emmanuel's imprisoning arms.

'In the name of heaven, what happened?' asked William as he tore open Noah's shirt and tried to rouse him.

Beth fell to her knees beside them, her knuckles pushed against her mouth, the cold grip of dread that Johannes had killed Noah rendering her speechless.

'*Moordenaar!* Papist murderer!' Johannes yelled.

William shook Noah hard and slapped his cheeks. 'Come *on*, Noah! Wake up!'

Noah's chest rose and the breath rasped in his throat.

'Thank the Lord!' said William. 'Take slow, easy breaths, Noah. You're safe now.'

Susannah pushed her way through the gathering of shocked faces crowded all around. Beth pulled herself to her feet and clung to her mother with shaking arms.

'Whatever happened?' asked Susannah, as she dabbed at Beth's nose with her handkerchief.

Beth stared in horror at the lock of Johannes's hair, torn out by the roots, that was still entwined in her fingers. Her voice broke. 'I c-c-couldn't make him stop.' She glanced at Noah, whose face was ashen. There were angry red marks around his neck as he continued to heave for breath.

Johannes, still lost to reason, flailed his arms, sobbing and screaming as Joseph and Emmanuel grappled with him.

Poor Joan's voice rose in a terrified wail, accompanied by anxious cries from Nellie Byrne, and Susannah went to soothe them.

'Emmanuel,' said William, 'put Johannes in the cell.'

'No!' Beth grasped her father's arm. 'You can't!'

'Beth, look at him! He's a danger to himself and to others. See what he's done to you and to Noah.' He tipped up her chin and gently felt her nose and cheek. 'Nothing broken but you'll have a black eye.'

'I don't care about that,' she said impatiently, brushing his hand away. 'Father, it's *Johannes!* Please, *please* don't put him in the cell.'

William's face was implacable. 'He nearly killed Noah. Tend to Noah's bruises while I sedate Johannes.'

Johannes, roaring and fighting like a man possessed by the Devil, was manhandled away.

Beth sat on the floor beside Noah until his breathing steadied. Eventually his eyes opened and she was shocked to see that they were red with burst blood vessels. Gently, she smoothed the hair off his forehead. 'Shh! Don't try to speak. You're all right now.'

After a while she helped him to his feet and supported him to the dispensary. Talking reassuringly to him with a calmness she didn't feel, she placed cooling compresses on to the swelling and empurpled skin of his neck, unsure which one of them was shaking the most. She poured out a measure of honey and glycerine linctus for him. 'Sip this,' she said. 'It will soothe your throat.'

'Your poor face!' croaked Noah. He reached up to touch her cheek; that was her undoing.

'I thought Johannes was going to kill you!' Her throat closed in a spasm as she choked back tears. A few more seconds and Noah's life would have been snuffed out.

Noah pulled her head to his shoulder, his breathing harsh in her ear as she struggled to contain the waves of trembling that had overtaken her.

'Johannes is never violent!' she said, as Noah patted her back. 'He becomes sad and miserable but I never thought it possible he could ever hurt anyone.'

'Shh, now!' whispered Noah.

Beth clung to him, squeezing her eyes tight shut to banish the picture of her beloved Johannes with the light of murder in his eye.

Chapter 16

The following morning Beth dressed quickly, her teeth chattering in the freezing air of her bedchamber, and then examined her face in the mirror. Her father had been right: she had a black eye a prize-fighter would be proud of.

Shock had set in the previous night after she went to bed. Cecily had wrapped her in the curve of her body and held her tightly while she shivered and wept. She was still unable to put out of her mind what Johannes had done to Noah.

Leaving Cecily to sleep, Beth went to find her parents as they breakfasted in the great hall. 'I can't believe that Johannes turned like that,' said Beth in disbelief to William. 'He's always so gentle. He'll be frightened in the cell and I must go and see him.'

'We gave him a strong sleeping draught last night and he's not yet awake. The question is: what are we going to do with him?' asked William, a frown creasing his forehead.

Susannah took Beth's hand. 'Evidently, he isn't to be trusted any more and I'm worried for the other guests.'

Beth stared at her, horror-struck. 'You won't make Johannes leave Merryfields! He didn't mean to hurt me. Christmastime is always difficult for him as it brings home to him how much he misses his family, and then he overheard Noah talking about his plans for the royal nursery which upset him terribly. Father, Mama, come to the studio with me now. I must show you something.' She took hold of their hands. 'Please!'

In the studio the great canvas still rested on the easel. With trembling fingers Beth turned it towards the light so that her parents could study it more closely. The painting was even more horrifying by the light of day and the terror of it sliced into her insides. 'He's told me many times of the atrocities the French carried out on the Dutch soldiers and how his brothers were killed and then his wife—' She broke off, her face scarlet, unable to use the word *raped*. 'His wife was attacked and died later, along with the baby she carried.'

William and Susannah stared silently at the harrowing panorama for a long time.

'Can't you *see* how distressed he must be to have painted this monstrous scene? He blames the Roman Catholics for his family's deaths. And then to hear that Noah is building a luxurious nursery for a papist prince, a prince who could be the means for the King to turn England into a Catholic country again . . . '

Slowly, William said, 'The poor man is caught in the living hell of his own memories.'

'Creating this terrible picture must have made it all come to life again for him,' said Susannah.

'Please,' Beth pleaded, 'I beg of you, you must let him stay at Merryfields! We are the only family he has left now.'

'I will make no decisions until I have spoken to him,' said William. 'Meanwhile, will you mingle with the guests this morning and try to reassure them? They're all upset by the disturbance.'

'Will you promise to call me as soon as I can see Johannes?' asked Beth.

'Of course.'

It was late afternoon before William accompanied Beth to the cell. 'He's quiet now,' he said, 'but he refused to talk about what happened.'

Johannes sat with his back to them and Beth was overcome with pity for him. The big man seemed somehow diminished; it wrung her heart.

Beth moved forward but William caught her by the wrist and held her to his side. 'Johannes,' she whispered.

His head jerked around. 'You came, then?' His face was as grey as ashes and his eyes dull.

As he stared at her a look of horror washed over his face. Burying his head in his hands, his shoulders heaved.

Beth shook her father's hand off her wrist and ran to embrace Johannes. She rested her chin on his hair and rocked him as he wept, murmuring nonsense words of comfort while tears fell in a stream off her chin.

'I'm sorry,' he sobbed. 'Can you ever forgive me?'

'Hush, now!' she soothed.

'Your pretty face is all bruised. I never meant to ... Hearing about the papist prince ... terrible changes are coming to this country where I thought I was safe! And my battle painting, the memories of that time still so clear in my mind ... ' He drew in a shuddering breath. 'I was there again, the blood slippery under my feet and my brothers all hacked to pieces ... '

'But Johannes, you must know that Noah is not a papist? His work is almost entirely building *Anglican* churches. But while he is working for Sir Christopher Wren, he must do as he is bid. His involvement with the royal nursery is most definitely not because he

129

wants a papist heir to the throne. Besides, the people of this country do not want Catholicism in England and will do everything to oppose it.'

'The question is,' said William, 'what are we going to do with you now?'

Johannes hung his head. 'I want nothing but to spend my time painting with Beth.'

'I need some time to consider the best course of action,' said William.

Johannes gently touched Beth's face. 'I'm so sorry, my little chicken. I was gripped by such a sudden terror I didn't know what I was doing. And I am sorry I hurt Noah too.'

Her heart breaking, she held his hand to her cheek. 'I know that, Johannes.'

Later, Beth and her parents sat in the solar, deciding what to do.

'We cannot risk Johannes attacking anyone again,' said William.

'That painting must be destroyed,' said Susannah, 'since it inflames his passions so dangerously.'

'But Johannes isn't dangerous!' protested Beth.

'Can we be sure of that?'

Beth went to look down at the garden, where John and Old Silas were busy clearing the flowerbeds of the last leaves. A twist of smoke rose up from the bonfire in the vegetable garden. Suddenly the solution came to her. 'You always say that busy hands make for a happy mind, Father.'

'Our successes at Merryfields have proved that.'

'Then we should let Johannes work. I do not think he truly cares if he never leaves the studio at all. There is that little storeroom where we keep the paints and props for the still life paintings. Johannes could have a bed in there. You can lock him in.'

'But ...'

130

'I am a calming influence on him, Father. I know him better than anyone and can alert you immediately if I think his behaviour is changing. Let Joseph stay with us for a while if you like, as a guard.'

'Beth speaks a great deal of sense,' said Susannah

William sighed. 'I see you two are in collusion against me.' He smiled at Beth. 'I will not risk your safety but in my opinion yesterday's furore was an exceptional incident. However, one more like that and Johannes will have to leave Merryfields. And we will burn the battle scene.'

'Must you?' asked Beth. 'Surely you can see it will be a great work of art?'

'But it would destroy its creator in the process,' said William.

Half an hour later, Beth stood beside John and Noah watching the canvas burn on the garden bonfire. The drummer boy writhed in silent screams as flames licked at the canvas, bringing to life the swirling smoke. The dying horse at the edge of the drawing blackened and then burst into flames as the breeze teased the fire into a blaze.

'It's terrible, the agony man inflicts upon another in the name of religion,' whispered Noah, his voice still hoarse.

Beth wrapped her arms tightly across her chest to prevent herself from snatching the canvas to safety and beating out the flames. Horrifying though it was, it had the potential to be one of Johannes's best works.

'I feel guilty about the destruction of such a painting,' said Noah miserably. 'If only I'd left for Richmond Palace a little earlier . . .' He sighed. 'In the circumstances I shall return to Fulham.'

Beth's stomach clenched. Confused, she realised she didn't want him to go but at the same time she couldn't help thinking that if he hadn't boasted about the proposed opulence of the royal nursery Johannes would not have been driven into such a passion.

John poked the canvas with a stick and it crackled and curled until before long it was nothing more than a glowing pile of ashes. He heaped another bucket of damp leaves on top and black smoke billowed over them in a cloud.

'It's a s-s-shame,' said John. 'Still, now he can finish your p-p-portrait.' He smiled, mischief in his eyes. 'I w-w-wonder if he has enough colours in his palette to paint your face, since your bruises display all the colours of the rainbow?'

Beth turned away so that he wouldn't see her cry.

Later that day William, Beth and Joseph escorted Johannes to the studio.

'My daughter has interceded for you but if there is any hint of violence I will have no choice but to send you away from Merryfields,' warned William.

Johannes looked around the studio as if he'd never expected to see it again. 'I will not disappoint you,' he said in a voice so quiet it was hard to make out the words. 'I was overtaken by the fit of the moment and am sorry for it.'

'Then I shall leave you. Joseph, you will stay here.'

Joseph stationed himself by the door with his arms folded.

Beth lifted her muslin-draped portrait from the floor and set it on the easel. 'Shall I lay out your paints for you, Master?'

A flicker of a smile raced across Johannes's face. 'Yes, Beth. I have work to do.'

They quickly fitted back into their old routine. Beth, with Orpheus at her feet, posed for Johannes every morning, while Joseph stood like a carved mahogany statue by the door. Sara brought Johannes a dish of food every dinnertime while Beth and Joseph went down to the great hall to eat, carefully locking the door behind them. Afterwards, Beth returned to prepare more paints for Johannes and then to continue with her own work.

'This is very good,' said Johannes one afternoon as he studied her latest painting of a yellow crocus. 'You understand now, I think, how to look at an object and decide how to paint it.'

Beth's heart swelled at his praise.

'Perhaps I have been selfish in keeping you as my apprentice when you have already reached a high level of skill. But still you must practise, practise every day. Nothing must stand in the way of your work.' He gripped her hands even tighter. 'To be a great artist you have to make sacrifices. Do you understand me?'

Johannes's love for her shone in his eyes as Beth lifted his clasped hands to her lips. 'I understand, Johannes.'

His grip relaxed a little. 'You are capable of great things, Beth. Your botanical paintings are excellent but you should experiment. Look beyond the flowers you love and try different styles and larger canvases! Paint life in all its different forms and settings. Be bold and brave!'

Early the following morning Beth persuaded her father that Joseph need not come to watch over her and William accompanied her to the studio.

Johannes was already bent over before his easel. Absorbed in his task, he barely glanced at them. The table at his side was untidy, as if he'd been at work for several hours.

Curious, she wondered how long it would be before she would be allowed to see her portrait.

'Johannes? Can we talk to you?'

Slowly he looked up and Beth was concerned to see that his eyes were strained and his face pallid with fatigue.

Johannes bowed his head. 'I am ashamed that I have caused distress, Dr Ambrose. You have all been so kind to me ...' He blinked hard and rubbed at his eyes with paint-stained knuckles. 'It is not my usual nature ...'

133

William clasped his arm. 'We know that. You may return to your room in the attic and take your meals in the great hall again.'

'I promise that I will trouble you no longer,' said Johannes.

'Then I shall leave you to your work.' William smiled. 'And I look forward very much to seeing my daughter immortalised in oils.'

'How is the portrait coming along?' asked Beth after William had gone.

'I worked all the night and hope to finish today. The background is complete.' He spoke in low tones and Beth had to strain to hear him.

Johannes sat her back in the same position at her easel, turned towards the window, with her feet touching the chalk marks he'd placed on the floor to note her position. He adjusted the window shutter until the light was right and tipped up her chin with his fore-finger. 'Now lick your lips and take a breath as if you are about to speak. Good.' He returned to his easel and where he began to work without speaking, the tip of his tongue protruding and an intense frown of concentration on his brow.

Some considerable time later, Beth had an itch on her nose. She stared fixedly up at Johannes as he painted her, not daring to move. Spots began to float in front of her eyes. At last, unable to stand it any longer, her hand moved involuntarily.

'Ach! Beth, can you not sit still for five minutes?'

'Johannes, it's been hours!'

He came to reposition her arm. He tilted her head a fraction towards the window and tweaked at the folds of her skirt. 'Now keep still!'

Outside rooks squabbled in the elm trees; Beth heard John's voice calling to Silas in the garden.

A couple of hours later every muscle in Beth's body was scream-ing but still she dared not move.

At last, Johannes stood back from the canvas. He studied it for a while, made to move forward with his brush poised but then changed his mind. 'It is done,' he sighed.

Beth stood up and stretched. 'May I see it?' Curiosity made her voice eager.

Johannes hesitated. 'Later. I would like to be alone now.'

Rebuffed, she studied his hair, streaked with paint and hanging in lank clumps around his face. She was overcome with love and compassion for him to see how old he looked. 'You look tired, Johannes. Can you rest a while?'

He took her hand and kissed it. 'My sweet Beth. You must not worry about me.'

'I do worry about you! Your health is not robust . . . '

He caught her up in a bear hug and kissed the top of her head. 'You may have a holiday from your work this afternoon and I shall rest now. I believe I have found the way forward again.' He held her at arm's length and smiled at her. 'Your portrait can never truly do you justice but nevertheless, I am pleased with it.'

He carefully covered the canvas again and untied his sacking apron.

Quietly, Beth closed the studio door behind her.

Chapter 17

During the afternoon Beth helped her mother in the apothecary, then went outside to the garden. She came across John tying up a rose bush that had fallen over in the last storm.

'The f-f-fresh air has put roses in your cheeks, Beth,' he said.

She folded her arms and buried her hands in her sleeves against the bitter wind. 'I came outside searching for a snowdrop to paint.'

'Go and look under the old oak tree. There is a c-c-cloud of snow-drops there.'

Snowdrops in full bloom and tight bud carpeted the ground under the oak tree and Beth examined them closely until she discovered a perfect specimen. Pleased with her find, she hurried upstairs to the studio to show it to Johannes.

Johannes was nowhere to be seen. She stood in the stillness of the room, remembering how exhausted he'd looked and guessed he must have returned to his attic to sleep.

The paintbrushes had been placed in a neat pile, wrapped in a turpentine-soaked cloth, ready for her to clean. Her portrait, covered in muslin, rested on the easel. After a moment or two she went towards it. Looking over her shoulder she lifted a corner of the cloth and caught a glimpse of the bottom of the canvas. It showed a corner of the intricately patterned Persian rug and part of Orpheus's flank, with every hair of his wiry grey coat seemingly painted individually.

The sound of footsteps along the gallery made her drop the muslin and retreat to the window, her heart clamouring in her chest. But the door didn't open and Johannes didn't materialise.

She cleaned the brushes and restored order to the painting table, all the while resisting the urge to peep again at her portrait.

The light was fading; it was too late to start painting the snowdrop now. She placed it in the little green glass bottle that John had dug up in the garden, the one he always insisted was Roman. Stepping back to look at it, she smiled to herself. She would start work bright and early the following morning.

Orpheus waited patiently outside the kitchen and grasped the opportunity to sidle inside as soon as Beth opened the door.

Phoebe, slicing cabbage at the table, smiled a greeting.

Peg flapped a cloth at Orpheus. 'Go on, you great brute, out of my kitchen!'

Orpheus slunk under the table, eyeing the soup cauldron from behind Phoebe's skirts.

'Have you seen Johannes?' Beth asked. 'He missed his dinner again.'

'Not seen him since the incident with Noah,' Peg said. 'He looked as miserable as a featherless chicken in the snow. I thought then that he might be heading for one of his funny turns again.' She pushed Orpheus away from the cauldron with her knee. 'Dratted dog, always sniffing round the soup! But then, a dog's never likely to be content with bread and water, which is all he's had for the past few days. Take Johannes an apple. There are still some that aren't too wrinkled.'

Beth put an apple, bread and a heel of cheese on a plate and carried it up to the attics. She knocked at the door of Johannes's room and waited.

Orpheus sniffed loudly at the gap under the door.

Beth knocked again. Silence.

'Shall we go in, Orpheus?'

The dog pricked up his ears and his tail stirred.

Very gently, Beth lifted the latch and peered inside Johannes's room.

The shutters were closed but the bedclothes were tossed into a heap at the end of the mattress. Johannes wasn't there. Beth stepped inside the room and opened the shutters to let in the last of the light.

She stared curiously around the plain, whitewashed room, bare except for the bed, a rag rug, a wooden chest and a small picture hanging on the wall above the fireplace. The painting, one of Johannes's own, showed a homely scene of his wife, Annelies, sitting in a doorway with her spinning wheel. Beth looked closely at her, studying her rosy cheeks and sweet smile.

Beth placed the plate of food on the trunk next to the bed. As she turned to leave she caught sight of a scrap of paper, half tucked under the trunk. She bent to pick it up and was surprised to see a smudged chalk drawing of herself sitting at her easel. It was sketched in vivid, flowing lines and caught her likeness well; perhaps it even made her look prettier than she was. Carefully, she placed it back where she had found it.

Beth glanced into all the attics and dormitories before going downstairs and through the inner court to look in the library and the parlours, stopping to ask the guests one by one if they had seen Johannes.

Emmanuel, replenishing the fire and lighting the candles in the great hall before supper, shook his head in answer to her question. Then she surprised Joseph and Sara in the pantry. They sprang apart and Sara blushed scarlet and ran from the room. Barely acknowledging Joseph's defiant grin, she simply asked him if he'd seen

138

Johannes. He had not, so she carried on to search the next store room after he shook his head.

Anxious now, she ran at full tilt into Clarence Smith, who was crossing the hall. She curtsied deeply as she apologised.

'Where are you off to in such a hurry, little maid?'

'I beg your pardon, sire. Have you seen Johannes this afternoon?'

Clarence adjusted his crown, which had slipped down over one eye. 'I did see him. Hmmm.' He tapped a finger against his cheek. 'A little after two, I believe. Looked as happy as a piece of week-old fish. Suggested that he made your dear mother a visit in the apothecary and took a purge.'

'I was with Mama most of the afternoon and we didn't see him.'

'Can't help you then. Too busy to pass the time of day, my dear! Important affairs of state to attend to!' He inclined his head graciously and set off towards the great hall.

Beth sat down on the hall bench. Johannes had looked so tired she could only suppose he'd fallen asleep somewhere. But where?

Orpheus scratched at the great oak door and whined to go out.

As Beth unbolted the door a gust of wind snatched it from her hands. The icy draught made her shiver. Johannes wouldn't have gone outside so late in the day, surely? It was dusk already and beginning to rain. She had no desire to go out in such blustery weather but where else was there to look? She hurried to the boot room to slip on her gardening shoes and wrap herself in her cloak before following Orpheus down the steps.

Darkness was falling and it was raining as she hurried down the lime tree walk, the big dog trotting at her heels. A crescent moon glowed silver in a deep sapphire sky. The cold wind whipped her hair across her face, puffing her cloak out like a sail behind her. Suppose Johannes had slipped and twisted an ankle? She called his name and stood still for a moment, her ears straining into the dusk for an answering cry. Nothing.

An owl hooted from the elm tree but otherwise the garden was silent except for the patter of rain and the rustle of dead leaves as they whirled and spun in the wind. Setting off again, she dashed around the perimeter walls until she came to the vegetable garden. There was no sign of John. The potting shed loomed up out of the increasing dark. She snatched open the door and recoiled in disgust as a cobweb draped itself across her face in sticky folds. But, except for garden tools, the dim recesses of the shed were empty. The rain drummed on the roof, making her reluctant to leave its shelter.

The gate to the orchard was open, banging back and forth in the wind. Orpheus, nose to the ground, thrust his way through the gate and Beth ran after him.

'Johannes!' She cupped her hands around her mouth as she called his name, the wind snatching her words away into the looming darkness. The dripping branches of the apple trees swayed and creaked eerily as Beth stumbled through the long grass. Now that it was becoming too dark to see clearly she tripped on a tussock and fell headlong on to the wet grass, winding herself. Dragging herself into a sitting position against a tree trunk, she gasped and wheezed, fighting for breath. Shocked and chilled through, she began to shiver violently. Then the rain began to come down in torrents and her wet hair clung to her cheeks like seaweed.

When at last she got to her feet she gasped as the dark silhouette of a fox streaked past her, eyes glowing green in the moonlight. Suddenly the orchard was unfamiliar to her, full of menacing shadows and unfamiliar sounds. Anxiety gave way to sudden fright. Rooted to the spot, she wondered how she would summon the courage to find her way home through the storm.

The wind howled through the trees and a sudden fierce blast nearly knocked her over. Without warning, something hard struck her on the back of the head. Flailing her arms in fright, she turned to see who, or what, had attacked her.

Her mouth fell open. She let out a sob, fumbled at the neck of her dress and pulled out her silver whistle. Eyes tight shut, she blew into it hard, again and again.

Orpheus crept out of the shadows, lifted his head to the moon and howled.

Johannes, hanging by his neck from the apple tree, swayed from side to side in the wind.

Chapter 18

Morning came at last. Beth, dry-eyed now, lay flat on her back with her hands behind her head, staring at the ceiling while Cecily slept beside her. The night had been never ending as she went over and over in her mind how she might have prevented such a tragedy.

Emmanuel and Joseph had come running when she blew her whistle, closely followed by her father and mother. Emmanuel had caught hold of Johannes's legs and lifted him up to take the pressure off his neck but his body was already cold.

Now, Beth sat up, suddenly filled with a terrible anger at Johannes. She hugged her knees so tightly that her fingernails bit into her skin. *How could he have done this to her?* He was so much more than her painting master, he was her friend. She had relied on him absolutely and loved him like a father. Surely he'd known how much she cared for him and how she would grieve if he killed himself?

Cecily stirred and stretched. 'Did you sleep at all?' she murmured, rubbing sleep from her eyes.

'A little.' Beth's mouth felt as if it was full of sand.

Cecily reached up to stroke Beth's cheek. 'Did Johannes seem so very miserable to you?'

Beth shook her head. 'I never imagined he would do such a thing.' Anguish squeezed her heart again. 'It's all my fault! I knew him best of all and should have guessed what he was planning.'

Cecily leaned her head against her sister's knee. 'But how *could* you have known? Perhaps you should be happy for Johannes because all his unhappiness has gone away now?'

Beth couldn't bear to go into the studio that morning. Misery engulfed her at the thought of Johannes being made ready for his coffin and she set off to find her brother in the garden.

John had left his work turning over the vegetable plot and begun to dig a deep trench in a sunny patch of the garden by the honeysuckle arch.

'Johannes liked to sit on the b-b-bench here with you,' he said. 'I think he'd like to be at rest h-h-here. Father has agreed to it.'

Beth hugged her brother, while a picture flashed through her mind of all the happy, lazy summer afternoons she'd spent with Johannes on the bench with their sketchbooks, the scent of honeysuckle in the air.

'I h-h-hate to see you so sad,' said John, kissing the top of her head.

Beth was struck all at once how he'd grown up since Kit had left them. 'Thank you for thinking of it.' She shivered. Since he took his own life Johannes would have to be buried in unconsecrated ground but perhaps he'd find peace in this place.

A shout from the orchard made them turn to see a figure hurrying towards them waving his feathered hat in the air.

'Noah!' A flicker of unexpected pleasure caught Beth by surprise.

'It's cold to be in the garden today,' said Noah as he kissed Beth's cheek. 'Isn't that trench too deep for planting potatoes, John?' He clapped John on the arm. 'I may not be a gardener but I do know that nothing grows if you bury it that far down! The smile faded from his face as he studied theirs. 'What is it? What have I said?'

Beth swallowed while she fought the urge to weep again. 'It's Johannes,' she said. 'We're burying Johannes.'

Stinging sleet carried over the garden wall on a vicious north wind needled the family and guests as they huddled together in the garden to lay Johannes to rest the following day.

William conducted the service and Clarence Smith gave a dignified eulogy, accompanied by the mournful cries of the rooks in the elm tree.

Beth, frozen in misery, stood between Noah and John, gazing down into the grave. John's hand, rough and callused from gardening, reached for hers.

Then William nodded at Beth and she scattered a handful of earth on to the coffin followed by a posy of snowdrops and the tightly rolled sketch of herself and the small painting of Annelies that she had found in his room. She was determined he wouldn't go lonely into eternity.

It began to snow in earnest, a thin white blanket already covering the coffin as Noah guided her back to the great hall where Peg served mulled ale and freshly made Dutch biscuits to the mourners. Johannes had been well liked and there were many reminiscences about his kind nature.

At last everyone drifted away to their various duties and pursuits, leaving only Beth and a white-faced Noah.

'I'm more sorry than I can say,' he said. 'And I feel I must bear a part of the blame for his passing.'

Beth swallowed and met his gaze

Noah bit his lip. 'I can see that you do blame me.'

Beth took pity on his misery and shook her head. 'There is no point in placing blame, not now. I will just miss him so. He gave a framework to my days and I don't know how to fill the space he leaves behind.' The pain of his loss pressed behind her breastbone so sharply that, for a moment, it hurt to breathe.

'You should not forget that you gave his life purpose at a time he suffered from a great sorrow.' Briefly, Noah rested his hand on her shoulder.

She closed her eyes for a moment, wishing she could fall into a deep and forgetful sleep. 'He could be a stern master but we had some very happy times.'

'Then those are what you must remember.' He glanced out of the window as flakes of snow pattered against the glass. 'Beth, I can delay no longer. I came only to make a brief visit on my way to Richmond Palace yesterday.'

'I'll walk you down to the river.'

He glanced again at the snow but didn't attempt to dissuade her. They fetched their cloaks and Noah tucked Beth's arm firmly into the crook of his elbow as they walked through the garden.

Before they entered the orchard Beth hesitated, her hand resting on the snow-covered moss on the old gate, remembering her fear the last time she had passed this way.

'Shall I lead on?' asked Noah, as if sensing her reluctance.

Almost unconsciously Beth stopped by the tree where she had found Johannes. She shivered and looked away.

'Is this the place?'

She nodded.

Noah touched the gnarled bark of the trunk, now dusted with snow. 'Do you see here,' he asked. 'Look at the lichen growing upon the branches.'

Beth took a closer look. The frosted lichen grew like clusters of crisp little grey-green stars, each one perfect and beautiful. The textured bark held a myriad of colours when you looked closely: silver, umber, burnt sienna and verdigris. Fleetingly, she wondered if, perhaps one day, she might make a painting of it. 'It's lovely,' she said.

'You see,' said Noah, 'there is always good in a bad situation, if you look for it.'

The boatman waited for Noah at the landing stage, his collar hunched up around his neck and his hat pulled low against the snowflakes that fell down from the leaden sky.

Noah kissed Beth goodbye, the slight roughness of his chin grazing her cold cheek.

'May I come again, perhaps in a week or two?'

She nodded and her heart lifted, just a little.

Sadness engulfed her as the boat drew away to the centre of the river. Arms folded against the cold, she waited until it had disappeared from sight before returning with dragging steps to the house.

Some days later Beth stood in the gallery, her finger on the latch, bracing herself to enter the studio for the first time since she'd found Johannes hanging from the apple tree. Taking a deep breath, she opened the door. Grey, early morning light illuminated the room as she stepped inside. The quietness pressed down upon her like the weight of water and she stood still, straining her ears for the echo of Johannes's voice. But there was nothing.

The studio was just as she had left it. She crossed to where her cloth-draped portrait rested upon the easel, hesitated for a moment and then threw back the muslin.

She drew in her breath sharply, clasping her hands over her breast. Seeing Johannes's last work carried with it a poignancy that almost made her cry out. He had lovingly painted every line and brush stroke with meticulous care and she suffered again the tragedy of his loss as a rapier-sharp blow.

The portrait showed her sitting at her easel with all the trappings of a painter's profession spread around her, the shadowy recesses of the room forming a frame for the shaft of clear sunlight that fell on to her like a waterfall from the tall windows.

But it was her own face that had her mesmerised. Her mouth was slightly open, her lips glistening as if she were about to speak. There was a hint of mischief in her blue eyes and a smudge of paint on the luminous skin of her cheek. Red-gold curls lay tumbled on her shoulders, drawing the eye to the way her paint-spattered dress was closely moulded to follow the curves of her slender body.

Was that portrait how Johannes saw her? It was like her and yet not like the self she saw reflected back from her mirror. This was a Beth who looked as if her life was bursting with the expectation of exciting possibilities; the personification of the Beth she wished to be.

'Oh, Johannes,' she whispered in anguish, 'why did you have to leave me?'

It was then that she saw the letter, wedged under the bottom of the canvas, where it rested on the easel. Sealed with a blob of red wax, it bore her name with the words *The Painter's Apprentice* underneath. Her heart lurched as she snatched it up, sliding her finger under the seal to prise it free. She unfolded the paper, which was covered in Johannes's writing, the thick black ink splattered and blotched in places.

Dearest Beth

However much you have sweetened the medicine for me, I will not spend the rest of my life confined to a madhouse or live in a country ruled by papists. Your family has shown me great kindness and I will not bring them such difficulties.

Passing on my knowledge to you was my reason to live but now your apprenticeship is finished. Always remember that your art is greater than your own happiness and you must willingly make sacrifices. Now you must look beyond your small dreams. Go into the world. Reach for the heavens and I know you will find you can go further than you believe possible.

Sweet Beth, you have been as dear to me as any daughter. Do not be sad for me since I die in expectation of being reunited with my family for all eternity.

Your Johannes

Beth choked back a sob. So Johannes hadn't forgotten her! If only she'd given in to curiosity that afternoon and peeped at the portrait then she would have found the note and maybe had time to save him.

But it did no good to think like that. What was done was done.

Chapter 19

March 1688

The studio was so cold that Beth's bones ached; in spite of wearing an old pair of gloves with the fingers cut off, she could barely grip her paintbrush. The insides of the windows were decorated with a delicate tracery of frost flowers, which she would have found beautiful if she hadn't been so miserable.

Day after day she had set up a new floral arrangement but as soon as she started to work nothing went right. The charcoal was too thick and left smudges behind, spoiling the clarity of the watercolour. She ground up a new batch of umber, carefully washing away any lumps of pigment, then ground the powder again, rinsing away the impurities, but a small grain still left a thick smear on the paper.

She cleaned the studio from the tops of the picture frames down to the wide elm floorboards, scrubbing away the last vestiges of paint splashes that decorated the floor around Johannes's easel. But when she had made everything gleam and she could procrastinate no more, the virgin sheet of paper on her easel appeared too pristine to risk sullying with her own clumsy daubs.

The truth of it was that she had lost the excitement for her painting that had burned within her over the past years and she was frightened. Johannes had always been on hand to encourage her, always making her look at her work with a fresh eye and never accepting anything but her best. Now she stood listlessly by the window watching the wind teasing the trees while she tried, and failed, to summon up her old enthusiasm. All colour had faded from her life, reducing it to shades of grey.

Glancing across the room, her eyes were drawn again to her portrait. Somehow, the picture seemed to radiate light, even in the gloom. She shuddered slightly, her sadness over Johannes's death settling around her like a cloak. His teaching and his friendship had filled the past four years. How could she ever close the gaping chasm he had left in her life?

She dropped her paintbrush on the table and hunched over with her fists tucked under her armpits for warmth. Her stomach churned with a gnawing emptiness as she watched her breath mist the air. Every moment felt as if she were waiting for Johannes and she kept glancing over her shoulder, expecting to see him standing at his easel. She missed him. She missed his untidy hair and his paint-grimed fingernails. She missed his quiet presence as he worked beside her and his acerbic comments when she failed to follow his instructions. She even missed the fusty, unwashed smell of his clothes. More than anything she missed the occasional shout of laughter and the wide smile on his homely face when he offered her a rare morsel of praise.

Sighing, she reached into her pocket and drew out again the letter that Noah had brought her, the thick paper creased from reading and rereading it. Bishop Compton's handwriting, however, was bold and clear.

The gardens are waking up after their winter slumber and there is much for you to see. Bring your brother John and your mother, too, as I believe there is a great deal to interest them here.

You may come on any day you choose as I have no official duties at present and spend all my time in the gardens pruning and planting. Don't forget to bring stout shoes if the weather is inclement!

Beth glanced out of the window again. Merryfields was her home and she loved it with every fibre of her being but perhaps now she had begun to comprehend why Kit had wanted to leave. The high brick wall that surrounded the lovely gardens allowed only a limited view to the outside. All at once she was filled with a great curiosity to see more of it. Besides, Johannes had told her to look beyond her own small world.

She made up her mind. Closing the studio door firmly behind her, she hurried downstairs.

Susannah, as usual, was in the apothecary.

Old Silas had come in from the garden and he leaned over the counter, dropping earth from his boots and nodding vigorously as Susannah explained how to use the embrocation she had dispensed for him.

When Susannah took the cork from the bottle the air was at once filled with the eye-smarting odour of grated horseradish, crushed mint, mustard seed and oil of bitter almonds. 'I mixed up a new batch for you as soon as I saw the first signs of spring,' she said. 'It's the same every year, Silas. You must take the digging gently until your body has accustomed itself to the work.'

'I knows that, see! But when the sun comes out and the shoots start growing, well,' he turned and winked at Beth, 'well, then the sap starts arising in Old Silas too, and I'm a-filled with the joys of spring and just has to be a-digging from sunrise to sunset.' He sniffed at the bottle of embrocation and his bushy white eyebrows shot up. 'If I don't keep digging, them weeds will grow as big as trees and Merryfields will be lost in a thicket.'

Susannah smiled. 'But if you work your back too hard you'll end up taking to your bed.'

'Let John do some of the heavy digging,' suggested Beth. 'And you can supervise him.'

The old man's face broke into a toothless grin. He nodded to Susannah and shuffled off back to the garden.

'Mama?' said Beth. She took the Bishop's letter out of her pocket. 'May we visit Fulham Palace? I know John would like to see the plants the Bishop has collected and you would be interested in the herb garden.' She glanced out of the window, 'And I would so enjoy a change of scene; to put the sadness behind me a little.'

Susannah sighed. 'I'm still heartsick about Kit's departure. Perhaps a visit to see the Bishop's garden would do me good, too.'

Early morning mist swirled over the river, touching them with cold, damp fingers and leaving droplets of moisture like diamonds clinging to their hair and clothes. Emmanuel and Joseph, wraith-like silhouettes at the front of the boat, pulled steadily on the oars propelling them through the vaporous air towards Fulham.

Beth shivered, huddled into her cloak. Her mother and John sat silently beside her, their features pale and indistinct in the ghostly haze. All sound was muffled, as if a great goose down pillow had drifted down from the heavens and was now suspended above them. A warning shout made them look up as a boat travelling in the opposite direction suddenly loomed out of the fog and skimmed past.

Emmanuel and Joseph shipped the oars to catch their breath and take a sip of ale from the flask wedged between their feet.

After a while a brisk breeze began to blow the mist away and soon a number of boats became visible on the water. By the time they reached Fulham Palace, a watery sun was shining.

Joseph jumped on to the landing stage. 'I'll find someone to tell

His Grace we're here.' He set off along a gravelled path through an avenue of elms.

John helped Beth and Susannah to disembark. They waited on the landing stage, watching the passing boats.

Before long the wooden jetty began to shudder beneath their feet and they saw Bishop Compton striding towards them.

'How delightful to see you again, Mistress Ambrose,' he said, offering his hand to Susannah.

'As you can see, we took you at your word and have arrived unannounced, Your Grace.'

'There's no need for formality to look at a garden, is there? I am usually out here from dawn to dusk. Such a lot to do at this time of year, isn't there, John?'

John flushed. 'C-c-certainly there is, sir! I am v-v-very much looking forward s-s-seeing all the exotics you have here.'

'Plenty of those and I do like to show them off. What a shame pride is such a sin!' He shook his head sorrowfully but his eyes were merry as he greeted Beth. 'And I see you have followed my advice and are wearing good, strong shoes.'

'I know how muddy the garden can be at Merryfields after the rain.'

'I knew you were a sensible girl.'

Beth smiled, amused as much by his easy manner as by the streak of dirt on his cheek and his homespun gardening trousers, all caked with mud. He rubbed his hands together. 'We'll take some dinner before we tour the gardens.'

The path led through a water meadow into a lightly wooded copse and then to a wooden bridge over a moat.

'This is the best time of year to see the moat, when the crocuses and wild flowers bloom,' said the Bishop. 'The water always stinks in the summer heat, in spite of the sluice to the river.'

The palace was a fine red brick building set in open ground, planted all around with young saplings. As they walked through an archway lined with great oak gates, the porter burst out of his gate-house, still chewing his dinner and wiping his mouth with a napkin.

'It's all right, Walter!' The Bishop clapped him on the shoulder. 'Some friends of mine have come to visit the gardens.'

The archway led into a large courtyard, enclosed on all sides by the palace and with a circular pool complete with a splashing fountain set in the centre. Crossing the courtyard, they entered a small vestibule through a stone arch beneath a clock tower. A wonderful aroma of roasting beef drifted in the air and Beth felt her stomach growl with hunger in response.

The chatter of voices echoed around the mediaeval beamed and vaulted ceiling of the great hall. A refectory table ran down the centre of the room and people were already helping themselves to the bread, roast meats and pies set out before them.

After they had finished their dinner the Bishop was not inclined to linger. 'There's a bank of Spanish daffodils that's still looking very fine and a cloth of gold crocus, which will interest you, John.'

Beth was pleased to note how the Bishop drew John out and spoke to him as one gardener to another.

John became animated as they discussed the best way to propagate roses and his stutter almost disappeared.

The tour of the gardens took a couple of hours, by which time Susannah had several cuttings from the herb garden and the Bishop had wrapped three oriental jacinths in damp sacking for John. 'Pot them up as soon as you arrive home and put them on a windowsill,' he said. 'I promise you, once they flower you will never forget their perfume. And for you, Miss Ambrose, an aconite and some crocuses. You shall paint them and let me see them next time we meet.'

Beth took the plants from him, carefully wrapped in a cloth to contain the earth around their roots. 'I will try to paint them,' she said.

'What's this? You sound doubtful.' The Bishop's kindly eyes bore into her.

'My tutor Johannes has died and since then I have lost my appetite for painting.'

'Noah told me the sad news. I understand that Johannes had not been well for some time.'

'I still feel his loss keenly.'

'Of course you do! But I've seen your special talent. You simply need some time to overcome your natural sadness. And a little inspiration, perhaps? Come with me, I have something to show you.'

The Bishop set off at speed back to the palace and they all trotted along behind. He opened a door into a passageway and then another door leading to a library, where he carefully took out a sheaf of papers from a drawer and spread them out on the table.

Beth drew in her breath sharply. The papers were covered by an explosion of colour: painted orange lilies, striped auriculas, anemones, purple tulips and more. 'But these are exquisite!'

'Alexander Marshal,' said the Bishop. 'He and his wife lived at the palace for several years and he painted many of the plants we grow here.'

'I should like to meet him.'

'Alas, he died a few years ago. But your own paintings are quite as good as these, Miss Ambrose.'

Covered in confusion, she shook her head.

'No false modesty, now! Take another look.'

Beth picked up one of the paintings, a gloriously pink-and-white striped tulip, and took it to the window to study it more closely. Each careful little brush stroke of carmine and madder and moss green glowed and the rendition was lively. She narrowed her eyes while she thought about her own work. These paintings were very good but were they really any more proficient than her own? She looked up to find her mother and the Bishop watching her intently. A tiny bubble of excitement began to fizz in her stomach. 'Perhaps it is time for me to try again,' she said.

'There are a great number of new species of plants here since Mr

Marshal died,' said the Bishop. 'It's my intention to document all the flowers that grow in the garden and publish this as a record for gardeners in the known world. If you came to live here at the palace your skill would allow me to achieve that ambition. What do you think, Mistress Ambrose?'

Susannah was silent for a moment. 'I believe my daughter has the artistic ability to carry out the task.'

'She has a talent which should be allowed to flower in the public gaze. What is your opinion, Miss Ambrose?'

'I'm not sure . . . ' She looked again at the marvellous painting of the exotic tulip and thought she might be able to paint again here, away from the place where Johannes's absence haunted her and with such a variety of different flowers to inspire her. But would it be too cruel of her to absent herself from Merryfields so soon after Kit's departure? She glanced again at her mother, saw the apprehension in her green eyes and made up her mind. 'Merryfields is my home,' Beth said, smiling reassuringly at Susannah, 'and I have no wish to leave it.' Carefully, she put the painting back on the table.

The Bishop sighed. 'What a pity! I had hoped . . . '

A strange mixture of regret and relief stirred in Beth's breast as she walked beside her mother. She was uncomfortable that she appeared to have disappointed the Bishop, who had been so kind to her. 'Your Grace?' she said.

He glanced at her, his ready smile playing about his lips. 'Changed your mind?'

She glanced at Susannah, who stared at the ground as she walked. 'No, it's not that. I wondered if you had news of Princess Anne?'

'Indeed! She was here not two days ago, in excellent spirits. It would seem that she is expecting a happy event.'

'So, it's true, then?' said Beth. 'I am very happy for her. She confided in me before she left Merryfields that it might be the case.'

'She has been disappointed before but I will pray for her,' said the Bishop.

Emmanuel was waiting for them at the landing stage and once they had said their goodbyes and settled themselves into the boat, he cast off.

Chapter 20

Beth stood before her portrait, now hanging on the studio wall. Her painted self stared back at her, a paintbrush in her hand and a mischievous invitation in her eyes. Where had all that self-confidence gone? Taking a fleeting look over her shoulder, she wondered if she would catch sight of Johannes's shadow hovering over his easel but the studio was as quiet as a tomb. The aconite and crocus plants rested on the painting table, their roots still wrapped in damp sacking. She laid them out on a piece of white linen, arranging them carefully so that the leaves and flower heads were seen to their best advantage and began to set out her paints and brushes.

Glancing up at her portrait again she caught her breath in surprise. She moved closer to study the canvas. On the wall behind her painted self was a mirror. In minute detail, there was a reflection of Johannes at work on her portrait. He wore his usual sacking apron around his broad middle and his blond hair stood up in spikes, touched with blue paint. It was Johannes's last joke: his own miniature portrait contained within her own.

Laughter bubbled up within her, breaking the uneasy silence in the studio. Johannes had thought she could paint; he'd even said there was no more he could teach her. It was up to her now to refine her skill and to be her own taskmaster.

Taking a deep breath, she picked up her brush.

A few days later, Beth was helping her mother in the apothecary. The memory of Johannes's impassioned plea in his letter to her reverberated in her mind. *Look beyond your small dreams. Go into the world and let people see your work. Reach for the heavens and I know you will find you can go further than you believe is possible.*

At last, she could bear it no longer. 'Mama? I don't wish to make you unhappy but I do so very much want to go and work at the palace. If I stay at home I know I'll always regret the lost opportunity.'

Susannah was silent for a moment. 'I've seen your new paintings. Henry Compton's aconite and crocuses seem to have set you on your way again. They are as fine as anything we saw by Alexander Marshal.' Susannah sighed. 'It's selfish of me to want to keep you by my side when you have a gift that the world should know about. If you wish to go I will not prevent you.'

Beth bit her lip. Excitement fought with trepidation again at the thought of it.

'Let us go together to talk to your father,' said Susannah.

William was in the library looking out of the window and Beth was concerned to see that his eyes were unnaturally bright.

'What is it, Father?' she asked, reaching for his hand.

He sighed. 'I was wondering what Kit is doing. It's a hard thing to accept that he may never return home. And I fear for Merryfields with no one to carry on my work.'

'But the funds from Princess Anne have helped, haven't they?'

'Not nearly enough. We must find another way to bring more

159

income into the household. We have the capacity for more guests but not the funds.'

'Then perhaps I can help,' said Beth slowly. 'I would like to accept Bishop Compton's invitation to work at the palace, after all. I'd meet people of importance and I can tell them about the work you do at Merryfields. Perhaps they may have relatives or friends who might come here.'

'No!' William's jaw clenched. 'I'm not having you racketing across the countryside to stay, unchaperoned, in a place full of strangers.'

'Father, it's not some terrible den of iniquity, it's a bishop's palace.'

William stood up, his brow thunderous. 'Do not presume to argue with me, miss!'

'Can't you *see* what an opportunity this is?'

'Silence!'

Sudden anger and despair made Beth clench her fists. 'Why do you have to stop me doing the one thing that's important to me? You've *never* loved me like you love your own children!'

William's face blanched and a muscle trembled in his jaw. 'That isn't true,' he said quietly. 'I've always thought of you as my own.'

'No, you haven't! I've never fitted in. I even *look* different from them.'

Susannah, her expression shocked, reached for Beth, who avoided her embrace and stumbled out of the room.

Beth ran outside, down the steps into the courtyard and through to the back garden, not stopping until she reached the potting shed where she threw herself, sobbing, on to a heap of sacks in the corner. She buried her face in the rough, earth-scented sacking and howled.

Probably ten minutes later she heard a noise behind her.

Mutely, John offered her a grubby handkerchief and sat down beside her. 'This is where I come, too, when I'm m-m-miserable,' he said. Do you want to talk about it?'

'No,' she sniffed, leaning against the reassuring warmth of him.

160

Then she told him all that had passed. 'I've always felt so different from you and Cecily and Kit because Father *isn't* my father,' she finished.

'Funny that,' said John. 'You see, I've always f-f-felt different from you and Kit and Cecily. Kit is my big brother: tall and handsome. Father really never sees me because Kit's star shines too brightly. He was so proud of the son who was going to be a doctor. And then Cecily is so very p-p-pretty and lively. And you, well you look so like our lovely mama and you have an extraordinary talent. Then there's m-m-me. I'm not handsome or clever. I always have earth under my fingernails and no one listens to me because I s-s-stutter. Sometimes I think I mean no more to Father than one of the g-g-guests.'

'Oh, John!' Beth hugged him so tightly he grunted. 'But you can make *anything* grow in the garden. You know how to make sick plants thrive and you guide and encourage the guests to make their own gardens. You never make fun of them or judge them when they behave oddly. And you *are* handsome. You must know that you are a younger version of Kit? Just look at yourself in the mirror!'

'Do you t-t-think so?' he asked.

'I do.'

He stared at her intently. 'Did you know there's a dead s-s-spider in your hair?'

William didn't come to take his meals in the great hall during the week following Beth's outburst but remained cloistered in his study.

Beth was pleased to avoid his company but she couldn't put out of her mind the memory of his hurt expression when she accused him of favouring his own children. She relived the incident over and over again, angry and self-righteous one moment and then overcome with guilt. Did he *really* favour them? She'd lived with those jealous thoughts for so long she couldn't remember where they came from, or even one example of favouritism to support her argument.

Perhaps it was only that she loved Father so much that when her siblings arrived she had been jealous, as a small child will be. These troubling thoughts twisted around in her mind like a spider twirling on a strand of silk in the breeze.

Early the following morning Beth found the door to William's study was firmly shut. She'd tossed and turned all night and knew that she would not be happy until she had spoken to him. Tentatively, she knocked and then went in.

William stood by the window, looking out at the garden.

'Father?' she whispered.

He whirled round at the sound of her voice, his face set. 'Beth.'

She didn't know how to begin. She wanted to run to him and bury her face in the safety of his chest, just as she had when she was a little girl. If she spoke, she thought she might cry so she simply looked at his shoes.

'Beth,' he said again. Then he took two strides across the room and crushed her to his chest.

Weeping, she clung to him. At last he let her go and held her at arm's length. 'Look at me, Beth!' he said. 'I've loved you from the first time I saw you when you were only a week or two old. You squinted at me as if you didn't much like what you saw and then smiled with milk dribbling down your chin. You captured my heart and hold it still. Love is a funny thing. It's not finite but it grows as much as necessary. Yes, of course I love your brothers and your sister but I do not differentiate between you. You are *all* my children.'

'I'm sorry,' she whispered.

'Let us have no more unhappiness.'

She shook her head. 'But I wish you could understand how much I wish to go to Fulham Palace.'

William sighed. 'I cannot stand to lose you, Beth, not so soon after Kit . . . ' He swallowed and cleared his throat. 'I do see that it is a wonderful opportunity for you but I cannot bear the thought of any harm coming to you.'

'None will!'

'I don't like the idea of you staying alone at the palace.'

'But it's too far to travel there every day!'

William bit his lip. 'If there was a way … Let me think about it. Meanwhile, shall we go down to the hall for breakfast? I think perhaps I could fancy an egg this morning.'

Puffs of white clouds drifted across a powder blue sky and Beth sighed as she leaned back against the sun-warmed garden bench and turned her face up to the spring sunshine.

'You'll grow freckles if you do that,' warned Cecily. 'Then no one will marry you.'

'I don't care if I have freckles and anyway, I've decided I shall never marry.'

Cecily squealed. 'Don't say that!'

'I owe that to Johannes. He begged me not to waste his training and if I have little ones there will be no time to paint.'

'I can't bear to think of you as a lonely spinster, living all alone and with no children to look after you in your old age.'

'Don't worry; I'll be a devoted aunt to all your offspring and they'll bring me sugared almonds for Christmas.'

'That's not *at all* the same thing, Beth!' Cecily suddenly pulled on her sleeve. 'Look, coming through the orchard gate.'

Beth opened one eye and then sat bolt upright. 'It's Noah!' Sudden warmth flushed her cheeks.

'And Grandmother is with him. Oh! I do wish I had put on my best dress this morning.'

Arm in arm, Noah and Lady Arabella made stately progress towards them, while Beth and Cecily smoothed their skirts and tidied their hair as best they could.

Cecily ran forward to kiss Lady Arabella.

Beth met Noah's ironic smile.

'Good morning,' he said. 'I am accompanying Lady Arabella to her house in Windsor to look at the proposed refurbishment work and we thought to call in to break the journey.'

'You are both very welcome,' said Beth. 'In spite of the sunshine it's cold on the river. Please, come inside and take some refreshments. Cecily, will you run ahead and tell Mama that Lady Arabella and Noah are here?'

'No need to run, child,' said Lady Arabella. 'It's not ladylike.'

'No Grandmother.' Cecily skipped off towards the house.

Lady Arabella sighed. 'Someone needs to teach that girl how to behave. She has a measure of good looks but she'll never go anywhere while she acts like a hoyden.'

Beth, in an attempt to give her mother time to ready herself for the surprise visit, engaged Lady Arabella in conversation to delay her progress towards the house. She showed her the newly flowering tulips in the great stone urns at either side of the pleached lime walk and the bank of crocuses. Naturally, these were of no interest to Lady Arabella.

'There is too much wildness and profusion in this garden,' she said. 'For myself, I prefer a garden designed in the French manner with low box hedges and coloured gravels.' She stopped to disentangle a stray bramble from her skirt. 'Really, I cannot abide a country garden. It's all far too untidy.'

Susannah opened the door just in time to prevent Beth from saying something she might regret. She noticed that her mama, slightly out of breath, had found time to change into her second-best gown.

'Welcome, Arabella,' said Susannah. 'And Noah. How kind of you to call.'

While Lady Arabella divested herself of her travelling cloak, Susannah whispered, 'Beth, fetch your father, will you?'

Beth slipped away to knock on the door of her father's study.

William looked up from his account books, his brow furrowed.

'Lady Arabella has descended upon us and Mama is asking for you.'

'What does that tiresome woman want now?' he sighed.

'She's taking Noah to Windsor to see what he can do to modernise Sir George's house.'

'I expect she wants to trick it up and make it more ostentatious to suit her affectations.'

'Noah won't let her do that.'

'Then he's a better man than most,' said William. He tucked Beth's hand into his own and they set off for the little parlour.

Susannah, her eyes shining, passed William a piece of paper. 'Noah had a letter from Tom and enclosed within was a letter for us. From Kit.'

Beth exclaimed in delight. 'Father, will you read it aloud?'

William unfolded the paper and held it to the light of the window.

My dear Mama, Father, Beth, John and Cecily,

I hope this finds you as well as it leaves me. I arrived here after a stormy passage but Noah's family greeted me with much kindness.

Uncle Tom is teaching me everything he knows about running the tobacco plantation, while Aunt Caroline is feeding me up as I became rather thin on the voyage. Noah's sisters, Abigail, Kate and Maryanne, are full of questions about their cousins and send their love to you all.

I wish I could show you the wealth of exotic plants and flowers here, Beth. You could paint something different and unusual here every day for a hundred years and still not catalogue it all! John, I have planted the seeds you gave me and hope to show my newfound family an English garden by the end of the season.

Mama and Father, please do not worry about me. I truly believe I have found the place where I want to spend the rest of my life.

Your ever-loving son, Kit

PS Remember me to the servants and the guests.

Susannah slipped her hand into William's, her eyes sparkling with unshed tears.

William fixed his gaze out of the window.

'I expect it's all very primitive,' said Lady Arabella with a supercilious lift of her painted eyebrows. 'But then, if you are not used to living in refined surroundings perhaps you do not draw such comparisons?'

'On the contrary,' said Susannah with a brittle smile. 'Your knowledge is quite outdated. My brother and his family live in an elegant house amongst a circle of educated and sophisticated friends.'

Noah turned his back to Lady Arabella and made a comical face at Beth. 'Come and sit beside me and tell me how the world goes with you,' he said. 'Bishop Compton told me that you refused his invitation.'

'I did,' she said. 'But then I changed my mind but Father will not consent to it. He believes it improper for me to stay unchaperoned at Fulham Palace.'

Noah studied his fingernails for a moment and Beth noticed how clean and well shaped they were. 'But you would still like to go there?'

Beth nodded. 'It's a rare opportunity to paint the marvellous botanical specimens in the gardens and for my work to be seen by many. I shall never achieve that if I stay at Merryfields. Johannes told me to reach for the heavens and I shall do my best to do so, although at present I can't see how.'

'Beth, has your mother never told you it's impolite to sit in corners whispering?' scolded Lady Arabella.

'We were simply talking quietly so as not to disturb you with our chatter,' said Noah. 'Beth was telling me that she'd had to decline Bishop Compton's kind invitation to stay at Fulham Palace since her father feels it would be improper for her to stay there unchaperoned.'

'Indeed it would!'

'So I wondered, dear Lady Arabella,' said Noah with a winning smile, 'if Beth might presume upon your kindness and stay with you in Chelsea? It's only a matter of three miles to the palace from your house and easily accomplished by public boat. She could visit each day to undertake her studies and travel back in the evening. Why, your house is so large you'd hardly know she was there.'

William cleared his throat. 'How very kind of you to offer, Arabella!' he said with a bland smile. 'It would give me great comfort to know that Beth is in your safe care. Just as your twins found a safe refuge here at Merryfields for so *much* of their childhood.'

'Well, I . . .'

'Oh, Grandmama, may I come too?' Cecily knelt at Lady Arabella's feet and clasped at her hands. '*Please* say yes! I'll be no trouble at all and you can teach me how to behave like a lady. I'm so sick of the country where nothing ever happens. *Please*, Grandmama?'

'Stand up at once!' said Lady Arabella. 'You certainly need to learn your manners.'

'Then that's settled,' said Noah. 'We must take our leave now if we are to reach Windsor in good time. We'll collect Beth and Cecily the day after tomorrow on our way back to London, won't we Lady Arabella?'

Lady Arabella stood up, flustered. 'I didn't . . .'

'Let me accompany you down to the landing stage,' said William.

'We'll all come,' said Susannah. 'Cecily, fetch Lady Arabella's cloak, will you?'

In no time at all Lady Arabella was safely seated in the boat.

William, his mouth twitching with suppressed amusement, shook Noah's hand.

'We'll arrive in the early afternoon the day after tomorrow, Beth,' whispered Noah, his eyes full of mischievous laughter. 'I suggest it wouldn't be a good idea to keep Lady Arabella waiting.' He kissed her cheek and climbed into the boat. Tenderly tucking a blanket around Lady Arabella's knees, he gave a jaunty wave as the boat pulled away.

'*Well*!' said Susannah. She caught William's amused expression; the two of them burst out laughing.

'I've never seen Arabella at a loss for words before,' said Susannah, wiping her eyes a minute later.

'That boy will go far,' said William. 'That was as smart a piece of trickery as I've ever seen.'

'Wasn't it?' said Beth, smiling to herself at how neatly Noah had solved her difficulty to everyone's, except perhaps Lady Arabella's, satisfaction.

Chapter 21

The next few days passed in a whirlwind of preparations. Cecily, in a ferment of excitement and chattering non-stop, swept a tangled mess of ribbons, hairpins and stockings into her trunk, followed by her ball dress and embroidered party slippers. Beth waited until she had left the bedchamber and then repacked her trunk with a more sensible collection of clean shifts, skirts and bodices.

Beth carefully cleaned and packed up all her paintbrushes and pigments and the small supply of precious vellum that still remained in the studio store. She placed her paintings of the aconites and the crocuses into a folio on top of the folded clothes in her trunk.

She took a last look around the studio and then stood before her portrait and the image of Johannes reflected in the painted mirror. 'I'm following your last instructions, Johannes,' she told him. 'And I'll do my best to make you proud of me.'

Closing the door behind her, she went downstairs for dinner.

Noah and Lady Arabella arrived soon after.

Joseph and Emmanuel carried the trunks down to the landing

stage and before she knew it, Beth was hugging her father and mother goodbye.

William handed her a purse full of coins. 'You will need this for your travel costs between Chelsea and Fulham. Keep it safe. Keep yourself safe.' His voice was brusque but his eyes were anxious.

Beth clung to him for a moment and he held her tightly.

Susannah hugged her. 'Look after your sister, won't you?'

Cecily began to weep.

'Oh, Cecily, please don't cry!' Beth spoke sharply because she was holding back her own tears.

'What a fuss about nothing!' said Lady Arabella crossly. 'That child always showed an excess of sentiment.'

At last they were away and Beth watched her parents waving until the boat rounded the bend in the river.

It was growing dark by the time they reached Chelsea.

Beth and Cecily stayed beside the river stairs with their trunks while Noah accompanied Lady Arabella to her house to arrange for her servant to fetch the luggage. As the sun dropped behind the trees they shivered, drawing their cloaks more tightly around them.

At last Noah and the manservant arrived, pushing a handcart.

'Beth, I'll wait for you tomorrow at about eleven o'clock at the palace landing stage,' said Noah.

'And you'll give Father's letter to Bishop Compton?' Suddenly feeling very alone, she clutched at Noah's sleeve. 'I hope he hasn't changed his mind about my visit.'

'I'm sure he hasn't. Until the morning, then.'

Beth watched him go with a hollow feeling in the pit of her stomach.

The manservant hoisted their boxes on to the handcart and trundled off at a fast pace over the rutted lane while Beth and Cecily trotted along behind.

The river was wide at Fulham and the tide was going out, leaving mud flats peppered with small islands of stones and detritus. Seagulls swooped overhead, their harsh cries echoing over the water. It was a grey and mizzly morning and Beth was relieved to see Noah already waiting at the landing stage for her.

She'd spent a nearly sleepless night in Lady Arabella's magnificent goose-down guest bed, anxiously wondering if she had made a dreadful mistake in leaving Merryfields. Would she even be able to paint at all in strange surroundings?

Beth scrambled off the boat, struggling with her easel and bag of painting equipment.

'Let me take those,' said Noah.

'Thank you.' She rubbed at a smear of mud on her skirt and broke into a trot to keep up with him. 'I also want to thank you for bamboozling Arabella into taking me in. You twisted her very neatly around your little finger and Father is full of admiration for you.'

He grinned. 'I'm glad to have helped but I never thought you'd really leave Merryfields' protective walls.'

'It's only for a while. The summer, perhaps. After all, Arabella is unlikely to allow me to stay any longer than that.'

'You'll never finish recording all Bishop Compton's specimens in a few months!' said Noah. 'There's a lifetime's work here for you. Alexander Marshal stayed for seven years and it would have been longer if he hadn't died.'

Noah led her through the Tudor archway into the quadrangle. The mellow red brickwork was attractively criss-crossed with grey brick diamonds but this time she noticed that many of the roof tiles were slipping and the glass was broken in one of the windows.

Their footsteps echoed as they walked briskly through the cobbled courtyard, past the fountain and into the palace.

Bishop Compton was in his library and came forward with a wide smile to greet them. 'Welcome, welcome, Miss Ambrose!' He took her hands in his. 'So, your parents have decided not to keep you at Merryfields after all?'

'They have given me their blessing to visit for a while.'

'Very good! Shall we accompany you to your new quarters?' He led them through a maze of rooms and up a narrow, creaking staircase to the first floor.

Beth glanced over her shoulder at Noah, he was struggling to keep up so she waited for him.

The Bishop stopped outside a low door and lifted the latch.

The room was not large but it had a good window, allowing the light, even on such a grey day, to reach every corner. Moreover, it afforded a pleasing view over the gardens towards the river. A table and chairs were pushed up against the wall and there was a large store cupboard. The worm-eaten floorboards were bare but newly swept and a fire flickered in the fireplace.

Beth smiled. 'I shall work very well here, I think.'

'Alexander Marshal always liked it,' said Bishop Compton. 'The window is tall and the aspect north-facing so the light remains clear.' He strode across the room to open another door, into a bedchamber. 'And this is also for your use.'

It was simply furnished with a chest, a chair and a bed dressed with plain linen hangings. Rush mats covered the floor, giving off a fresh, green scent. A deep window seat overlooked the courtyard and Beth imagined herself curled up on it while she read a book. 'It's delightful,' she said.

'These rooms are entirely at your disposal so, if your father changes his mind, you may stay here any time you wish.'

Rummaging in her bag, Beth withdrew the illustrations she had completed of the aconite and the crocuses. 'I brought these to add to your collection.'

Bishop Compton studied the paintings, his face expressionless.

Beth began to feel nervous. What if her work wasn't good enough and he sent her home?

Then he looked up. 'Just as I expected,' he said. 'I have found a painter worthy of continuing Alexander's work.'

The knot in Beth's stomach lessened.

Henry Compton rubbed his hands together, brisk again. 'What are you doing today, Noah?'

'I'll take my dinner with Beth but then I go to Whitehall.'

'Then I propose that this afternoon, since it's raining now, you would perhaps like to study Alexander Marshal's paintings, Miss Ambrose? Tomorrow, if the weather is better, I'll take you to meet George London, my gardener, and he will show you where to find the choicest specimen plants in the garden. You would do well to make a friend of him.'

'Indeed, I will.'

'I've laid out Alexander's paintings in the library. Should you wish to bring some of them to your studio to study, please do so. I know you will take great care of them. My secretary is waiting for me so I'll leave you to settle in and Noah will bring you down to the hall for your dinner.' He lifted a hand and hurried away.

Noah hoisted the bag of painting equipment up on to the table. 'What in the name of heaven have you in here, Beth? Stones?'

'That'll be the grinding slab. Some of the unground pigments are heavy, too.'

'Shall I set up your easel by the window?'

'If you would.' Beth opened the store cupboard and found a pot of paintbrushes, miscellaneous bottles of turpentine and linseed oil and a flat box nearly full of different mineral and vegetable pigments: carbon black, terre-verte, copper carbonate, Spanish ochre and gamboge.

'Look, Noah!' she said with a delighted smile. 'I've found a box of treasures. These must have belonged to Mr Marshal.'

'The Bishop told me that he'd left them there for your use.'

'Such supplies are expensive and I'll be pleased not to keep asking Mama to send them to me.'

After Beth had unpacked and set up her new studio, Noah took her on a brief tour of the palace, which formed a square around the courtyard.

'I shan't take you up to the attics,' he said. 'It's all storerooms and most of the servants sleep there, poor things. Roof leaks. Buckets all over the place. I told the bishop that he must carry out repairs or the whole building will rot but his income isn't sufficient for the scale of works required.'

Downstairs they wandered through a warren of still rooms, storerooms, wash houses, a brew house and a dairy. There was a housekeeper's room, a servants' hall, butler's pantry and a great hot smoky kitchen bustling with scullery maids.

In the bakehouse a young woman was just removing a fragrant tray of golden apple turnovers from the oven and Beth closed her eyes for a second as she breathed in the enticing aroma.

'Hello, Judith,' said Noah. 'Those look good!'

Judith pushed a dark curl back under her cap. 'New-baked for your dinner.' Tall and big-boned, she stared curiously at Beth.

'This is Beth Ambrose, who is coming to work on Bishop Compton's flower paintings,' said Noah.

Judith, her ruddy complexion flushed from the heat of the fire, smiled so widely at Beth that her hazel eyes were almost lost behind the apples of her cheeks. 'Welcome to Fulham Palace,' she said. 'Come and share a slice of pie with me one afternoon, if you're not too busy.'

'I'd like that,' said Beth, taking straight away to Judith's down-to-earth manner.

In the hall, Bishop Compton was deep in conversation with two men as he ate so Beth and Noah found a place for themselves amongst the other guests.

'What are you doing at Whitehall this afternoon?' asked Beth, as she dipped her coarse brown bread in a flavoursome mutton stew.

'Sir Christopher Wren is inspecting the works on the Queen's apartment and the terraced garden. I hope to take instructions from him to work on the court house in Windsor.'

'That would allow you to visit Lady Arabella's house at the same time.'

'Exactly.' Noah sighed. 'Mind you, I think Lady Arabella may be a harder task master than Sir Christopher. I do hope Sir George has deep pockets for the ambitious schemes she envisages.'

Despite the drizzle, Beth walked down to the river with Noah and waited with him until his boat arrived.

'Perhaps I'll see you tomorrow?' she asked, suddenly not wanting him to leave.

'Certainly.'

She waved goodbye and hurried back to the palace.

The following morning the rain had stopped and George London and his apprentice were pruning in the rose garden when Beth and Bishop Compton found them. The gardener nodded at his apprentice, who bundled a pile of thorny trimmings into a barrow and wheeled them away.

The Bishop drew Beth forward. 'George, this is Miss Ambrose, the young lady I mentioned who is come to continue Alexander's work.'

George London took off his hat and rubbed his hand clean on his homespun breeches before offering it to her.

'Mr London.' Beth's hand was crushed in his hearty grip.

'Welcome to the gardens at Fulham Palace, Miss Ambrose.'

'They're beautiful. I'm certain to find a great deal of inspiration here.'

'George, I'd like you to show Miss Ambrose the new varieties of plants we're growing,' said Henry Compton. 'She will need your expertise to find the best specimens.'

'Although,' said Beth, 'I noticed when I studied Alexander Marshal's paintings yesterday that they often show less than perfect specimens and his work doesn't suffer in the least from that approach.'

'Quite right, Miss Ambrose.'

George London's ordinary, middle-aged face looked quite different when he smiled, thought Beth. 'I have already noticed some brightly striped auriculas and some delightful pink flowers growing in a carpet under the cork oak tree,' she said. 'They have dark leaves in a heart shape with crinkled edges and the flowers look as if they have been blown inside out in the wind.'

'That'll be the cyclamens. And the spring flowers are coming in now the weather's more clement. You'll need to keep your eyes open as they'll arrive thick and fast.'

'Probably more quickly than I can paint them,' said Beth with a rueful smile. 'I'll not pick anything from a plant where there is only a single bloom.'

'I'd appreciate that. Some of the plants we have here are rare and in some cases may be the only one in the country. We need to collect the seeds for propagation.'

'Bishop Compton was telling me that you are both members of the Temple Coffee House Botany Club,' said Beth.

'I wouldn't miss our weekly meetings at the Rainbow Inn for anything. You never know who will have recently travelled abroad and returned with exotic seeds or plants for sale or exchange.'

'I can see you're busy,' said Beth, 'so I'll take a walk around the garden now and perhaps I may pick two or three of the pink cyclamens to study?'

George London nodded and turned back to his rose bushes.

'There's a great deal more to George than simply being a gardener,' said the Bishop.

'He was apprenticed to John Rose, King Charles's gardener. and he's travelled extensively in France and Holland to further his knowledge. He and his business partner own the largest nursery in England, too. Over a hundred acres at Brompton Park.'

'I've heard my brother John talk of the nursery,' said Beth, 'but I didn't realise it was Mr London who owned it.'

'I'm going to see how my latest consignment of trees are settling in. Come and find me if you need anything.' Bishop Compton strode off.

Beth spent a happy half-hour wandering through the grounds taking note of interesting plants for future reference before returning to the cyclamen growing beneath the cork oak. She picked three blooms in different stages of development and carried her prizes carefully back to her new studio.

Anticipation began to build inside her. Much as her heart was at Merryfields, her visit to Fulham Palace offered her new and exciting opportunities to further her skills. Humming to herself, she put on her old painting apron and set to work.

Chapter 22

April 1688

Beth was deeply absorbed in capturing in watercolour a particularly delicate shade of green on the undersides of the petals of an Illyrian sea daffodil and nearly jumped out of her skin when a pair of hands appeared from behind her and covered her eyes.

'Guess who?' said a voice.

'Cecily? Is it you?' asked Beth, perplexed. 'What are you doing here?'

'It's not Cecily!' said the voice, full of laughter.

Beth turned to see that Princess Anne stood before her, eyes alight with mischief. She sank into a deep curtsy, her heart beating like a hammer on an anvil.

'Please rise, Beth. We are quite alone and there is no need to stand on ceremony. Bishop Compton told me you were here and I couldn't resist coming to find you. Such pretty pictures you are painting! But do you keep well, my friend?'

'Very well, as you see. And your own health?'

'God is smiling on me and I await the birth of my baby with great happiness.'

'That pleases me more than I can say,' said Beth, taking Anne's proffered hand. 'But you must not tire yourself.' She pulled out one of the chairs from the table for Anne to sit on. 'So tell me your news.'

'George is so very happy about the child but, of course, it's not our personal delight that matters.'

'Of course it matters!'

Anne shook her head. 'The succession is the important thing. Although my sister Mary is the heir, so far, she has no surviving children. Should this state of affairs continue, in time I would be queen and so my child may be most important to the state. I pray, oh how hard I pray for a son! We *cannot* have a papist on the throne.'

'How is the Queen?' asked Beth.

'Advancing in her pregnancy,' said Anne, her face tight with resentment. 'But I tell you,' she said, 'there is something most strange about it all. Her priests are so *very* sure that the child is a boy.'

'But no one can possibly know until the babe is born.'

The Princess lowered her voice. 'Not unless there is terrible wrong doing afoot. My father is absolutely determined to have a son, a *Catholic* son, to be his heir. When a man is so very unyielding, the people should question his intentions. And there is a great deal of gossip at Court. Not once has my stepmother allowed me to touch her belly to feel the baby within. Not once!'

'Is that significant?'

'I am her stepdaughter. I carry a child myself. What would be more natural than to allow me to feel her baby move?' Anne's lips tightened. 'I am banished from her bedchamber. She allows no one near her when she is dressing or bathing. I tell you, there is something most odd about this so-called pregnancy.'

Beth stared at Anne in consternation. 'Do you mean that you fear the Queen may not be with child?'

Anne stood up abruptly. 'I wish with all my heart that it is so. The Queen tells us she is to give birth but there is too much mystery. I believe either she merely stuffs a cushion under her bodice or that when the baby is born, should it be a girl, it will be smuggled away and a boy child substituted instead.'

There was a long silence while Beth assimilated this terrible idea. 'She would never be able to do that,' she said, at last. 'Someone would know.'

Anne sighed. 'You understand nothing of life at Court, Beth, my dear. My stepmother is the Queen and my father is the King. He is irrational and deeply stubborn in his beliefs.'

'But what could they do?'

'Everything has its price. And everyone. Besides, a newborn, soothed with a good feed and a drop of brandy, could be smuggled into the birthing chamber in a warming pan. No one would be the wiser. I shall only believe that the Queen has truly given birth to a son if I am present when he is parted from his mother.'

'Time will show us the truth,' said Beth, still struggling with the dreadful vision of some poor cottager's infant son drugged and crammed into a warming pan.

'Indeed it will!' said Anne, standing up. 'But I am disturbing you in your work.' She took Beth's hand, turning it over in her own. Pouting a little, she said, 'I had hoped you might wear the ring I gave you.'

'It's far too beautiful to wear every day,' stammered Beth. 'I save it for special occasions.'

'Wear it every day, Beth. How many of us know when the Good Lord will see fit to gather us into His arms?' She laughed. 'Don't look so worried; I'm sure He will spare you a little longer.'

After Anne had left, Beth returned to her work, staring with unseeing eyes at the half-finished painting of the Illyrian sea daffodil while she went over and over what Anne had said. What she was suggesting was a monstrous political deception on the King's part. But was it simply a figment of Anne's overworked imagination?

Joshua and Samuel were at home when Beth returned to Chelsea that evening. She followed the sound of laughter into the drawing room and found them playing cards with Cecily.

'You cheated, Josh!' protested Cecily as her uncle cleared the table of cards.

'He always cheats,' said Samuel.

'That certainly used to be true,' said Beth as she entered the room.

'Beth!' Joshua ran towards her and lifted her up, knocking her hat over her eyes.

'Put me down!'

'Not until you say you're sorry!'

'What for, telling the truth?'

'It's not true! I don't *always* cheat, only sometimes. Not like my angelic twin.' He lowered her to the floor. 'Anyway, you're late,' he said. 'You'd better hurry up and change before supper.'

'I'll come upstairs with you,' said Cecily. 'Grandmama has guests for dinner tonight and she bought me a new lace shawl today. We had *such* fun shopping at the Exchange ...'

Cecily prattled away as she accompanied her sister upstairs but Beth's thoughts were with Anne's terrible accusation. Was it really possible that the King and Queen were desperately intent upon deceiving the nation? She supposed she would never know unless the child was a girl, in which case perhaps Anne's mind had been turned by her own pregnancy.

'Beth? Are you listening to me?'

'Sorry, Cecily, what did you say?'

'Harry de Montford is coming for supper. Oh, and Grandmama's doctor and Harriet and her horrid husband will be here.' Cecily clasped her hands to her breast and sighed. 'Harry de Montford is so very elegant, don't you think? He has become fast friends with Josh and Sam and they are up to all *kinds* of fun together.'

'Mischief, I expect you mean.'

'There's no malice in high spirits, Beth. Just because you lead such a staid life and you're always buried in your painting . . .'

'At least I'm doing something worthwhile, Cecily, not simply frittering my time away shopping and playing cards.'

'That's very unkind.' Cecily's eyes glistened with sudden tears. 'It's not a crime to make myself pretty or to enjoy myself. At least I shall find a husband, while you will remain an old maid, your eyesight fading as you sit alone painting in a freezing attic.'

'Now who's being unkind?' Wounded, Beth turned away from her sister's accusing eyes while she opened the clothes press. There was a glimmer of pale blue silk amongst her more workaday cotton dresses and she pulled out one of the gowns Anne had given her. Perhaps it was too fine for supper in Chelsea? But it would please her to see Cecily and Arabella raise their eyebrows in surprise at seeing her in such a beautiful gown.

The air reverberated with Cecily's sighs, which Beth ignored, as she shook the folds out of the skirt and changed in silence. Then she unwrapped Anne's sapphire ring from the little velvet purse she had made for it and slipped it on. It really was very beautiful, she thought, as she held her hand out in front of her. Anne was right; she should wear it and enjoy it every day.

'You're looking unusually modish tonight, Beth,' said Cecily at last, with more than a suggestion of a pout. 'No one will notice that I have a new lace shawl.'

Beth relented. 'It's very pretty and sets off your shoulders beautifully.'

'It does, doesn't it?' said Cecily, smiling again as she studied her reflection in the looking glass. 'I wonder if Harry will like it?'

'He's bound to,' said Beth with a dry smile. 'He likes all pretty girls. Men like Harry de Montford are not always to be trusted.'

'And how do you know that, miss?' Cecily lifted her chin in defiance at Beth. 'What experience have *you* of men's promises?'

There really was no satisfactory answer to that, thought Beth.

The other guests were assembled in the drawing room. Harry de Montford leaned gracefully against the mantelpiece and the twins lounged on the tapestry armchairs.

Lady Arabella frowned at Beth and Cecily. 'Ah, there you are! At last.'

The two sisters were presented to Lady Arabella's daughter, Harriet, who appeared to have no memory of having met them before, and then to her husband, Francis Crawford, a bow-legged, elderly man with thinning hair and a sour expression. He wore a lemon yellow coat with a black and sulphur striped waistcoat and bored the company with dry tales of his business dealings in the mercer's trade.

Beth suppressed a giggle at the irreverent thought that he looked like a bad-tempered wasp.

'And this is Dr Edmund Latymer,' said Lady Arabella. 'He's been such a help to me as I suffer so from fits of anxiety.'

Dr Latymer, perhaps a year or two older than Beth, had a pleasant, if unremarkable face. He was quietly dressed in olive-drab but the quality of the lace at his wrists was excellent.

Beth reflected that Lady Arabella liked to surround herself with young men who were of use to her.

Lady Arabella and Sir George led the way into the dining room.

Harry de Montford held out his arm for Beth but somehow Cecily, a dazzling smile upon her lips, was between them, ignoring Dr Latymer's offer to lead her in.

Harry led Cecily away with a mocking lift of his dark eyebrow as he looked back over his shoulder at Beth.

Dr Latymer stepped forward. 'May I?'

Beth took his arm with a smile and was sorry to discover that he walked with a bad limp.

'Old hunting accident,' he said dismissively. 'Happened when I was a young and impetuous youth. Changed my life, though. A doctor saved my leg and it was then I decided to study medicine.' His lips curved in a self-mocking smile. 'As only the third son of an earl, my father was happy to let me do what I pleased.'

Lady Arabella's dining table, laid with polished silver and gleaming glass, shimmered under the soft glow of a myriad of scented beeswax candles. Beth thought she had never seen so many silver salts, sweetmeat and syllabub glasses, crisp damask napkins and matching knives and forks for each person.

Sir George presided at the head of the table, smiling benignly as he deftly carved the haunch of venison. Liveried manservants silently poured wine as their mistress chattered brightly to her guests.

Beth found herself placed between Harry de Montford and Edmund Latymer.

'How very lovely you look tonight,' said Harry lifting her fingers to his lips.

Cecily scowled at Beth from the opposite side of the table.

Harry held Beth's hand, studying the heavy sapphire ring that flashed on her finger. Really, the man was impossibly handsome! His close attention made Beth feel uncomfortably flustered. 'I believe you have become fast friends with the twins?' she said, pulling her fingers free of his.

'Indeed. They have taken me to visit some of the delights of the city that I hadn't already found for myself.'

'I can imagine.' Beth caught Joshua's sardonic glance from across the table. 'I do hope they aren't leading you into wicked company?'

'I suppose if that were the case, Miss Ambrose, then I would hardly admit to it, would I?'

'Tell us how you are faring at Fulham Palace,' Samuel asked. 'Still painting your little flower pictures?'

Beth gritted her teeth. 'I am continuing with my botanical studies,' she said. 'The Bishop of London is very pleased with what I have produced so far ...'

'The Bishop of London!' Lady Arabella's laugh was shrill. 'Did you hear that, Sir George? I cannot imagine why you bother with him, Beth. Of what use is he to you when the King himself has rusticated him in disgrace?'

'He has provided me with my own studio and allows me free rein to select any of the plants and flowers from his gardens for me to paint,' said Beth in quick defence.

'But will he find you a husband or a position at Court?' Lady Arabella raised one painted eyebrow and fixed Beth with her gimlet glare. 'No, I thought not. If you wish to advance in the world you must look elsewhere.'

Beth opened her mouth to make a sharp retort but then thought better of it since it was only by Lady Arabella's grace that she was able to visit the palace every day.

'But you must admit, Lady Arabella,' said Harry de Montford, 'that Miss Ambrose is looking very well tonight. Perhaps she has no need of a bishop's help to find herself a husband.'

Discomfited, Beth turned again to Edmund Latymer who was watching Cecily's every move on the other side of the table. Cecily was entirely oblivious to him, as she twirled her fan to attract Harry's attention. 'My father is a doctor, too,' she said.

'How interesting!' Dr Latymer turned his attention back to her. And where does he practise?'

'At our family home, near to Richmond village.' The doctor's grey eyes were kind, she thought. 'He takes in guests who suffer from melancholy and helps them to overcome their sorrows.'

'And is he successful at that?'

'Usually. But some of the guests never go back to their families, if indeed, they have one.'

'Doesn't that make your home an unhappy place to be?' Dr Latymer's expression was concerned.

'On the contrary! They become part of our larger family and are protected from the outside world. You see, some of them have been cast out by their relations and if we didn't offer them a home they might otherwise be sent to Bedlam.'

Dr Latymer considered this. 'Are there never ...' he shrugged, 'upsets?'

'Sometimes.' Beth at once pictured Johannes's attack on Noah.

'You come from an exceptional family, Miss Ambrose.'

Why, Edmund Latymer's face wasn't unremarkable at all when he smiled.

Chapter 23

April arrived with a flurry of showers interspersed with brilliant sunshine. Beth's daily boat trip between Chelsea and Fulham in all weathers often meant that she arrived at her destination cold and wet but on this sunny morning the wind across the wide stretch of river didn't pinch at her cheeks with icy fingers. Lambs skipped in the meadows beside the river and the trees were clothed in soft new greenery.

When Beth arrived at the studio she felt that the day was full of promise and her fingers were itching to take up her paintbrush and set to work. She found a letter from her mother resting on her easel; she guessed that Noah must have brought it the previous night on his return from Richmond. Sorry to have missed him, she opened it with eager fingers, and read that Father had a head cold but sent his love and that Mistress Fanshawe had called at Merryfields, bringing news of their neighbours, the Beauchamps, dyed in the wool Royalists and Catholics.

Charles Beauchamp took up a new post in the army not two months ago. That would never have been allowed when Old Rowley was on the throne, whatever his private inclinations may have been with regard to religion. No doubt the Beauchamps hope to be further elevated following this recent state of affairs. Who knows where it will end?'

The other great news is that Joseph and Sara plan to wed in May. They say that their day will not be complete unless you return home for the ceremony.

Beth smiled to herself as she folded the letter again. It was hardly unexpected that Joseph and Sara were to marry; somehow it had always been understood, right from when they were children, that they belonged together.

A few hours later, Beth sniffed the air as the scent of roasting pork drifted in through the open window. Her stomach grumbled with hunger as she put the finishing touches to her study of a bunch of grape hyacinths, each tiny azure bell delicately shaded with violet. She swished the brush in a pot of water and wiped it dry on her apron.

Chattering voices and leisurely footsteps echoed along the corridor. Beth had already learned enough of the palace routine to know that members of the household were making their way towards the great hall for their dinner and she set off to join them. She knew several of them well enough by now to smile and pass the time of day.

A little while later one of the Bishop's hunting dogs sniffed around Beth's feet looking for crumbs while she ate her roast pork. A sudden a wave of homesickness washed over her as she wondered if Orpheus missed her.

She was finishing her apple pie, her homesickness magically forgotten while she ate the crisp pastry and thick, yellow cream, when George London appeared at her elbow.

'Miss Ambrose, there's a tulip you might want to see. It's an oddity.'

Hastily, Beth swallowed her last mouthful of pie. 'Indeed I should like to see it. Shall I come now?'

A slow smile spread across George London's weather-beaten face. 'Finish your dinner first. Come and find me down in the garden when you're ready.'

After she had finished her second slice of pie, Beth hurried outside. The gravel glistened with rain from a recent shower but the sun was out again and a fresh breeze stirred the treetops. Beth followed the path to the walled garden where several men were industriously digging and hoeing the neat rows of vegetables, while two gardener's boys stretched a long piece of twine between them to mark a straight row in which to plant seeds. Beth spied George London turning over a great heap of manure from the stables.

He stopped work as he saw her approaching. 'Busy time in the vegetable garden.'

She wrinkled her nose at the acrid fumes emanating from the manure. 'My brother John will be sowing his carrot seeds now.'

'Let me show you the strange tulip I found,' said George London, planting his spade into the dung heap. 'It's near the dove house.'

They walked around the side of the palace and into the outer court, bounded on two sides by the curve of the moat and on another by the stables. A great noise of hammering came from the forge; Beth saw the blacksmith through the open door, a great giant of a man all glistening with sweat amidst swirling smoke and steam.

'Nicholas Tanner,' said George London. 'Strong as an ox, that one.'

A brick dove house with a tiled roof was set in the middle of the court with two stone urns at its base, each filled with a blaze of red and white tulips.

'Have a look at the urn on the left,' said George London, 'and see what you can find. It's a curiosity.'

A flutter of doves arose from the dove house as she approached. Beth bent to study the flowers, which had elongated heads, very different to the rounded Tradescant tulip. There was an elegant curve to the tips of the white petals and Beth noticed that the red stripes were uneven, almost blotched in places. Some of the petals were shaded with a delicate green and the strap-like leaves had misshapen, jagged edges as if a naughty child had hacked at them with scissors. 'The irregular colouring makes them very unusual,' she ventured.

'That's true. There's a great interest at present in flowers with uneven stripes but look again and tell me what you see.'

Beth stared at the flower-filled urn and suddenly noticed something. 'It's this one!' she said triumphantly. 'How very odd!'

George London cut through the stem of one of the tulips with his pocket knife and handed it to her.

'I've never seen such a thing,' she said. She ran a finger over the leaf, which sported a red and white stripe down its length.

'I've only seen it twice in all the time I've been a gardener.'

'Thank you so much for finding it for me.'

But George London had already touched his hat and set off back towards the vegetable garden.

Carefully, Beth carried her prize back to the studio and arranged it on a piece of white linen. Hurriedly she laid out her paints and mixing bowl determined to make good progress on the painting before the extraordinary tulip began to wilt.

***

Beth was chatting to George London one day as she finished her dinner, a tasty chicken and leek tart, when Noah slipped on to the bench beside her.

'This is an unexpected pleasure,' she said.

'I've been at Whitehall this morning and heard some news. I came straight here to tell Bishop Compton. The King has issued the Declaration of Indulgence again.'

Beth frowned. 'I thought there was such an outcry last time that nothing happened?'

'Nevertheless, all the clergymen have been instructed by the King to read it out in their pulpits next month.'

George London's jaw clenched in anger. 'It's simply another step towards the papists taking over the Church of England. Once there's no requirement to affirm the oath for the established church, we'll have Roman Catholics in positions of control in the army and the navy and the universities. The King will not rest until he's turned us all into Catholics.'

'But he can't do that, can he?' said Beth. 'It's against the law. The Test Act forbids it.'

George shrugged. 'The King is determined to have the final word and disregards whatever laws Parliament makes, if they don't suit him. When you think of the King's cousin, Louis, and the Revocation of the Edict of Nantes and the resulting religious persecution I am fearful for what may happen.'

'We all knew that King Charles had Catholic leanings,' said Beth, 'but he was always careful never to impose them on the people.'

Noah smiled ruefully. 'After his father was sent to the scaffold I suppose he was particularly cautious but King James is a very different kettle of fish from his brother.'

Then, a buxom girl with creamy skin and black hair sauntered up to them. 'Afternoon, Noah and George,' she said, regarding Noah with a sleepy smile. 'Are you going to introduce me to your little friend?'

'Hello, Lizzie. This is Miss Beth Ambrose, lately come to the palace,' said Noah. 'Beth, this is Miss Lizzie Skelton, the bee-keeper's daughter. She works in the palace laundry.'

George stood up. 'Since I have some seedlings to transplant I'll leave you two ladies to become acquainted.' He headed off towards the garden.

'I must go to my chamber. I have some drawings to finish,' said Noah, pushing back his chair. 'See you both later.'

Beth saw Lizzie's appraising glance as she watched Noah hurrying away. 'You're that painter girl, aren't you?' Lizzie said, stretching rudely across Beth to pick up an apple from the fruit bowl, her immodest neckline exposing far more of her charms than was seemly.

Beth nodded.

'Noah told me about you. He's a fine gentleman,' said the girl, her sloe-dark eyes gleaming as she looked Beth up and down. 'I'm going to ask him to show me some of those buildings he keeps talking about. Perhaps he'll take me to London in a carriage.'

'I don't think he has a carriage,' said Beth, itching to slap the insolent girl's face.

The girl looked disappointed. 'Maybe he'll buy one if he knows I'll go to London with him. I like the city. Such shops as you've never seen and the theatres and parks!' She bit into the rosy side of the apple with sharp little teeth and studied Beth speculatively. 'Not planning on keeping him for yourself, are you?'

'Certainly not!' A scalding blush raced up Beth's throat and lodged on her cheeks.

'Aha! Like that, is it?'

'No! I ...'

'Well, spoils to the victor, then.' The girl dropped the half-eaten apple on to Beth's plate and sauntered away, her hips swinging.

Beth stared at the apple with loathing. Perhaps she'd take a walk in the garden to calm down before she returned to work.

Beth found it strangely difficult to settle to her painting that afternoon. She'd discovered a delightful little heart's-ease blooming in the shade of the elm walk and the pretty flowers with their tiny faces should have inspired her but her heart simply wasn't in it. She arranged the specimens carefully to show off their leaves and blooms to their best advantage and sketched them, sighing all the while. The image of Lizzie Skelton's sleepy eyes making up to Noah insisted on intruding continuously upon her thoughts, irritating her like a burr chafing under her bodice.

Putting down her sketchbook, she made herself busy preparing a new batch of paints, attacking the pigments with force, as if hammering and grinding them on to the porphyry slab would dispel the annoying image of Lizzie Skelton's complacent smile.

A cloud of ochre powder settled all about her, making her cough. Wrists aching, she put down the muller and washed the pigment off her fingers. As she was drying her hands the studio door opened and with a jolt of pleasure she saw Noah.

'I've finished my drawings,' he said. 'It's still sunny and I've brought ginger ale and some sweet custard tarts.' He held up a small basket to show her. 'We're going on a picnic.'

'A picnic? It's only April,' protested Beth, laughing in delight at the idea.

'Where's your spirit of adventure? Wrap up warm and we'll go down by the moat.'

Passing the fountain in the empty quadrangle, Noah's booted footsteps echoed from wall to wall as he strode across the cobbles, Beth hurrying along beside him. 'I often like to imagine how this might have been in old Queen Bess's day,' he said. 'Can you picture the commotion when she arrived here with her retinue?'

'It must have been a marvellous sight,' said Beth.

'Of course, the palace wasn't in such a sorry state of decay in those days. The Bishop says he'd rather spend what money he has on the gardens and, any other money he can raise, he sends to the building fund for St Paul's cathedral.'

'I should love to see St Paul's. When do you think it will be finished?'

'Years from now. It's an expensive undertaking, particularly when you take into account all the other costs of rebuilding the city after the Great Fire.'

'Noah, you're walking too fast!'

He slowed down while Beth caught her breath. 'Sir Christopher goes everywhere at such a tremendous pace I have to stride out so as not to be left behind and it's become a habit. I've never met a man with such energy!'

They made their way through the rose garden and past the bowling green until they came to a gate leading into the pasture known as the Warren. The coarse grass was flattened underfoot to form a rough path, which led to the moat.

Noah spread out his cloak with a flourish on the grass and Beth arranged her skirts carefully over her ankles, wondering if he had ever brought Lizzie Skelton on a picnic there. The very thought of Noah taking Lizzie Skelton anywhere troubled her; she realised with sudden dismay that she was jealous. Unwilling to examine the thought, she pushed it away. After all, Noah was here with her now and Lizzie was in the laundry.

Noah rummaged in the basket. He took out four custard tarts wrapped in a clean napkin and then eased the cork in the bottle of ginger ale with his thumbs. 'The last time I had a bottle of this it exploded,' he said as the cork shot off with a loud *pop* and flew into the moat.

Beth snatched a tankard out of the basket to catch the ale before it all fizzed out of the bottle.

'Well caught!' laughed Noah. He lifted his tankard. 'A toast! Here's to the coming summer and plenty more picnics.'

'Must you really return to Virginia this autumn?' asked Beth, speaking her thoughts aloud.

Noah hesitated. 'There's still a great deal for me to learn here. Perhaps I'll stay until the following spring.'

The thought made her smile. 'I can't bear to think of you leaving us, although I know Kit will be pleased to see you,' she said, biting greedily into the creamy sweetness of a custard tart.

'I expect Kit's having a fine old time. My sisters and our neighbours Hannah and Amy Sharpe will be asking him to squire them to all the parties and dances.'

Noah was quiet for a while, contemplatively watching the ginger ale cork bobbing up and down on the turgid green water.

'Since coming to the palace, I understand now why Kit wanted to leave Merryfields. Perhaps I judged you too quickly when I blamed you for Kit leaving us. If you dream of something greater for your life, you have to take risks, don't you?'

Noah picked up her hand, the Princess's sapphire sparkling on her finger. 'The world is an uncertain and worrisome place at present. You were brave to leave the safety of Merryfields.'

Although embarrassed that her hands weren't as clean and white as a lady's should be, Beth idly imagined what it would be like to entwine her fingers with Noah's. 'It's an exciting prospect for me, here at Fulham, to become a known artist, through Bishop Compton's associations with other botanists. An opportunity I never looked for but now hold precious. I am set upon this course and will let nothing divert me.'

'So you are still intent upon remaining a spinster?'

'I must,' she said.

Noah let go of her hand and sighed. 'I only hope it makes you happy, Beth.'

'Johannes left me a letter when he died,' she said. 'He told me to go out into the world and look beyond my small dreams. And now I have.'

Chapter 24

It was a breezy day in mid-April when a consignment of trees arrived for Bishop Compton.

Beth looked up from her easel when she heard cartwheels roll over the cobbles and a deal of shouting below. Hurrying to the window, she leaned out of the casement and saw what looked like a small wood moving into the quadrangle. Then she realised that it was a cart heavily loaded with trees, their branches tied up with rope and the whole swaying dangerously from side to side.

George London and his gardeners were already in attendance and, as she watched, Bishop Compton came out to inspect the delivery.

Beth hung out over the windowsill until the last of the trees had been unloaded on to a handcart and taken away.

Later that afternoon, she took a walk through the garden and found Bishop Compton and George London supervising the digging of a hole deep enough to accommodate the roots of one of the new trees.

'Miss Ambrose! Good day to you!' called the Bishop.

'I'm curious to see what new delights have arrived.'

'This one is a sweet gum tree and I'm reliably informed that the leaves turn a glorious red in the autumn. You shall take a leaf then to immortalise in paint.'

'I shall look forward to it.'

The planting hole was pronounced large enough and one of the gardeners tipped a barrow load of well-rotted manure into it, before George London and the Bishop carefully manoeuvred the sapling into place.

The Bishop himself backfilled the earth around the roots and vigorously trod it in. 'There!' he said with satisfaction as he stamped his boots and rubbed his hands together to remove the earth. Taking a knife from his pocket he cut the rope that secured the branches of the sapling and they sprang free. 'George, give it good drink and that's a job well done.'

Then Bishop Compton narrowed his eyes as he looked over Beth's shoulder. She turned to see a man hurrying towards them.

Dressed in a travelling cloak and a fine feathered hat, his high boots jingled with spurs as he walked over the grass. 'Your Grace.' Bowing, the man handed the Bishop a letter.

As he scanned the contents the Bishop made a small exclamation of dismay. 'This is ill news indeed! If you will excuse me, Miss Ambrose?'

She watched him walk back towards the palace, his shoulders sagging, and wondered what could have disturbed him so.

Late that afternoon, Noah came to the studio as Beth was cleaning her brushes.' I wondered if you'd like to visit the site of St Paul's cathedral on Sunday?'

She couldn't contain a smile of pleasure at the thought of such an excursion.

'I know you will appreciate how magnificent it will be.' His face shone with enthusiasm. 'The stonework is very handsome but all the decorative details will take years to complete.'

'I'm very interested to see you in your natural setting at work.'

'If you're finished for today I'll walk you down to the boat.'

The sun, partly obscured by the clouds, was low in the sky as they ambled through the gardens. In the distance, men were still planting one of the new saplings and all was quiet except for the cooing of the doves and the swish of their feet through the long grass. A chill dampness was beginning to arise from the ground.

Beth kept her gaze on the path ahead but she was conscious of Noah's silent presence so close beside her. She could feel the warmth coming from him in the cool air and smell the faint scent of leather from his damp boots. Then their fingers brushed accidentally sending a sudden shock up her arm. He glanced at her and rapidly looked away again. She held her breath as if she was waiting for something momentous to happen but Noah didn't look at her again.

The boatman appeared, ghostlike out of the white mist that hung over the river. 'Best get on, miss,' he said. 'The fog's coming down fast.'

Reluctantly, she said goodbye to Noah.

He handed her into the boat and she wasn't sure, but she wondered if he held her hand a moment longer than necessary.

'Until tomorrow,' he said.

As the boatman pulled away Beth looked back over her shoulder at Noah, until he was hidden by the swirling mist.

It was almost dark when she arrived at Chelsea. With some relief, she heard a loud 'Halloo' and then saw the light of a lamp glowing steadily brighter in the vaporous gloom.

The twins, Cecily and Harry de Montford, all arm in arm and very merry, were coming along the path towards her.

'We came out to look for you,' said Samuel. 'The fog came down so suddenly and Cecily was worried about you.'

'I'm very glad of the light home.'

Samuel slipped his arm through hers. 'Careful, the path is slippery.'

Harry de Montford took Beth's other arm and pressed himself close to her side as they walked. He carried with him the heavy perfume of expensive hair pomade, bay rum and orris root but the pervasive nature of it made her nose wrinkle in distaste. It occurred to her how much she preferred Noah's clean, uncomplicated male scent.

'So, you're moving in high circles now, Beth,' Harry de Montford said. 'Do you see much of the Bishop of London?'

'I see him in the gardens on most days and sometimes he comes to the studio to look at my work.'

'Have you met anyone of interest to you in the Bishop's household?' asked Harry. His dark eyes were brightly inquisitive. 'I'm sure there must be a dozen young men all curious to meet the beautiful lady painter.'

'Not at all,' stammered Beth.

'Come now, why so modest?' He captured Beth's hand and studied the sapphire ring glinting in the lamplight. 'Not only beautiful but talented and wealthy.'

Beth frowned, wondering if he was teasing her.

'You must have many suitors?' he persisted.

Beth snatched her hand away. 'I do not look for suitors.'

'Perhaps I should snap you up myself?' His smile was bland but Beth thought the look in his eyes was as calculating as that of a lizard about to shoot out its tongue to trap a fly.

'Beth is *far* too good a catch for her father to consider a match for her with a ne'er-do-well such as you, Harry,' said Joshua.

It wasn't long before they saw the candles glowing in the windows of Arabella's house. Beth, relieved to come in out of the clinging damp air, went to warm herself by the drawing-room fire.

Harry de Montford came to stand close to Beth, stretching out his hands towards the heat of the flames.

'Shall we play a hand of cards?' Cecily asked.

'Not tonight, Cecily,' said Joshua. 'We're going into the city.'

Harry nudged Joshua. 'And Sally Fisher would be most unhappy if you're late, wouldn't she, Joshua?'

'All the young ladies would be sorry, I believe,' said Samuel, snorting with laughter.

Cecily appealed to Beth with tragic eyes.

'You must take care,' said Beth. 'The fog is thick over the water.'

'Will you be very late back?' asked Cecily.

'Very early, more like,' replied Joshua. 'If indeed we come home at all tonight.'

'Well, go on then!' Cecily stamped her foot. 'Leave us to a lonely evening all by ourselves.'

Harry took Cecily's hand and raised it to his lips. 'Don't take on! I'll escort you to the city another time.'

Mollified, Cecily fluttered her eyelashes and formed her mouth into an adorable pout. 'Will you really?'

'Undoubtedly,' said Harry with a lazy smile.

After they had gone, Beth and Cecily went upstairs to change for dinner.

Cecily sat on the edge of their bed and sighed. 'Isn't Harry the most handsome man you've ever seen?'

'Quite probably,' said Beth. 'But he is too familiar.'

Cecily stared at her with blank incomprehension. 'Not at all! And he doesn't treat me like a child, unlike *everyone* else I know.'

'Well, if you stamp your feet and behave like a child what can you expect? He said perhaps he should snap *me* up as I haven't any suitors,' said Beth, deciding it best not to spare Cecily's feelings. She really ought to have the measure of the man.

'And you're not even looking for a husband! I'll *never* forgive you if you steal him from me, Beth!'

'Don't worry about that.' Beth stretched out her hand and studied her sapphire ring. 'But you mustn't take his honeyed words seriously, Cecily. Harry de Montford is an incorrigible flirt.'

'No he isn't! Besides, I'm sure that once he falls in love with me he'll marry me, even when he knows I don't have a dowry.'

Beth embraced Cecily. 'For goodness' sake, don't place all your hopes in Harry, sweetheart.'

Beth was staring contemplatively out of the studio window, barely noticing the peaceful scene set out before her. She admitted to herself that she spent as much time daydreaming about Noah as Cecily did about Harry. It was a fruitless waste of time, of course, since Noah's passionate and single-minded ambition would return him to Virginia, just as her own ambition would not allow her to deviate from her painting. But then, sitting so closely together by the moat the other day, he'd expressed the concern that spurning marriage for the sake of art might not make her happy and this had left a worm of doubt in her mind. She had spent far too much time of late imagining what it would be like if Noah kissed her.

Sighing, she turned away from the window to study again the paintings she'd produced in the month since she'd arrived at the palace. She laid them out in rows upon the wide shelf which lined the room and walked slowly past them, her footsteps echoing into the silence.

'What do you think of them, Johannes?' she whispered. 'Should I make this my life's work? And if I do, will it make me happy? *Must* I give up all ideas of marrying and having a family?' She often held imaginary conversations with Johannes while she was working. It was surprising how often his imaginary answers solved her problems but today she heard no reply.

Behind her, someone cleared his throat and she saw Bishop Compton, in his gardening clothes as usual, standing in the doorway.

'Am I disturbing you, Miss Ambrose?' He glanced through the open door to the bedchamber. 'Were you talking to someone?'

Beth coloured. 'No, I . . . that is . . . I was talking to myself.'

'Ah! I do that, too. I have conversations with Our Lord; usually when I have some knotty problem.' He smiled but his eyes looked weary. 'Sometimes I even believe He answers me. I've brought you something,' he said. He held out a small cloth bag. 'I have been remiss since I forgot to discuss your salary with you. You will need to purchase paints and materials and then there are your travelling expenses and other costs incurred by being away from home.'

'I had not expected—'

Henry Compton held up his hand. 'You are continuing Alexander Marshal's work and you should be remunerated for it.'

Beth's eyes widened at the bag's weight. 'Thank you,' she said. 'I will be relieved not to have to ask my father for financial assistance with the purchase of studio supplies.' Hesitating a little, she said, 'I saw the messenger arrive yesterday and I wondered if I might ask if everything is well?'

Henry Compton rubbed a hand over his eyes. 'I am sorry to tell you that it is not. Princess Anne has miscarried her child.'

'Oh, no!' Beth pressed her fingers to her mouth. 'I saw her only a few days ago and she was well and so happy.'

'No longer, I fear.'

'I had hoped that this time . . .'

'She has been sorely disappointed before but there are much greater issues afoot, as the Princess herself is aware. If she could have brought forth a healthy son it might have done a great deal towards safeguarding the security of the succession. As it is, we shall have to wait and see if the Queen produces the son her priests are predicting.'

Bishop Compton's face was grim. 'I fear for every man, woman and child if the King has a male heir. Affairs will quickly spiral out of control as he will never allow Parliament to temper his obsession to return this country to a Catholic state.' He began to pace the floor, agitation apparent in every step. 'And with the weight of France and Spain behind him he will do this by force, if necessary. The people will resist. There will be civil war.'

'War?' Beth felt her face pale.

'You're too young to remember what it was like last time but already the King has manoeuvred his papist toadies into positions of importance. No one, or their possessions, will be safe.' He looked straight at Beth. 'How will you feel if he confiscates Merryfields from your family and gives it as a bribe to a Roman Catholic?'

'He couldn't! It wouldn't be fair!'

'Fair?' The Bishop gave a mirthless laugh. 'Don't expect justice from the King while he is gripped with this fixation. He believes he is above the law. King Charles may have been a secret papist but he learned that the people of this country will not have a tyrant Catholic on the throne. His Majesty is determined there shall be an absolutist monarchy, just as in France. Mark my words, there will be terrible bloodshed if the Queen has a son.'

Chapter 25

On Sunday morning Beth dressed carefully in one of the gowns that Princess Anne had given her. She peered into the mirror, pleased to see that the dress, made of the finest wool the colour of lapis lazuli, made her eyes look as sapphire as her ring.

'You look enchanting,' said Cecily, eyeing the embroidery on Beth's skirt with jealous eyes. 'Would you like to borrow my shawl that Grandmama bought for me?' She rummaged in the coffer for a piece of lace, as delicate as a spider's web, which she draped around Beth's shoulders. 'There! I knew it would be perfect.'

'Why, thank you, Cecily.' Touched, she kissed her sister's cheek.

'And perhaps you will lend me one of your fine gowns that the Princess gave you? I think the green one would suit me, don't you?'

'I might have known you wanted something from me!' Beth glanced at her reflection again and smiled. The lace shawl really was very pretty.

'We'll be a credit to Grandmama, won't we? All heads will turn to look at us when we arrive at the church.'

'Cecily! We don't go to church to be admired.'

'Don't we? I don't know why you're scolding *me* when you're all dressed up in your best things.'

Across the fields, the church bells began to peal.

'Have you forgotten I'm going with Noah on an excursion to the city after church?'

'To look at St Paul's, you said.' Cecily took the green gown out of the coffer and stepped into the skirt. 'What a waste of a trip to the city! Don't you want to go to the shops?' Cecily sighed and turned her back for Beth to pull her bodice laces. 'Don't ruin your beautiful dress, traipsing around a building site.'

Beth said nothing but she did wonder if, in this instance, vanity had perhaps overridden her usual good sense.

Smoothing down her skirt with a self-satisfied smile, Cecily gave Beth a sharp look. 'Is there something you're not telling me? You don't usually care much what you wear; it all ends up covered in paint anyway. Why this sudden change?' She gripped her sister's arm. '*Please* tell me it's not Harry!'

'I'm not remotely interested in Harry.'

A wide smile broke out across Cecily's face. 'It must be Noah then!'

'Don't be ridiculous! Just because I'm going to look at St Paul's with him ... '

'It is Noah! It is! Your blushes give you away, Beth.' She hopped up and down in delight.

'Stop it, Cecily. And hurry up and put your shoes on or we'll be late for church.' Beth turned away from her sister's prying eyes and hurriedly pinned up her hair with clumsy fingers. It was true. Cecily had only said what Beth had been too afraid to admit to herself.

She was saved from having to enter into any more conversation about the matter when Samuel hammered on the door.

'We're just coming,' said Cecily.

'Mama and Sir George are leaving. Mama says she has no intention of sitting at the back of the church because you've made them late.'

They scrambled down the stairs and hurried along the lane towards the church.

The bells were still ringing as they walked up the aisle. Lady Arabella raised an eyebrow when they slipped into the pew beside her.

As the bells ceased Beth felt a touch on her arm and looked up to see Noah standing in the aisle.

'Move along a little,' he whispered.

The service seemed interminably long to Beth as she sat wedged into the pew with Cecily on one side of her and the warmth of Noah's thigh pressed tightly against her other. She kept her eyes firmly upon the parson but a pulse fluttered in her throat.

She stood and knelt and made her responses almost unconsciously while she came to grips with this strange new feeling. Was this what drove perfectly sane women into foolish behaviour in the presence of the object of their desire? Sneaking a sideways look at Noah from under her lowered lashes, she was disconcerted to find him looking back at her. He glanced away but Beth noticed that the tips of his ears had flushed as pink as the delicately furled and velvety petals of her favourite cabbage rose.

The service came to an end at last and Beth shivered at the light touch of Noah's hand on her elbow as they filed outside into the sunshine.

Lady Arabella held out her hand to Noah and he lifted it to his lips, causing Beth to experience a sharp stab of jealousy.

'My dear Noah!' said Lady Arabella, deftly elbowing Beth aside and gripping Noah's arm. 'I understand you are taking Beth into the city today?' You'll not be too late back, I hope? I wish to discuss some further ideas for the improving of our house in Windsor before we go to the service in the chapel at St James's this evening.'

'My wife talks of nothing else but the proposed renovations,' said Sir George with his usual urbane smile. 'The house has served my family for generations but I have been persuaded that it is time to make changes.'

'Of course it needs changes, Sir George,' said Lady Arabella. 'It's damp and draughty and extremely old-fashioned. I intend to enrich the drawing room with new panelling and decorative plasterwork to the ceiling.'

Noah gave a small bow. 'I shall be delighted to discuss the additional works with you later.'

Beth swallowed her disappointment. She had so looked forward to this precious day out and Lady Arabella was going to cut it short to suit her own avarice for self-aggrandisement.

Lady Arabella clapped her hands together. 'In fact, I have a better thought! Sir George and I insist you join us for dinner before you go out and we can discuss my ideas afterwards.'

'How very kind,' said Noah, 'but unfortunately Beth and I have a prior engagement with Sir Christopher Wren.'

'I'm sure he won't mind if you arrive an hour or two late.'

'Nevertheless, we must decline your invitation. I regret to say that Sir Christopher is a busy man and sometimes of an impatient disposition.' Noah leaned forward to Arabella, his eyes twinkling conspiratorially. 'Since I rely upon his good nature for my opportunity to learn from a man of such stature, I fear I cannot take the risk of offending him.'

'We quite understand,' said Sir George, deftly prising Lady Arabella's fingers off Noah's sleeve and tucking them in the crook of his own elbow. 'My dear, shall we return home? I intend to open a bottle of the best wine in the cellar, in celebration of His Majesty's tolerant and liberal-minded stance relating to those of all faiths. We'll see young Leyton when he returns Beth into our care later on today.'

Lady Arabella pursed her lips in disappointment. 'Well, go on then, if you must, Noah! Cecily, you shall walk by my side and keep me company this afternoon.'

'Yes, Grandmama.' Cecily fell into step beside Arabella.

'Shall we go, Noah?' said Beth. 'I wouldn't wish us to be late and displease Sir Christopher.'

They took the path towards the river and, once Lady Arabella and the others were out of sight, Noah let out a sigh of relief. 'I thought we'd never escape. A fearsome woman, your step-grand-mother!'

'What time is your appointment with Sir Christopher?'

'I don't have one. Did you really want to spend the entire after-noon indoors with Lady Arabella, discussing the finer points of embellished plasterwork, on such a lovely day?' Noah's brown eyes sparkled with amusement. 'I thought not.'

Noah had arranged for a covered skiff to wait for them at the public stairs. Beth rested her feet on a floating plank and hoped the scummy water in the bottom of the boat wouldn't soak into her shoes and the hem of her beautiful skirt. Then the boatman pulled away to the middle of the river, which shone like molten lead in the sun. Forgetting her small worries, Beth began to simmer with excitement at the joy of being out and about on such a glorious spring day.

Noah pointed out Westminster Abbey, Whitehall Palace and other landmarks of interest as they passed.

'Princess Anne's apartments are in the Cockpit in Whitehall Palace, aren't they?' she said.

Noah nodded. 'Bishop Compton told me of her sad news. He had pinned a great deal of hope on the child being a son.'

Beth stared at the windows of the palace, glinting gold in the sun-shine. Perhaps Anne was sitting lost in melancholy thought by one of them, watching the river traffic pass by.

The sound of church bells floated across the river and Beth turned her face into the invigorating breeze. The sun shot sparks of copper off Noah's chestnut hair as it whipped about in the wind and he laughed when a sudden gust made Beth snatch at her hat. She gave a great sigh of contentment at the prospect of a whole day in Noah's company.

The river was quiet since it was a Sunday; there were no wherries ferrying passengers from Gravesend to the shires and few barges queuing up at the quays to unload their wares. The tide was against them so the boatman had to work hard, straining against the stream but, after they passed Bridewell, he began to row towards the shore. The boat cut through the stinking rubbish that bobbed about on the oily green water, collecting up in mounds against the beach of exposed tidal mud. Before long they were tying up at Blackfriar's Stairs.

'I thought we'd walk past St Bride's and approach the cathedral from Ludgate Hill,' said Noah.

Beth gathered up her embroidered skirts in an effort to keep them from trailing in the bilge water and stepped off the boat. The stench of the mud was overpowering as they picked their way along the slippery jetty towards the stairs. Seagulls screamed raucously from above, swooping down over the scattered detritus.

Beth lost her footing on the slime-covered timber then gasped as Noah caught her, snatching her against his chest. Her cheek was pressed against the slight roughness of his jaw and his arm was tight around her waist. His hair smelled of the open air together with an underlying male muskiness that set her senses reeling. Her heart began to pound and she wondered if she'd ever be able to breathe again, overtaken with an almost irresistible desire to turn so that their lips could meet.

'I thought you were going to fall on your face in the mud,' he said, releasing her.

His gaze was fixed on her but Beth daren't look at him. 'I would have fallen, if you hadn't been there,' she murmured, making a show of brushing imaginary mud off her skirts.

He tucked her arm firmly through his so that her hip brushed against his as they walked.

Unable to speak for the tumultuous thoughts tumbling around in her head, it was all Beth could do to keep moving. In spite of everything she believed in, in spite of dear Johannes's advice, she was irresistibly drawn to Noah.

Barely noticing her surroundings, she clung to Noah's arm as they made their way along the narrow lane leading away from the river.

'There's St Bride's church,' he said. 'It's one of Sir Christopher's projects, too.'

Beth forced herself to concentrate as she looked at the pale stone building. 'There's no steeple.'

'The funds are still being raised for that. The church itself was built in only nine years, making it one of the first to reopen after the Great Fire. There's an interesting story about how it was completed so quickly.' He smiled in amusement. 'It was because Sir Christopher built the Old Bell Tavern nearby.'

'How did building a tavern make the building works finish faster?' asked Beth.

'The tavern was for the labourers so that they were close to hand and could work longer hours.'

'What a mine of information you are, Noah! But it was a gamble for him. The labourers might have spent so much time in the taproom that they were too drunk to work.'

Noah laughed. 'Sir Christopher likes to talk about what happened after the fire. A new city had to be built very quickly to provide homes and to allow businesses to continue. It's fascinating,' he said as they climbed up the hill. 'You can be walking along a street full of higgledy-piggledy timber-framed buildings and then, halfway along, the houses change to a flat-fronted brick terrace. You can see the extent of the Great Fire very clearly.'

'Mama watched St Bride's burn,' said Beth. 'It was terrifying. The whole landscape was unrecognisable under rubble and burning thatch. She says she'll never forget the roaring of the fire and the smoke and the feeling of utter helplessness as St Bride's went up in flames. It was the church where she was christened and where she married my father. Henry Savage, that is.'

'And your birth father died of the pestilence just before the fire, I believe?'

Beth nodded. 'I wish I'd known him. Mama never speaks of him.'

'But she is happy with Dr Ambrose?'

'Devoted. And he has been a kind and loving father to me, in spite of anything I may have said to you before.'

Noah looked at her consideringly. 'I have never seen him act with any less affection for you than for your brothers and sister.'

'But I'm ashamed to say that after Johannes died I accused him of that.'

'Sometimes we say things we don't mean when we are grieving,' said Noah.

'I hurt Father badly.' She drew a quivering breath at the memory. 'But in the end we talked of it and it lanced the boil of my hurt. And I realised that, for all that time, I'd been wrong.'

Noah smiled. 'Then there's no need to look so woebegone.'

She sighed, suddenly embarrassed at opening her heart to him. Looking around her at the houses, all lightly brushed with sooty deposits, she said, 'It's almost impossible to imagine the destruction caused by the fire now. It's even harder to imagine that these buildings are only twenty years old. They look as if they've been here much longer.'

'City smoke is the culprit,' said Noah. 'It amazed me when I arrived in this anthill of a city as I'd never smelled anything like it in Virginia where the air is so clean and there's so much more space.'

'I wish I could see Virginia. I'd love to be able to picture Kit in his new home.'

'Who knows? Perhaps one day you'll visit.'

They reached the top of the lane and turned into Ludgate Hill, a much wider cobbled road, full of people and carriages.

'I recognise this,' said Beth. 'This is where Cecily and I came with Lady Arabella for the St Cecilia's Day concert. Some pigs were being driven to market and they upset a fruit stall. There was chaos because the traffic was blocked.'

'Watch out!' Noah steered her out of the path of an oncoming carriage.

The Portland stone of the new St Paul's cathedral shone white in the sunshine but it was clear that there was a long way to go before it would be ready to use. The entire building was criss-crossed with timber scaffolding and mountains of sand were heaped on the ground.

'This cathedral will be a proud testament to the power of the Anglican faith,' said Noah. He stood with his hands on his hips looking up at the stonework.

'A new beginning,' said Beth. 'What a sight it must have been when the old St Paul's burned!'

'Sir Christopher said the lead melted off the roof and ran like a molten river down the hill,' said Noah, a faraway look in his eyes as he imagined the scene.

'How long will it be before the new cathedral is finished?' asked Beth.

Noah shrugged. 'The foundation stone was laid thirteen years ago and it might be finished in another twenty, if there are sufficient funds. Shall we go inside?'

He led her around the back of the building and lifted up a large piece of sacking hanging from the timber scaffolding. When they ducked underneath it Beth saw a small door in the wall. Noah extracted a key from underneath a nearby block of stone. 'Here we are!'

Beth followed him inside; as he closed the door all street noise was muffled. The musty smell of new mortar and damp stone assaulted her nostrils. From the perimeter walls of the cathedral, already in place, she could see that it would be shaped like a gigantic cross. The walls soared above her but were still open to the elements. Blocks of dressed stone lay stacked on the ground, together with more sand and workmen's tools.

She craned her neck to look upwards at the sky so far above. 'It makes me dizzy,' she murmured. Her whisper echoed around them in the silence and she shivered and glanced over her shoulder, suddenly overcome with the feeling that this was a place of veneration, full of spirits not only of saints and worshippers past but of the future also.

Noah's eyes were fixed on her. 'So you sense it, too,' he said quietly. 'I knew that you would feel the same reverence resonating in the air as I do.'

When she met his gaze she found herself powerless to drop her eyes. A pulse began to beat in her throat and she wondered if he could see it.

He drew a deep breath and looked away. 'I love to come here on a Sunday when the workmen are all at home. It's quite different during the week when it's full of shouting men clambering over the scaffolding and heaving wooden beams up in the air.' He removed the remains of a workman's lunch, a half-eaten pie and an apple core, from a block of stone, then spread out his handkerchief for Beth to sit on.

They sat side by side, awed by the stillness. '*This* is why it's so important to me to be an architect,' he said, passion throbbing in his voice. 'This sense of making history. In years to come, when the cathedral is finished and made beautiful with carved wooden screens and decorative floors and embellished ceilings, people who worship here will wonder about those who built it. Not just Sir Christopher, who will never be forgotten, but Ned or Dick who sat here before us and ate lunch,' he smiled, 'or most of it, anyway, and then carried on building the walls. I will have played my small part in it, too.'

'I wish you could do that here rather than in Virginia.' She bit her tongue, afraid he would read her feelings too clearly.

'Of course, I could spend my whole life learning from Sir Christopher.' He looked intently at her. 'There are many reasons to stay.' He sighed and his gaze slid away. 'And others to return. Architects with a vision of the future are needed at home. I believe I can make a real difference there. You do understand?'

She nodded, her throat suddenly closing up as she tried not to cry.

'Yes, I'm sure you do,' he said, all fervour gone. 'You have a lifetime's work laid out before you at Fulham Palace and will let nothing stop you.'

'No,' she said, wondering why the thought of freedom from a wife's cares and spending her entire life painting made her suddenly feel so miserable.

They sat for a little longer, each alone with their thoughts, until Noah sighed and stood up. 'Shall we go? I know a tavern not far from here that serves an excellent steak and oyster pie.'

Noah was right; the tavern served a hearty dinner and Beth enjoyed the unaccustomed luxury of roasted quails, steak pie with fragrant gravy and lemon flummery washed down with a glass of canary wine. There was a noisy party at the table next to them, full of jokes and laughter, who insisted they join them in finishing their jug of wine and then waved them off with ribald good humour.

They left the smoky warmth of the tavern and ambled along Cheapside to settle their dinner and watch the other people enjoying their Sunday promenade before they cut through the side streets to Paul's Wharf.

A pervasive melancholy settled over Beth. 'The day has passed too quickly,' she said as they climbed into the boat. 'I've had such an enjoyable time.'

Noah took her hand. 'Then we shall come again another Sunday.

There is much to explore in the city. Let's make the most of the time I have here.'

'I'd like that,' she said, trying to ignore the hollow feeling in the pit of her stomach at the thought of how quickly the time would pass before his return to Virginia.

Chapter 26

May 1688

Beth breathed a deep sigh of contentment. The gardens were truly lovely at this time of year and the air smelled sweetly of honeysuckle and damp grass. Everywhere she looked, George London's men were busy watering and weeding and she felt a stab of guilty pleasure that she was enjoying a break from her own work. New flowers appeared in the garden every day as the weather became warmer, meaning she'd had to work quickly to record as many of them as she could. The Bishop regularly visited her in the studio, as pleased as she that her collection of botanical studies was growing so rapidly.

A haze of purple and white double columbines grew in the shade of an oak tree, their heads nodding on delicate stems in the breeze. She bent to pick a small collection of the most perfect blooms to paint that afternoon, wrapping their stems in a damp cloth to keep them fresh.

She wandered over to the wooden bench against the kitchen garden wall and sat down for a moment to enjoy the peace. It was one of her favourite places from which to rest and survey the grounds. There were niches set at intervals along the wall, each one containing a woven willow skep of bees. The humming of the bees sounded lazily in the air as Beth closed her eyes, her face turned up to the sun.

Drowsy in the early summer warmth, she let her thoughts, as usual, return to Noah. They had made another Sunday expedition to the city, the Tower this time, and had visited the lions in their cage. Beth had felt sorry for them as they paced up and down, enduring insults and rotten eggs from some of the visitors.

Noah had laughed at her when she said she'd like to set them free. 'And have every man, woman and child in the city run screaming through the streets?' He'd hugged her briefly, his touch bringing a blush to her cheeks. 'And if you took them back to Africa they'd be too old and mangy to survive in the jungle.'

Then the taunting crowd broke into screams as the largest lion shook his mane, opened his mouth wide and roared. Slowly, he turned round behind the bars, lifted his tail and projected a stream of urine at the main perpetrator of the insults. The crowd roared in delight.

'I think the King of Beasts can look after himself, don't you?' said Noah, his eyes twinkling with merriment.

Every moment of time that they spent together was intensely precious to Beth, a golden time before he returned to Virginia. He came to see her in the studio at the end of each day and they had fallen into the routine of walking around the garden so that she could show him whatever had come newly into flower. Often they sat under the oak tree by the moat, feeding the ducks and discussing the events of their day.

But, in spite of all the time they spent together and Noah's solicitous attention to her, he never said one word to betray what he felt, or didn't feel, for Beth, leaving her utterly mystified. He looked at her with tenderness and surely he must know that she was smitten by him? She was beginning to wish she'd never made such strong protestations that she would never enter the married state. Although she supposed that was still true, she couldn't help feeling that she *did* want to love and be loved.

Sighing, Beth glanced at the sun high in the sky. Time to return to work. Passing by the bakehouse, she stopped for a moment to sniff the appetising perfume of vanilla and cinnamon and apple on the air. Judith Tanner, wrapped in a clean apron, leaned against the doorpost with a mug of ale and waved a friendly greeting.

'Something smells delicious,' said Beth.

'Apple pies, cinnamon biscuits and custard tarts for dinner.'

'You have been busy!'

'Ah well, there's always work to be done in the pastry kitchen. 'How are you finding life at the palace?'

'It was strange at first, being away from home, but I'm settling in now. And I keep very busy.'

'I'd love to be artistic, like you. May I see your paintings one day?'

'I'd be delighted to show you. Come by the studio any time you're free.' Beth smiled. 'Have you been at the palace for long?'

'Always. My father was the palace blacksmith until he died and my brother, Nicholas, took over. You may have seen him around the stables?'

'I have,' said Beth. She remembered glimpsing a swarthy giant of a man in a leather apron toiling over the smithy fire in a swirl of acrid smoke like some heathen god arising from the underworld.

'Fancy a cinnamon biscuit?' Judith disappeared inside for a moment and returned with a handful of biscuits. 'There's a couple of broken ones and one that was a bit too close to the fire but you won't mind that, I suppose?'

Beth held out her hands. 'Thank you. I shall enjoy these.'

Beth set off, cutting through the passage by the coal store into the quadrangle. Biting into a biscuit's crisp sweetness, she crossed the courtyard on her way towards the main entrance.

A door slammed behind her and the porter hurried out of his lodge to unbolt the great oak gates. He shouted out to his son, who hurried off towards the stables.

Curious, Beth heard the rumble of wheels on the drive and then saw a carriage approaching the archway. Two splendid black stallions trotted briskly through the gateway and came to a halt within a few feet of her.

The ostler ran forward to take charge of the horses, while the coachman jumped down and unfolded the carriage steps. A liveried footman set off at a smart pace towards the palace.

After a moment or so, two richly dressed ladies descended, followed by a maid.

Beth caught her breath as she recognised Princess Anne. Unsure what to do, she froze back against the wall.

While they waited, Princess Anne did not speak to her companion, a fine-featured lady with fair hair and an aristocratic bearing, but simply stood still, with her eyes on the ground.

Beth was filled with pity as she noticed Anne's sallow complexion was unusually pale and drawn and that she had become very thin. Then, as she watched, she saw the Princess falter. Her eyes turned up and she began to sway.

The companion squealed in consternation and the ladies' maid, holding the princess's large jewel case against her breast, watched in wide-eyed horror.

Without pausing to think, Beth ran forward and caught the Princess a moment before she sank to the ground. 'Quickly! Help me!' she called to the maid.

The maid thrust the jewel case into the arms of the Princess's companion. Half carrying, half dragging Princess Anne between them, they managed to prop her up on the carriage steps.

Now wasn't the time for Court niceties, thought Beth, as she pushed the Princess's head between her knees.

The maid scrabbled in her pocket for a bottle of smelling salts, which she waved under the Princess's nose.

Feebly, Princess Anne batted her hand at the bottle and turned her head away. 'What happened?' she murmured. Her hair had come loose from its pins and fell around her shoulders.

'You fainted, that's all,' said Beth. She smoothed a loose strand of hair off her face. The companion, her face outraged, bustled forward. 'Take your hands off her! At once!'

The Princess blinked furiously for a moment while she looked at Beth. 'Beth? Is it you?'

Beth sank into a deep curtsy. 'Your Royal Highness.'

'Do you know this person?' asked the blonde lady.

'Indeed I do,' murmured Princess Anne. 'This is my friend, Miss Beth Ambrose. You must remember, Sarah? I told you about how kind to me she was when I stayed with her family at Merryfields.'

The lady's frosty expression thawed a little.

The Princess turned back to Beth. 'May I present Lady Sarah Churchill?'

Beth curtsied to Lady Sarah and was relieved to see Bishop Compton hurrying across the quadrangle to join them. In the hubbub of greeting, Beth moved away and watched as the party made their way towards the palace entrance.

Then Princess Anne stopped. 'Beth, come with us, won't you?'

Taken by surprise, Beth remained motionless for a moment but the Bishop beckoned to her and she followed them inside.

Refreshments had been prepared in the Bishop's private parlour. Beth found herself sitting beside the Princess with a glass of wine in her hand.

Bishop Compton drew up a footstool at the Princess's feet. 'I am sorry to see you brought so low,' he said.

'It is not simply a weakness of the body but also a sickness of the spirit.' She buried her face in her handkerchief and her shoulders heaved. 'The King *gloated*, I can use no other word for it, when he heard I had miscarried my baby. The way is clear for him now to introduce us to his imposter son next month.'

'And the King still seems certain that the child is a boy?'

'Absolutely, resolutely, *stubbornly* certain. Such confidence in the outcome can only be born out of trickery.' She blew her nose and wiped her eyes.

Bishop Compton's expression was grave.

'We travel to Bath to take the waters,' said Lady Sarah. 'And to pray for the Princess of Denmark's return to good health.'

'Will you return to London in time for the birth?' asked the Bishop.

Princess Anne, her nose red and her face tear-stained, said, 'In my present condition, I could not bear to be there when the Queen is brought to bed, in spite of the King's command in that respect.'

The Bishop looked thoughtful. 'If you are not in the birth chamber to verify your so-called half-brother when the Queen's time comes, there will be many who will question the prince's validity.'

A flicker of a smile appeared on the Princess's face. 'Indeed, I believe that to be the case. But I must not allow anything to stand in the way of recovering my health. I wish to visit my sister in The Hague to take comfort from her but His Majesty will not permit it.' She stood up and smoothed down the disarray of her hair. 'And now I shall rest before I continue my journey.' She turned to Beth. 'I have cause again to be grateful to you and thank you for your prompt action when I was indisposed.'

'As always, I am at your service, ma'am.'

The Princess glanced at Beth's hand. 'I am pleased to see that you wear my ring.'

'I am honoured to do so.' Beth curtsyed deeply; when she looked up the Princess, Lady Sarah and Bishop Compton had gone.

The room was silent. She stood motionless, watching dust motes whirling in a shaft of sunshine from the window, then held her hand up to the sunlight and studied the glittering sapphire of the Princess's ring.

Later that afternoon, Beth carefully added another delicate purple stripe to her study of the columbines. She used her favourite squirrel-hair brush, only a few hairs thick, applying the watercolour with tiny strokes. The contrast between the white and the dark purple petals was truly beautiful and complemented the soft greens of the leaves.

She pushed back her chair and studied the painting. Should she put another wash of colour on the leaves? What would Johannes have advised? Perhaps not. Decisively, she stirred her brush in the pot of water and shook it dry. The painting was finished.

'Very pretty!'

Noah was leaning against the door, his arms folded. She blushed as she was almost sure he was referring to herself and not her painting. 'You made me jump,' she said. 'Imagine if I'd knocked over the pot of water and spoiled the painting!'

'That's a fine greeting!'

'Have you been there long?'

'Long enough.' He unfolded himself from the doorway. 'This is lovely, Beth.'

She nodded. 'I've never seen this variety of columbine before with the double flowers and the star-like form.'

The floor creaked and Beth's heart sank when she saw Lizzie. She found herself unaccountably irritated that Lizzie wore a low-cut bodice and the creamy skin of her full breasts strained over the top like freshly baked dumplings. She felt she could almost bite into them herself, so heaven only knew what Noah was thinking.

'Hello Noah,' said Lizzie. She licked her lips and gave him a slow smile. 'Haven't seen you since the other evening.'

'Hello Lizzie,' he said. Spots of bright colour appeared on his cheeks as he shuffled his feet.

Lizzie stared at Beth, her face entirely expressionless. Then she drew a deep breath, expanding her chest even more, if that were possible. 'Ah well, must be getting on. Some of us have better things to do than mess about with paints. See you at supper tonight, Noah.' She bathed him in the radiance of her smile and left.

Tight-lipped, Beth collected up her brushes and the mussel shells containing the remains of her paint and briskly washed them. 'You seem to have found an admirer, Noah.'

He shrugged, giving her a sheepish smile. 'I think perhaps I have. She's very interested in architecture.'

'Really?' Beth raised her eyebrows in disbelief.

'Yes, really. She makes a point of seeking me out to talk about the projects I'm working on in the city.'

'And does she do the talking about architecture or do you do all the talking and she simply listens?'

'Well . . . ' He frowned. 'Perhaps I do run on about my latest work. But she's always fascinated. She even said she'd like to come to the city with me to learn more about what I'm doing.'

'I'm sure that she did.'

Noah changed the subject. 'Shall we go for our walk now? We can take our sketchbooks, if you like?'

'I've finished here.' Jealousy was a painful emotion, she reflected and, apart from the usual sibling rivalries, not one she'd experienced before.

They went to sit in their favourite place beneath the oak beside the moat, where the late afternoon sun restored Beth's good humour. She missed the summer afternoons when she and Johannes had sat, sketching and chatting, on the garden bench at Merryfields, and following the same pursuit with Noah made her recall those happy times.

Noah leaned back against the rough bark of the tree, sighing in contentment. 'I've spent the afternoon smoothing over petty squabbles between stonemasons and joiners,' he said, 'and I've looked forward to being here with you all day.' He opened his sketchbook and began to draw the tree canopy above.

Beth, drawing the bulrushes clustered on the bank of the moat, watched Noah's charcoal slip from his fingers as he drifted into a doze. A soft breeze stirred the branches above, dappling the filtered sunlight over his fine, straight nose. A lock of auburn hair fell across his forehead. Smiling, Beth turned to a new page in her sketchbook.

Twenty minutes later, absorbed in smudging the graphite with her thumb to mould the shadows beneath Noah's cheekbones, she realised that he was awake and regarding her with lazy eyes.

'So I am to be the subject of your next work?' he smiled. 'Something of a change from a flower portrait.'

'Johannes told me to experiment. And you were sleeping so peacefully that I thought I'd attempt your likeness.'

'May I see?'

Beth handed him her sketchbook.

'You have captured me,' he said after a moment. 'This is clearly the face I see in the mirror when I shave every morning. But I believe you have made me look unnaturally heroic.'

Beth flushed. It was true that as she sketched the line of his jaw she had imagined him as the knight in one of the tales of chivalry she had enjoyed as a child.

'It will serve to remind you of me after I have returned to Virginia,' Noah said. He drew up his knees to his chin and turned to stare at the moat, his face set.

'Perhaps then,' said Beth with a lightness of tone that she didn't feel, 'perhaps you should draw me and then you won't forget me, either?'

'I shan't forget you. How could I?' he asked, turning to face her again.

Covered in confusion, she couldn't meet his eyes. 'May I see your sketchbook?' she asked. As she turned the pages, she was fascinated to see how his drawings differed from her own.

'You don't attempt to make an exact likeness of what you see?'

'You see the oak leaves above? I've used them as an inspiration for a carved stone corbel I'm working on.' He came to sit beside her and took back the book. 'And look, if I draw the leaves like this ...' Snatching up her graphite stick, his hand moved rapidly over the page as he sketched a garland of oak leaves. 'This will make an excellent length of plaster cornicing or a carving to decorate a chimneypiece.'

'It's very handsome,' said Beth, fired by his enthusiasm.

'One day,' he said, 'I'll use these details when I build a house of my own.'

'What a shame I'll never see it,' said Beth.

Then a cloud passed in front of the sun and she shivered.

Chapter 27

A few days later the boatman tied up at Merryfields and Beth and Cecily jumped on to the landing stage, eager to see their home again. After Beth pulled on the bell they waited impatiently until the gate in the wall opened.

'Joseph! How are you?'

A wide grin spread across Joseph's face as he took their bags. 'All the better for seeing you two young ladies again! I wasn't sure if you'd come.'

'What! Miss your wedding?'

'Tell me, has Sara made a beautiful dress to wear?' asked Cecily.

'She's been closeted away in secret with Peg every evening,' said Joseph. 'Strangely, she always seems to have little bits of thread caught in her hair so I expect there's something afoot in the sewing department.'

They walked through the orchard towards the house and Beth felt a pang of sadness as they passed the apple tree where she had found

Johannes hanging. Refusing to let such a thought mar a happy event, she pushed it away.

When Joseph opened the orchard gate to the garden Beth stood still, gazing at Merryfields. The faded red bricks glowed in the golden sunshine, the twisted chimneys reached up towards an azure sky. Oh, how she had missed it! The gardens were as neat as ever, though she was surprised how small they looked now that she had become used to the extensive grounds at Fulham Palace.

John and Old Silas were weeding one of the flower beds. Silas waved when he saw them and John ran to greet them.

'Beth! Cecily!' He hugged them both together. 'I've m-m-missed you both so much!'

'Mind my new hat!' said Cecily, straightening the brim and stroking the feathers back into place. 'You're all covered in earth!'

'Let me look at you.' He held her at arm's length. 'My little sister has grown into a b-b-beautiful lady.'

'Do you really think so?' asked Cecily eagerly. 'Grandmama is teaching me everything she knows about how to behave in polite society so that I can find myself a rich husband.' She glanced at Beth. 'I'm determined *one* of us Ambrose girls must marry well.'

'Come on in,' said John, linking arms with Beth. 'You c-c-can't imagine how strange it's been with both of you away, especially with Kit in Virginia, too. I don't like being an only child. Mama and Father are pacing about indoors waiting for you to arrive and I'm d-d-determined to sit you down with me for a couple of hours, Beth, while you tell me all about G-G-George London.'

'There's a great deal to tell. I painted a particularly beautiful auricula, red and yellow and bronze, and mentioned how you would love to grow some here so Mr London has sent you a gift of some seeds. I've brought my painting, too, to show you how they will turn out.'

John hugged her tight. 'So you d-d-didn't forget me, then, while you've been away?'

'Of *course* not!'

Joseph had gone on ahead with their bags and now Beth saw her mother hurrying towards them with Orpheus at her heels. Beth ran to her with her arms wide and pressed her face to Susannah's soft cheek, breathing in her familiar perfume of rose and lavender.

Eyes bright with joy, Susannah kissed Beth before gathering Cecily into her embrace, too. 'Welcome home, my beautiful girls,' she said.

Orpheus jumped up to rest his paws on Beth's shoulders and lick her face.

'Down, sir!' Beth bent to fondle his ears and pat his wiry coat. 'So you missed me, too?'

William was waiting for them in the little parlour and Beth was moved to see the pleasure on his face as he greeted them. 'Come and sit by me and tell me all your news, or are you too grand now, Beth, since you've been living in a palace?'

'It isn't anything like as grand as it sounds, in fact, parts of it are in worse repair than Merryfields,' she laughed.

'What news from the city?'

'All the talk amongst the household is of unease about the standing army being so large when we are not at war. Bishop Compton is worried that the Jesuits have twisted the King's promises to alter nothing in the established Church.'

'I never thought to hear you interested in politics, Beth,' said Susannah.

'I never was. Only now, when I hear about happenings at Court from Josh and Sam or about events from Bishop Compton, it *is* interesting when I hear how these affairs may change how we all live.'

'Have you been very homesick?' asked Susannah.

'At first,' said Beth, 'but I've made friends now and Noah usually comes to see me at the end of the day before I return to Chelsea.'

'Don't you want to hear what I've been up to?' asked Cecily. '*Much* more interesting than Beth's crumbly old palace!'

'You don't find it too irksome to stay with Lady Arabella?' asked Susannah.

'Irksome!' Cecily laughed. 'It is not irksome at all. She takes me shopping to the Exchange and we visit her friends for coffee and we've been to the theatre with the twins and Harry de Montford. Why, Grandmama Arabella has quite adopted me!'

William raised one eyebrow. 'It seems you are having a fine old time.'

Cecily's eyes sparkled. 'I certainly am. Grandmama's dressmaker is making me a new gown of yellow taffeta and I love going into the city. It's all so exciting! And then the twins bring back all *kinds* of scandalous gossip from the Court, too.' She lowered her voice. 'Only the other day Harry told me that Josh had told him that the King had a common whore brought up the back stairs to his private quarters ...'

'Cecily! That's quite enough!'

'But, Father, it's true!'

William's face had darkened with anger. 'Is it not bad enough that your uncle should relate such a wicked and treasonable tale, without you repeating such a thing?'

Cecily gave a long suffering sigh. 'Yes, Father.'

'Perhaps you should retire to your chamber for a while to reflect upon a proper mode of conduct for a young lady?'

'You're sending me to my chamber?' Cecily's expression was incredulous.

'If you behave like an ill-mannered child you must accept the consequences. I cannot think that Lady Arabella would like to hear such words pass a young *lady*'s lips.'

'Mama?' Cecily looked to her mother for support and found that it was not forthcoming. Pouting, she stood up. 'Oh well, I must hang up my new skirt to let the creases fall out before the wedding.' She closed the door a little too firmly behind her.

'What was Harry de Montford thinking of to relate such disgraceful tittle-tattle to a young girl,' asked William, shaking his head in disbelief.

'Cecily is extremely taken with him,' said Beth. 'Of course, he can be very charming.'

'Is Arabella maintaining proper control over your sister?' asked Susannah, with a worried frown.

'Lady Arabella likes to surround herself with handsome young men but she wouldn't allow it if they paid more attention to Cecily than herself.'

Susannah gave a wry smile. 'That does sound exactly like Arabella.'

'Shall we forbid Cecily from returning to Chelsea?' asked William.

'You must do what you think right, Father, but I believe it might be better to let Cecily enjoy herself a little longer. I cannot imagine that it will be long before she becomes disenchanted with both Lady Arabella and Harry de Montford's capricious and shallow ways. Quite apart from a prolonged fit of the sulks if you drag her away from her new friends, should Cecily not come to this under-standing herself?'

William thought about this. Then he turned to Susannah. 'What is your opinion, my dear? Instinct tells me that, although I would prefer to keep Cecily close to hand, Beth has the matter in a nutshell.'

'And Beth can keep a watchful eye on her.' Susannah sighed. 'When she was a child, Cecily wasn't called So-Silly by her siblings without good reason.'

'Unlike our Beth, who shows such good sense,' said William, reaching for her hand.

Beth flushed with pleasure. William's praise was precious to her. 'I will endeavour to curb any excesses on Cecily's part,' she said.

❦

The following morning, Joseph and Sara's wedding day, the Ambrose family and the guests and servants gathered in the hall in their Sunday clothes before they walked to church.

Phoebe, quietly dignified in a turquoise turban and gold hoops in her ears, clung to her son's arm, her ebony skin glowing with pride.

The bridegroom wore a blue velvet coat and fidgeted nervously with the lace at his throat.

'L-l-last day as a free man,' joked John, punching him on the arm.

Joseph nodded and gave a sickly grin, his brown face paler than usual.

The church bells began to peal.

'Shall we go?' said William, holding out his arm to Susannah.

The church was dressed in flowers from the garden at Merryfields and the bride, wearing a blue dress with embroidered butterflies on the petticoat, was as sweetly charming as only a blushing bride can be. Emmanuel's proud smile as he tenderly accompanied his daughter down the aisle tugged Beth's heartstrings.

Cecily cried prettily into a lace handkerchief all the way through the service. 'I wish I was being wed today,' she whispered to Beth. 'But I would wear white flowers in my hair and have a green silk dress to match my eyes and ribbons on my sleeves.'

'Marriage is far more important than the clothes you wear,' said Beth severely. But she, too, watched Sara and Joseph exchange their vows with a tear in her eye. She had grown up with both of them and witnessed their love develop. A strange melancholy took possession of her. She would never be a bride like Sara, with all the hopes and dreams that marriage promised. There would never be a husband to care for her and share her life. She would never have children to love. She sighed deeply and Cecily nudged her.

Beth sat up straight. It was no good to go into a decline; this was the path in life she had carefully chosen to prevent her special gift from being wasted. Anything else would make a mockery of Johannes's faith in her talent.

After the ceremony, the wedding breakfast was laid out in the great hall and the family and guests feasted on chicken pies, roasted lamb, a great pike and a selection of jellies, syllabubs and sweet pastries. Afterwards there was music and dancing.

Beth was amused to see Old Silas take Nellie Byrne for a turn around the floor.

Orpheus, who took against the fiddler and howled every time a new tune began, had to be banished to the stables.

At last the sun began to streak the horizon with gold as the day grew to a close. Clarence Smith proposed a final toast to the bride and groom and William made a speech to wish them a long and fruitful marriage. Then the party processed outside and threw rice and rose petals at the happy couple as they made their way up the stairs to the room they would share over the stables.

Phoebe and Peg cried tears of joy in each other's arms and speculated on how long it would be until they became grandmothers.

The guests returned to their dormitories and Cecily, having imbibed two glasses of wine, fell asleep with her head upon the table.

Beth and Susannah set to work with Jennet, Phoebe and Peg to restore order to the great hall.

'What a perfect wedding,' said Beth as she carried a teetering pile of plates into the scullery.

'They do look happy, don't they?' said Peg, her arms in water up to the elbow as she washed the pots.

'You only have to see the way they look at each other to know it's the right choice,' said Beth, wondering why her own spirits had suddenly sunk so low.

Peg blew a loose strand of fair hair off her face. 'I knew when I met my Emmanuel that he was the one for me and I was only fourteen then.' She smiled dreamily as she scrubbed the plates and Beth could see the eager young fourteen year old girl again in her freckled face. 'And he's still the one for me, even after twenty years. He always could make me laugh, even when life is difficult. Laughter, that's the secret of a happy marriage.'

Beth awoke with the dawn chorus and slipped out of bed so as not to disturb Cecily. She pulled aside the curtain to peep through the casement. The sky was a hazy blue suffused with pink and mist shimmered over the grass. The scene was so delicately pretty she longed to paint it and spent several minutes wondering how she might capture the veil of peachy clouds all edge-lit with purest gold. Suddenly desperate to be outside, she scrambled into her clothes and tiptoed barefoot out of the bedchamber.

Orpheus, materialising out of the shadows, fell into step beside her. Once outside the stone steps were cold and rough under her feet as she breathed in a lungful of sweetly scented air.

She picked up her skirts and sprinted across the lawn with Orpheus loping along at her heels, her heart swelling with the pleasure of an early summer morning at Merryfields. All alone, she could run with the joyful abandon of a child. At last she reached the orchard where, out of breath, she slowed to a walk, the hem of her skirt heavy with dew against her bare ankles. Leaning against the rough bark of an apple tree, she let her breathing steady while she watched the mist lifting off the grass in the early warmth of the sun. The orchard was full of birdsong and sunlight and it was hard to imagine it as the dark and frightening place it had been when she had found Johannes.

After a while she set off again, gathering a posy of flowers as she walked. Stopping by the honeysuckle arch, she bent to place the posy beside the wooden cross which marked Johannes's grave. She sat quietly for a while on the bench where they had liked to sketch and said a prayer for him. Eyes tightly shut, she pictured his homely face and wished that he were beside her to enjoy the day. Sighing, she stood up. Soon the household would be stirring and it would be time for her to leave Merryfields.

As she sauntered past the stables, a casement up above opened and she saw Sara, naked as the day she was born, leaning out of the window to take the morning air. Her curly black hair fell unbound to her breasts and the sun touched her cinnamon skin with gold.

Joseph appeared and rested his chin on the top of her head, wrapping his arms around her waist. Sara turned to face her husband, holding up her face to be kissed.

Beth shrank back into the doorway of the hay store and averted her eyes until they withdrew into their room, not wishing to intrude. Then she crept away, a bitter worm of envy eating into her heart.

Chapter 28

At the end of the afternoon Beth heard the bell of Fulham church ring the hour. She glanced up from her sketch of the beautiful scarlet star anemone with its layers of narrow, backward-curving petals and velvety, charcoal stamens. She had ground a large quantity of red pigment in preparation and would start to paint it the next day. Freeing her hair from its confining ribbon, she combed it with her fingers. She had prepared a picnic basket earlier on containing a large lardy cake, the sugar glaze glistening invitingly, a flagon of cider and two beakers. She stared at the lardy cake, wondering if it would show if she pulled off a little piece from the side.

She didn't have to wait long before Noah pushed open the studio door. 'I'll just wash the brushes and cover my paints,' she said, 'and then I'll be ready.'

Noah perched on one end of the work table swinging his foot while Beth tidied up. Then he went to look at the wide shelf where she had laid out her paintings. He picked up one of these, a striped red and white tulip with a rounded bowl of curled and twisted petals, parted a little to expose the dark, velvety stamens within.

'That's a variety of tulip, which was collected and grown by John Tradescant,' said Beth. 'It's exquisite, isn't it?'

Noah carried the painting to the window, where he studied it for some time.

Beth watched him covertly while she busied herself wiping the table.

'Well, what do you think of it?' she asked. 'You've been looking at it for so long you're making me nervous.'

He turned to face her. 'It's plain to me now why you are so passionate about your painting. This is no mere hobby. You have skills equal to, or greater than, any man. And your proficiency has grown in these last weeks.'

Pleasure bubbled up inside her at his praise. 'Thank you, Noah,' she said quietly.

'Nevertheless, your decision to remain a spinster is still a great sacrifice to make.'

She sighed. 'Marriage brings children and I cannot allow that to divert me from my purpose.'

He frowned a little. 'To forgo the comfort of marriage may be a greater sacrifice than you know.'

'Perhaps.' To avoid the intensity of his look, she took off her apron and snatched up her cloak.

'Just a minute,' said Noah. 'Come here.' He took out his handkerchief and steadied her chin with one hand while he carefully wiped her cheek.

His fingers were warm against her skin and she could smell the outdoors on his coat. They were so close that she could see the tawny bristles in the cleft of his chin and the golden flecks in his amber eyes, which were fixed on her mouth. She licked her lips, her pulse beginning to skip.

Then, outside, a horse neighed and someone called across the quadrangle.

Noah blinked and hastily stepped back. He held up his hand-kerchief to show her the streak of red paint upon it.

'Thank you,' she said, all at once unable to meet his eyes.

'Come on then, my lady!' He made a mock bow and proffered his arm.

They walked briskly along the passage and down the back stairs. Beth was relieved that the ill-lit stairs concealed her heightened colour from Noah.

Down by the moat, seated on the blanket, Noah opened the cider while Beth tore the lardy cake into pieces.

'How was your visit to Merryfields?' asked Noah, taking a piece of cake.

'The wedding was such a happy occasion,' she said. A picture of Sara and Joseph entwined naked in each other's arms by the open window flashed into her mind again. All at once she wasn't hungry any more and carefully put down her piece of cake. 'It's a wonder-ful thing to see two people so much in love,' she went on quietly. 'It must be awful to marry someone you don't love.'

'People marry for many other reasons than love,' said Noah. 'Companionship, money, convenience ...' He wrapped his arms around his knees and stared at the river. 'Family expectation.'

'Can you imagine spending the rest of your life, day and night, for years and years until one of you dies, with someone you don't feel passion for?'

'Lots of people have to,' said Noah shortly.

'Well, I'm not going to be one of them.'

'You've made that plain enough. Your work is so important to you that you won't even marry for love.' He reclined on to his side and threw a few pieces of his lardy cake into the river for a family of ducks that paddled hopefully nearby.

If there had been any reason for it, Beth would have thought that Noah was cross with her. 'That doesn't mean I want a life without love, though,' she said.

'I didn't believe you to be so shameless, Beth!'

'I'm not! But Joseph and Sara are so happy together.' She picked a crumb off her finger, unable to look at him. 'I'm envious of what they have. Sometimes I can hardly bear the thought of not having a husband of my own.'

'Then you'd better decide what you do really want.'

'But it isn't fair! A man can have a wife and still carry on with his own life but a woman has to look after the house and the children and there is no time for anything else.'

'A home and children are more than enough to satisfy most women. Certainly all the young women of my acquaintance, except for you it would appear, do their utmost to find a husband to give them the position in society they crave.'

Frustration at his lack of understanding made her voice sharp. 'Noah, imagine if you were a woman, would you want to give up *your* dreams of becoming a great architect in order to cook the dinner and mend the bed curtains?'

Noah stared at her. 'Now you're being ridiculous.'

'Am I? Do you imagine that it is impossible for a woman to have dreams as great as those of a man?' She glared at him until eventually he looked away and an awkward silence sprang up between them.

After a while, Beth sighed. 'Let us not argue.'

'I have no wish to do so.' He touched her cheek with his finger. 'Tell me more about your visit to Merryfields.'

'Well, Cecily managed to provoke Father into sending her to her room in disgrace,' she said. She related some scandalous piece of gossip about the King that she'd heard from Harry and the twins. Father wasn't amused.'

'Harry shouldn't relate such gossip to Cecily; she's little more than a child. Some say that the King's carnal desires are *why* he works so tirelessly to be a good Catholic: it's in atonement for his sins.' Noah's eyes were laughing. 'And others say that his paramours are all so ugly and horse-faced that his penance is here on earth.'

Beth smiled, relieved that his good humour had apparently been restored. 'I'm glad you can talk about such things with me.'

He lay down on the blanket beside her and squinted into the sun in the blue dome of the sky above. 'Unlike Cecily, I can rely on you to understand when it is appropriate *not* to talk about them.'

'She is not at all worldly wise. She certainly has no interest in current affairs or any understanding of what the King's ambition to make this country follow Rome could mean for us all.'

'But you have grasped the seriousness of the situation.'

'It's hard not to, living at the palace, isn't it? Since the Bishop is so stalwart an Anglican and Lady Arabella espouses the papist cause, I have become more acutely aware of the looming crisis if the Queen gives birth to a son.' She sighed. 'I worry about Cecily. I'm not sure I like your friend. He has a silver tongue but I cannot trust him.'

'He isn't really my friend. I knew of him in Jamestown, of course, and we travelled to England together. His family home is a large tobacco plantation on the other side of the town. His father is from wealthy French Catholic stock but he's drunk most of the fortune away and the plantation is in decline. Harry was sent to England to find a rich wife to restore the family fortunes.'

Beth lay down beside him, conscious of the small space between them. 'I suppose I should be relieved,' she said, wondering if he would think her shameless if her arm brushed against him. 'Since he's searching for a rich wife I can be sure he'll leave Cecily alone.'

Noah yawned and reached for her hand. 'The sun is so warm it's making me sleepy.'

Drowsy with cider and warmth, Beth watched his face as he dozed, drinking in the sweep of his lashes curved upon his cheek, the dimple in his firm chin, learning every freckle and plane of his face. Her hand still lay curled in his and she lifted it to her lips and kissed it. Would it be like this, she wondered, to lie next to your husband every night and be able to open your eyes in the morning to see his beloved face on the pillow next to your own? A sharp sense of loss pierced her heart at the thought that she would never experience such a joy.

She dozed for a while and then sat up, drained the last of the cider from her beaker and brushed the crumbs from the rug. The remainder of the lardy cake had gone stale in the sun so she threw it into the river for the ducks, which descended on it with a flurry of wings and a deal of raucous quacking.

Noah yawned and stretched.

'It's later than I realised,' said Beth. 'Lady Arabella will be vexed with me for being late for supper.'

'Shall I accompany you back to Chelsea?'

'Really, there's no need.'

Noah whistled for the next passing boat. His face rested against hers as he kissed her goodbye and she yearned to turn her head, just a little, so that her mouth, instead of her cheek, would meet his lips but her courage failed her.

As the boatman pulled away towards Chelsea, Beth looked back towards the river bank and saw a young woman walk across the grass to Noah and link her arm in his. Lizzie Skelton.

Beth hovered outside the half-open dining room door. There was a low buzz of conversation and a peal of high, artificial laughter that Beth recognised as Lady Arabella's company laugh. There must be guests for dinner. As if it wasn't bad enough that she was eaten up with jealousy over Lizzie and Noah, now she'd have to face up to a scolding. Taking a deep breath, she opened the door.

A sea of faces turned towards her. At least a dozen were sitting down to supper at a table laid with the best glasses and linen. The air was laden with the aroma of roasted meats, heady perfume and red wine.

'I'm sorry to be late,' said Beth, wishing now that she'd taken the time to change.

Lady Arabella's mouth tightened before she remembered to paste a wide smile upon her painted face. 'Tardy, as usual, Beth! No matter. Seat yourself now so that our conversation is not interrupted any more than needs be.' She smiled again at the assembled company. 'Beth appears to have inherited her mother's unfortunate dress sense and forgetful attitude to punctuality.'

'I beg your pardon, Lady Arabella, Sir George. I left Fulham Palace later than usual and I didn't wish to make myself even later by changing for dinner.'

'So I see. There is a place laid for you between Samuel and Dr Latymer. I'm sure Dr Latymer has seen worse sights while tending the sick in the slums. Isn't that so, Doctor?'

'I'm often kept working late myself,' he said, his limp apparent as he pulled out a chair for Beth. 'Come and tell me all about what you've been doing today, Miss Ambrose.'

Seething at Arabella's barbed comments, Beth sank down on to her chair. Dr Latymer made general small talk and listened to her commonplace replies with great concentration, just as if what she said was the most interesting thing in the world, and she was grateful for his kindness. She cast a glance around the table, noting that Lady Arabella's daughter, Harriet, was there with her sour-looking husband. Harry de Montford was watching her with one eyebrow raised, while Cecily hung on to his sleeve and fluttered her eyelashes at him. Joshua had pushed away his dinner and morosely concentrated on draining his wine glass at frequent intervals. Sir George smiled blandly, while he listened to a loud-voiced man with a red face, already into his cups. Beth reflected that for all the opulence of the table and the expensively dressed guests there was less comfort to be found around Arabella's table than at the simplest turnip soup supper at Merryfields.

At last the evening drew to a close and Beth was able to escape to her bedchamber.

Cecily dallied downstairs until Harry de Montford took his leave and then came, yawning, to bed. 'What a lovely party!' she said. 'I'm having *such* an agreeable time here in Chelsea; I don't ever want to go home. I'm going to find myself a rich husband and then I shan't have to return.'

'Don't set your sights too high, Cecily. You know there is no dowry for you.'

Cecily dragged most of the blanket over to her side of the bed. 'What do I care? I shall find my rich husband and he will have enough for both of us.'

'Someone like Harriet's husband?'

'Ugh! Certainly *not*; he's a horrid wizened old dwarf!'

'Without a dowry you cannot hope for a young and well-favoured man, Cecily, never mind one with a fortune.'

'I can and I will!'

'Even a girl as pretty as you may find that difficult.' Beth reached out in the dark to touch Cecily's shoulder.

'I *will* find a good husband, Beth.' She pushed her sister's hand away and turned her back. 'Just you wait and see!'

Irritatingly, since she was so tired, Beth could not sleep. The picture of Lizzie Skelton sidling up to Noah on the river bank danced behind her closed eyelids and, when she did eventually fall into a restless doze, Lizzie taunted her in her dreams.

The following morning Beth returned to the palace to find the quadrangle ringing with the sound of horses' hooves and the grind of coach wheels on the cobbles. A dozen or so richly dressed men were striding about, their voices echoing off the walls and their velvet cloaks blowing in the wind like so many flags. Ostlers ran hither and thither leading the horses to the stables.

Lizzie Skelton was watching the goings-on from a doorway on the other side of the quadrangle and gave Beth a hard-eyed stare. Then Bishop Compton arrived to welcome the visitors into the palace.

Curious, Beth stood back until they had all disappeared inside and peace returned. She set off for the studio but stopped by the bakehouse to look for Judith.

'Apple turnover?' asked Judith, taking a tray out of the oven.

'I ought to be working,' said Beth, sniffing the mouth-watering aroma of newly-baked pastry as she drew a stool up to the table. 'I called by to see if you knew what's happening? The courtyard was full of visitors.'

'Important guests are expected and the kitchens are busy.' Judith lowered her voice. 'The Bishop is incensed that the King has tried to force the clergy to read the Declaration of Indulgence in the churches again. It's illegal, for a start. The noblemen you saw are here to discuss what might be done.' Judith bit her lip. 'But it's meant to be a secret meeting so you'd better not talk about it.'

'Who would I talk to about it, anyway?'

Judith sprinkled sugar on the apple turnover and put it on the table.

'What a picture of perfection!' said Beth. 'It's almost a shame to eat it.'

'Go on with you!' Judith's ruddy complexion flushed even more at the compliment.

'I saw Lizzie Skelton casting her eyes over the guests in the quad-rangle,' said Beth as she bit into the crisp pastry.

Judith raised her eyes to the ceiling. 'You want to watch out for her. She likes men and she isn't fussy about whose man she steals. You've never seen such a flutter of eyelashes and a tossing of the hair when she sets her cap at some poor fellow. He'd have to be a strong man to resist her wiles. Chews men up and spits them out for break-fast, that one. And I'll give you a word of warning.' Judith leaned closer. 'My poor brother suffered by her and recently I've seen her making up to Noah in the evenings after supper.'

Beth stared contemplatively at the last mouthful of her turnover and suddenly wasn't sure if she could finish it. 'In any case,' she said, 'it won't do Lizzie any good. Noah is returning to Virginia in the autumn.'

'I'd heard that.' Judith eyed her speculatively. 'I daresay there'll be several broken hearts when he leaves.'

Beth stood up and dusted the crumbs off her mouth. 'I must go. There's a beautiful star anemone waiting to be painted.'

The upstairs corridor was deserted. Firmly, Beth banished all thoughts of Noah and Lizzie and set her mind to thinking about whether she would use a plain white backcloth or the green watered silk for her anemone painting, Humming under her breath, Beth lifted the latch of the studio door and then stopped, frozen, on the threshold, barely able to comprehend what she saw.

At first she thought there must have been a terrible accident, even a murder. Her heart began to rattle in her ribcage and she clapped a hand to her mouth so prevent the sudden sickness from erupting. A scream began to gather in the back of her throat before she realised that the awful staining dripping from the table and pooling in a sticky pond on the floorboards was not blood, after all.

All her paintings, swept off the side table, were strewn over the room. Vermilion pigment had been scattered over everything and then water from the ewer hurled over the whole. Even the lovely star anemone had been crushed and mangled underfoot.

Beth let out a primitive cry of distress and, heedless of marking her skirt, fell to her knees in the lake of scarlet paint to snatch up one painting after another, only to discover that every one was ruined. The hundreds of hours she had pored over her specimens, painstakingly studying them and capturing them on paper with every part of her heart and soul, had been utterly wasted. The delicate early snowdrops, the boldly striped Tradescant tulips, the little aconite, every single one was destroyed.

Bewilderment overwhelmed her. Who could have done such a thing? But then she recalled Lizzie Skelton's hard-eyed stare of earlier that morning. Could it be Lizzie? All at once she yearned desperately to feel Johannes's comforting arms around her; only he could truly understand the crushing pain she felt. But Johannes had gone from her life for ever. Misery and sorrow pierced her heart leaving her weak and shaking. Gathering an armful of her precious paintings to her breast, she began to rock, sobbing soundlessly.

Then a sudden noise behind her made her glance fearfully over her shoulder. Noah, his face ashen and his eyes wide and shocked, stood in the doorway.

She whispered his name and he knelt in front of her, his hands resting on her shoulders with as much care as if she were made of glass.

'Beth, my sweet Beth! Where are you hurt? What happened?'

'I'm not hurt,' she said.

He stared at her, disbelieving. Slowly, he dipped his finger in the pool of red paint around their knees and rubbed it between his fingers. He closed his eyes and let out his breath. 'I thought you'd been stabbed. Sweet Jesus, I thought you'd been stabbed!'

Then she was in his arms and his mouth was on hers. He held her so tightly she could hardly breathe. A sweet shaft of desire shot through her pelvis making her quiver with a pleasure so intense it was almost pain. Her knees buckled and she sagged against him.

He sighed, catching her up against his chest, his breath on her cheek.

She tipped her head back as his burning kisses moved down her throat and his hands caressed her back. Forgetting the horror of what had happened, she felt herself opening up like a flower, wishing that time would stand still and that the moment would never end.

At last he lifted his head and stared at her with dazed eyes, his breath coming fast. They swayed together with the sound of her blood pumping in her ears. 'My sweet, precious love.' His voice cracked and he buried his face in her neck. 'I thought I'd lost you.'

After a while, he gave a deep sigh and released her. 'I'm sorry. I shouldn't have ...'

Still shaking with a strange mixture of shock and ecstasy, she looked at him, confused.

'I'll help you clean up the mess,' he said. He fetched water and they set silently to work, bundling the spoiled paintings into a heap and vigorously scrubbing the floor. Noah carried bucket after bucket of blood-coloured water downstairs to the drain.

Exhausted, Beth brushed a wisp of hair out of her eyes. Her hands were stained scarlet, along with the front of her skirt and she kept her eyes averted from it to avoid the painful reminder of her sorrow.

'I think it was Lizzie Skelton who did this,' she said.

'Lizzie?' Noah's face was puzzled. 'But why would she?'

Beth's cheeks warmed. 'She's jealous of me. She wants you for herself.'

'But I've never encouraged her to think ...' He broke off and pursed his lips. 'I shall make enquiries as to her whereabouts when this happened.'

At last they closed the studio door behind them and Noah led Beth through the gardens to the landing stage. Strangely taciturn, he hailed a boat to take them back to Chelsea.

They sat side by side in the boat, the two inches of space between them as wide as a chasm. Grim-faced, Noah stared out over the water while Beth, still trembling, watched him covertly, not understanding why he didn't speak to her with words of love. His severe demeanour bewildered her and she wondered for a moment if shock had turned her mind, causing her to imagine that he had kissed her.

Lady Arabella screamed when she saw Beth's stained clothes and hands.

'It's not blood. There was an accident with a pot of paint,' said Noah, hastening to calm her.

'Go straight upstairs before the neighbours see you,' said Lady Arabella.

'I'm sorry, Beth,' Noah murmured after she had gone. 'Sorry for the loss of your paintings and for the way I behaved.'

Puzzled, she went to embrace him but he merely pecked her on the cheek.

Disconcerted, Beth watched him leave without looking back. Then she retreated to her bedchamber and lay on the bed in a daze, attempting to make sense of the day's happenings.

Chapter 29

Two days later Beth's heart began to gallop when she saw Noah waiting for her as she arrived at the palace.

'The Bishop is asking to see you,' he said, as she stepped off the boat. She waited for him to kiss her or at least mention what had happened between them but he wouldn't look at her directly. Ignoring the wretchedness that lodged like a stone in her breast, she made the effort to keep her voice steady. 'I heard yesterday that a messenger came from the Archbishop of Canterbury to see him,' she said. 'And that Bishop Compton had gone to Lambeth Palace.'

'He returned less than an hour since,' said Noah, 'and asked me to bring you to him.' He strode off along the path, Beth hurrying to keep up with him.

A short while later he opened the door to the library, ushered Beth into the Bishop's presence and left without so much as a backward glance.

Henry Compton had his back to her as he stared out of the window, his hands clasped behind him.

Beth waited for several moments, wondering if she should cough to draw attention to herself. When finally he turned, his expression was sombre. 'Miss Ambrose. Noah told me what happened to your paintings.'

She nodded, her throat closing up again with emotion. The distress of finding her work destroyed was all mixed up with the joy she had felt when Noah kissed her and she still alternated between anguish, elation and uncertainty.

'I am sorry to have been away when it happened,' said the Bishop, 'but there are matters afoot which required my urgent attention. I have, of course, now made enquiries but I must tell you that Lizzie Skelton was with Daniel Fairweather, one of the stable boys, at the time of the incident and no one noticed anyone untoward near your apartments.'

'I see,' said Beth, thinking how easy it would be for Lizzie to wheedle a stable boy into giving her an alibi.

The Bishop poured wine into two glasses and handed one to Beth. 'Please, sit awhile.'

Awkwardly, Beth perched on the edge of her chair, while Bishop Compton appeared lost in thought. She held the glass up to the light and studied the colour of the wine, lighter pink at the edge next to the glass but with layers of deep ruby richness in the centre. Idly, she wondered what pigments she would have to mix to achieve the effect. Rose madder, perhaps, with a touch of ultramarine ...

'What *is* the world coming to?' sighed Bishop Compton at last. 'What will happen to us all? Your exquisite paintings destroyed! The law of the land flouted by the King himself! Malice stalks the very corridors of this palace and I fear for the souls and well-being of us all. Such times as we live in ... ' His voice drifted away until he was lost in contemplation again.

Made bold by the warmth of the wine creeping into her cheeks, she ventured, 'All the talk in the palace is of the King's wish for the clergymen to read the Declaration.'

249

The Bishop's gaze snapped back to her. 'And what do *you* think of that?'

'I'm only a simple country girl, Your Grace . . .'

'. . . with the wit to think for herself. You must have an opinion?'

She hesitated. 'Last year, when the King first published the Declaration, I couldn't understand why it caused such an uproar. But now that I have gone about in the world a little, I see that this isn't about religious tolerance after all but simply a way for the King to break down the established Church of England. He desires to rid us of Parliament, seize absolute power and fill the government offices with papists.' She stopped, wondering if she had said too much, but the Bishop smiled approvingly at her.

'And the mood of the people encourages me to believe that the time has come to put a stop to it.' He drained his glass of wine and banged it down on the table. 'The King will dismiss those who disobey his order to read the Declaration on Sunday. It's outrageous and it's illegal.' Bishop Compton paced back and forth, his jaw tense and his face pale.

'But what can be done?'

'I have been in close discussion with the Archbishop of Canterbury, together with the Bishops of Ely, Peterborough and Bristol, amongst others. There is no secret of it now, for the news will soon be in every alehouse and on every street corner. Last night we signed a petition requesting the King to excuse us from complying with his order. We shall present it to him on Friday, two days before the Declaration is due to be read in the churches.'

Beth turned over the words in her mind, while she worked out exactly what this might mean. 'But . . .' She tried again. 'But will this not anger the King greatly, Your Grace? Already you have been suspended . . .'

Bishop Compton smiled without a speck of humour. 'I will not turn over to show my belly like one of the old king's lap dogs. We shall have to wait and see what transpires.' He sighed, running a hand through his greying locks. 'Meanwhile, will you take a turn in the garden with me? The garden soothes troubled thoughts, I find.'

They walked slowly together, pointing out newly opened flowers and stopping to pull up an occasional weed. Bishop Compton bent to pick a scarlet and white star anemone. 'You must start afresh and paint this, Miss Ambrose. Did you ever see anything lovelier?'

She took it from him, a shiver of sadness running through her as the scarlet petals rekindled the memory of the lake of vermilion paint which had ruined her recent work. 'I'm ready now to start work again,' she said. 'I had not the heart for it before.'

Bishop Compton squeezed her hand. 'That's the way, Miss Ambrose. Have faith and keep on going; that's all any of us can do when circumstances are set against us, isn't it?' He set off across the grass, his arms swinging by his side like a soldier.

Beth watched him go before she returned indoors, cradling the anemone in her hands.

She paused outside the studio, her hand upon the latch, and was seized by a sudden reluctance to open the door, fearful of what she might find. After a moment she lifted her chin and went in.

All was as it should be, except for the empty shelf where her paintings had been displayed.

Beth rubbed the toe of her shoe across one of the scarlet spots still staining the studio floor. Why was Noah so cold towards her? Had she done something to anger him? Perhaps she had been too forward in returning his kisses and her passion had repulsed him?

Without conscious thought, she set out her paints on the work table. The vermilion pigment, which she had so painstakingly ground last week, ready to paint the first star anemone, had all been wasted in the destruction of her work. Heaving a sigh, she took out another lump of raw pigment and dragged the grinding slab towards her.

By the end of the day she had made good progress with her painting, which relieved some of her sadness for those she had lost. She had no intention of losing her latest work, however. There was no lock on the studio door but she discovered a key in the door to the bedchamber. She carried the easel and her new painting into that room, then emptied the cupboard in the studio of all her paints and equipment and placed them in the press beside the bed. Carefully, she locked the bedchamber door and tucked the key into her bodice.

The church bell rang the hour but Noah did not come. Beth sat by the window, watching and hoping. How *could* she have misunderstood him so?

The church clock chimed again. Beth unwound herself from the window seat, rubbing pins and needles from her legs. She must return to Chelsea. The prospect of Arabella's censure made her hasten as one of her step-grandmother's sharp set-downs was almost unbearable in her present frame of mind.

The following Saturday morning Beth and Cecily were surprised to find that Joshua and Samuel were at the breakfast table before them. Lady Arabella, dressed in a blue morning gown with lace ruffles and a smile of satisfaction, sat at Sir George's side.

'You're unusually bright and early, twins,' said Beth as she took some bread.

'There's news afoot,' said Samuel. 'Sir George heard it himself, didn't you, sir?'

Sir George bowed his head in acquiescence. 'A deputation arrived for an audience with the King last evening.'

Beth paused, her coffee cup halfway to her mouth. She had an inkling of what the news might be.

'A deputation of seven bishops, eight if you count Bishop Compton—'

'Which we do not,' interrupted Lady Arabella with a sharp glance at Beth, 'since he is already disgraced. He was refused admission to the King's presence, along with the Archbishop of Canterbury.'

'This deputation presented a libellous petition to His Majesty at ten o'clock last night,' continued Sir George in smooth tones. 'It consisted of some nonsense requesting permission to refrain from reading the Declaration in the churches. The King was deeply displeased and astonished that the clergy oppose his will.' He leaned forward and spoke in a voice so soft that it was hard to hear. 'His Majesty was moved to say that the bishops' actions amounted to rebellion.'

'Rebellion? Just because the clergy don't want to read some boring paper in church?' Cecily's eyes were wide with amazement.

'I have rarely seen His Majesty so angry.' There was a gleam of spite in Sir George's eye. 'He called them all trumpeters of sedition and commanded them to return to their dioceses.'

'If they know what's good for them, they will comply with His Majesty's orders,' said Lady Arabella.

Then a knock on the front door echoed through the house and a few moments later the maid ushered Noah into the dining room.

Beth felt the heat rise up her throat and set fire to her cheeks. She stared at the bread on the plate in front of her, her heart clattering against her ribs. She waited for her blush to subside while the others greeted him.

'What have you there, Noah?' asked Samuel.

Noah handed him a sheet of paper. 'I stayed last night in the city and on my way back to Fulham this morning I saw these leaflets being distributed,' he said. 'It's a copy of the Memorial handed to His Majesty. The printing presses must have been turning almost from the moment the delegation left Whitehall.'

Arabella tweaked the paper from Samuel's hand and read it. 'It's a disgrace!' she fumed, passing it to her husband. 'Do you go to Court today, Sir George?'

'I am not yet decided ...'

'His Majesty must know that you await his pleasure, should he require your services.' Her eyes were bright and calculating. 'You would do well to remind him that you support him in *all* his decisions.'

'Just so, my dear.'

'Beth, I came to see if you and Cecily would accompany me to church tomorrow?' said Noah. 'I had a mind to go to Westminster Abbey.'

'Cecily, I had expected you to stay with me tomorrow,' said Lady Arabella with a frown. 'Harriet is coming and you promised to amuse her children, don't you remember?' She narrowed her eyes. 'Besides, Harry de Montford said he may call upon us.'

'Then I had much rather stay and play with the children,' said Cecily. 'You won't miss me if you're with Beth, will you, Noah?'

'Perhaps you would prefer to stay with your sister, Beth?' asked Noah.

'No, I should like to accompany you,' said Beth.

Noah kissed Lady Arabella's hand and bowed to Sir George. 'Until tomorrow, Beth.'

On Sunday morning there seemed to be more boats on the water than usual when Beth arrived at the public stairs at Chelsea. Her stomach churned at the prospect of being alone with Noah and she ruminated on different ways to broach the subject of his apparent demonstration of love followed by his subsequent withdrawal from her.

At last she saw Noah waving as his boat approached the stairs. He seemed more at ease than on the previous day and Beth's anxiety began to release its sharp grip upon her.

'I was lucky to find a boat today,' he said. 'It would seem that everyone is out upon the water this morning.'

'Why is that?' asked Beth, puzzled. 'It's a pleasant day for an outing but not so remarkable as to account for the crowds.'

'I think most are on their way to their churches to see if the

Declaration is going to be read. There's a deal of curiosity amongst the citizens.'

The sun appeared from behind the clouds and the river stench lifted off the oily green water as the boatman pulled his way through the floating detritus.

The short trip to Westminster Stairs was swiftly accomplished but the sight of a press of boats all jostling to unload their passengers greeted them. Tempers were being lost and voices raised as the watermen used their boathooks to push away rival craft.

Three young men were arguing loudly with their boatman as he failed to shove his way closer to the stairs fast enough to please them. One of the men leaped to the next boat and then the next, using them as stepping stones as he bounded towards the bank. His friends whistled and cat-called after him before they followed suit. One of them landed with a thump on to Beth and Noah's boat, rocking it so hard that it took on water. Their boatman yelled and swiped at the miscreant's legs but he'd already jumped on to the next boat with a shout of merriment.

Beth gathered up her skirts out of the bilge water and clung to the side of the boat. 'That's the sort of high-spirited mischief I expect from Joshua and Samuel,' she said. 'I daresay those young men didn't have the benefit of a father's discipline, either.'

Noah returned her smile and passed her his handkerchief to blot the splashes from her skirt.

At last their turn arrived to disembark. Once on the stairs they had to push their way through the throng; Noah gripped Beth's arm firmly and used his elbow to ease their passage through the noisy mass milling around in Old Palace Yard.

A crowd of people were waiting to file into the Abbey. Beth's hat was knocked over one eye and she heard Noah's sharp intake of breath as a corpulent woman dressed in purple silk pushed past him and stepped on his toe.

At last they were through the doors. The Abbey was crammed but

Noah smiled winningly and persuaded an elderly couple to squeeze together to make room for them.

Beth, pressed closely against Noah, remembered again how he had held her so tightly that afternoon in the studio. She kept her eyes modestly lowered for fear he would read the longing in her expression.

The expectant rustle of the congregation quietened as the choir began to sing and the service began.

Beth craned her neck to look at the stone columns soaring up to the pointed arches. Light slanted into the Abbey through the beautiful windows so far above, making a wonderful sense of peace and calm descend upon her.

Then Dean Spratt stood in his pulpit with a sheet of paper in his hands. He was a well-built man whose purplish complexion indicated that he enjoyed fine wines. His gaze flittered around the congregation. 'His Majesty, King James,' he said in sonorous tones, 'has instructed that the Declaration of Indulgence is to be read in all churches today. Listen well.'

'He *is* going to read it!' whispered Noah.

Dean Spratt lifted his chins and started to read.

Almost immediately the congregation began to murmur. The shuffling of feet and the whisperings grew louder and louder until the noise completely drowned out the Dean's voice. He faltered for a moment, his hands trembling so much that the paper shook, then continued to read.

There was further disturbance as two men stood up and walked out, their boots clipping noisily along the stone floor. Before they even reached the doors, the rest of the congregation rose as one man.

The choir began to sing again, valiantly attempting to conceal the sound of the congregation's dissent as they marched angrily down the aisle.

Beth and Noah were swept along in the general exit. As they reached the doors Beth glanced over her shoulder to see that Dean

Spratt still in his pulpit, reading the Declaration to the empty pews.

Outside the Abbey the congregation stood about in groups, full of excitement and righteous indignation.

'Sir Christopher knows Dean Spratt well,' said Noah as they pushed their way through the chattering crowd. 'He anticipated that the Dean would read the Declaration today. Thomas Spratt's tastes are too expensive to risk his living by displeasing the King.'

'Will the King dismiss all the clergy who refuse to read the Declaration?' asked Beth. 'And what will happen to them? Who will take the services?'

Noah shrugged. 'Perhaps he intends to replace the ministers with Catholic priests.'

'But he can't!' Beth was outraged. 'We'll not have papists in our churches! If the King allows that, before we know it we'll have France and Spain knocking at our door. Who knows where that would end? Bishop Compton is right: there would be bloodshed.'

'Over the next two or three weeks we'll discover how many of the clergy refuse to obey the King's orders.'

'It worries me that Princess Anne thinks the King so set on this course. What if there is civil war again?'

Noah looked at her with a half-smile. 'How different you are now from when I first arrived at Merryfields. You were determined then never to step outside its walls. He linked his arm through hers as they stepped over a pothole. 'There are great things ahead for you, Beth, I'm sure of it. Losing your paintings was a setback but you will go on to create even better works of art.'

'I hope so,' she murmured, wondering if he would mention how he had held her in his arms that day.

'And you must let nothing come between you and your ambitions.'

Beth glanced at his face again and saw that his jaw was set. There was a tight knot in her chest. She wasn't at all sure any more that she wanted a life without love so that she was free to dedicate herself to art. 'And what of your ambitions?' she asked. 'Shall you definitely return to Virginia this autumn?' She held her breath while she waited for his reply, the knot in her chest tightening even more.

He chewed at his lip. 'My mother has written to me, urging me to return. They all miss me.'

'Your family?'

He hesitated. 'And my friends.'

'You have family and friends here, too.'

Noah's grip on her elbow tightened but he didn't look at her. 'There's the Goat and Compass. Shall we take some dinner?'

At the busy inn and they sat crushed together at the end of a table full of noisy people. Her usual greedy appetite deserted her as she nibbled her steak pie, nearly choking on the rich gravy and crisp pastry as she came to terms with the fact that not only was Noah returning to Virginia but he didn't appear to have any regrets about leaving her behind.

Chapter 30

June 1688

Two weeks later, the great hall resounded with the anxious chatter of the household. Beth and Judith sat side by side picking at their stewed carp and buttered cabbage, listening to snatches of conversation taking place between the gardeners and the stable boys, the housekeeper, the laundry maids and the secretaries.

'It seems the whole world is holding its breath waiting for the birth of the Queen's child,' said Judith.

'And to see which of the clergy has read the Declaration,' said Beth.

'Nicholas talks of nothing else until I'm fit to shake him,' said Judith with a sigh.

As Beth finished her nutmeg custard and stewed apple, Bishop Compton drew himself to his feet and rapped on a glass with his knife.

The buzz of conversation slowed and then ceased. All eyes turned towards him.

'There has been much speculation on the news from the

parishes,' said Bishop Compton. 'I can tell you now that I have collected reports from all parts of England. The Bishop of Worcester has declined to distribute the Declaration to his diocese, as did the Bishops of Winchester, Exeter, Norwich, Salisbury and Gloucester. Only three clergymen read the Declaration in the great diocese of Chester.'

A cheer went up from the lower end of the table as the gardeners and stable boys stood up, shaking their fists in the air.

The Bishop held up his hand until they subsided. 'Out of twelve hundred parishes in Norwich the Declaration was read in only four parishes. It is clear that a spirit has been awakened in this land which the King had not expected. It is possible, of course, that the clergy in this fine country of ours may still be *broken* by His Majesty's orders but *they will not bend!*'

A roar of approval drowned out the Bishop's voice and the dogs began to bark as the members of the household stamped their feet and whistled.

Beth, her eyes shining, kissed Judith on both cheeks. 'We needn't worry any more. The King is sure to bow to the opinion of the clergy and the people, isn't he?'

Judith shrugged 'Of course it's good news,' she said. 'But when did His Majesty ever bow to the opinion of the people if it didn't suit him?'

Beth looked around at the happy, shining faces of the household as they laughed and exclaimed in delight and a quiver of unease ran down her back. Was Judith right? Was this celebration entirely too premature?

❦

Beth was full of bittersweet hope for the future again when Noah slipped back into his previous habit of visiting her at the end of each working day. His delight was plain to see as her collection of new paintings grew but, nevertheless, Beth sensed that he kept a distance between them. She watched him carefully, searching to read meaning into his conversation but without finding the answer she sought.

'What variety of iris is this?' he asked one afternoon. 'It's quite different from the one you painted last week.'

'That was a mourning iris, so dark a purple it's almost black. This Siberian flag iris is George London's favourite. I like the contrast between the mauve-veined drooping petals and the purple upright petals, don't you? And then there's the calyx, so crisp and delicate it's like paper half-burned in the fire.'

'You've captured it beautifully.' He smiled at her, his brown eyes warm. 'I love to see you show such animation when you talk about your painting. It's a happy thing to find such satisfaction in your work.'

'Yes, it is. But . . . ' She hesitated. How could she say that she was beginning to realise that she wanted more from life than painting? She wanted someone special in her life to love. She wanted children. She wanted Noah. 'But I do sometimes wonder if Johannes was right.'

'In what way?' His expression was guarded.

She met his gaze steadily, even though her heart was thumping. 'Is it not possible to find a path between the two ways? Must it be so absolute?' She sighed. 'A man is able to fulfil his ambitions, while still enjoying family life. Why cannot a woman?'

'You know why.' His voice was terse. 'Children need their mother.'

Having come this far, Beth wasn't going to give up. '*I* didn't suffer while Mama worked in the apothecary. *And* she helped Father with the guests at Merryfields. Phoebe looked after us but Mama was always there if we needed her. With the right husband, perhaps a woman *can* achieve her ambitions?'

There was a long silence. 'And what kind of a husband would that be?' he asked at last.

'A man who had his own interests and ambitions but who would allow his wife to follow her own heart. A man who would support her and love her and value what she did.' The words she wanted to say but couldn't were, 'A man like you!' She held her breath, a pulse fluttering in her throat like a bird frantic to escape its cage. Would he see her argument for what it was; tantamount to a proposal?

'Beth?' He was very still, staring at her paint-stained hands clasped against her apron.

She waited, scarcely breathing.

Outside, a horse galloped into the courtyard and then a man began to shout. Noah let out his breath with an audible rush as he went to the window.

Beth could have cried with frustration.

'There's a messenger,' Noah said. 'Sancroft's livery.'

'The Archbishop of Canterbury's man?' Curiosity piqued her interest.

Noah nodded. 'I wonder what this means?'

Hastily, Beth covered her paints with a damp cloth while Noah took her painting into the bedchamber, which she carefully locked.

They hurried downstairs to discover George London standing in the corridor outside the library.

'We saw the Archbishop's messenger arrive,' said Noah.

'It's bad news, all right.' George London's expression was serious. 'The bishops who signed the petition to the King were all summoned to Whitehall this afternoon.'

He'd barely finished speaking when the library door flung open and Bishop Compton strode out, his cheeks crimson with fury. 'So, you've heard the news? The bishops have taken legal advice. They'll refrain from admitting anything incriminating and hold their ground, assuring His Majesty of their loyalty to the Crown, but they will neither withdraw the petition nor confess to any wrongdoing.'

'Will that be enough to appease the King?' asked Beth.

Bishop Compton ceased pacing and sighed. 'It is a risky course of action. We can only hope and pray. I go now to Whitehall and will wait until there is more news.'

'May we come with you?' asked Noah.

The Bishop shrugged. 'Why not? I'd welcome your company.'

The river at Whitehall was crammed full of small boats. The news that the seven bishops had been summoned before the King had spread as quickly as the Great Fire had taken hold of the city twenty years before.

The Bishop's boatmen had to use all their skills to work the barge through the mass of small crafts, shouting, 'Make way for the Bishop of London!' The sheer size and weight of the barge made the rowing boats scurry out of the way as the barge forced its way to the shore.

Bishop Compton pointed out the Archbishop of Canterbury's barge, already moored by the stairs, and the boatmen manoeuvred them into an adjacent position.

A chattering crowd congregated on the banks, the air humming with an excitement that was almost palpable. A group of apprentices on a nearby skiff, in high spirits due to the leather bottle of wine they passed between them, started to sing. Someone piped up with a penny whistle and before long a fiddle joined the merry refrain.

On another boat Beth saw a family unpacking a picnic hamper, just as if it were a feast day. The children squabbled over a loaf of bread and threw their chicken bones into the river to join the rest of the rubbish bobbing about in the water. She wished they had brought their own provisions for what might prove to be a long wait. Bishop Compton, hunched over in the stern, was silent, his gaze fixed on Whitehall Palace, ignoring the raucous singing. Every now and again his lips moved in silent prayer.

Noah, Beth and George London barely spoke, in deference to the

Bishop; after a while the boisterous horde ran out of songs and settled down to wait.

An hour passed, then another.

A dead fish, bloated and stinking, floated past and Beth began to feel the need to find a privy.

The crowd started to mutter and become quarrelsome as it waited so long without news.

A chilly breeze picked up across the wide expanse of the river; the sun began to lower itself towards the horizon while the river slapped fretfully against the side of the barge. Beth shivered, wrapping her arms around her waist.

Silently, Noah took off his coat and draped it over her shoulders.

With a grateful glance she hugged it to her, luxuriating in the residual warmth of his body against her skin. His coat smelt slightly of smoke and dust and she wondered if he'd laid it down on a pile of stone or bricks while inspecting a building site earlier that day.

All at once a murmur ran through the crowd. The noise built up to a collective groan. 'What is it?' asked Beth.

Bishop Compton squinted into the setting sun. 'The crowd is moving.'

'I'm going to find out what's happening,' said Noah. He pulled on the mooring rope and jumped out when the barge bumped the bank.

Beth caught her breath as he slipped on the muddy steps but he scrambled up and thrust his way through the multitude. In a moment he had disappeared as surely as if the waters of the murky river had closed over his head.

There were distant angry shouts. Beth narrowed her eyes as she searched for Noah's bright hair amongst the crowd.

Bishop Compton stood up, his legs braced apart as he stared towards Whitehall. 'The news cannot be good,' he said.

George's face was pale and set. 'I fear that the King is stubborn enough to insist on his way.'

'Surely the people and the clergy will never allow it?' said Beth.

'How can the people decide what is right when the King himself is set upon destroying the Church? My uncle died in the civil war,' said George. 'Family turned against family. The terror of it was that no one knew who their enemies were and I fear it happening again.'

'Perhaps the King will see reason, after all,' said Beth.

'When did he ever?' asked George.

There were more shouts from the sullen crowd and several skirmishes broke out. Then Beth glimpsed Noah as he emerged from the sea of people 'Noah's coming!'

Noah forced his way to the Bishop's barge through the swarming multitude. Beth's heart turned over when she saw his rapidly swelling eye socket and blood running from his nose. 'What happened?'

'Sedition,' he said. 'Rebellion against the King and his government. The bishops are to be charged with seditious libel!'

'Damn the King!' Bishop Compton slammed his hand on to the side of the barge.

'They're to be taken to the Tower,' said Noah, his voice muffled as Beth mopped at his bleeding nose with her handkerchief. 'The bishops have refused bail.'

'The Tower?' Beth dropped the handkerchief, apprehension gripping at her stomach. 'Will they be beheaded?'

'They'll have to be tried first,' said Bishop Compton, his mouth set in a grim line. 'But can we believe in justice any more?'

'Why have the bishops refused bail?' asked Beth. 'Surely anything would be better than being sent to the Tower?'

Bishop Compton smiled, just a little. 'Perhaps that was a shrewd decision.'

Before Beth could ask what he meant by that a rousing cheer went up and the crowd parted to reveal the seven bishops, grey haired and bent with age. Twenty or so heavily armed soldiers led the prisoners down to the Archbishop of Canterbury's barge.

There was a cacophony of cat calls and shouts of 'Shame!' The King's men were jostled, one tripped up by a protester's foot.

'Scared?' A man in the crowd taunted one of the soldiers. 'Do you think these old men are so dangerous they'll overpower you?'

The cheering people rushed forward, stretching out their hands to touch the bishops' cloaks. The hullabaloo was such that it was impossible for Henry Compton's voice to be heard when he called out to the prisoners. But then Archbishop Sancroft saw him and lifted a hand only to be shoved in the back by a soldier as he stepped on to the barge.

The Archbishop of Canterbury's barge set off slowly with prisoners and soldiers aboard. The bishops waved as the crowd roared its approval and support.

'God bless you for standing by the Protestant cause!'

'Blessed martyrs!'

Bishop Compton shouted at his boatman to follow. The jolting and jarring of the barge as it shoved its way through the flotilla of smaller boats meant Beth had to snatch at Noah's coat when it flew off her shoulders after a particularly hard knock.

A great cry went up from the people lining the banks. They surged forwards with outstretched hands to the Archbishop's barge, impeding its progress. Someone screamed and fell into the river; others followed, splashing through the mud and wading chest deep into the filthy water in their efforts to touch the bishops for their blessings.

Church bells began to peal, one after another.

'Have you ever seen such a thing?' shouted Noah over the din.

'Seven brave men,' bellowed George. 'Surely the King cannot find against such a weight of public opinion?'

Scores of boats set off in convoy to accompany the Archbishop's barge to the Tower. It was a little quieter in the centre of the river but cheering crowds lined the banks all the way.

'It would seem that Archbishop Sancroft has been very shrewd in his refusal to accept bail,' said Bishop Compton. There was a wry gleam of amusement in his eye. 'The sympathy of the people is even more firmly behind the bishops now as the wicked tyrant, His Majesty the King, packs them off to a horrid dungeon in the Tower.'

It was very late by the time Noah escorted Beth back to Chelsea and their ears still rang from the noise of the crowd. He held her hand to guide her, since there was little moonlight.

Beth curled her fingers around his and wondered if he might kiss her goodbye in the shadows but when they reached Lady Arabella's house it was ablaze with candles.

'I shall have to be careful what I say about today,' said Beth, as they waited upon the step for the maid to open the door, 'since Sir George and Lady Arabella's sympathies lie so strongly with the King in this matter.'

'It's been a momentous day, hasn't it?'

He lifted her hand to his lips and she moved closer, her pulse skipping as she anticipated his kiss.

Then, as they heard the servant's footsteps approaching the door, he bent and swiftly kissed her cheek. 'Goodnight, Beth,' he said.

Before she could reply, he had disappeared into the darkness.

In the event, Lady Arabella wasn't remotely interested in anything Beth had to say and barely noticed how late she was. All the candles were lit and the household gathered in the drawing room, discussing the events of the day.

'These trouble-making bishops have been a thorn in the side of the King for far too long,' pronounced Lady Arabella, 'but you can be sure now that he will not allow them to continue to make difficulties.'

'What will happen to them?' asked Cecily.

'They have been charged with seditious libel,' replied Sir George. 'Treason,' he said, in the face of Cecily's blank incomprehension.

'Treason? But won't they have their heads cut off and put on stakes over Tower Bridge?' She shuddered theatrically.

'I certainly hope so!' said Arabella. 'Once these rabble-rousers are removed from office there will be nothing to stand in the way of a new order in government.' She smiled fondly at her husband. 'The King will wish to have about him those of like religious beliefs, whom he can trust to support him in his endeavours. And Sir George and the twins will be ready and waiting to answer His Majesty's commands.' She patted Sir George on the arm. 'Won't you, Sir George?'

'Just as you say, my dear.'

'I see very great things ahead for this family,' said Lady Arabella.

Beth could stand Lady Arabella's self-satisfied smile no longer. 'It's late,' she said. 'I'm going to bed. Are you coming, Cecily?'

The following evening Sir George sent a message to say that he and the twins would not be home for supper.

Lady Arabella held up the note in hands shaking with excitement.

'What is it, Grandmama?' asked Cecily.

'The news we have all been waiting for,' said Lady Arabella, her pale eyes glittering like ice diamonds. 'The Queen ...' She paused for effect.

'Yes? squealed Cecily.

'The Queen is brought to bed!'

'She has given birth?' asked Beth.

'Not yet. We must wait a little while longer. But she is abed and in travail.' Lady Arabella took a deep sigh. 'Poor soul! I remember those times so well. Sir George and the twins will remain at Whitehall until she is delivered.' She whispered, 'Sir George hopes to be one of the witnesses at the birth. I impressed upon him the importance of his presence.'

Beth pictured the priests and courtiers all crowded into the birth chamber, waiting to see if she would be safely delivered of the expected prince. She sighed, wondering if Princess Anne had been set into a turmoil over the news. Poor lady!

Lady Arabella yawned. 'It's too late to wait any longer. Sir George will let us know soon enough how the Queen fares.'

Beth awoke when the front door slammed. Grey dawn light filtered in through the shutters and there were voices downstairs. Pulling on her wrap, she ran down to hear the news.

The twins, glassy-eyed, leaned against each other in the hall. There was a strong smell of rum.

Sir George was pale after a night without sleep but he carried with him such a glow of complacency that it left Beth in no doubt that the new prince had indeed arrived safely. Her heart constricted at the thought of the future trouble the little prince brought with him. Why, oh why, could the babe not have been a girl?

Lady Arabella hurried down the stairs. 'Sir George, Sir George! What news?'

He caught her up into his arms in an unusual display of affection. 'The very best, my dear. A prince!' he said.

Lady Arabella squealed and kissed his cheek.

'A beautiful little Catholic prince,' beamed Sir George.

The twins, reeking of rum, lurched towards their mother and collapsed into a giggling heap on the hall floor.

Chapter 31

Later that morning Noah came to find Beth in her studio and lingered in the doorway. 'The Princess of Denmark has returned from Bath and is visiting the Bishop on her way to Whitehall. She's asking for you.'

Beth twisted the sapphire ring on her finger, relieved that she had remembered to put it on that morning but wishing she had worn one of her better dresses. 'How is she?'

'As you will imagine, distressed by the news of Prince James Francis Edward's arrival.'

'Then I'd better not keep her waiting.' Hastily she covered her prepared paints with a damp cloth to prevent them drying out.

'Perhaps I'll see you later,' said Noah and left before she could reply.

Forsyth stood outside the Bishop's parlour and gave Beth a nod of recognition before announcing her. Princess Anne, her lady in waiting, Lady Sarah Churchill, and Bishop Compton were seated by the window.

Beth curtsied to the Princess, noticing that her eyes were red and swollen. The birth of the new prince must have upset her greatly.

'I am in need of some of your calm good sense, Beth,' said the Princess. 'You have no doubt heard that the Queen has, apparently, been delivered of a son?'

'I have, Your Royal Highness.'

'I refuse to believe the child is my half-brother.' The Princess wiped her eyes. 'Very few Anglicans witnessed the birth. I understand the King peopled the birth chamber almost entirely with Catholics. And now my sister Mary is no longer heir to the throne but this . . . this papist imposter is to take her place!'

'It was one thing to have a Catholic king, knowing it to be of short duration until a Protestant heir took his place,' said Bishop Compton, 'but this changes everything. In time, Princess Mary, with the Prince of Orange at her side, would have safely restored England to the Anglican faith. But now . . .'

Princess Anne twisted the sodden handkerchief in her lap. 'We *must* do something.'

'There is a great deal of support for the bishops now that they are confined to the Tower,' said Bishop Compton, narrowing his eyes. 'I've been receiving reports that many of the nobility are visiting them during their imprisonment.' He smiled. 'Messages of support and sympathy arrive every day. Even the guards are drinking to the bishops' health.'

'If ever there was a time to force the King to retract, this is it,' said Princess Anne.

Bishop Compton glanced at Beth, then back to the Princess. 'We must see the outcome of the trial. After that we will know what to do.' He shrugged. 'Who knows, perhaps the King will see sense and drop the proceedings.'

Princess Anne rubbed at her temples. 'My head aches so! Shall we take a walk in the garden, Beth, like we used to at Merryfields?' She stood up. 'You may remain here, Lady Sarah, as I shall not need you.'

Forsyth followed at a discreet distance while they walked in the sunshine. Princess Anne opened her heart again to Beth, pouring out her misery at her childless state and her anxieties for the future. 'I cannot help but feel at fault,' she wept. 'If only my baby had lived! Or if my poor sister could have a child …'

'You cannot blame yourself!'

'Perhaps God is seeking to punish me? What will become of us all now?'

It grieved Beth to see Anne in such distress; she took the sobbing woman into her arms and patted her shoulder. 'Perhaps God has some other great plan for us all?' she said, offering her handkerchief.

The Princess wiped her eyes and linked her arm through Beth's. 'You always make me feel calm again. Our friendship is important to me. Circumstances make it difficult to see you as often as I should wish but you are always just the same, kind Beth,' she said, kissing her cheek.

Over the Princess's shoulder, Beth caught a glimpse of Lizzie Skelton, open-mouthed at the sight of her in the Princess's arms. Trying not to laugh, she watched Lizzie walk into a rose bush.

The following Sunday, Noah, wearing a new hat with a dashing green feather in the crown, called again at Lady Arabella's house to ask her permission for Beth to accompany him to church.

'The truth is,' Noah said, as they walked briskly along St Martin's Lane later on, 'Bishop Compton asked me to attend the service at St Giles in the Fields today. He believes the rector is not holding fast to the Church of England and asked me to report back to him.'

'St Giles?' Beth was out of breath as she hurried along to match Noah's pace. 'Isn't that the rector who caused the Bishop to be disgraced?'

'It is. There have been such comings and goings in the evenings at Fulham Palace, Beth! Something's in the air … Messengers.

Secret meetings. Peers of the realm and gentry arriving under cover of darkness and leaving in the middle of the night.'

'It sounds exciting!'

Noah gave her a worried glance. 'And perhaps treasonous? Careful!' He snatched her arm to prevent her from stepping into a pile of steaming horse dung. 'Sometimes the Bishop acts more like the soldier he once was than a minister of the Church. He's planning some kind of campaign, I'm sure of it.'

There was a good turnout at St Giles and Noah and Beth sat in silence while they waited for the service to begin.

Noah tapped his fingers on his knee, his energy and impatience barely reined in.

Beth eyed him covertly, studying the line of his profile. A shaft of sunlight from the window fell on to his hair, burnishing it with fiery copper lights. She had never painted a portrait but all at once she was possessed with the idea that she must attempt it. She had the graphite sketch she had made when they were sitting by the moat but she wanted a faithful likeness that would capture the tones and shadows of his skin and the colour of his hair so that she would never forget him after he had gone. A sudden pain gripped her with the force of a blow to the stomach as she remembered that she would never see him again once he returned to Virginia.

'Beth?' Noah whispered. 'What is it?'

She shook her head and pressed her lips tightly together, frightened that she might start to howl, like a small child deprived of a precious toy.

Noah gave her worried sideways glances but then the service began and she took several deep breaths and concentrated fiercely on it.

The rector began to read the prayers for the King and Queen and to give thanks for the safe arrival of Prince James Francis Edward, while the congregation sat in sullen silence, omitting to make the usual responses to the prayers. When the prayers finished the rector began his sermon, further praising the King and Queen and the new prince.

A whispered conversation in the pew behind Beth and Noah made heads turn to stare. Feet shuffled, a prayer book was dropped, several staccato coughs rang out. Someone laughed and the murmur of voices blossomed until the rector's voice was completely drowned by the volume of conversation.

Several members of the congregation stood up and left the church; within a few minutes the rest had followed.

'Well!' said Noah, 'this will be something to report to the Bishop, won't it? The birth of the Prince isn't good news at all as far as the people are concerned. The King plans a magnificent firework display next week to celebrate it and it'll be interesting to see how the people respond. Shall we go together?'

Beth nodded. 'I'd like that.' She would have walked barefoot across Hackney marshes if it meant spending time with Noah.

'I wondered if you'd like to go on an excursion this afternoon?'

'An excursion?' Her spirits lifted.

'I've arranged to hire a horse and I thought we'd take a picnic to Islington village.' They bought eel pies, still warm from the oven, from the pie shop in Drury Lane.

It was hard for Beth to resist opening the parcel and taking a bite. She waited impatiently outside the Rose and Crown while Noah went inside to purchase some ale.

A sway-backed grey mare waited for them at the stables. She eyed them with disfavour, curling back her lips to expose yellow teeth and backing off when Noah took hold of the reins.

'You want to watch old Meg,' said the stable boy. 'Make sure you tie her up nice and tight if you stop anywhere or she'll be away.'

Noah set his lips in a line of grim determination and grasped hold of Meg's bridle. He leapt up on to the horse's back before she had time to object and Beth was impressed to see how quickly he brought her under control.

Beth tucked the picnic into the saddlebag and the stable lad hoisted her up to sit behind Noah. She settled herself on to Meg's broad back, wrapping her arms around Noah's waist.

'All set?' Noah glanced back over his shoulder.

She nodded and Noah nudged the horse's flanks with his heels.

Meg refused to budge.

'Stubborn old girl!' said the stable boy, thwacking her on her rump.

Meg tossed her head and shot off at a cracking pace out of the stable yard into the road.

Noah hauled on the reins, which steadied the horse to a more sedate pace along Holborn.

It had been a few years since Beth had ridden. She and her siblings had shared a couple of ponies when they were young but they had been too expensive to keep.

It was very pleasant to be sitting high up and so close to Noah. Meg clumped along past the gardens of Gray's Inn where people strolled the paths in groups, enjoying their Sunday walk after church. Beth leaned against the warmth of Noah's back and the green feather of his hat tickled her cheek, making her smile.

They passed Leather Lane with its stinking tannery before they turned off Holborn into Hatton Gardens.

'These are splendid houses, don't you think?' asked Noah. 'Abraham Arlidge has been building these houses around squares for the past twenty years for merchants who don't wish to live in the city but still need to be close to their businesses.'

'Some of them aren't finished,' said Beth, peering into the empty shell of a building.

'Mr Arlidge himself showed me some of the houses since I expressed an interest,' said Noah. 'There were several ideas of note, which I will bear in mind when I build my own house.'

Beth sighed. Noah's own house would be in Virginia.

They passed across the narrow bridge over the Fleet river and on through Clerkenwell. Cattle grazed in the fields and there were market gardens on either side of the road as they plodded up the hill to Islington.

Noah pulled up beside an elm tree at the edge of a field. He dismounted and tied Meg securely to the tree trunk.

Beth slid off the horse into Noah's waiting arms. He held her close for a moment and she studied the firm line of his jaw, too hesitant to lift her gaze to meet his eyes. Perhaps now he would kiss her again? She remained motionless, sure that he would feel the rapid beat of her heart against his chest. But then he released her.

Swallowing in disappointment and cursing herself for not being braver, Beth thought that Lizzie Skelton would not have hesitated. She would have simply offered Noah her lips. Sighing, she took the pies out of Meg's saddlebag.

They found a good picnic spot in the soft lush grass with a view of the distant city spread out below.

From inside his coat, Noah took a sheaf of papers which he laid on the ground for Beth to sit on.

She broke the pies into halves and offered a piece to Noah. 'What have you there?' she asked, picking up one of the papers, an architectural drawing in pen and ink.

'It's a plan of a room.' He turned the cross-shaped drawing in his hand to show how the walls had been projected upwards from each side of the plan, complete with details of panelled wainscots and cornices, windows and doors.

'Let me show you,' he said, folding the paper up at the sides to make a box. Small cuts in the paper at the corners allowed the edges to slot together and keep the box square.

'Oh!' exclaimed Beth in delight. 'It's a room with no ceiling.'

Noah smiled. He continued to fold up more boxes until he had assembled a number of them. 'I thought these might amuse you.'

'They do! Just look at the details of the fireplace, all carved around with oak leaves.'

'I took that idea from the sketches I made of the oak tree by the moat at Fulham Palace.'

'I remember!'

'This is the house I want to build. My father has set aside a piece of land for me on the side of a hill with a view of hazy blue mountains in the distance.' He spoke quietly with a faraway expression in his eyes. 'There's a stream at the foot of the hill and wild flowers grow in the woods. All you can hear is birdsong and yet my family home and our neighbours are only a five-minute walk away. It's the place in the world I love best; the place where I intend to end my days.'

Beth closed her eyes for a second, imagining the serenity of the setting, with its mountain views and the birds singing in the trees. All at once she longed to see this place.

'You would like Virginia, I think,' Noah said. 'The land is so fertile and the climate so kind that everything grows well. There are more lovely flowers than you can imagine; you would never be at a loss for some new bloom to paint.' He bent over the boxes and began to place them side by side on the ground. 'I'll begin my house by building the front parlour with a dining room behind. Our summers are hotter than yours so they'll have high ceilings and tall windows to allow the breeze to cool the air.' He added a smaller box. 'And here is the kitchen. There will be two bedrooms on top and a roof of cedar shingles. The whole will be clad in timber.'

'Not brick?' asked Beth, curious.

'Only for the chimneys. Brick is expensive to make in Virginia because we don't have the right kind of clay but there's plenty of good timber. I want my house to look as if it has grown out of the landscape.'

'And what are all these rooms for?' Beth picked up one of the spare boxes and studied the careful rendering of a well-proportioned drawing room with elegant drapes at the windows and finely detailed shutters. On each side of the chimneypiece there were deep alcoves fitted with shelves for books.

'I shall build a small house at first but as my family grows,' he hesitated, his cheeks growing pink, 'then I shall build more rooms.' He bent over the little house so that she couldn't see his face any more while his fingers restlessly continued to assemble the boxes to make a larger dwelling. 'A fine drawing room, a hall with windows to the front, four more bedrooms and a boudoir for the lady of the house.' He picked up some of the smaller boxes. 'A wash-house and quarters for servants. And there'll be stables for a horse and buggy.' He glanced at Meg, fully occupied with tearing up mouthfuls of long grass.

'It's wonderful,' said Beth. She tried to sound excited for him but all the pleasure in it had evaporated at the thought of Noah living in that lovely house with a lady that wasn't herself. 'You have it all planned down to the last detail.' She mustn't allow herself to cry. 'And have you also picked out the lady of the house?' Her voice sounded as bright and hard as diamonds.

He began to unfold the little rooms, laying the drawings hastily into a neat pile on top of each other. 'Perhaps I shall never build it, after all,' he said. 'It has been merely a pastime to keep me occupied during my time away from home.'

'It would be a shame not to build such a beautiful house.' Beth had seen it so clearly in her mind and the thought that it might never exist made her unbearably sad.

Noah smoothed the drawings flat. 'I must take you back to Lady Arabella before it becomes late.'

'There's plenty of time,' protested Beth.

'Nevertheless, we should go.' Silently, he helped her to her feet.

Meg allowed Noah and Beth to mount her with little more than a contemptuous flick of her mane and then set off at a steady pace down the hill towards the city.

Noah barely spoke all the way back; Beth began to wonder if she had offended him in some way. His body was rigid under her encircling arms and when Meg lost her footing in a pothole and Beth fell hard against his back, he didn't even glance behind.

The pleasure of the excursion was entirely lost for Beth, whose eyes pricked with unshed tears. The eel pie churned uneasily in her stomach as Meg swayed from side to side.

Once the countryside was left behind and they reached the streets on the outskirts of the town, Meg lifted her head and began to trot. She picked up speed so that it was all Noah could do to prevent her from breaking into a canter. They entered the stable yard at a spanking pace with Meg's shoes striking sparks off the cobbles.

'She always smells the stables and hurries back at the speed of lightning,' said the stable lad.

After Beth watched Noah pay the boy, they started back towards the river. He was entirely preoccupied as they passed through Lincoln's Inn Fields, unresponsive to Beth's tentative attempts to make conversation. He ignored the blind beggar in Wich Street who clutched at their feet, never noticing Beth turn back to drop a coin in his begging bowl.

Noah absent-mindedly took Beth's arm as they crossed the Strand, all crowded with carriages, horses and pedestrians, and guided her to a short cut towards the river stairs through a dark alley, stinking of decomposing vegetables. Shutters hung askew from the windows and the rotting timber of the houses only added to the atmosphere of decay.

Noah was still quiet, speaking only to warn Beth of a horseman approaching at speed. They shrank back to flatten themselves against a wall as the horse trotted past them down the alley.

'Noah?'

'Yes?' He didn't look at her.

'Have I angered you?'

'Of course not,' he said, his tone of voice abrupt.

'Then why do you not speak to me?' She blinked furiously, refusing to cry.

He glanced at her and his expression softened. 'Perhaps I *have* been preoccupied.'

'You've barely spoken since we left Islington.'

'Sorry.' He sighed. 'It's not your fault. I'm wrestling with a problem and don't know how to proceed.'

'Can you not talk to me about it?'

'Oh, Beth!' A fleeting expression of anguish passed over his face.

'Noah, what *is* it? One minute I feel you care for me and the next you ignore me. You're like a weathervane twisting from north to south and I . . . ' She suppressed a sob. 'I don't know what you want of me.'

'Don't cry! I can't bear to see you unhappy.' He gathered her into his arms and his lips were on her hair. She turned her face up to his, her heart singing with joy again. His mouth came down on hers and she forgot the noisome alley and the scattered filth underfoot and lost herself in the sweetness of his kiss.

At last he released her and held her at arm's length, his breath fast and uneven. 'Beth, I . . . '

'Yes, Noah?' she breathed. She reached up to touch a muscle flickering in his jaw.

Catching her hand, he turned it over to drop a kiss on her palm, making a delicious shiver run down the small of her back. He curled her fingers over to capture the kiss. 'I've treated you unfairly,' he said unhappily. 'And I don't know what to do for the best.'

'Please tell me what troubles you. Perhaps I can help?' she entreated him.

He shook his head. 'Not yet. Come on. We'll be late.'

They emerged from the alley into the light again almost before Beth could register her disappointment that he hadn't said more.

A boat was immediately available but by the time the boatman had pulled away, Noah was lost in thought again. Beth was as bewildered as before. What *was* it that caused him to blow so hot and cold?

Chapter 32

The great hall echoed with the clatter of knives and the hum of conversation as Beth looked for a quiet space to sit. She'd struggled to concentrate on her work that morning, endlessly pondering on Noah's changeable behaviour, and she didn't feel much like making idle chatter. She passed by a space on the bench next to Lizzie Skelton; her back crawled as she felt the girl's gaze following her.

Then George London waved at her and she took the seat beside him. George quickly realised she was in a contemplative mood so he turned to chat with his neighbour. Beth toyed with a bowl of mutton stew but the small globules of fat floating on the surface nauseated her. She picked up an apple and began to peel it, more for something to keep her busy than from hunger. She watched the knife slicing through the skin and the ribbon of peel falling on to the table in a coil. Perhaps, if she managed to peel the whole apple in one long piece, Noah would come to see her today.

A shout silenced the conversation for a moment before the babble of voices grew again.

'The Bishop is coming!'

Bishop Compton swept into the great hall, banged his knife on the table and called for quiet.

The household turned expectantly to look at him.

'I have come straight from Westminster to bring you news,' said Henry Compton, his face grave. 'The seven bishops appeared before the King's Bench today and have been charged with seditious libel against the King.' He held up his hand as an angry murmur broke out again. 'They have been released from the Tower on bail but must return to the Court two weeks from now on the twenty-ninth of June.'

'For shame!' called out George London.

Beth had almost finished paring the apple when the long ribbon of peel fell away from her knife and broke into two pieces. She stared at it in dismay.

The Bishop sat down and the noise levels rose as the household discussed the news with lively indignation.

'I've been praying that the King wouldn't proceed to persecute the bishops,' said George London. 'Mark my words, Miss Ambrose, trouble lies ahead.'

'Civil war?'

George sighed. 'I'm very much afraid so.'

After dinner Beth, too unsettled to return to the studio, decided to take a walk.

Judith Tanner was slumped on a stool outside the pastry kitchen with her clogs off. 'How are you?' asked Beth.

'Been rushed off my feet this morning. No time for dinner today. Fancy a piece of gingerbread?' Judith divided into two the slab of cake that rested on her aproned knees.

Beth took the proffered piece. 'I couldn't eat my dinner today so I'll be glad of this later.'

'We're all a bit off our food, aren't we? What with the waiting for news. Nicholas couldn't stand not knowing what was happening and he upped and went to the Palace Yard at Westminster this morning.'

'When the bishops were being questioned?'

Judith nodded. 'There was a big crowd and when they came out of the church, the bells began to ring. Nicholas said everyone was cheering. Some people thought it meant that the charges had been quashed and when they found out it wasn't so, they were angry.' She brushed gingerbread crumbs off her plump knees. 'There'll be Pope-burnings in the street tonight, I shouldn't wonder.'

'Best to stay indoors if feelings against the papists are running high.'

'Scared to go out then?' said a sneering voice behind Beth.

Lizzie Skelton leaned against the coal house door.

'Not at all!' said Beth.

'Saw you were off your dinner today. Thought you might be frightened, that's all.'

Judith noticed Beth's discomfiture and hurried to turn the conversation. 'I was telling Beth that Nicholas waited for the bishops to come out of the Court today,' she said.

A slow smile spread across Lizzie's face. 'Ah, Nicholas! Haven't seen him for a while.'

'He's barely left the smithy since you bewitched him, made him fall in love with you and then ditched him to move on to yet another paramour,' said Judith tartly.

'That wasn't witchcraft.' Lizzie smiled again, running her pink tongue over her full lips. 'I just knows what a man likes.'

'And you offer it so generously. Charitable of you, I'm sure!' Judith turned back to Beth, ignoring Lizzie. 'As I was saying, that *toady* the Bishop of Chester is entirely in the King's pocket and when he came out into the Palace Yard, one of the men, not knowing who he was but seeing his bishop's mitre, imagined he was one of the seven accused. He begged the Bishop for his blessing. A bystander asked the man if he knew who had blessed him. "It was one of the seven," the man said. "No it wasn't! It was the Bishop of Chester." The man who'd been blessed was furious. "Popish dog, take your blessing back again!" he roared. Everyone in the crowd fell down with laughing and the Bishop of Chester scuttled back inside again before he risked being hung up on a gatepost.'

Beth smiled but then her expression grew serious again. 'But in spite of the people's support, the bishops are still in danger.'

Judith sighed. 'And only the good Lord knows what will become of us if they're executed.' She slipped on her clogs and stood up. 'Come and see me tomorrow. I'm making walnut biscuits.'

Beth turned to find that Lizzie was standing in front of her, hands on her hips.

'I've seen you walking out with Noah,' said Lizzie accusingly.

'Have you now?' said Beth.

'I saw him first and I told you I wanted him for myself.' Lizzie regarded Beth through gypsy-dark eyes full of animosity.

Anger flared in Beth's breast. 'I think perhaps we should leave Noah to decide for himself if he's interested in you.'

Lizzie smiled slowly. 'Oh, he's interested in me, all right.'

Jealousy gripped Beth like a steel trap. Had Noah succumbed to Lizzie Skelton's charms and was that why he said he'd treated her unfairly? How could she possibly compete with Lizzie's lush sensuality? Unable to find the words to wipe the complacent smile off the other girl's face, Beth pushed past her and hurried away through the herb garden.

She came to a stop at last down by the moat, still seething. The moat smelt rank in the early summer warmth. Sitting on the grass, Beth stared at the floating duckweed. Her cheeks burned with anger at how inadequate the other girl made her feel. There was no doubt in her mind that Lizzie knew how to please a man, if she wished. Lizzie's voluptuous charms, so freely offered, would be hard for any man to resist.

♣

Two days later Noah still had not come to see her. Beth made discreet enquiries but all she discovered was that Judith had seen him at supper in the great hall but hadn't spoken with him. On the evening of the firework display, there was still no sign of him and Beth returned to Arabella's house with a heavy heart.

The family was gathered together in good humour in the parlour as they discussed the proposed celebrations.

'I hear that the King has spent twenty-five thousand pounds on the fireworks for tonight,' said Joshua.

Sir George smiled. 'His Majesty has spared no expense to ensure that the people will be able to celebrate Prince James's birth in the proper manner.'

Beth wondered if the King intended the lavish firework display to buy the hearts and minds of the populace.

Lady Arabella smiled. 'This is truly a great day for the nation.'

'I can't even *imagine* twenty-five thousand pounds,' said Cecily, wide-eyed. That many coins would fill a whole house.'

Joshua grabbed hold of Cecily and whirled her around. 'And it's all going up in smoke tonight.'

'I thought Noah was coming to take you to the fireworks this evening, Beth,' said Cecily, laughing as she pushed Joshua away.

'I expect he's working late again.' Beth wondered for a moment if he'd decided to take Lizzie Skelton instead.

'Harry isn't coming either. I'm *so* disappointed. He sent a note but he *promised* me he'd come!'

'Never mind; you'll have us to squire you to the celebrations.' Samuel pinched Cecily's cheek. 'Don't look so cast down!'

'Sir George and I have been promised a place on Lord Danby's barge,' said Lady Arabella. 'And we intend to be seen to be happy for their Majesties.'

'Then I shall accompany you, Cecily,' said Beth, having no intention of allowing her younger sister to roam the streets of London at night with the twins as her only protection. 'I should not wish you to become lost somewhere in the city if Joshua and Samuel are distracted and set off on some mad pursuit of their own.'

After supper, Lady Arabella, wearing a new velvet cloak, all perfumed, painted and be-ribboned, left in the coach with Sir George.

Beth and the twins walked along the lane, with Cecily skipping along beside them. A queue of people was waiting for transport by the crowded river.

After a while, Beth's eye was caught by someone on one of the boats waving at them. 'Look, it's Noah!' she said, her spirits soaring.

In a few minutes Noah's boatman had tied up at the stairs.

'I hoped I hadn't missed you,' Noah said, smiling at Beth in a way that made her heart race.

The river was teeming with boats as they made their way towards Whitehall. The setting sun painted the water with golden reflections and the bank was lined with crowds. Several barges and a myriad of small boats were moored up side by side, across the width of the river.

'Can't go no further,' said the boatman. 'We'll have to stop here.' He shipped the oars, took a chunk of bread and a raw onion from his pocket and began to eat his supper.

'I've missed our evening walks,' Beth murmured to Noah, wishing that they were on their own. 'I wasn't sure if you were coming tonight.'

'Sir Christopher has kept me very busy but I was determined to keep my promise to accompany you to the fireworks.'

Noah's warm smile embraced her; she forgot her anxiety of the past days and looked forward to enjoying an evening in his company.

Joshua and Samuel began to chat to a party of young men in an adjacent boat and before long were sharing one of their bottles of wine. The young men, full of high spirits, took it in turns to toast first Cecily and then Beth, their laughter ringing out and mingling with the expectant chatter emanating from the other boats.

'Cecily, behave yourself!' admonished Beth as her sister flirted scandalously with her would-be suitors.

'Let her be!' murmured Samuel. 'She may as well be happy while she can.'

'What do you mean?'

Samuel rubbed his nose and shrugged. 'She's set her heart on Harry de Montford, hasn't she? Well, Harry had a letter from his father. He's been told to stop wasting time and find himself a rich wife. At once. The plantation is going to rack and ruin.'

'Harry can't go out and find himself a rich wife just like that! Wives aren't stocked in the haberdasher's you know.'

'But he *has* found himself a rich wife. Not top quality, I grant you. Her father is a butcher.' Samuel rubbed his finger and thumb together. 'But there's a large dowry for little Miss Plumridge.'

'I see.' It was hard for Beth not to feel relieved, although she dreaded the impending histrionics when Cecily found out.

Meanwhile, Cecily was having a fine time. She trilled with laughter and jumped up and down, rocking the boat so that Beth's shoes filled with dirty water, and then exchanged places with Noah so that she could be closer to the young men in the next boat.

As the sun began its descent the excitement amongst the crowd grew. The fireworks had been set up on barges in the middle of the river outside Whitehall and it was possible to see the outlines of three giant figures.

Noah nodded towards them. 'I heard that the King planned for two female figures to represent Fecundity and Loyalty and also one of Bacchus since the wine will be flowing tonight.' There was a gleam of amusement in his eyes. 'But, unknown to His Majesty, Anglican supporters have modified the effigies to represent Anne Boleyn, Henry the Eighth and Queen Elizabeth. Then they started a rumour that the figures are to be publicly blown up as a symbol to undo all that they did to give birth to the Church of England.'

'So the firework display may aggravate the tension?'

'Very likely, especially if the wine is flowing.' He glanced at the men in the adjacent boat, who were drunk enough to be amusing but not yet drunk enough to be argumentative.

Beth spared a thought for Princess Anne. If the Princess was at home in her apartments in the Cockpit, it would be a bitter thing for her to watch the celebrations, not only because her own baby was lost but because she so firmly believed that her father had foisted a Catholic changeling upon the nation. In her eyes, her sister had been denied her right to the throne. Beth shivered. What if the Princess was right?

The sky turned cobalt, faintly streaked with orange in the west. A sprinkling of silver stars appeared and a faint mist, damp and clinging, began to rise from the river. Anticipation stirred amongst the crowd and snatches of song, rallying cries to battle, floated over the water.

When, at last, a fanfare of trumpets sounded in the distance, Cecily jumped up to peer at the milling crowd on the river bank in front of Whitehall. The crowd parted and a few people cheered.

'Look!' Cecily cried. 'It's the King and Queen.'

Beth strained to see the distant figures, curious to see the King and Queen who were so disliked by the nation. Torch-bearers illuminated the Queen, a dark-haired, slight figure in a blue gown, who rested her hand on the King's forearm as they made their way through the crowd.

'Huzzah!' shouted Joshua and Samuel, waving their hats in the air.

A family in a nearby boat turned to stare at them, muttering amongst themselves and Beth felt uneasy that they might imagine her to be a papist.

The lamplit party, led by their Majesties and surrounded by courtiers, made its way slowly through the press of people and on to the royal barge. The crowd remained mutinously silent.

'Not exactly a rapturous welcome,' Noah murmured.

The trumpets blew another fanfare and within moments the fireworks exploded in a dazzling display of colour and light against the deep indigo of the night sky.

Beth stared open-mouthed as the three giant firework figures began to move, their limbs jerkily bending and stretching in a strange dance while fountains of sparks coloured massicot yellow, rose madder and verdigris burst out of the huge effigies with a great hissing and whistling.

Firecrackers burst across the water and women and children screamed in terrified delight. The acrid scent of gunpowder hung in drifts over them all.

Joshua put his fingers to his lips and emitted a piercing whistle while Cecily shrieked and buried her head in Samuel's shoulder.

Beth clasped her hands over her ears as a rocket detonated with an ear-splitting bang high above them in a shower of green and white sparks. Noah was looking at her, his face serious in the warm, reflected glow of the fireworks.

'Not frightened?' he shouted over the noise.

She shook her head. 'I've never seen such a spectacle! What a wonderful painting it would make.'

The remains of the firework figures were merrily ablaze. A final flurry of rockets screeched up into the blackness of the sky to explode with the might of thunder, dissolving into a myriad of crimson falling stars like a deluge of rubies.

A momentary silence fell as they drifted down; Beth was speechless with the wonder of it. Then Cecily sneezed as their boat was enveloped in a thick cloud of gunpowder smoke.

A round of cannon fire started, provoking a cheer from the barges moored near to the royal party.

'That'll be Sir George and Mama,' said Joshua with a grin. 'Mama is determined that the King will see she is a loyal supporter in these difficult times.

No sooner had the cannon fire stopped than the church bells began to peal. One after the other they joined in until a crashing cacophony of sound reverberated over the water. The clamour was deafening.

At last the bells ceased and the boats began to disperse.

'Hey!' One of the young men in the neighbouring boat stood up, rather unsteadily, and waved his bottle of wine at Cecily. 'We're going to the Old Bell for a lil' drink. Why doan you all come with us? Make a party.'

'Can we, Beth?' Cecily's voice was bubbling with excitement. 'Please say yes!'

'It's not a good idea, Cecily.'

'Listen to your sister,' said Noah. The conduits are running with wine and there will be fights before the evening is out.'

'Please!'

'No, Cecily!' said Beth, more sharply than she meant to. 'Have you *no* sense?'

'It won't hurt to take a little walk in the city,' said Joshua.

'Then you shall go by yourselves.' Noah spoke to the boatman, directing him to row as best he could to the river bank. 'And in the interests of your own safety, Joshua, I'd take care not to put it abroad that you support the Catholic persuasion.'

Joshua let out a snort of derision. 'All right, Sobersides. We shall do better without you.'

'We only converted because Sir George said we had to if we wanted a place at Court,' protested Samuel. 'The same as Lord Salisbury.'

'But I *want* to come with you both!' Cecily caught hold of Joshua's sleeve.

Samuel took her hand and kissed it. 'Perhaps Noah is right. Do go home, there's a good girl.'

'You want to be rid of me!' Cecily pouted. 'You want to go racketing off into the city, drinking and looking for girls.'

'That is also perfectly correct,' said Joshua, hardly able to contain his laughter.

The boat wasn't able to reach the stairs since so many other boats were trying to do the same thing. Eventually Joshua and Samuel jumped on to the muddy shore with whoops of glee and ran off into the night.

'I hope they'll be all right,' said Beth, worry creasing her brow. 'Arabella will be sure to blame me if something happens to them.'

'You could hardly stop them, could you?' Noah put his arms around them both but Cecily huffed and puffed and turned sulkily away.

Joshua and Samuel returned at first light the following morning, waking the whole household as they hammered on the front door. The scullery maid let them in and they stumbled into the hall, singing loud enough to wake the saints.

Beth, hearing the commotion, forgot any idea of trying to sleep any longer. Tiptoeing on to the landing, she peered over the banisters.

Joshua had a bloody nose and Samuel's breeches were singed and blackened with smoke.

'Doan you wag your finger at me, Mama,' said Joshua.

Yawning, Cecily leaned against Beth and looked over the banisters too.

Then the door to Sir George's chamber was flung back and his footsteps clipped along the landing.

Beth and Cecily shrank back so that he wouldn't see them.

'There was a bonfire in the street,' said Samuel to his mother, 'with an effy . . . ' He looked puzzled for a moment and then his face broke into a wide grin. 'I have it now.' He spoke slowly, concentrating on the words. 'There was an *effigy* of the Pope burning on the fire.'

'A pope burning!' Lady Arabella's eyes were wide with outrage. 'They burnt an effigy of the *Pope*? But that's *monstrous*!'

'S'all rig', Mama.' Hiccoughing, Joshua clasped her to his bloodied coat and patted her head. 'We pissed on the fire to put it out.'

'Made 'em all as mad as hornets.' Samuel sank down on to the bottom step convulsed with giggles. 'But we fought 'em off.'

Sir George thundered down the stairs, grasped hold of Joshua's arm and dragged Samuel to his feet by his collar. 'You should both be utterly ashamed of yourselves, coming home in this condition!'

Beth began to feel concerned since his normally bland face had turned an alarming shade of magenta. His ire was all the more disturbing since he rarely showed any emotion other than complacency.

'After all your mother and I have done to position this family so well at Court and then you go out and bring disgrace upon us!' he shouted. 'What if the King hears about you brawling and misbehaving in the street?' Rage made him shake the twins until their teeth chattered.

'Sir George, I beg you ...' Lady Arabella pulled on his dressing gown sleeve but to no avail.

'Ignorant curs!' He banged the twins' heads together and then dropped the young men, groaning, on to the hall floor. 'Madam,' he turned his fury upon Lady Arabella, 'Have your sons taken to the stables at once. I'll not have them in the house until they recover their manners.' He marched off upstairs again, slamming the bed-chamber door so hard that Beth thought he might bring the ceiling down.

'Now look what you've done!' shrieked Lady Arabella at the twins. 'Ungrateful boys! How can you risk your places at Court with such foolishness?'

'But Mama,' protested Samuel, 'no one from Court was there.'

'You never know who is watching,' she snapped back. 'Once you've sobered up you will come and prostrate yourselves in front of Sir George. *Is that quite clear?*'

'Yes, Mama,' said Samuel, still rubbing at the bump on his head.

'Oh dear! I think I'm ...' Joshua vomited copiously all over his mama's Persian carpet.

Beth and Cecily judged it best to retreat to their bedchamber and quietly closed the door on Lady Arabella's hysterical tirade.

Chapter 33

At dinner time the conversation in the great hall was all of the trial and the possible outcome. As tempers frayed, fisticuffs broke out between the baker's boy and one of the gardener's apprentices, setting the dogs to snarling and fighting amongst themselves. Nicholas Tanner hauled the boys outside by their collars and returned grim-faced to his beef stew.

During the afternoon Beth worked on her painting again but her heart wasn't in it. Noah had gone to Westminster with Bishop Compton and George London to await news of the trial. Every time she heard anyone arrive in the courtyard below she leaped up to peer out of the window but Noah, George and Bishop Compton didn't come. Eventually, she walked down to the river to wait on the landing stage. She squinted into the setting rays of the sun, dazzled by the reflections coming off the water as she scanned the river for signs of Noah.

Still there was no sign of a boat bringing Noah, George and the Bishop. When darkness fell she returned to sit with Judith in her room.

They listened to the church clock chiming the hours through the night. As the first streaks of dawn showed in the east, they fell asleep curled up together on Judith's bed.

Then a great shout down in the courtyard woke them.

Rubbing sleep from her eyes, Beth ran to the window. 'It's the Bishop!'

The whole household, full of excited chatter, turned out to follow Bishop Compton into the great hall.

Beth looked all around but couldn't see Noah or George London.

Bishop Compton stepped up on to the dais and raised a hand for silence. 'My friends!' he called. He waited until the noise died down and a sea of anxious, expectant faces turned towards him. He stood still, expressionless, until the last whisper had faded away.

Beth held her breath.

Then the Bishop threw his fists into the air and shouted with all his might, '*Not Guilty!*'

An explosion of cheers and yells of delight resonated up to the highest beams. Nicholas Tanner caught hold of Beth's waist with his brawny great arms and whirled her around in a mad dance of delight. She saw Lizzie Skelton kissing the steward, who didn't seem to be objecting. And then she saw Noah and George.

Noah's face was flushed with exhilaration. 'Beth! I thought you'd have gone back to Chelsea last night,' he said, raising his voice over the general euphoria.

'I waited for you' she shouted back. 'I had to know what happened.'

Beth found herself in his arms and he kissed her forehead. She turned her face up to his and met his eyes; slowly, he bent his face towards hers. She quivered in blissful anticipation of his kiss but then three loud bangs sounded as the Bishop thumped his fist on the table.

One by one the shrieks of glee died away until at last there was silence again.

Beth glanced at Noah as he let her go, frustrated that the longed-for kiss had been interrupted.

'Ten hours,' said the Bishop in sonorous tones. 'Ten hours for sixty peers to testify for the bishops! Such a crowd has never been seen before at the Court of the King's Bench. His Majesty is left in no doubt that the public would not accept such a charge.'

George London, standing beside Noah, cheered and waved his fist in the air.

'The jury sat all night to decide that seven old men are not guilty of sedition.' He thumped the table again. 'It was a charge which should never have been brought against them in the first place,' he thundered.

The apprentices whooped and drummed their heels on the floor.

'When the foreman of the jury, Sir Roger Langley, pronounced the seven "Not guilty", Lord Halifax threw his hat in the air.' Bishop Compton beamed at the assembly. '*Ten thousand* people roared their delight and the noise was so great that the roof of Westminster Hall nearly cracked.'

Another cheer burst from the household. The dogs began to bark again and there were cries of jubilation.

'You should have heard it,' Noah said into Beth's ear. 'It sent a shiver down my spine. The cheering of the crowd shook the very air. It grew and grew until it spread the news over all of London. I don't doubt it reached all quarters of the kingdom. People were dancing in the street and lighting bonfires.'

Bishop Compton banged loudly on the table again. '*But*,' he said, 'while this is a triumphant victory, the battle of Protestantism against Popery may not yet be won.' His expression grew sombre again. 'Now we must wait to see how His Majesty the King responds to this momentous event.' He stepped down from the dais and strode from the hall, his cloak flying out behind him.

George London yawned widely. 'We didn't sleep at all last night while the jury was out,' he said, 'and I'm fit to drop.'

'You must be tired, too,' Beth said to Noah.

'Tired but I'm not sure I can sleep. I can still hear the bells ringing and the cannons firing in my head. I wish you'd seen the crowds, Beth.' His eyes were fever-bright. 'The King can be in no doubt now that his subjects will not have papist rule in England.' He took her arm. 'Shall we walk outside?'

They went out through the quadrangle to find half a dozen richly dressed men galloping through the gates, spurs and swords jingling. Stable lads ran to take the horses while the visitors clapped each other on the back and exchanged hearty greetings.

'That's the Earl of Shrewsbury,' said Noah. 'And Lord Lumley. They have an axe to grind with the King since he ousted them all from the army and replaced them with papists.'

Bishop Compton came out to greet the guests and Beth and Noah watched while he ushered them inside.

Suddenly the quadrangle was quiet again.

They walked out through the archway by the porter's lodge to the Dovehouse Court and stable yard. The stable lads hurried to and fro carrying water for the visitors' horses.

'What's happening, do you think?' asked Beth as they walked on again.

'I'm not sure,' said Noah, 'but on our return from Westminster the Bishop said that it was time to put an end to the King's foolishness.'

'What did he mean by that?'

Noah shrugged.

They sat on a bench watching the doves flitting in and out of the dove house. Before long, soothed by the bird's billing and cooing, Noah fell asleep with his head on his chest.

Beth watched him as he slept and was overwhelmed with tenderness for him. Asleep, he looked curiously vulnerable. His auburn curls fell over his shoulder and there were tiny freckles, so small that they looked as if she might have painted them on his cheeks with her favourite squirrel-hair brush. She ached to take him in her arms and tell him how she loved him. After a while, she felt drowsy too and, unable to resist, rested her head on Noah's shoulder. He sighed in his sleep and murmured her name. Then Beth dozed too.

Something tickled Beth's nose. Still half asleep, she rubbed at her face.

'A pretty sight!' said a voice.

Beth opened her eyes to find Princess Anne smiling down at her. Blinking in the light, she scrambled to her feet.

'Your Highness . . . I didn't expect to see you.'

'I thought not.' Her eyes sparkled with laughter. 'So there is an understanding between you and Noah? I think you well matched.'

'Oh, no,' stuttered Beth, 'that is . . . '

'Shall I wake him?' asked the Princess. She held up the grass stalk with a seed head as soft as a silken tassel, which she had used to tickle Beth's nose.

'He stayed awake all last night outside Westminster Hall, waiting for the jury to make a decision, Your Highness.'

'Then I shall allow him to sleep. Shall we walk? It is the most excellent news, isn't it?'

'None better.'

'The jury would not have kept Noah awake all night if it hadn't been for the King's brewer,' said the Princess. 'He was too frightened to risk losing his contracts to the Crown to decide against the King.' She smiled. 'But the other jurors eventually persuaded him to change his mind.'

'The decision was a victory for the people.'

'So it was.' The Princess sighed. 'But I fear that the King will still not see sense. This is the first time an English monarch has lost such an important case in law and it will anger him.' She bit her lip. 'My father is monstrously stubborn when he's angry.'

'He *is* the King and in the end the people must follow him, I suppose,' said Beth.

'But *must* they?' The Princess stopped and turned Beth to face her. 'Even if it is against God's wishes and against our faith? Should one misguided and stupidly obstinate man be allowed to force a whole nation of people into suffering a religion they abhor?'

'But nothing can be done if that is the King's wish.'

'I believe it can.' The Princess's face glowed with suppressed excitement. 'My sister Mary and her husband, our cousin William of Orange, must come to the throne.'

Beth stared at her, shocked. 'But the King is still alive and, since the birth of the Prince of Wales, your sister is no longer his heir.'

'But she should be!' Princess Anne's mouth set in a determined line. 'Only that way can the people be sure that the Church of England will endure. Do you not see? If that changeling prince, for I *cannot* own him as my brother, if James Francis is ever allowed on the throne, England will return to papist rule for all time.' She took a fierce grip on Beth's arm. 'Can you keep a secret?' She shook her head. 'Of course you can, you've already proved that to me. Listen carefully, Beth. At this very moment, one Arthur Herbert is travelling to The Hague with an invitation to the Prince of Orange.'

'An invitation?' Beth was bewildered.

'An invitation from Bishop Compton, the Earls of Danby, Shrewsbury and Devonshire, Edward Russell, Henry Sidney and Lord Lumley, all asking the Prince of Orange to land on our shores with sufficient troops to defend them and himself. He must move quickly as, once the King has replaced all the officers in the army with papists, it will be too late.'

'You're talking about,' Beth hesitated, 'an invasion?'

'An *invitation* to defend the Anglican faith against popery.'

'I don't understand.'

'The French have ceased trade with the Dutch. If Prince William combines his forces with those of England, they can form a Protestant crusade against the Catholic power of the French *and* pre-serve the Anglican faith in both England and Holland.'

Shock made Beth silent. She stared at Princess Anne's shining face. Beth swallowed. 'But it's treason.'

Princess Anne shook her head. 'No, it's revolution.'

Stunned, Beth still said nothing.

'I must be patient now until I receive news from my sister,' said the Princess. 'We have corresponded secretly for some time, despite His Majesty's wishes. Prince William has made it known to me that he will do all in his power to defend our faith and preserve my sister's claim to the throne, *if* he can be assured that it is what the people of England want. The bishops' trial is all the proof he needs. I fervently hope to see my sister, and William, on these shores very soon.'

'The King will send his army to meet them.' Beth shook her head. 'There will be bloodshed.'

'The Prince of Orange has a large army. And as soon as he knows the people of England will no longer accept the King's popery, he'll come and rescue us from this great threat.'

A turmoil of fear and hope mingled in Beth's thoughts. 'If it could only be done without great loss of life ... without civil war?'

'I believe it can. And now I must return to talk with Bishop Compton. Do not look so afraid, my little friend. For the first time in a long while I feel hope for the future. Hope for *all* our futures.'

'I will pray that you are right.'

Watching her walk away, Beth relived the conversation, hardly able to believe that she had been made privy to such dangerous knowledge. The Princess must have a great deal of faith in her.

Noah had gone from the bench in the Dovehouse Court when Beth returned to look for him. She was almost relieved as her mind was still whirling with the Princess's terrifying secret and she would have found it hard not to share it with him.

She retreated back to her studio where she spent the rest of the day staring at the walls. At last, she tidied away her paints and set off for Chelsea.

Cecily was alone in the parlour, yawning as she played a game of Patience. Her eyes lit up when she saw Beth and she ran to her and smothered her in kisses.

Gratified to receive such a welcome, Beth hugged her. 'I've missed you, too.'

'You can't *imagine* what it's been like here,' confided Cecily. 'Sir George has been in a terrible fret ever since he heard about the acquittal of the bishops and Grandmama is tiresomely cross.'

'It's wonderful news that the bishops have been freed.'

'Not in this household,' said Cecily gloomily. 'Sir George is still not speaking to the twins and Grandmama *dare* not let them back into the house until he says they can. They've gone off to lodge with Harry in the meanwhile. And now Grandmama and Sir George are going out to supper and leaving me all alone.'

'Then we shall have a cosy evening together, just the two of us,' said Beth, almost laughing in relief at not having to face Lady Arabella while her thoughts were elsewhere.

Chapter 34

July 1688

July opened with a heatwave. The milk soured and the meat turned. The gardener's apprentices constantly grumbled about the blisters on their hands from their endless toil of carrying water to the Bishop's precious specimen trees.

One sweltering afternoon at the end of July, too hot to work, Beth was lying barefoot and daydreaming in the shade of the oak tree down by the moat, her bodice laces loosened. A flagon of cider sat at her side. Noah had been conspicuous by his absence most of the month; she missed him so badly that her work had suffered.

A deep sense of frustration had risen up in her since there had been no opportunity to see him alone. Every day she listened to the ticking clock in her head that carried her closer to the time that Noah would leave. And every day had brought her closer to the certainty that her happiness would never be complete without him.

'Beth?'

She opened her eyes and sat up, disoriented, to find Noah smiling down upon her.

'Did I wake you?' he asked softly. He'd taken off his coat and slung it over one shoulder.

The top buttons of his shirt were undone so that she glimpsed the brown skin of his chest. She wondered what it would be like to kiss him there, tasting his warm, salty skin with the tip of her tongue. 'I haven't seen you for a while,' she said, hoping her wanton thoughts weren't plain to read on her face.

He sat down beside her. 'There's been a lot to do. Progress is slow on the building sites when it's so hot. The men drink more ale and then they fall asleep, or even worse, fall off the scaffolding.' He wiped his forehead with his handkerchief. 'I'm tired of having to chastise them; it's too hot to work but I want to be sure my projects are finished before I return.'

A cold chill snaked down Beth's back, in spite of the heat. 'Return to Virginia?'

Noah nodded. 'Autumn will be upon us sooner than we expect.' He drew a deep, sighing breath, his eyes sad.

'Must you go, Noah?' She wondered if he heard the pleading in her voice.

'I have to, Beth.'

'But *why*? Are you not happy? There's work enough here to keep you for years to come.'

He didn't look at her. 'I promised I'd return this autumn.'

'Promised who?'

He looked away. 'My family. Myself. My future is in Virginia, Beth.' He plucked a daisy from the grass and twirled it between his finger and thumb, his face closed.

'I can't bear it!' All she could think of was that the man she loved was leaving. 'I thought you cared for me?'

'I do,' he said. His voice was quiet. 'I do care for you, Beth.' Savagely, he began to pull the petals off the daisy, one by one.

'Then ...' She gathered up all her courage and spoke before she could change her mind. 'Then stay.'

He threw the mangled daisy to the ground and stood up, his face pale and set. 'I cannot,' he said, shaking his head. He lifted a hand in farewell as he walked away.

Shock at his dismissal of her rendered her still for a moment but then her fear of losing him made her scramble to her feet. Picking up her skirts, she ran barefoot across the grass after him. She caught hold of his sleeve and when he turned she saw that his eyes were anguished. 'Can you not see how much I love you?' she begged. She waited, holding her breath.

'Yes, I can see that.'

'And . . . and can you not love me, too?' she asked in a small voice. She shrivelled inside a little, dreading a polite rebuff.

'Love you?' His voice was full of pain. 'Of *course* I love you. I've probably loved you since the first day I saw you but . . . '

Relief and elation suffused Beth with sudden joy. *He loved her!* That was all she needed to know. She threw her arms around his neck and kissed him. He was curiously still for a moment, then he groaned and returned her kisses with such passion that she trembled with yearning. Entwined, they sank down on to the grass.

Noah's hands were fanned against her waist and Beth strained against him, revelling in the feel of the heat and the hardness of his body pressed so close to hers.

'My sweet, lovely Beth.' His breath was hot in her ear. 'I dream of you at nights. You cannot imagine how I long for you.'

'I love you so much, Noah! And I've been so miserable, not knowing if you loved me or not.'

He kissed her neck in the soft hollow above her collarbone, while his hands ran urgently down her thighs; she melted at his touch, wanting the moment to never end. She pulled his shirt free from his breeches and slid her hands inside to stroke the warm, naked skin of his back. He smelt of sunshine and a musky male scent which set her senses reeling.

All at once there was a loud splash followed by a shout nearby.

Beth gasped and Noah let her go as they both sat bolt upright.

One of the palace hunting dogs was swimming in the moat and Nicholas Tanner was running towards them.

Beth pulled grass out of her hair and glanced at Noah's scarlet face as he steadied his breathing and hurriedly tucked his shirt back into his breeches.

The dog scrambled up the bank, splattered them with mud as he vigorously shook himself dry and then rolled on his back in the grass with apparent enjoyment.

Grinning, Nicholas Tanner came to stand beside them with his arms on his hips. 'Did old Poacher give you a soaking?'

'I'm tempted to jump into the moat myself,' said Noah, standing up. 'God knows it's hot enough.'

Nicholas whistled to the dog. 'I'll leave you to it, then,' he said with a knowing smile. He ambled off, the dog at his heels.

Mortified, Beth stood up and shook out the creases from her skirt.

'Beth, I'm sorry,' said Noah. 'I behaved abominably. I should have known that anyone could pass by and see us like that. Your reputation ...'

'Then you'll just have to make an honest woman of me,' she said, glancing at him from under her eyelashes.

He said nothing but stared at her with anxiety in his toffee brown eyes.

Beth's smile faded and her heart began to thud erratically. Had she made a terrible mistake and assumed too much?

'You said you'd never marry,' he reminded her.

'But that was before I fell in love with you.' He didn't respond and an icy tremor of dread clawed at her insides. She watched him close his eyes for a moment, as if to pray for the courage to say what had to be said. But then he smiled and a tiny flame of hope rekindled in her heart.

'Love strikes when you least look for it,' he said quietly. 'Or perhaps even want it.' There was a tiny tic at the corner of his eye; Beth longed to lean forward to kiss it away.

'I certainly wasn't looking for love,' she said.

He took her hand and swung it between them as they walked over the tussocky grass of the orchard. 'But if true love does come, surely it's wrong to ignore it?' He didn't look at her but spoke as if debating with himself. 'True love is such a rare and precious flower that you may never find again. Somehow you have to rearrange your life to allow it to bloom.' He shaded his eyes against the sun. 'However difficult that may be.'

'Yes,' she said, a pulse fluttering wildly in her throat.

'And I do want to spend the rest of my life with you, Beth.' He looked at her then and lifted her hand to his lips. 'Oh, how I want that!'

She let out a pent up sigh of relief and it seemed to her that all the birds in the orchard began to sing. He did love her after all. 'But Johannes was right in a way,' she said. 'If I am to continue with my painting, I'll have to work at it constantly, just as you must work at your skills in architecture. But cannot there be a balance?'

'I understand how necessary it is to your happiness for you to have the freedom to paint. We will, we *must*, find a way.'

Another thought occurred to her making her stomach churn with anxiety again. 'Noah, there's one thing you must know,' she said. 'I have no dowry.' She waited for two long seconds before he threw his head back and laughed as if she had said something especially amusing.

'That's the least of our worries!'

Beth made a sound halfway between a sob and a laugh. Noah loved her and everything was going to be all right.

'I will speak to your father,' said Noah, 'but until then we must keep our love a secret.'

She took a deep lungful of the overheated air, joy threatening to overflow into tears. All at once the world was full of promise again.

Johannes had been wrong; it was plain to her now that Noah was essential to her happiness. Strengthened by his love and encouragement, she knew she would achieve artistic goals she hadn't yet dreamed of.

Beth travelled back to Chelsea in a state of euphoria that evening and even Lady Arabella's disparaging comments at the supper table failed to dampen her elation.

'It's not so much fun here any more,' complained Cecily as they undressed for bed. She took off her busk and rubbed at the angry red weals on her waist.

'You shouldn't lace so tightly when it's hot. It'll make you faint,' said Beth. 'Sir George is worried and that makes Lady Arabella short-tempered.'

'I don't understand why he's so *angry* all the time. He never used to be.'

'He's worked hard to make the King notice him but it's plain now that the people of this country will no longer support the appointment of Catholics into senior positions.'

'Oh well, it's probably a passing storm. Anyway, the King can do whatever he likes, that's what Grandmama says.' Cecily passed Beth her nightshift and frowned. 'You look more cheerful, anyway. You've been so distracted of late that you never seemed to hear me when I spoke to you. Has something happened?'

Beth couldn't contain a wide smile. 'Noah has declared his love for me.'

Squealing in delight, Cecily threw herself into her sister's arms. 'I knew it! I knew it!'

'But it's a secret and you mustn't tell anyone yet.'

Cecily's face fell. 'Why ever not?'

'Because Noah must speak to Father first.'

'So you're not going to be a miserable old spinster, after all?'

'It would appear not,' said Beth, laughing.

'Oh, *how* I wish Harry would declare himself to me!' sighed Cecily as she climbed into bed.

Beth suffered a pang for her sister's sake. Harry de Montford would disappoint poor Cecily. Pretty as she was, would she ever find a man who loved her enough to take her without a dowry?

'Goodnight, Beth.'

'Night, Cecily.' Beth blew out the candle and lay with her hands behind her head, smiling into the dark.

'Beth? You won't go and live in Virginia, like Kit, will you?'

'Don't worry about that. There's plenty of building work going on in this country and Sir Christopher Wren needs good architects.'

'That's all right then,' yawned Cecily.

Beth lay awake for a long time, her joy suddenly tinged with anxiety. Something she and Noah hadn't discussed was where they would live.

August came and continued to be hot. The grass scorched brown and the Bishop's prized snakebark maple withered and died. The palace household moved about their tasks with a weary lassitude, leaving corners unscrubbed and windows fly-spotted. Even the bees drifted lazily from flower to flower as if it were all too much bother. The moat and the privies stank, pervading the air with the foul stench of decay.

Judith came to visit Beth in her studio. 'Have you heard what happened?' she asked, panting after the exertion of hurrying up the stairs. Her cheeks shone in the afternoon heat like ripe plums.

'No, what?' Reluctantly, Beth laid down her paintbrush, casting a glance at the half finished study of a creamy lily with orange stamens quivering with pollen. The paint dried out rapidly in the heat and she needed to complete the pale green wash of shadow under the curve of the petals. Ever since Noah had declared himself, she had found it easy to paint again. Johannes would have been proud of the way her work had become so assured and at the same time so prolific.

Judith peeled a strand of damp hair off her forehead and tucked it behind her ear. 'The Dutch stock market has crashed.'

Beth wrinkled her brow. 'I don't understand.'

'Nicholas says it's because Prince William of Orange is leaving his borders undefended against the French. He's been secretly amassing his forces for months and is risking everything to come to England to restore Princess Mary to her rightful place as heir to the throne. What do you think of that!'

Beth stared at Judith, while she absorbed the news. So Princess Anne's secret was true.

'Beth, don't you see?' Judith shook Beth by her arms. 'Prince William is going to save us all from the papist threat!'

Bishop Compton spoke to the household at dinnertime, confirming the news.

Afterwards, Nicholas Tanner, who had joined Beth and his sister, picked at his roasted chicken in near silence, while the great hall resonated with excited conversation.

'Nicholas?' said Judith, catching his sleeve. 'It's good news, isn't it?'

'It may be,' he said. He wiped the sheen of perspiration off his forehead with a brawny arm. 'But can we be sure that the Prince of Orange will simply land on our shores and put Princess Mary on the throne without meeting any resistance? The Bishop says the King is amassing a great army at Hounslow Heath. He's not simply going to hand over his crown to Princess Mary, is he? He'll fight. To the death, if necessary.'

Judith's face paled. 'Nicholas, you won't have to fight, will you? Surely you're needed in the smithy?'

'I may have no choice,' he said in a low voice. 'We may all have to fight. And how will we know our enemies? There are Catholics all over the country, ready to kill for their cause.'

Beth shuddered, suddenly picturing Sir George coming after her with a pike in one hand and a musket in the other.

Two weeks passed and Beth saw little of Noah, apart from a few snatched kisses on some evenings as she hurried back to Chelsea. He continued to work long hours and on some days she didn't see him at all. The thrill of his declaration had worn off a little to be replaced by a niggle of doubt. Why did he not come to see her more often? She wanted to shout aloud the secret of their love and begin to make plans for their marriage but nothing could move forward until he had gained Father's permission.

One evening, determined to pin him down, she waited on the landing stage until at last she saw a boat carrying him towards her. She was relieved to see his face break into a smile when he saw her.

'I thought I might have missed you again,' he said. 'It'll be dark soon. Jump into the boat and I'll accompany you back to Chelsea.'

It wasn't quite what Beth had in mind, as she didn't want a boatman listening in when she spoke to Noah on private matters.

The warm breeze gusting across the river was pleasant after the suffocating heat of the day, in spite of the summertime reek of the river. She sat hand in hand with Noah, watching the great golden orb of the sun sink in the sky.

'I've hardly seen you,' she said.

'There were drawings to finish for St Paul's and a great many meetings with stonemasons and carpenters.'

She wasn't sure but she thought he sounded defensive. 'I'm not complaining,' she said. 'It's just that I've missed you.'

He smiled briefly and squeezed her hand.

There was another important matter to discuss. It had troubled her a great deal but it must be raised. 'Noah, I need to talk to you about something.'

He turned to face her. 'You don't want to go to Virginia, do you?'

Mutely, she shook her head.

'I thought not.' He shrugged and his mouth set in a thin line. 'Then we'll stay here. I know you want to be near your family.'

It was as easy as that! Beth sighed in relief but then, strangely, she visualised Noah's house that would now never be built on the foothills of the mountains in Virginia and experienced a profound sense of loss. When she glanced at him he was staring at the water again, his face unreadable. Full of guilt, she struggled to find something to say to appease him. 'There is important work for you to do here,' she ventured.

'That Sir Christopher will claim as his own.'

They sat in silence for a while, Noah's knee jiggling up and down as he stared out over the water. At last he sighed. 'Beth? I need to go home to Virginia.' The words tumbled out of him as if he'd had to find courage to say them.

'Go home? Now? Just when we ...' She was confused.

'There's some unfinished business I must attend to,' he said. 'That's why I've been so busy of late, trying to tie up all the loose ends here. I must return to Virginia for a while. I'll be back as soon as I can. Then I'll speak to your father and we'll be married.'

'Why don't you speak to Father before you leave? You'd be away for months. *Must* you go?'

'Yes, I must.'

'I don't understand.'

'No,' he said. 'I don't suppose you do.'

The light was fading rapidly but she was still able to see his face, set and anxious. What business could possibly be so important that he had to return to Virginia? She was intensely curious but something in his expression prevented her from asking. 'But you will come back for me?' she asked, gripping hard on to the side of the boat.

'I promise,' he said.

She had to be content with that.

Chapter 35

August 1688

A week later, Judith poked her head around the studio door. 'A little bird told me it's your birthday. Can I come in?'

'Please do!'

Judith carried a large cake which she presented to Beth with a flourish. 'A birthday cake for you. Almond and honey.' She beamed as Beth's eyes widened at the sight of the cake generously studded with toasted almonds and the whole frosted with powdered sugar.

'What a beauty!' gasped Beth.

'Thought you'd like it. There's half a pound of Mr Skelton's best honey in there; you can taste the lavender.'

Judith and Beth were just finishing their second slice when Noah arrived. 'If there's any left, I'd like some too,' he said.

'Perhaps we can spare you a very *small* slice,' teased Beth.

Judith licked crumbs away from the corner of her mouth. 'If I don't hurry back to the kitchens there'll be no pies for dinner.'

Noah waited until the door closed behind her before enfolding Beth in his arms. 'Happy birthday, sweetheart.'

She slipped her arms around his neck and held up her face for his kiss.

'You taste of honey,' he said a moment later. 'I'm exceedingly fond of honey.'

He kissed her again, taking his time, and her knees were weak with longing when he released her.

'You have bewitched me,' he whispered. 'How can I bear to leave you, even for one minute?'

'Don't, then. Stay with me!'

He ran his fingers into her hair, cupping her face while he covered her cheeks in tiny, hot kisses. Sighing, he let her go. 'I have something for you.' From inside his jacket he pulled out a box about four inches square.

Beth lifted the lid. Inside was a silver bracelet, wrapped in a wisp of forget-me-not blue silk. Exclaiming in delight, she saw that the catch was fashioned like a pair of clasped hands. 'It's beautiful!'

He fastened it around her wrist. 'Imagine that these clasped hands are mine, holding you until I return.'

He kissed away her tears of happiness with a touch as gentle as a feather. 'I'm working at St Paul's again and I'd better leave now,' he said, 'or I shan't be back in time to accompany you to the playhouse this evening.'

She cut him a slice of cake to take away for his dinner. 'Don't be too late!' she cautioned, as she kissed him goodbye.

After he had gone, she picked up her paintbrush and stared unseeingly at the plump mauve peonies which awaited her attention. Had she done the right thing in expecting Noah to stay in England after they were married? His dreams were so clearly set on building a new Virginia but she could just as easily paint flowers there as at home. It was clear to her now that she produced her best work when she was happy and she *would* be happy if she was with Noah. But would Noah's work suffer if she forced him to change his plans?

Of course, if she went to Virginia the prospect of saying goodbye to Mama and Father was terrible but they would still have Cecily and John to look after them in their old age.

She chewed the end of her paintbrush while she imagined living in the handsome house Noah envisaged. Kit would be so happy to have her close to hand and she was sure Noah's family would welcome her. And then there were the flowers. When she saw the variety of astonishing and exotic plants and trees that were regularly arriving at Fulham Palace from Virginia, her heart began to race at the artistic opportunities that would be open to her. Perhaps she could even make her own book of flower painting; a collection illustrating all the exotic local species?

There was a lot to consider but deep inside her a bubble of excitement began to grow and grow. Going to Virginia would be the start of a great adventure. Noah had already proved his love for her by forgoing his ambitions and agreeing to live in England but perhaps the greatest wedding gift she could give to him was her heartfelt support for what he truly wanted?

Beth left the palace in good time to change for the planned birthday outing to the playhouse with Cecily, the twins and Harry de Montford. When she arrived at Chelsea, Lady Arabella's maid told her that Cecily was not at home, having gone to the New Exchange with the mistress.

Beth took time over her appearance, putting on the lovely aqua silk dress given to her by Princess Anne and dressing her hair in an artfully simple way that took a great deal of effort. She smoothed her hands with the lavender hand cream made by her mother for her birthday present and rubbed precious attar of roses behind her ears. The Princess's ring sparkled on her finger and she kissed the gleaming silver of Noah's bracelet.

When she was ready she studied her reflection in the mirror, wondering if the low-cut neckline was too daring since the tight lacing accentuated the swell of her breasts. But it was her birthday and she wanted to look ravishing for Noah. More than anything she wanted him to desire her as much as she desired him. Her nights had been disturbed of late as she lay wide-eyed in the dark, yearning for his touch, and when she finally fell asleep her dreams made her blush when she remembered them in the morning.

She walked slowly downstairs, taking pleasure in the sound and feel of her silken skirts swishing around her ankles as she walked.

In the parlour, Joshua and Samuel were playing a hand of cards and Harry leaned against the chimney piece cleaning his nails with a knife. Beth paused in the doorway to reflect on the pretty picture that they made: the twins, so blond and identically good-looking, contrasting so dramatically with Harry's olive skin and black hair.

As elegant as ever, Harry slid the knife into a sheath inside his coat of topaz velvet. He kissed her hand, never taking his dark eyes off her face. 'You are looking exceptionally fine, tonight, Miss Ambrose.' he said.

The touch of his lips, the faint graze of his stubble on the back of her hand, made her shiver. The intensity of his gaze always unsettled her and she could quite see why Cecily had lost her head over him.

'How kind of you to grace us with your presence,' she said, unable to meet his eyes and looking instead at his full lips. As he continued to hold her hand, she cursed inwardly as a blush began to warm her cheeks. 'I hear that you have been spending a great deal of time of late with the butcher's daughter.'

'Why, how gossip travels!' Harry raised an eyebrow at Samuel.

'And how is Miss Plumridge? Is she soon to become Mistress de Montford?'

'I think not.' Harry leaned a little closer to whisper. 'Delightful though she is, plump little Miss Plumridge resembles, just a shade too much, one of her father's pigs.'

'Most ungallant of you!'

'But you, my dear, are in extraordinary good looks tonight.'

'Once you wash the paint and charcoal smudges off her, it's plain to see that my niece is a pretty little thing,' drawled Joshua with a mischievous smile.

'Pretty as paint,' added Samuel.

'Why, thank you, Uncles! That's the kindest thing you've ever said to me.'

'We promise not to make a habit of it,' said Joshua. 'Don't want to turn your head.'

Footsteps ran along the hall and Cecily threw open the door. 'Am I going to be late?'

'Not at all,' said Beth. 'Besides, Noah won't be here for a little while yet.'

Then Lady Arabella hurried into the parlour. 'Joshua and Samuel, Sir George wants to see you in his study.'

'What now?' grumbled Joshua.

'At once, if you please! Do not let me have to remind you that you owe your positions at Court entirely to Sir George.'

The twins followed their mother from the room without a backward glance.

Harry smiled at Cecily. 'You look charming, as ever. But perhaps you will wish to wear something a little more festive as it is Beth's birthday?'

'I certainly do!' Cecily leaned forward conspiratorially. 'Grandmama was persuaded to buy me a new gown. It's gold with red ribbons and it makes me look so lovely I shall amaze you all.'

'I'm sure you will, Miss Cecily.' Harry smiled lazily at her. 'We don't want to be late and you will need a little time for your *toilette* if you are to amaze us. Off you go now!'

'I'll be back soon,' said Cecily, closing the door behind her.

'Well, well! We're all alone,' said Harry, regarding Beth with heavy-lidded eyes.

All at once Beth found that the air in parlour was very warm. 'Not for long,' she said with a lightness she didn't feel.

'Perhaps not.' His expression grew thoughtful. 'But maybe for long enough.'

She sat very straight-backed and wished she were somewhere, anywhere, else. 'I should see if Cecily needs help to dress.'

'No, stay! I had meant to take more time to . . . ' He hesitated and flickered a smile at her.

Beth narrowed her eyes. If she didn't know him better, she'd have thought him nervous.

'Hell and damnation, Beth! Don't look at me like that!'

'What are you trying to say, Harry?' She spoke in as cool a voice as she could muster.

'You're a sensible girl and, unusually, not susceptible to my flattery. So I see no merit in waiting.'

'Waiting for what?'

'I will not insult you by treating you like an innocent.'

'Like Cecily?'

'Perhaps.' Amusement crinkled the corners of his eyes but then he grew serious again. 'I know all about you from the twins, you know. They tell me that, for a woman, you are an unusually gifted artist. Not only gifted but wealthy and ambitious. And that you have declared you will never marry.' He stood up and walked slowly towards her, standing rather too close for her comfort. 'Is it true?'

She allowed a hint of a smile to play upon her lips as she thought about Noah. 'I certainly did say that.'

He reached out his forefinger and she froze as he ran it slowly down the side of her cheek, pausing to touch the corner of her mouth. 'What a waste that would be!' His voice was soft as he fixed her again with his compelling gaze. His finger continued its unhurried journey down her chin and the side of her neck. 'Have you no desire for a husband? Or a lover?'

His dark eyes still bored into her and all at once she found herself completely unable to look away. She couldn't think clearly, as if she were a mouse spellbound by a snake. He caressed the hollow of her neck causing small thrills of pleasure to radiate over her skin. She began to tremble.

'It would be a terrible thing for a beautiful woman such as yourself never to experience the sensual delights of love, don't you think?' He leaned over her, his whispering breath hot and moist against her ear. 'Clandestine afternoons behind closed shutters, the silken touch of skin on skin, bare limbs entwined together in shuddering ecstasy ...' Slowly, so slowly, the warmth of his fingertip trailed lower and lower towards her décolletage.

A shaft of desire clutched her at her, deep inside. Her eyelids fluttered closed and her breathing quickened.

Swiftly, Harry slipped his hand inside the neckline of her bodice and bent to lick her creamy flesh.

Gasping, she reared up, the spell broken. 'Don't touch me!'

Harry threw back his head and laughed. 'I wondered how long you'd let me continue. And don't tell me that you didn't like it.'

Beth's chair was hard back against the wall and Harry was standing so close that she was unable to rise without pressing herself against him. 'You are no gentleman,' she said, her heart thudding in fear and humiliation.

'How very true! Now listen to me: I have a proposition for you.'

'I do not care to listen to any proposition you may make. Please, stand aside.' A wave of heat flooded over her and she glanced down to see the scarlet flush of shame mottling her breasts.

'Hear me out.' He rested his hands heavily on her bare shoulders, holding her down. 'Your problem is that a husband would expect you to place your energies into managing his household and bearing his children but you want to spend all day painting. So, to avoid argument, you have decided to remain unmarried.'

'Take your hands off me!' She tugged at his wrists, desperate to pull his hands away from her naked skin but he only gripped her all the harder.

'Look at me!' His persuasive voice was like honey, rich with secret pleasures. 'You are a beautiful woman and I cannot believe you will wish to spurn the delights of physical love all your life. An unmarried woman cannot afford to make, shall we say, a little mistake. And these things do happen. Artist or not, you will not want a bastard child clinging to your skirts.'

'How dare you!'

'There is a perfectly simple answer to your dilemma.' He leaned forward until his face was two inches from her own. 'You can marry me.'

'Marry you!' Beth opened her eyes wide in astonishment. Curiosity momentarily overcame her anger. 'Why would you want to marry me?'

'For your beauty and charm.' He smiled. 'And your money, of course.'

'My *money*?'

He glanced at the sapphire on her finger. 'This ring alone, that you wear so casually every day, would keep us for years. Joshua tells me your family is very rich. And then there is your family connection with Lady Arabella and Sir George, who move in the highest of circles.'

Beth shook her head in disbelief. What had possessed Joshua to tell Harry that her family was wealthy? Pure mischief, she suspected.

'Listen to me, Beth!' He voice throbbed with passion. 'I will not deny that my family is currently financially embarrassed but together we can both live the lives we want. You may paint all day if you wish. At the plantation in Virginia we shall have slaves to take care of domestic matters. We needn't trouble each other at all.'

'You call that a marriage?'

'A business proposition. My father's estate shall be restored and you will lead a life of artistic freedom. If you wish to take lovers, I shall not be jealous. And should there be a little bastard I shall own it as mine. Who knows, perhaps you will even invite me into your bed? I promise you, I can bring you to heights of pleasure you have only dreamed of.' Harry bent to kiss her mouth, pressing her back in the chair and forcing his tongue between her teeth. His beard rasped her lips and he tasted of stale wine and corruption.

She recoiled and raised a hand to slap his face.

His eyes glittering like jet, Harry caught her wrist in a grip of iron. 'I like a woman with spirit. So much more fun when there's a challenge.'

'*Nothing* would induce me to marry you.'

'I understand you need a little time to consider my proposal.'

'You disgust me,' she hissed. 'And all this time you have played with Cecily's feelings . . . I tell you, even if I hadn't already given my heart to another, I would rather marry the Devil than you!'

The colour drained from Harry's face with such speed that Beth would have laughed if she hadn't been boiling with rage.

'You've given your heart to another?' He squeezed her wrist until she whimpered. 'Who?' He twisted her arm sharply, shoving her hard against the wall. 'Who is it?' He was so close to Beth that a fleck of spittle landed on her face.

She flinched and turned her face aside.

'It's that damned red-headed cousin of yours, isn't it?' He shook her wrist again. 'Isn't it? I *thought* Noah was sniffing around you with the face of a moon-sick calf. God's teeth, as if that family didn't have enough money of their own already!'

He relaxed his hold on her a fraction and Beth took her chance. With all her strength she twisted back sharply to face him, ramming her elbow forcefully into his crotch.

Caught by surprise, he doubled over, moaning and cursing.

Heaving him aside, she scrambled to the other side of the room. 'Now get out!' she said. 'And don't come near me, or my family, again.'

Slowly, Harry stood upright again and walked towards her, his face contorted by spite. 'Well, then! Did Noah forget to tell you about Hannah Sharpe? You'd better ask him about his plans to marry *her* this Christmastide.'

Beth gasped, his word like a kick to her stomach. 'It isn't true!'

'I'm afraid, my dear, that it is. So, you see, you had much better be *my* wife.' He reached out to touch her throat and she stepped back. 'You may act as if you are outraged but I sense you are ripe for the plucking. And I assure you, I am the man to do it.'

He came at her again then, forcing her back against the wall, his eyes slitted with lust.

Beth drew in her breath as he seized her hair, yanking her head towards him. She tried to scream but he covered her mouth with his own, kissing her savagely.

She struggled wildly in his hard embrace, trying in vain to push him away.

Laughing, Harry scrabbled at the neckline of her bodice, tearing at the fragile silk until he could scoop out her breast with his greedy hand and bend to suck on her nipple.

Her mouth freed, Beth screamed and kicked, beating at his head with her fists. Then, over his shoulder, she saw Cecily's shocked face in the open doorway and behind her, Noah.

Noah hurled himself at them with a roar, dragging Harry away from Beth and punching him on the jaw.

Beth gathered up the torn silk to cover her naked breast and fell back, shaking, while Cecily began to shriek.

Grunting, the two men grappled together, locked in a fierce embrace as they crashed around the room, upsetting a table and shattering a vase of roses. They knocked pictures off the walls, ornaments went flying and they became entangled in the curtains, which were ripped from their hooks as they staggered against the window.

Noah was scarlet with fury and although the smaller and leaner of the two men, he was driven by rage. At last he wrestled Harry to the ground, straddled him, and sat on his stomach. 'I'll make you sorry you ever touched a hair of her head,' he yelled, banging Harry's head again and again against the floor.

Harry kicked and struggled but he was running out of steam. Flailing his arms, he reached inside his coat to pull out his knife.

Beth, still trembling with shame and disgust, saw the blade glint.

Harry raised the knife high, aiming it at Noah's chest.

Cecily gave a blood-curdling scream.

Beth snatched up a chair which she swung with all her might at Harry's arm to deflect the blow.

The knife clattered to the floor.

'Son of a whore!' Harry yelled.

Noah let go of Harry's throat. Blood, flicked off Noah's cheek, and spattered on to Lady Arabella's pale blue silk upholstery.

Sir George, Joshua and Samuel came running into the room and wrenched the two men apart.

Noah's face was running with blood and Harry nursed his wrist, moaning.

'This is an absolute disgrace!' bellowed Sir George. 'You will leave this place at once!'

The twins dragged a cursing and struggling Harry out of the room.

The front door slammed.

Lady Arabella appeared and burst into loud lamentations at the sight of the devastation that had been her parlour.

Cecily rocked backwards and forwards, shrieking hysterically.

Beth ran to her and gripped her in a tight embrace but Cecily caught her breath on a sob and pushed her away. When Beth glanced at Noah she bit back an exclamation of horror. 'You're hurt!'

Noah's cheek had been sliced open in a terrible wound stretching from his ear to his jaw.

Beth turned to Lady Arabella. 'We need clean water and bandages. At once!'

Lady Arabella's expression was coldly unforgiving. 'Take him into the kitchen. And I do not expect to see him in my house again. Ever.'

The cook exclaimed in dismay when she saw the blood streaming down Noah's cheek and soaking into his shirt. She sat them down in the scullery, dismissed the kitchen maid and brought a basin of water and clean cloths herself.

'Now you call me if you need any help,' she said. 'Poor young gentleman, you'll bear that scar until your grave.'

Noah sat silent and pale-faced while Beth, sick and trembling, cleaned the gaping wound. She pulled the edges of the skin together as best she could, wrapped the bandage under his chin and over the top of his head, concentrating all the while on her actions and thrusting away again and again of the awful memory of Harry's revelation about Noah's betrothed. 'You must see a doctor,' she said.

'I'll never forgive myself for not being there when you needed me,' said Noah.

Beth couldn't meet his eyes. She was defiled by Harry's touch.

'If you hadn't gone for Harry with that chair he'd have stabbed me in the chest. I might have died.' Noah reached out to take her in his arms.

Beth stepped back. 'Don't!' she said, her chin quivering. How could she possibly bear it? An agonising pain began to grow somewhere deep in her belly, blossoming upwards as if she was being eviscerated.

'Beth?'

'When were you going to tell me about your engagement to Hannah Sharpe?' she asked in a light, conversational tone, praying that Harry had lied to her out of spite.

He froze, his brown eyes wary. 'Hannah?'

'Yes, Hannah. I believe you mentioned she is your neighbour? But you forgot to tell me she is also your betrothed.'

Noah's arms fell down to his side and he seemed to shrink. 'Who told you? Harry, I suppose?'

'Who else?' Her last vestige of hope died. Then rage came seething up and boiled over. 'Do you have so little respect for me that you could not tell me the truth?' she hissed. 'You encouraged me to fall in love with you, knowing all the while that you would break my heart!'

'It wasn't like that!'

'Yes, it was exactly like that.' There was a deep sense of unreality about their conversation. Was it only that morning they had exchanged passionate kisses and she had been so certain of his love?

'I never meant to fall in love with you.'

His voice was quiet and full of pain. For a second she longed to comfort him in her arms, overcome by the knowledge that his handsome face was ruined by the hideous wound.

'I tried not to fall in love with you. And you were so set on living at Merryfields and remaining a spinster that, when it was too late and I already loved you, I still thought my life could carry on as before.'

Beth's throat began to constrict while deep in her chest a knife twisted, cutting out her heart. 'Forget me, as I shall forget you. And go home to Hannah. I'll not be instrumental in breaking a betrothal.'

'Beth . . . '

'Please, just go!' The tearing sensation in her breast grew worse and she was nearly choking from holding back an eruption of weeping.

'I'll always love you. Nothing will ever change that.' He stared at her for a long second and then, white-faced, left the room.

She stared at the basin of water, crimson with Noah's blood. Suddenly faint with shock, she rested her head on her arms on the scullery table, amongst the dirty pots and pans. Strangely, she couldn't cry after all but her mind raced. Everything fell into place: Noah's reticence in spite of the fact that he seemed to love her, his moodiness and odd behaviour when he talked to her about his dream house. And then his urgent desire to return to Virginia.

The scullery maid looked in with anxious eyes.

'Come in; I've finished now,' said Beth.

Chapter 36

The hall was silent and empty. Beth caught sight of herself in the mirror. Her eyes were wide and dazed and there were red marks on her shoulders. A loosened lock of hair hung over her breast. Hardly knowing what she was doing, she pinned the curl back into place while she fought down a wave of sickness.

Lady Arabella stood by the window in the parlour. 'I shall have to redecorate and have new furniture.' She closed her eyes, shuddering. 'Look at my chairs all spattered in blood and the curtains torn and defiled! And Sir George has left me alone amongst the wreckage and hurried off with the twins back to Court.'

'Where is Cecily?'

'The foolish child ran after Harry de Montford.'

Beth caught her breath. 'You didn't stop her?'

'She'll soon come running back with her tail between her legs.'

'But Harry is dangerous!'

Lady Arabella raised her eyebrows. 'I can only say, Beth

Ambrose, that men are *not* dangerous unless a woman flaunts herself and encourages him to indulge in his baser instincts.'

Too angry to speak, Beth swept from the room, barely resisting the desire to slam the door behind her.

She ran helter-skelter down the lane towards the river stairs, heedless of the stones cutting into her satin slippers and the brambles snatching at her silken skirts. The sultry heat of the day had barely abated and perspiration pricked under her arms and ran in rivulets between her breasts.

A stitch pulled sharply in her side but, panting hard, she forced herself on. Dread at the thought of seeing Harry again consumed her but the fear of finding that he had assaulted Cecily was even greater. She prayed that he'd already caught a boat back to the city before Cecily reached the river stairs.

As she sprinted towards the end of the lane she caught a glimpse of Cecily's new gold and red dress through the trees. Then she saw that Harry was at her side.

Sobbing, Beth raced on, bursting out through the copse on to the river path.

Cecily clung to Harry's coat front and he had one arm around her waist.

'Let her go, Harry!' Beth heaved for breath, her heart thumping.

Harry's face twisted into a sneer. 'Your sister and I have an understanding,' he said.

Cecily, her eyes shining with joy, smiled widely at Beth. 'Harry says he made a terrible mistake. It's me he loves and we're going away to be married.'

Shock coursed through Beth's veins. 'Didn't you *see* what he did to me, Cecily?'

An expression of distaste flashed across Cecily's face. 'Harry explained that. It was unforgivable of you to throw yourself at him like that, especially when you know that it's me he loves. I never realised you were so jealous of me, Beth.'

'Jealous?' Beth laughed. 'He doesn't love you at all, Cecily.'

'Of course Harry loves me. He never even *asked* me if I have a dowry so that proves it!'

It was too much for Beth. She grasped her sister's arm and shook it. 'No, it doesn't!'

Cecily, still clinging to Harry's coat front, turned her face up to his. 'You do love me, don't you?'

Harry had become very still. 'Well now,' he drawled. 'No dowry?'

Cecily shook her head. 'None at all.' Her smile wavered as he prised her fingers free of his coat.

'Then I've been misinformed.' His lips tightened into a thin line. 'I shall have to take Joshua to task about that. I'm afraid, my dear, that you must seek a husband who'll overlook such an impediment.' Without even a backward glance, he hurried towards the landing stage, where a boat was waiting.

Cecily stared in disbelief as he vaulted into the boat. 'Harry!'

Beth snatched at her sister's wrist. She noticed the gown of golden silk was adorned with vulgar knots of scarlet ribbons, the bodice cut far too low for a young girl. No matter, there would be no further opportunity for Cecily to flaunt herself in front of Harry de Montford.

'Don't leave me, Harry!' Cecily screamed, fighting to free herself from Beth's grasp. She wrenched her hand away and ran to the landing stage but the boat had already reached the middle of the river. 'Harry, come back!' Cecily broke into a storm of noisy tears, her mouth open in a square of sorrow as she wailed and wept.

Beth went to comfort her but Cecily shook her off. 'This is all *your* fault!' she spat. 'And now he's gone for ever! I can't live without Harry. I want to die!'

'Don't say such a terrible thing!'

Cecily pulled at her hair and began to shriek again, lost in despair. 'I cannot bear the pain!' she howled. She turned to face the river and held her arms out at her side.

Before Beth could react, Cecily threw herself in the river with a noisy splash.

'Cecily!' Beth watched in horror as she sank below the surface. A second later Cecily's head reappeared. She flailed at the water, then sank again.

Beth didn't hesitate. She kicked off her shoes and jumped from the landing stage. She gasped as she went under, bobbed up and burst into the light once more. Cecily had already been dragged some yards away by the current.

Beth hadn't swum in the river since she was a child, when she hadn't been hampered by long skirts. She struck out towards Cecily, fighting against the current as the weight of several yards of waterlogged silk dragged her down.

Cecily thrashed and screamed and sank and came up for air but her cries were becoming weaker and each time she became submerged she stayed under the water for longer.

Cecily's panic was so great that when Beth reached her she was only able to catch hold of her arm and was kicked in the stomach for her pains.

Cecily's head went under the water again and she came up choking.

Thoroughly frightened now, Beth saw that Cecily was weakening. Her eyes were wide with terror and her face turned grey as she took great whooping breaths, fighting for air. Then her eyes closed and she slid down below the surface of the water.

'No!' screamed Beth. Taking a deep breath she dived down into the green depths of a dim and silent world. Her skirts billowed around; and she felt them catch on an underwater branch. The silk ripped as she frantically kicked her feet to thrust herself in Cecily's direction. Slimy weed wrapped itself around her legs, tugging at her ankles.

She thought for a moment that she had grasped Cecily's skirt but as she rose to the surface she saw it was only a piece of old sacking. She dragged in a lungful of air and went down again.

There was a movement below her and she reached out. Her fingers caught hold of something. It felt tougher than weed and she pulled on it until Cecily's face, pale and still, loomed up out of the murky depths. She dragged on Cecily's hair to heave her up towards the surface.

Cecily remained motionless, her eyes closed.

Coughing and choking, Beth's own strength was fading and it was an almost impossible task to support her sister's weight. She slipped into a dreamlike state where all movement was slowed down. All she knew was that she must keep Cecily's face out of the water but that she couldn't turn her over.

Suddenly, the river churned beside her and Cecily was dragged from her arms.

'I have her,' Noah said. 'Float on your back and I'll fetch you in a minute. Can you do that?'

She nodded, too shocked to answer. Rolling on to her back she found that she floated and only needed to kick her legs to propel herself towards the bank. After a moment, her head nudged a clump of reeds; she grasped them and pulled herself up. Tripping over her sodden skirts, she barely had the strength to crawl out of the water, never mind to stand.

Noah had placed Cecily face down on the bank and was pressing the water out of her lungs. She lay waxen white and deathly still and a dread such as Beth had never experienced before clawed at her, rendering her speechless.

Grim-faced, Noah continued to press rhythmically on Cecily's back.

A terrible trembling began in Beth's hands, spreading up her arms and throughout her body while she whispered the Lord's Prayer.

At last Noah sat back. 'Beth,' he said in a voice full of sorrow, 'she's gone.'

'No! Don't stop!'

He hesitated only a fraction of a second before bending over Cecily again.

Beth closed her eyes, rocking herself back and forth in an agony of despair. She pictured Cecily as a little girl climbing on to her knee to be told a story, saw the excitement in her lovely green eyes as she dressed for her first ball and wondered how she could possibly tell Mama and Father that she hadn't been able to save her.

A cough made her snap her eyes open.

Noah pushed down on Cecily's back until a trickle and then a gush of green liquid came from Cecily's mouth. Her foot twitched; she moaned.

Beth sobbed and snatched her sister's hand, hope flaring in her breast. She smoothed a sodden strand of black hair off Cecily's face.

Cecily coughed again, more violently this time.

A few minutes later she was sitting up, encircled in Beth's arms. Beth wept and shook and covered her sister's face in kisses, hardly daring to believe that Cecily had come back to her again.

Noah cleared his throat and Beth saw that blood and tears ran unchecked down his own face. After a while, he lifted Cecily to her feet. 'Can you walk?' he asked, 'or shall I carry you?'

Cecily collapsed against him, burying her face in his shoulder.

Noah hoisted her into his arms and carried her along the path.

Beth, too full of emotion to speak, trailed her wet skirts behind them.

Noah carefully deposited Cecily on the front steps of Lady Arabella's house. 'Will you be all right from here?' he asked.

Beth nodded. 'I daren't ask you in. Go on back to the palace and put on some dry clothes. And ask Judith to change your bandage,

332

will you?' The blood had soaked through the dressing and was dripping off his chin, staining his shirt-front.

Noah caught her hand and before she could stop him, pressed it to his lips.

Though it broke her heart all over again, she pulled it away. 'Thank you for saving Cecily. There aren't the words . . .' She took a deep breath to steady herself.

Noah glanced at Cecily, drenched and motionless, staring at the ground. 'Look after her.'

Numb, Beth watched him walk away. When he disappeared from sight, she led her sister indoors, deeply thankful that Lady Arabella was nowhere to be seen.

Cecily made no protest as Beth undressed her. She lay in bed with her eyes shut, shivering and icy cold.

Beth picked the sodden mess of Cecily's golden dress up off the floor. The dye had run from the knots of vulgar scarlet ribbons and blotched the silk with ugly stains.

Cecily whimpered and Beth sat beside her, stroking her hand until she slept.

Moving as slowly as an old woman, Beth unlaced her own bodice and took off her soaked and ruined dress. The neckline was torn and there was a gaping rent in the skirt. No matter. It was tainted with grief and shame; she would never wear it again.

Pouring water from the ewer into the basin, Beth washed herself. She paid special attention to her breast, scrubbing so hard that her skin became reddened and sore. Revulsion made her shudder as she remembered Harry de Montford's wet lips, violating her with his touch.

When at last she felt cleansed she slipped a freshly laundered nightshift over her head. The cotton caught over her face and she was overcome with panic again as she recalled her frenzied groping underwater to find Cecily. Freeing her face she ran to the window to lean out and gulp in the warm night air.

After a while, her breathing steadied. She leaned her forehead against the cool stone of the window frame. Somewhere out there in the dark was Noah: Noah who had stolen her heart and deceived her. The pain of his betrayal rose up in her again and she grasped at the heavy window drapes, pressing them to her mouth to muffle the terrible cry that forced its way out of her, a long drawn-out howl of the utmost misery and despair.

Chapter 37

After a near-sleepless night, Beth left Cecily in bed and arrived early at Fulham Palace, intending to bury herself in her work. Even at eight in the morning the sun bore mercilessly down on the top of her aching head. In the Dovehouse Court, Lizzie Skelton and the other laundresses were desultorily hanging out the wet sheets, which flapped in a wind as hot as the open door of a bread oven. Dust whirled in eddies, landing in gritty deposits on the clean linen.

The heat in the studio was stifling so Beth opened the windows to let out the flies that repeatedly banged their heads against the glass. It was no cooler inside even with the windows open.

Beth sat before her easel and studied the lovely crimson and white York and Lancaster rose she intended to paint but the velvety petals had become tipped with the brown of decay overnight. She rested her chin on her hand and stared at the spoiled bloom through a mist of tears. Only yesterday she had been so happy. She touched a finger to her mouth, bruised from Harry's assault on her, and shuddered in disgust.

During the long morning, Beth had to use every ounce of self-discipline to keep on working. The heat and the breeze caused the paint to dry instantly she touched brush to paper, making it hard to lay down even washes of colour. At dinnertime she threw down her paintbrush with relief.

In the great hall Judith waved at her and Beth slipped on to the bench to join her friend.

'You're quiet today,' Judith said, after a while.

'It's so hot. Everything feels as if it's too much trouble.'

'The weather must break soon, surely?' Judith wiped perspiration off her top lip. 'It makes everyone short-tempered. Nicholas . . . ' She sighed.

'What?'

'He's so anxious all the time. He doesn't sleep and he's sure the world is about to fall down around our ears. He's heard that the army in Ireland has been entirely purged of Protestants now.'

'I suppose the King is preparing for if the Prince of Orange comes.'

'The King's army numbers more than thirty-four thousand men in the three kingdoms now. Can you imagine that?' Judith's broad brow furrowed. 'What if the Prince of Orange hasn't enough men to help us? The Dutch army will arrive tired and seasick even before they march, while the King's army will be fighting fit, rested and well fed.'

Beth picked at her plate of salad greens. Nothing seemed to matter to her now, not when Noah had betrayed her.

'Beth? Did you hear me?'

'Sorry, Judith. The Prince of Orange is a seasoned soldier. I cannot imagine he would come to help us if he wasn't confident that his army would win.'

That evening, Beth left the palace early to be sure to avoid meeting Noah. It would be far too painful for both of them and serve no useful purpose. She dragged her feet along the river path through the sweltering sunshine and waited listlessly for a boat. When she arrived back at Lady Arabella's house, Cecily still lay in bed and turned her face to the wall when Beth tried to persuade her to come down for supper.

Beth said little when Lady Arabella quizzed her about Cecily, only that she'd slipped into the river by mistake. Any hint of a possible elopement would ruin her sister for ever.

After supper Beth sat with an unread book on her knee, staring out of the parlour window while she counted the ways in which she missed Noah.

'Cecily appears to have retired to bed in a fit of pique,' said Lady Arabella. 'She fancied herself in love with that Harry de Montford, I suppose. I never was so taken in by a young man! Unless, of course, I count Noah.' She stared intently at Beth, a half-smile upon her painted lips. 'Cecily told me that Noah also made you false promises, Beth?

Beth stared at her book, unable to speak.

'I can't say I'm surprised,' continued Lady Arabella, 'he is a Leyton, after all. I would, however, strongly advise you to put a smile on your face if you intend to find yourself a more suitable husband. No man likes a sour-faced woman.'

Beth resisted saying that she wondered then that Lady Arabella was on her fourth husband.

That evening Cecily grew feverish and worsened over the following days.

Beth sat beside her and carried up trays of soup, which she never touched.

On the fifth day Cecily's temperature and racking cough gave Beth real cause for anxiety. It wasn't only that Cecily was obviously unwell but, apart from the occasional, 'Please', 'Thank you', or murmured, 'You're so kind to me, Beth', she barely spoke or ate.

During the night Cecily moaned and muttered and Beth couldn't bring her to proper consciousness. Thoroughly frightened, she hurried to the twins' bedroom and shook Samuel awake.

'Sam, I'm worried about Cecily. She's burning with fever.'

Samuel dragged on his dressing gown and came to look at her. 'I'll send one of the servants to fetch Dr Latymer right away,' he said.

Samuel returned to sit with Beth while they were waiting. He glanced anxiously at Beth as Cecily's breathing rasped in her throat as she tossed and turned. 'She's very hot,' he said.

'This might never have happened if Joshua hadn't told Harry that Cecily and I had large dowries,' said Beth.

Samuel shifted uneasily in his chair. 'It was only one of Josh's jokes.'

It seemed an age until Dr Latymer limped into the sickroom. He felt Cecily's forehead and looked down her throat. Then he listened to her chest, looking grave. 'It's an inflammation of the lungs.'

'Is it serious?'

He nodded. 'She's dangerously hot. We must bring down her temperature or she'll convulse.' He took a phial of birch-bark medicine from his bag and dripped a dose on to Cecily's tongue. 'You must give her five drops of this every three hours.'

During the small hours of the night the heat of Cecily's fever grew so intense that Beth was unable to reduce her temperature, despite continual sponging with cool water. She became so frightened that she pulled back the sheet and soaked Cecily's nightshift, hoping that as her body heat evaporated the water it would take away the fever.

Beth listened out for the church clock, counting out the lonely hours until she could drip another dose of medicine on to Cecily's tongue. Exhausted and frightened, she rested her head in her hands while Cecily's breath came in painful gasps and wheezes.

She must have dozed for a moment but was woken when Cecily went into such a paroxysm of coughing that she stopped breathing entirely for a second or two, causing Beth to experience the utmost terror. Supporting her sister in her arms, Beth willed her to breathe while she longed for her mama.

It was past four in the morning when she heard footsteps on the stairs and she burst into tears of relief when she saw Dr Latymer open the door.

'She's failing and I don't know what to do.'

Dr Latymer made a steaming bowl of friar's balsam and tenderly supported Cecily against his chest, while Beth prayed the inhalation would ease her breathing.

'You're worn out,' he said. 'Close your eyes for a while and I'll watch over her.'

'You're very kind, Doctor.'

Beth slept in the chair for an hour. When she woke she stared into the dim light for a moment, wondering where she was. The room was quiet. She couldn't hear Cecily's tortured breathing any more. Sudden terror made jump to her feet. 'Cecily?

'Shh! She's sleeping,' whispered Dr Latymer. 'The fever has broken.'

Tears of release flowed down Beth's face and the doctor patted her back and lent her a handkerchief. Beth confessed to him the whole sorry tale of Cecily's near-drowning.

'It was obvious that poor Cecily was very taken with that scoundrel, de Montford. A sensitive girl such as she would take it very hard when he rejected her after raising her hopes so. The loss of a first love is very painful.'

'I blame myself for not sending her home to Merryfields.' Beth wrung her hands, wondering if her own spirits would ever recover from the loss of Noah's love.

Cecily lay back on the pillow and stared at nothing for two days.

'I'll ask Lady Arabella to instruct her cook to make some beef tea,' Dr Latymer said, worry etched around his eyes. 'And you should go outside for some fresh air. I'll sit with your sister if you want to go and see how Noah's wound is healing.'

'Oh no! I don't wish to disturb him.' The thought of seeing Noah again was too painful.

'From what you say, it was a very nasty wound to his face and could fester. Bring him here if you'd like me to look at it.'

Secure in the knowledge that Cecily was in safe hands, Beth returned to Fulham.

Judith's round face broke into a wide smile when she saw her. 'Where have you been?'

'My sister had a fever. Did Noah come to see you?'

'I bandaged his cheek for him.' Judith shivered. 'What a horrible wound! He said he fell off a horse and sliced it on a flint but I haven't seen him since.'

Beth went to find young Jem, the porter's boy, and asked him to run up to Noah's room and tell him that she had arrived. A pulse throbbed in her throat while she waited, wondering how she could face him with any equanimity, but when Jem returned he was alone.

'Not there, miss,' he said. 'His room's empty and he wasn't at dinner yesterday, neither.'

Beth went into the palace again. Hesitating for only a moment, she knocked on the library door.

Bishop Compton opened the door himself. 'Ah, Miss Ambrose! Come in, come in!'

'I'm sorry to disturb you but I wondered if you'd seen Noah?'

'Not since yesterday when he came to say goodbye. He's returned to Virginia.'

Beth stifled a cry and her knees began to tremble.

The Bishop reached out to steady her. 'Miss Ambrose, are you unwell?'

She drew a deep breath. 'I knew that he was going, of course,' she said, trying to keep her voice steady. 'But my sister has been ill and I haven't seen him for a few days. I thought he'd still be here.'

'You've just missed him,' said the Bishop sympathetically.

Stumbling out of the library, she hurried through the quadrangle into the garden, fighting back the storm of tears that threatened to engulf her. How could she bear it? She darted through the rose garden, catching her skirt on the thorns, before breaking into a run along the avenue of pleached limes.

Lizzie Skelton stood on the path in front of her. 'Hey!' she called.

Beth ran around her and didn't stop until she reached the walled kitchen garden where she leaned her forearms against the sun-warmed bricks and sobbed. All she could think of was that she would never see Noah again. She brushed away a bee that landed on her wrist.

'Hey!'

Beth turned to see Lizzie walking towards her and hastily wiped her eyes.

'Didn't you hear me calling you?' Lizzie stuck her chin out at Beth. 'It's all your fault!'

'What's my fault?' The air was heavy with the drowsy buzzing of the bees as they flew from the lavender bushes and in and out of the skeps lodged in the wall alcoves.

Lizzie stood with her hands on her hips. 'I told you to keep clear of Noah, didn't I? I had a chance with him until you spoiled it for me. And now he's gone.'

Beth tried to sidestep Lizzie but found her path blocked again.

'Don't need your sort around here.' Lizzie's face was ugly with spite. 'What really gets my goat, apart from you stealing Noah, is that the Bishop pays you more in a month than I earn in a year. And for what? Messing about making stupid pictures of flowers! I ask you, what use is that?' She licked her full lips and smiled. 'Still, I got rid of them, right enough, didn't I?'

Beth stared at her. 'So it *was* you?' Shock and outrage made her tremble.

'None other! You shoulda seen it!' Lizzie cackled with laughter. 'Covered the whole lot of 'em with red paint. Does that make me an artist, too?' She plucked a stalk of grass and minced about pretending to use it as a brush to paint imaginary pictures in the air.

A terrible anger grew in Beth's breast, building up like the pressure of steam in a covered pan, and then erupted, obscuring her vision with a scarlet haze. She grasped hold of the girl's black hair and slapped her laughing face.

Lizzie, shrieking like a she-devil, raked at Beth's cheeks with her fingernails.

Beth ducked aside but Lizzie tripped over her foot and fell headlong against the wall, catapulting one of the skeps out of its alcove.

Almost at once, a shimmering cloud of angry bees swarmed out of the skep and settled on to Lizzie, covering her with a dark pulsating shroud.

Beth stood helplessly by until Lizzie's terrified screams brought the gardeners running. They formed a chain of buckets to the rainwater cistern and doused Lizzie in water while Beth ran for the beekeeper.

Much later, Beth returned to Chelsea, Lizzie's screams still echoing in her ears. The dozen or so bee stings that she had received on her own arms throbbed enough but she could hardly imagine the pain that Lizzie must be enduring. The poor girl's face had swollen up so much that her eyes had almost disappeared. Lizzie's father had scraped out the stings and anointed her with a thick white paste to soothe her lumpy, red skin but he shook his head, anxious that the shock would be too great for her.

When the Bishop had come to discover the cause of the commotion Beth had explained to him how Lizzie had boasted of her malicious deed and her own part in the girl's misfortune.

'Justice appears to have been done,' he said, 'but perhaps this might be a good time for you to make a visit to Merryfields, just until Lizzie recovers?'

The idea of returning to Merryfields brought Beth a great deal of comfort. Cecily was in such low spirits that it was a serious cause for concern. What could be better for her than to be nursed back to health by Mama and Father? As to herself, Beth knew that she had hardly begun to grieve for Noah yet and a spell with those she loved around her would console her a little.

Dr Latymer, comprehending some of Beth's distress, was in full agreement with her decision to take Cecily home to Merryfields.

'I shall accompany you myself,' he said. 'It will be my pleasure. Besides, I like what I hear of your father's work and I should like to meet him.'

Beth went straight to the dispensary to find her mother.

'Sweetheart! What a lovely surprise!'

'Mama, Cecily has been very ill and we've brought her home.'

Susannah's welcoming smile faded. 'What ails her?'

'A severe inflammation of the lungs. The fever has gone but she's very frail.'

Susannah called for Emmanuel and they hurried down to the landing stage.

'Who is that?' asked Susannah, as they neared the boat. 'I thought you'd come with Noah.'

A sharp pain twisted in Beth's insides at the mention of his name. 'It's Dr Latymer, who has been attending Cecily with every possible kindness.'

Susannah glanced at Beth but then she saw Cecily reclining on the boat cushions with her eyes closed, pale and still.

Dr Latymer limped forward to greet Susannah. 'Good morning, Mistress Ambrose.'

At the sound of her mother's voice Cecily opened her eyes and even smiled faintly when Susannah kissed her.

Emmanuel gently lifted Cecily into his brawny black arms and carried her as lightly as if she were thistledown.

The word went around that Cecily and Beth had come home and the guests arrived from all parts of the garden to join the procession back to the house.

Poor Joan wept when she saw how fragile Cecily had become. Clarence Smith patted her hand and begged her not to worry as he would send for the best physicians in his kingdom to attend her.

John left his pitchfork quivering in the compost heap and ran to Beth's side.

'Cecily's been ill and I've brought her home,' she said, her voice muffled against his chest.

'Nowhere b-b-better,' he said. 'I'll fetch Father.'

Later, after Dr Latymer had left and Cecily was asleep, Beth sat in the solar with her parents.

'Beth, what is it?' asked William. 'What has happened?'

'It's all my fault,' she whispered. 'I promised you I'd look after her.'

'I think you'd better explain.'

She struggled to know where to begin.

'I saw a great deal of Noah at Fulham and ...' She swallowed, seeking the courage to declare everything. 'I fell in love with him. Then he told me he loved me and that he would speak to Father.'

Susannah smiled. 'I'm so happy for you, sweetheart!'

Beth shook her head. 'He was curiously reluctant, almost as if I had forced him into declaring himself. And then,' she shuddered, 'Harry de Montford asked me to marry him.' She closed her eyes at the memory of his compelling gaze and how she has almost succumbed to his awful attraction. She could never tell Father of how he had touched her.

'Harry?' William looked bewildered. 'I thought Harry was interested in Cecily.'

344

'He wasn't interested in either of us, as it turned out. When I refused his proposal Harry became very angry.' Unconsciously, she fingered the remains of the bruises on her wrists. 'I told him that I'd given my heart to another. He guessed it was Noah and he told me ...' She caught her breath on a sob. 'He was so spiteful; he told me that Noah is going to marry a girl in Virginia called Hannah.' The pain of Noah's deceit sliced into her again; a pain so intense that she couldn't understand why it didn't kill her.

Susannah gasped. 'Is it true?'

'Noah never mentioned this to you?' William's lips set in a thin line and anger burned in his eyes.

Beth shook her head. 'I confronted him and he admitted it.'

'I am truly sorry,' said Susannah, 'but I can't see how this made Cecily so ill.'

'Joshua had spun Harry some tale that Cecily and I had large dowries. Whatever he said, Harry believed him. And so, after I refused him,' she drew a deep breath and steeled herself to look at her mother, 'he persuaded Cecily to elope with him.'

'God's teeth!' William stood up abruptly, scraping his chair on the floor.

'But when I ran after them and told Harry that Cecily has no dowry, he threw her aside just as if she were an old stocking. Cecily was distraught. She ...' Beth could hardly bring herself to say the words. 'She said she wanted to die and then threw herself in the river.'

Susannah covered her mouth with her hand to suppress a mew of distress, shock apparent in her eyes.

'I went in after her. The mud was all stirred up by the current and I couldn't see where she was. I kept diving under the water until at last I caught hold of her by her hair.' Beth sobbed as she relived that terrible moment. 'I tried to pull her up but our skirts were so heavy.' She closed her eyes, remembering. 'But then Noah came. If it hadn't been for Noah, she would have died,' concluded Beth, the words tumbling out of her.

'However badly Noah has behaved towards you,' said William, 'it seems we must be grateful to him.'

Beth wiped her eyes on the back of her hand. Admitting Noah's betrayal to her parents intensified her pain and she could no longer pretend to herself that it was all a horrible dream. He had gone and she would have to learn to live without him.

Chapter 38

September 1688

September came, bringing melancholy mists as a harbinger of the autumn to follow. Beth stayed a month at Merryfields. Cecily's recovery was slow but there were signs that her spirits were recovering. She still wept a great deal; a flow of soundless tears completely unlike the noisy and dramatic scenes of the past.

'I'm sorry, Beth,' she murmured one day. 'I've been a great trouble to you all, haven't I?

'We only want the old Cecily back again,' said Beth as she brushed her sister's hair.

'That Cecily has gone.' Her lip quivered. 'I was so selfish and vain then. All I could think of was shopping for fine clothes and dreaming of a husband who would give me a grand house. And you? Will you ever be able to forget Noah?'

Beth shook her head. 'But at least my way is clear now. I must continue with my painting and be the best artist I can be. An artist Johannes would have been proud of.' She spoke bravely but there was a great void in her insides.

'I'll never forget Harry, either. Not because I love him but because I must never forget the lesson he taught me. He was utterly heartless and used his cruel charm to bring me down.' The hint of a smile curved Cecily's lips. 'You may not believe me now but I shall dedicate myself to helping Mama and Father in their work. Dr Latymer said I could be of use to them.'

Dr Latymer had visited Merryfields every week to check on Cecily's progress. Afterwards, he and William could be seen walking around the gardens deep in conversation.

Beth hid her surprise. 'Then, do you not think it time to rise from your bed?'

Cecily clutched the sheet, pulling it up to her chin. 'I suppose I cannot be of use if I stay here.'

'Indeed not. Shall I help you to dress?' Beth held her breath.

There was a long pause. 'Thank you, Beth. I should like to come downstairs for dinner today.'

Cecily not only went downstairs for dinner but she managed to eat all her soup and a slice of plum tart. The guests fluttered around her like moths to a candle and she smiled through her tears as they welcomed her back to the world.

Beth was kept busy helping Peg and Jennet to preserve the great glut of orchard fruit. She peeled apples and plums and picked black-berries for pies and jellies until her fingers were stained purple. But in the whole month she never picked up a paintbrush once.

Restless, she sought out William in his study and found him in conversation with Dr Latymer.

'Ah, there you are, sweetheart!' said William. 'We've been dis-cussing a new treatment for the falling sickness that Edmund has read about. It may help Old Silas.'

'And there is another patient of mine who would benefit from a period of rest at Merryfields,' said Dr Latymer. 'I shall speak to her husband about it. He would be generous, I'm sure, if she could be helped. I'm convinced that the family atmosphere at Merryfields is what makes it so successful for the guests. When you compare your guests to the inmates of Bedlam ...' He closed his eyes and shuddered. 'The peace at Merryfields is incomparable and I relish my visits here. London is so full of turmoil at present. The King has suspended Parliament and the Prince of Orange is readying his troops to sail to England. So many of my patients are sick with the worry of what will happen to us all.'

'You are most welcome to visit us at Merryfields whenever you can escape your duties,' said William.

'Cecily is improving,' said Beth after the doctor had left, 'and I wish to return to Fulham Palace to continue my work. Autumn is upon us already and I've missed all the flowers that bloomed during the past month.'

William held out his hands to her. 'Must you go?'

'When I'm not working I have too much time to think,' she said, wondering again if Noah's ship had already arrived in Virginia.

The bakehouse was as warm as Judith's welcome.

'How I've missed you!' she said, pulling Beth into her floury embrace.

'What news? Tell me about Lizzie Skelton. Is she well again?'

'She is. And she's left the palace, thank the Lord! She was a troublemaker if ever there was one. Gone to the city to seek work as an actress, would you believe.'

'Perhaps she'll even be successful. I don't like her but I didn't wish to see her so badly stung.'

'After what she did to your paintings, she escaped lightly in my opinion.' Judith bent to take a tray of fragrant saffron buns out of the oven.

'What news have you of the Prince of Orange?'

'The whole world feels as if it's holding its breath, waiting,' Judith said. 'But the worst thing is the continual false alarms that he's landed. It feels as if we're all living on the edge of a precipice until he arrives.'

'The wind is still blowing in the east, so who knows when he'll be able to sail?' said Beth.

'They call it the Catholic wind.' Judith smiled grimly. 'And the weather will worsen the longer he leaves it.' She sighed. 'Ah well, best get on. Standing here worrying about it won't feed the household.'

Beth left the warm kitchen to hurry through the palace grounds. Autumn leaves, whipped up by a blustery wind, whirled and eddied around her feet as she traversed the quadrangle. Winter was not far away. Would the Prince of Orange's army ever be able to make the crossing?

Her thoughts turned again to Noah being tossed about on stormy seas on his long journey to Virginia. He'd said he suffered horribly from seasickness and she imagined him prostrated in his bunk, a stinking bucket by his side with no one to tend him. But perhaps he'd already arrived and was even now kissing Hannah Sharpe? The very thought of that pierced her to the quick.

A liveried manservant stood outside the Bishop's library. Beth recognised him at once as Forsyth.

'The Princess of Denmark was enquiring after you, Miss Ambrose,' he said, 'but Bishop Compton said you were away. Shall I announce you?'

Before she'd had time to think, Beth found herself curtsying to the Princess.

Princess Anne offered her hand. 'Beth, how delightful! I understood you had returned to Merryfields?'

'My sister was ill and I stayed with her until she recovered, Your Highness.' Beth dropped a curtsy to the Bishop.

'So the secret I asked you to keep is now common knowledge,' said the Princess.

'News that the Prince of Orange is readying his troops reached us even in the country at Merryfields.'

The Princess glanced at Bishop Compton, her sallow cheeks suffused with colour. 'There has been a report that the Prince of Orange will arrive weeks sooner than my sister had led me to believe. The King is in a state of the utmost consternation and has sent for reinforcements from Ireland and ordered the standing army in Scotland to march south.'

'The measure of the King's alarm is that he has offered to restore me to my former position,' said the Bishop with a wry smile. 'He says it is time for *old friends* to return to Court.'

'Will there be fighting when the Prince of Orange arrives?' said Beth.

'Inevitably,' replied the Bishop, 'but we hope that the strength of his forces will be great enough to persuade the King's army to lay down their weapons before there is too much bloodshed. I understand from Princess Mary that her husband's agents have taken steps to ensure that his forces will meet limited resistance.

'George and I are now firmly decided,' said Princess Anne, 'that we will stand with my sister and the Prince of Orange against the King. The Netherlands and England shall unite in a Protestant crusade against my father and the combined threat of the Catholics and King Louis of France. But meanwhile, George has accepted a position as an uncommissioned volunteer. It pays to keep close to one's enemies.'

'And what of the King's General, John Churchill?' asked Bishop Compton.

'Sarah Churchill has been my close friend since I was a child,' said the Princess, 'and we look into the secrets of each other's hearts. Lady Sarah and her husband will join with us.' She smiled. 'The King will be greatly displeased.'

Chapter 39

November 1688

It was the first week of November and Beth yawned as she stared out of the studio window. She'd slept badly due to a violent storm in Chelsea, which had banged the shutters all night long. A bitter wind, heralding winter, had whistled its way through the casements and moaned down the chimney. Sleepless, she'd huddled under the blankets, rigid with cold.

It had been two and a half months since Noah had left; two and a half long months for her to lie miserably awake each night and to stare unseeingly at a blank canvas by day.

The botanical paintings she had finished in the brief period when she thought Noah loved her were propped up on the shelf. Always self-critical, even she could see how confidently the paintings were rendered, each bloom so lifelike that the fragile petals begged to be touched.

And then there was her recent work. On the table was a vase containing a magnificent hothouse lily, the double form, shaded from saffron through ochre yellow to cinnabar, like a glorious sunset. On her easel rested her half-finished image of it. The painted petals might have been carved from wood and she'd carelessly smudged one of the leaves. She stared at it for an age, while the fear that she might never be able to paint again rose up until it nearly choked her.

In sudden despair she tore the canvas off the easel and threw it to the floor. She covered her eyes with her hands, tears of wretchedness seeping between her fingers.

Later, a sound outside made her wipe her eyes and glance out of the window again. As she watched, a man on a black horse galloped across the quadrangle, his spurs and sword a-jingle and his cloak flying behind. Beth pressed her forehead to the glass to see what was happening.

The horseman waved his hat in the air and shouted out the news for all to hear. 'The Prince of Orange has landed!'

Beth pushed open the casement and hung over the sill, watching the palace household pour out of the doorways to greet the messenger, cheering and calling out to him. They crowded around him, plying him with questions and pulling at his mud-spattered clothes to catch his attention.

Beth ran downstairs and caught up with Bishop Compton as he hurried across the quadrangle. The Bishop smiled briefly at her. 'News at last!' he said.

The messenger slid down from his horse, exhaustion plain to see on his ashen face.

'Robert Collier,' he said. 'I've ridden without stopping from Tor Bay to bring you the news.' Collier, barely more than a boy, swayed and closed his eyes.

'Give the man some air!' commanded the Bishop. 'Fetch hot wine and refreshments to the great hall.' He guided the lad indoors.

Beth and Judith joined the rest of the household gathered in the great hall, all eager to hear the news.

The Bishop stood on the dais with the messenger. 'Robert Collier here is come to give you an account of the Prince of Orange's armada,' he said.

Collier, his young face flushed, waited until the whispers and coughs died down. 'It was foggy,' he said. 'And then the wind blew away the mist and there were nigh on four hundred ships all crowded together.'

A cheer went up from the gardener's apprentices.

'I climbed to the top of the church tower in Brill to look out over Tor Bay. Storms were still sweeping down from the sea. The smaller ships, bucking in the rough water and shaking the spray out of their sails, were nigh overwhelmed.' Collier took a fortifying sip of wine and continued.

'A whole host of us ran down to the beach and saw the Prince of Orange and his guard disembark. They climbed up the hill to the south of the beach with their flags flying and trumpets playing. The soldiers, some dripping wet and others rolling and falling over from being so long at sea, left the ships and formed into their regiments.

'We watched as the ships were unloaded. You've never seen such piles of provisions: hay for the horses, tents, artillery and explosives! Horses, whinnying in terror, were lowered off the decks into the sea to swim ashore. The men of Brill cheered and women waved as the soldiers marched past, accompanied by drum, flute and trumpet.'

'And what of the King's fleet?' called out George London.

Collier shrugged. 'I heard that the same west wind, the *Protestant* wind, that sent the Dutch armada to us, pinned the King's fleet back in the estuary.'

A roar of approval reverberated around the great hall.

Bishop Compton held up his hand for silence.

'What will happen now?' shouted out Nicholas Tanner.

The Bishop waved a pamphlet in the air. 'This is a copy of a Declaration issued by the Prince of Orange. It says that his aim is to maintain the Protestant religion, install a free parliament and

354

investigate the legitimacy of the Prince of Wales. It is to be hoped that the King will cooperate.'

'And the Dutch army?'

'The Prince of Orange's army will march to Exeter, where they hope to remain while the soldiers and the horses refresh themselves. After that ... ' Bishop Compton shrugged. 'We will have to wait for news.'

When Beth arrived at Chelsea that evening she found Lady Arabella in a flood of tears with Sir George ineptly fluttering about her.

'My babies!' Lady Arabella clasped her hand dramatically against her brow. 'Joshua and Samuel have gone to war!' She began to wail, angrily brushing Sir George's ministering hands away.

Beth stared at her.

'Don't gawp at me like that!' shouted Lady Arabella. 'They left me a note! Can you imagine that? Their own mother and they left me a note!' She began to roll from side to side, tearing at her hair and uttering ululating cries.

Beth turned to Sir George. 'A measure of brandy, perhaps?' He nodded, his perpetual smile fixed, but his glance flickered from Beth and back to his keening wife with panic in his eyes. Beth pushed him in the direction of the decanter.

Lady Arabella had worked herself into a fine fit of hysterics and refused to be consoled. Beth tried speaking calmly to her, then with more authority, but her step-grandmother was far too engrossed in her troubles to listen. At last, Beth gave a mental shrug and slapped her, hard, on the cheek.

There was a deathly silence during which Beth took the opportunity to thrust Sir George's glass of brandy to Lady Arabella's lips before she could react.

Lady Arabella took a deep breath and then sank the brandy in one.

'The Prince of Orange has landed,' said Sir George. 'Joshua and Samuel have gone to aid His Majesty's cause.'

'The twins are no more suited to being soldiers than ...' Beth struggled to find the words, 'than a bumble bee!'

'Ah!' said Sir George, the smile back on his face again. 'But collect a swarm of bumble-bees together and you need to be very careful of their stings.'

Beth had no answer to that.

Beth wasn't entirely surprised when Joshua and Samuel turned up in Lady Arabella's drawing room again one day at the end of November.

'You can have no idea of how hard a camp bed can be,' complained Joshua.

'Or how cold,' added Samuel, as his mother cried tears of joy and pressed him to her bosom.

'Please tell me you haven't deserted?' begged Sir George in a dangerously quiet voice.

'Of course not!' Joshua raised his eyebrows. 'Why ever would you think such a dreadful thing of us? We've merely slipped away for a night or two in order to bring you the news.'

'Won't you be missed?' asked Beth.

'There's such confusion on Salisbury Plain that no one will notice,' said Samuel.

Sir George covered his eyes with his hand. 'And what news is so important that it causes you to abscond, albeit only for a night or two?'

'At least *we* didn't creep off in the dead of night to join the Dutch! But the Earl of Clarendon's son, Viscount Cornbury, did.'

'That was very ill of him,' said Sir George. 'He shall be sorry for it when the Prince of Orange runs home with his tail between his legs.'

Lady Arabella coughed and nodded meaningfully at Sir George, sending a glance at Beth. 'Beth, fetch my cream wool shawl, will you? It's turned a little chilly.'

Reluctantly, Beth rose to her feet.

'And ask Cook to send in a tray for the twins immediately. The chicken pie and the cold mutton will do.'

Beth hurried to the kitchens, seething that Arabella was sending her away when there was such interesting news to be heard.

'We was going to have that pie for our dinner,' grumbled Cook as she foraged in the larder.

Leaving her to it, Beth raced up the stairs two at a time in a way Lady Arabella would not have approved of and snatched the shawl from her lady's maid before running downstairs again. The drawing-room door was ajar so she had no qualms about peering through the narrow opening to listen to the conversation.

'The Prince of Orange has gained an additional twelve thousand recruits since he landed so His Majesty came to stiffen the troops by his presence . . . ' Samuel poured a glass of wine. 'But King James is taken very poorly. He has continual nosebleeds, great gushing fountains of blood, in spite of an ice-cold gate key placed down the back of his neck.'

'Everything is ice cold in the camp,' added Joshua. 'The royal physicians say it's a sickness of the spirit that the King suffers.'

'Are there other desertions?' asked Sir George.

Beth listened intently, hoping for news she could impart to Bishop Compton.

'You haven't heard the half of it!' Joshua drained his entire glass of wine in one gulp. 'There was Thomas Langston who was with the Duke of Alban's cavalry . . . '

'And the Duke of Grafton and Colonel Berkeley,' said Samuel, tucking into a monstrous great slice of chicken pie.

Sir George's smile wavered.

'Morale is very low amongst the men,' said Joshua, through a mouthful of boiled mutton. 'No one knows if his commanding officer or the man standing next to him is friend or traitor.'

'And we can all hear the King's lamentations coming from his tent. It's most unnerving.' Samuel put down his bread, as if he'd suddenly lost his appetite.

Joshua took up the story. 'And then, in the early hours of this morning, Lord Churchill went to join the Prince of Orange and his men at Axminster.'

'Closely followed by Prince George of Denmark.'

There was silence.

Then Sir George, not smiling at all and his face bone white, said, 'So now both the King's daughters and their husbands have abandoned him?'

Joshua shrugged, his cheek bulging with bread. 'His Majesty is expected to return to London in the next day or two but meanwhile he's given orders that both Princess Anne and Lady Sarah Churchill are to be arrested.'

Beth gasped. If the King thought that Princess Anne had betrayed him what dreadful fate might befall her?

'When?' asked Lady Arabella.

'Tonight. At the latest, tomorrow morning,' said Joshua. 'They will merely be kept under house arrest at first but Lady Sarah, at the least, will be sent to the Tower.'

'They must be prevented at all costs from joining their husbands!' said Sir George. 'How will it look for the King if both his daughters and the wife of his most important brigadier-general are supporting the Prince of Orange?'

An icy chill of fear gripped hold of Beth. Members of the royal family were not excluded from charges of treason. The Princess and Lady Sarah were in terrible danger.

'My dear,' said Sir George to his wife, 'I fear the tide may have turned against us.' He was unable to conceal the tremor in his voice. 'Go straight away to your maid and bid her pack. Tell the housekeeper to close up the house. We will leave for Windsor this very afternoon.'

Lady Arabella remained motionless for a moment. 'But if the Princess of Denmark and Sarah Churchill are restrained we have little to fear.'

'Quite so but nevertheless …' he drummed his fingers on the table. 'Nevertheless, I believe we will withdraw and remain at Windsor until matters become clear.'

Lady Arabella scraped back her chair and Beth shrank back behind the door as she hurried from the room without another word.

'As for you,' Sir George said to the twins, 'you had better return to Salisbury.'

'I suppose so,' said Samuel doubtfully.

'At least until it's clear on which side of the fence we prefer to sit.'

The twins and Sir George left the room. Beth was forgotten.

What should she do? What *could* she do? One thing was clear: the Princess must be warned and there was little time to lose. Suddenly spurred into action, she ran up the stairs as fast as her skirts would allow.

Hastily, she packed a bag, sweeping the items off the dressing table in one go and stuffing her clothes on top.

She found Lady Arabella in her bedchamber, surrounded by piles of petticoats, gloves and gowns, while her maid ran back and forth weeping all the while.

Barely turning to look at her, Lady Arabella merely said, 'We are returning to Windsor and you must go home.'

Beth lost no time. Luck was with her when she reached the landing stage and she hailed a boat heading for the city almost at once. Willing the boatman to row faster, she gripped the bag upon her knees so tightly that her knuckles were white, while thoughts whirled around in her head. How could she possibly accomplish what she had to do?

At last she made a plan. She scrambled off the boat at Whitehall stairs and hurried into the nearby New Exchange, where she bought a pretty box tied with a blue satin ribbon and filled with candied plums in paper cases. Scrabbling in her bag, she found a sketchbook and a stick of charcoal. She wrote a brief note and then, without hesitating, slipped off the Princess's sapphire ring. Wrapping the ring inside the note, she folded it as small as she could and slipped it into one of the paper cases before retying the ribbon around the box.

She hurried through the streets until she came to the rambling collection of buildings that made up Whitehall Palace. Unsure where to go, she asked one of the guards, who directed her through the gatehouse to the fourth door along. She found herself in a central courtyard garden with trees and rows of statues A cold wind snatched at her hair and she hugged her cloak closely around herself as she hurried to what she hoped would be the right place.

Taking a deep breath she knocked on the door. Two long minutes passed before the door opened to reveal a smartly dressed maid with frosty blue eyes.

'I am servant to Lady Sarah Churchill,' said Beth, holding up the box of candied fruits, 'and bring a small token of her esteem for the Princess of Denmark.'

The maid frowned. 'I don't know you.'

Beth smiled uneasily. 'I'm Lady Sarah's new maid and I was worried I'd come to the wrong door.' She spoke in a confidential tone. 'And I don't think I want to suffer the sharp side of my lady's tongue.'

The maid laughed and her expression softened. 'I hear she doesn't suffer fools gladly. She's lodging with her brother-in-law, the Earl of Tyrconnel, isn't she? When is she coming back here then?'

Beth shrugged. 'Maybe this evening. You know how it is; the mistress never tells you anything.' Beth glanced along the side of the building. 'There are so many doors and I don't know how I'll ever find my way out again.'

'You should have gone to the servants' entrance, which is the next door along,' said the maid. She held out her hands. 'But I'll take your package and make sure it's given to the Princess of Denmark, if you like?'

Beth clutched the beribboned box to her chest. 'I'd rather hand it to her myself.'

The maid laughed. 'The Princess doesn't receive *maids*!' She looked at Beth's crestfallen face. 'Don't worry! I'll deliver it. I'm Mary Forest, by the way.'

'And I'm ...Kate Smith.' There was nothing else for Beth to do but hand her the box of sugar plums.

By the time Beth had waited her turn for a boat at the public stairs, darkness had fallen. It was damply cold and eerily black on the river, with only the sound of the creaking rowlocks as the oars slipped in and out of the brackish-smelling water. A screech owl calling to its mate on the bank made her jump and the boatman laughed.

'What's a young maid like you a-doing out on your own in the dark?'

'My father is waiting for me,' she lied, suddenly anxious.

'Then I'd best deliver you safely, hadn't I?' He hawked and spat into the water before turning his attention back to his rowing.

There was a lantern on the landing stage at Fulham which she snatched up to guide her to the palace but she had gone no more than a few yards when the light flickered and died. She waited until her eyes adjusted to the darkness, then fumbled her way through the grounds. An icy wind rattled the branches of the trees and a fox slunk out of the bushes and streaked across the grass on its way to the chicken yard.

She found her way into the quadrangle and knocked on the porter's lodge.

'You're late, Miss. Shouldn't be out here all alone in the dark.'

'I need to speak to the Bishop. Is he here?'

'He arrived but ten minutes since.' The porter unhooked a ring of keys from the hook and made his way with measured steps across the courtyard to unlock the great entrance door to the palace.

Slipping into the hall, Beth raced along the passage to the library, wasting no time before knocking.

The Bishop opened the door wide. 'Miss Ambrose?'

'I came at once,' she said, 'I didn't know what else to do.'

'Tell me.' Henry Compton's voice was gentle.

'It's the Princess. She's going to be arrested.'

'How did you hear this?' He narrowed his eyes.

'I lodge with my step-grandmother, whose husband is Sir George Vernon.'

'Secretary to the Earl of Salisbury?'

Beth nodded. 'My uncles have been with the army on Salisbury Plain. They came this evening to tell Sir George of the desertion of the Prince of Denmark and Brigadier-General Churchill to the Prince of Orange's cause.'

'So soon? I wasn't expecting ... '

'I heard that the King is even now travelling to London but has sent orders for the arrest of Princess Anne and Lady Sarah tonight or tomorrow morning. I went straight to Whitehall to speak to her but the maid wouldn't let me in.'

'You did well to come and tell me.'

'I sent a message to the Princess. I said that she was to pretend to go to bed early and that you would come for her tonight.'

'Did you, by God!' He gave a shout of laughter.

'I was so frightened that harm might come to her.' Beth shivered and blew on her hands, still aching with cold from the river trip. 'Of course, she may not find the message. But I do know she can't resist sugared plums.'

The Bishop gave her a quizzical glance and then paced across the floor to stir the ashes of the fire into a blaze with the toe of his boot.

'What else did your uncles tell you, Miss Ambrose?'

Beth related the tales of confusion and disorder on Salisbury Plain and how the King suffered from debilitating nosebleeds.

'Since there have been so many desertions already, the Prince of Denmark and Lord Churchill must have decided to act even sooner than planned,' said Bishop Compton. 'But that leaves us with the difficulty of removing the Princess and Lady Sarah to a place of safety. I thought we had several days yet.'

'I came as soon as I could.'

Bishop Compton squeezed her shoulder. 'You did the right thing.' His kindly eyes bored into her. 'But I believe I have to ask you for further help before I can convey the princess to Nottingham.'

'Anything!'

'Good girl!' I am known in Whitehall and if I go to fetch the Princess at this late hour, His Majesty's servants will be suspicious. I cannot risk precipitating her arrest.'

'What can I do?'

'A maidservant may pass unnoticed in Whitehall Palace.'

'And you wish me to fetch the Princess to you?'

Bishop Compton smiled. 'I always knew you were quick. Will you do this?'

'Of course but we must hurry!'

'I will send George London with you but the coach will have to remain out of sight of the palace. Lady Sarah will be in her apartment ... '

'No, she is not. I believe her to be with the Earl of Tyrconnel at present.'

'Then I will warn Lady Sarah and join you later at Whitehall. Lady Sarah's children have already been sent to the country.'

'How will I find the Princess? I should have asked her to meet us outside Whitehall.'

The Bishop shook his head. 'The King's servants spy on her and anything out of the ordinary will be immediately reported to the Queen. No, you did the right thing because now we know she will be in her bedchamber with a maid on a truckle bed outside her door.'

'Then how will I reach her?'

'Earlier this year, when the Prince was born, I suggested to the Princess and Lady Sarah that we make provision for an event such as this. And my instinct has proved right. There is now a secret staircase between the closet in the Princess's bedchamber and that of Lady Sarah's apartment below.'

'No one knows of this?'

'Only the Princess, Lady Sarah and myself. And, of course, the carpenter who has now gone to join the Prince of Orange's men at Axminster.'

'So I must go into Lady Sarah's apartment and reach the Princess by the secret stairs?' She pushed away the terrifying thought of what might happen to her if she was caught.

'Precisely!'

Chapter 40

It wasn't until later, when Beth was hanging on to the straps as the coach shuddered and jolted its way through the dark on the road to Whitehall, that she wondered how she was to gain access to Lady Sarah's apartment. Lady Sarah wouldn't be there and the door would be locked. Perhaps she could throw stones up at the Princess's window and she would come down the secret stair and let herself out? But how would she know the right window?

These uneasy thoughts rolled around in her head as she fought back nausea while the carriage bounced along the rutted road at break-neck speed.

After some time the coach slowed and lights were to be glimpsed outside. Beth rubbed away her frozen breath from the window and peered into the dark.

At last they came to a halt with only a creaking sound to be heard as the swaying coach settled on its leather straps. Then it rocked violently as George London jumped down from his perch on top and wrenched open the door.

Beth released her fierce grip on the hanging strap and climbed unsteadily down to the ground. 'My bones are nearly rattled to pieces,' she said.

A number of carriages bowled past and three men, arm in arm and singing a bawdy ditty, emerged from a nearby tavern. Two ladies of the night called to them from the shadows.

'Charing Cross,' said George London, his breath clouding the icy air. 'I daren't take the coach any closer. The Bishop will be here soon with Lady Sarah. Will you be all right?'

Beth nodded, feeling far from all right.

George London led her across the road. 'You need to cut across there, between those two trees, and you'll come to Whitehall. Go through a small archway and you'll find a garden with statues.'

'I know it,' said Beth, through teeth chattering with cold and apprehension.

'We'll be waiting for you.'

Keeping to the shadows, she set off, her palms suddenly damp with fear. She hurried between the two trees to find the Palace of Whitehall in front of her, its white stonework gleaming in the pale moonlight. Ranks of doors and windows punctuated the front face of the building and she hesitated, wondering which way to turn. Turning left, she walked swiftly along until she reached the corner. She had approached from the other side earlier in the day and didn't recognise anything. Where was the archway?

She retraced her steps, taking it more slowly, until she found it. She turned the iron handle, making it squeak loudly into the night. Glancing over her shoulder, she paused only long enough to see that she was unobserved, then entered the garden.

A group of men chatted together, not far from where she stood; she hesitated but they were arguing a point with good-natured laughter and no thought for anyone but themselves.

Taking a deep breath, she skirted close to the edge of the build-ing, walking purposefully with her head down, just as if she had every right to be there. Once she had reached the opposite side of the courtyard, she counted the doors until she reached the fifth one.

She tried the handle with shaking hands and barely suppressed a gasp as it opened. Standing motionless in the pool of dim light which spilled from the doorway, her heart thumping in her chest, she fought down an almost irresistible desire to run away, to return to Merryfields and never leave the safety of its walls again.

Footsteps clipped along the path and Beth glanced wildly around to see a cloaked man striding towards her. Without any other thought than to escape, she jumped over the step and closed the door behind her. She leaned against it, the pulse in her throat nearly choking her.

Outside, the footsteps marched past and faded into the distance and she breathed again. A long passage stretched out ahead of her, dimly lit by candle ends set on sconces at intervals along the walls. Green doors lined the passage on each side. Panic almost overwhelmed her. How could she possibly know which one led to Lady Sarah's apartment?

She tiptoed to the first door and listened. A mumble of voices came from behind it, followed by a shout of laughter. Not that one; Lady Sarah was away so the apartment would be empty. The sound of a viol came from the next door but the one after that was silent and no light came from underneath it. Stealthily, she turned the handle.

'Oh, it's you!'

Beth let go of the handle as if it were a red-hot coal and spun around, her knees quivering like junket.

The maid she had met earlier in the day stood there with a pile of folded laundry in her arms. 'What are you doing?' A frown wrinkled her forehead.

Beth took a deep breath. 'Oh Mary! It is Mary, isn't it?' she gabbled. 'I'm so pleased to see you. Lady Sarah asked me to come on ahead and prepare for her arrival but I have no idea which is the right door.'

'But Lady Sarah arrived an hour or two since.'

Beth stared at her in dismay. The Bishop must not have reached Lady Sarah in time to warn her.

Beth had to think fast. 'Then I'm in a great deal of trouble, aren't I?' she wailed. She clasped her hands to her breast. 'Mary, what am I to do? I don't know London at all, I come from a little village in the country, and I became so lost. And a most disrespectful man jumped out of an alley and made an improper suggestion to me and I ran away and couldn't find my way back. What if my lady turns me off without a reference?' Tears of genuine fright rolled down her face.

'Here!' Mary thrust a clean handkerchief at her from the pile of laundry she carried. 'She might not be too angry. But you'd better catch up with your duties sharpish. Follow me!'

Still sniffing, Beth followed Mary's neat figure along the passageway until she stopped outside a door. 'There's no light inside. Perhaps you're lucky and Lady Sarah is upstairs with the Princess of Denmark. She might not even have missed you.' Mary held out her hand. 'Key?'

A scarlet tide rose up Beth's face as she struggled to find a plausible explanation for its absence. She bent her head and fumbled for her pocket, drawing it out through the placket in her skirt. Pulling the drawstring open, she whispered, 'It's gone!'

'Are you surprised?' Mary's mouth was disapproving. 'Look at the size of that hole in your pocket! You're going to have to change your ways, my girl, if you're to work for a fine lady like Lady Sarah! What was she thinking of to employ such a country bumpkin? Wait here!' She bustled off down the corridor.

Beth tucked her pocket away again with shaking hands, thanking the Lord that she'd been too lazy to repair it.

Another serving maid came along and glanced at Beth curiously.

Dry-mouthed, Beth smiled to cover her anxiety and watched with relief as the maid entered another door.

Mary was a long time returning.

Sick with nerves, Beth tried the handle of the service door to Lady Sarah's apartment, wondering if she could put her shoulder to it and break it down. But, even if she had the strength, the noise would bring everyone running. In desperation, she knocked quietly at the door but no one answered.

Then she heard Mary's soft-soled shoes coming along the passage.

'I borrowed this but I must take it back straight away,' Mary said, putting the key in the lock.

It turned with a satisfying *clunk* and Beth sent up a silent prayer of thanks as Mary pushed open the door. Beth glanced into the darkness, suddenly afraid again.

'For goodness' sake!' Mary snatched up a candlestick from a nearby shelf and pushed it into Beth's hands. 'Now go!'

'Thank you. I don't know how I'd have managed without you.'

'Neither do I.' Mary's smile softened the tartness of her words.

Quaking from the top of her head to the tip of her toes, Beth slipped into the apartment and closed the door behind her.

She stood in the darkness, every muscle tense, listening. Somewhere outside a dog barked but inside the apartment the air was heavy with silence. There was faint smell of decaying vegetation. Slowly, she lifted her guttering candle and looked around.

Furniture loomed up from the shadows, a large cabinet, a day bed and a round table on which rested a vase of dead flowers. Suddenly a hint of movement caught her eye and she froze. A woman stood on the other side of the room, watching her. Beth exhaled in a shuddering gasp and lifted the candlestick higher, as did the other woman. A mirror. Her reflected self clutched a hand to her breast.

Moonlight fell from the window and painted a pale lozenge on the floor. Beth took a step forward, skirting around it. A door. Slowly, slowly, she lifted the latch but the scraping sound of it echoed all around her and she remained motionless, ears straining into the darkness, but there was nothing but silence.

The rug under her feet was thick and luxurious and the room she

369

entered carried the expensive bouquet of orris root, attar of roses and face powder. A lady's bedchamber. Her heart thudded wildly in her breast and she breathed so shallowly that a feather a few inches before her face would not have stirred. She pressed her back against the wall, gathering the courage to leave its safety and venture across the floor. The bulky shape of the bed emerged in the flickering candlelight and Beth ran her fingers down the heavy damask drapes, crusted with embroidery.

Where was the secret stair? She hadn't thought, until now when it was too late, to ask the Bishop how to find it. The bedchamber appeared perfectly square with no possible place for a hidden staircase. Fear fluttered under her bodice. She could not return without the Princess and Lady Sarah.

She tiptoed all around the bedchamber as cautiously as a cat, feeling for a jib door in the panelling but without success. Her nerves stretched to breaking point, she began to press and pull frantically at the mouldings, searching for a hidden catch. It was no good. Her breath came fast as she fought down the rising panic. How long would it be before the King's men arrived? If she didn't find the stair the Princess and Lady Sarah could not avoid arrest. Lady Sarah would certainly be taken to the Tower and beheaded. Even the Princess would not be immune from the King's anger. And Beth Ambrose would be to blame.

Taking a deep breath, she stopped scrabbling at the panelling. The marble of the chimney piece was cold under her hands as she clung to it for support. Studying the bedchamber again, she suddenly remembered Noah's drawings of the house he wanted to build in Virginia. There had been alcoves on either side of the carved chimneypiece. There were no recesses beside this fireplace, only a flat wall hung with tapestries. That was it!

She pulled aside the tapestry to the left of the chimneypiece and found the door straight away. Almost sobbing in relief, she opened it and stared in disbelief at the small chamber, empty save for a broken chair and a chest. No staircase. She backed out of the room and went to the right of the chimneypiece to snatch aside the other tapestry. Yes! Another door. She wrenched it open, whimpering in relief when her candle illuminated a narrow, winding staircase.

The treads were treacherously steep and there was no handrail. Holding her skirts bunched up in one hand and the candle in the other, she climbed the stairs, stopping at the top before another door. Slowly, she lifted the latch and pushed the door against the heavy tapestry that covered it.

Another dark room, lit only by coals glowing in the grate. She'd expected to find Princess Anne waiting for her. Holding the candle high, she surveyed the bedchamber. The bedlinen was thrown back as if the Princess had risen in haste and a chair was overset on the floor. A picture hung askew and a glass lay on its side on the dressing table. Milk still dripped over the edge on to the rug.

Dread rose in Beth's throat. Had the Princess already been snatched from this place and transported to the Tower? Then a tiny noise, a mere whisper of sound, made her head jerk up as she strained to listen. There it was again! She crept across the carpet and lifted a corner of the tapestry which hung on the wall to the left of the chimneypiece. She ran her fingers over the wall seeking, and finding, a recessed handle to the jib door. As she pulled the door open, there came a muffled sob.

Princess Anne, terror upon her face, and a weeping Lady Sarah huddled together on the floor in the corner of the closet.

Relief flooded over Beth.

Princess Anne sobbed again and held out her arms. 'Beth, thank God it's you! We thought they'd come for us.'

Beth helped the two women to their feet. 'We must go quickly.'

'Prince George and Lord Churchill left us behind,' said the Princess, gripping Beth's hand so hard that she winced. 'They went to join the Prince of Orange sooner than expected and they left us behind!'

371

Beth heard the rising edge of hysteria in her voice and spoke as calmly as she was able. 'Bishop Compton is waiting for you but we must leave quietly now.

'What if the King's men find us?' Lady Sarah trembled so violently that her teeth chattered. 'I don't care if my husband's estates are forfeit but my children are in the country. The guard came to the Earl of Tyrconnel's house and placed me under house arrest this afternoon.'

'Lady Sarah slipped away to warn me,' whispered the Princess.

Convulsed by another fit of weeping Lady Sarah clasped her hands over her belly. 'If they take me to the Tower what will happen to my children? Will they behead me even before this babe is born?'

'We must be very quiet and not let the soldiers catch us,' said Beth in as brave a voice as she could manage. 'Any of us.' The prospect of being left to rot in the Tower or being taken to the scaffold herself made it hard to breathe. 'Come!' She held out her hands to them.

'Where are we going? I have nothing with me,' said the Princess.

'There's no time!' Fear made Beth speak sharply. 'Fetch your plainest cloak and then we must hurry. The King returns to London so we must outpace him.'

The Princess and Lady Sarah put on their cloaks, standing still like obedient children while Beth pulled up their hoods.

'Ready?' she said.

'Wait!' The Princess turned back to her chest and lifted out her jewel case. She scooped out handfuls of glittering necklaces, bracelets and rings, stuffed them into a small cloth bag and thrust the whole into her pocket.

Barely able to contain her impatience, Beth led the two women down the staircase into Lady Sarah's apartment. 'Stay here while I look outside.' Very carefully, Beth opened the door to the service corridor just a crack. She heard footsteps and hastily closed it again.

The footsteps died away.

Beth edged the door open again and listened. Hearing nothing, she peered through the crack. The corridor was deserted. 'Now!' she said.

They slipped into the corridor and hastened towards the outside door. Beth's mouth was dry, her hands clammy with fear. Every footstep resounded in her head and her back crawled as she imagined a thousand eyes watching her. She drew the door bolts with shaking hands, glancing fearfully over her shoulder to see if the grating of the metal had alerted the servants. The cold night air had never been so welcome. The courtyard garden was deserted but Beth fought down her longing to run hell for leather straight across it and instead guided her charges around the perimeter in the darkest shadows. She could hear Princess Anne's breath coming in shallow pants.

At last they reached the gate in the wall and then they were running, running across the frosted grass, through the trees towards Charing Cross as if the hounds of hell were behind them.

Two men materialised out of the darkness and came purposefully towards them. One caught at Beth's arm and she yelped and gave him a sharp kick to his shin before she was able to shake him free. He swore under his breath and snatched hold of Lady Sarah.

The Princess shrieked and struggled in the arms of the other man.

'Let her go!' Beth rained blows on to the head and shoulders of Princess's attacker. She was damned if she was going to assist the Princess in escaping from the King's men only to allow her to be ravished by a common felon.

The assailant let go of the Princess and turned his attentions to Beth, imprisoning her arms in her cloak and holding her close to his chest in a grip of iron.

'Run!' Beth screamed to the Princess, increasing her struggles to free herself.

'Be still, you little hellcat!'

Beth kicked and squirmed. The assailant's mouth was close to her ear, his breath on her cheek. 'Stop it and I'll let you go. It's me, George London.'

Beth became still. 'How could you!' she spat. 'You scared us half to death!'

George London turned her to face the other man. 'There's no time to waste.'

'The Princess has a fine defender in you, Miss Ambrose,' said Bishop Compton.

The Princess leaned on one of his arms and Lady Sarah on the other.

'Please, let us leave at once.' Lady Sarah's voice trembled.

Beth's heart still raced but her knees had turned to jelly and she was grateful for George London's support as he and the Bishop escorted them to the waiting coach.

Lady Sarah, half swooning, was carried into the coach by George London and the Princess settled opposite her.

Beth stood back as George climbed up on to the top of the coach.

Bishop Compton took Beth's shaking hand. 'You have been fearless tonight, Miss Ambrose.'

'On the contrary,' she said, 'I have never been so terrified in all my life.'

The Bishop raised her hand to his lips. 'The mark of true courage is to do what you believe to be right, no matter what the consequences and no matter how frightened you are. I salute you.'

Unable to speak for fear of tears, Beth only nodded.

'Now hurry up and climb into the coach,' said the Bishop. We're going to Nottingham. You didn't think I would abandon you in the middle of the night on the wicked streets of London, did you?'

In the moonlight Beth caught a glimpse of his teeth as he smiled.

'Though I fear for any footpad who meets *you* in the dark,' he added, rubbing his bruised shin.

The coach began to roll away even before the door banged shut.

Beth looked out of the window to see the Bishop mount his horse, Lucifer, his sword glinting against his thigh. Really, she thought as they careered off into the night, Bishop Compton was much more of a soldier than a man of God.

Chapter 41

December 1688

A few days before Christmas, two horsemen clattered up the lane and set up a great hullabaloo until Joseph ran to unlock the gate.

'It's the twins!' said Cecily, peering out of the solar window.

Joshua and Samuel blew into Merryfields like a whirlwind, bringing in great draughts of cold air with them and dropping clumps of mud from their boots all over the floors.

'We're off to join the Prince of Orange's men at Nottingham,' said Joshua.

'Changing horses?' asked William, with an ironic lift of his eyebrow.

'It's chaos in London. Not at all safe to be out in the streets. Riots and burnings everywhere,' said Samuel. 'All the Catholic churches are being pulled down by the rabble. It shows a great lack of judgment to be a papist at this time. Even Mama agrees it's time to change sides.'

'The Queen and the Prince of Wales escaped to France last week,' said Joshua. 'She disguised herself as a washerwoman and the baby Prince as a bundle of laundry, would you believe? The King has flown the nest and thrown the Great Seal into the Thames. Lord Salisbury's house has been sacked and ...'

'The King has gone?' asked William.

'Flown like a bird!' said Joshua. 'Once his nosebleeds stopped he travelled back to London to find that the Princess of Denmark and Lady Sarah Churchill had escaped to join the Prince of Orange at Nottingham.' He struck a pose with his hand to his brow. 'The King fell into a fit and cried out, "God help me, my own children have forsaken me!"'

'That was his turning point; the moment when he knew all was lost,' said Samuel.

William glanced at Beth.

'The stuffing was quite knocked out of him,' continued Joshua. 'It quickly became apparent that he was in no fit mental state to be king any more. Convinced that he'd be beheaded like his father!'

'And what of the Prince of Orange?' asked Beth.

'He's made no claim to the throne. There's been little bloodshed. But the nation hasn't a king.' Samuel shrugged. 'Or a parliament. *Someone* needs to take control.'

'And what's the point in supporting King James if he isn't here? By fleeing, isn't that tantamount to an abdication?'

'I don't understand,' said Cecily.

'It means,' said Samuel kindly, 'that since King James, the *former* King James, has gone, together with the young Prince of Wales, Princess Mary is heir to the throne again.'

'And of course, as her husband and in the line of succession in his own right, who knows but if the Prince of Orange will share the throne with her?'

The twins stayed for the night and prepared to leave in the morning for Nottingham with their saddlebags stuffed with bread, apples and half a ham.

The family gathered in the frosty courtyard to say goodbye to them.

'There was something I meant to tell you, Beth,' said Samuel. 'I've had news of Harry de Montford.'

A shiver, which had nothing to do with the cold weather, passed down Beth's back.

'He's gone. Married a Catholic heiress. Her father couldn't wait to get her out of the city and to safety.'

'Safety! With Harry?'

'They sailed to Virginia last week.' Joshua gave Beth one of his irrepressible smiles. 'She's a shrew with a sharp tongue by all accounts.'

'Then I have no compunction in hoping she causes him to suffer a lifetime of scoldings!'

The twins waved their hats in the air and galloped away.

Susannah closed her eyes and sighed. 'I tried my best with them,' she said, 'but they clearly owe much to their mother.'

William drew Beth to his side as they walked back into the house. She leaned against him, happy at their new-found closeness since Bishop Compton had sent for him and he had travelled to Nottingham to bring her safely home.

'How does it feel to know that your swift and brave action in helping the Princess to escape has changed the destiny of the nation?' he asked.

Beth thought for a moment. 'It might never have happened, of course, if the Princess hadn't found my note.' She smiled. 'I knew her sweet tooth would lead her to it hidden in the box of sugar plums.'

***

Further excitement ensued that afternoon when a cart rolled into the courtyard bearing a number of large crates. The carter was insistent that the consignment was to be given only to Miss Beth Ambrose.

'This is for you, miss,' he said, pulling a small packet from his mud-spattered cape.

Curious, Beth turned the packet over in her hand to see a great red seal fastening it.

'What is it? Who sent it, Beth?' Cecily jumped up and down in excitement.

Carefully, Beth broke the seal and took out a letter.

My dear Beth

There are not the words to thank you enough for what you have done for me and for Lady Sarah. We are now quite recovered from that terrible, rackety journey through the night and are safely back in the arms of our husbands.

I shall never forget seeing your sweet face when you crept up the secret stair to find Lady Sarah and myself huddled together in my closet in desperate fear for our lives. And I shall never forget dear Bishop Compton galloping alongside the coach, pistols and swords in his belt, ready to defend us to the death! I count myself most fortunate in my friends.

It isn't clear yet what the future holds but now that the King has run to France, I dare to hope for better times for us all.

Please accept the enclosed as a token of my gratitude. In addition, please tell your dear father that I intend to make over a sum of money to him, sufficient to continue his excellent work at Merryfields, now and in the future.

Beth drew in her breath sharply and glanced at William before turning back to the letter.

The boxes contain some gifts for your family, the guests and servants at Merryfields in the hope that they will have the best Christmas dinner they have ever eaten.

A very merry Christmastide to you all!

I remain, your good friend,

Anne

Beth handed the letter to William to read and then tipped out the contents of the packet. A stream of blue ice tumbled into her palm.

Cecily gasped and Susannah's eyes widened.

As Beth lifted up the necklace blue fire sparked from the sapphire droplets in the winter sunshine.

Speechless, she turned to her mother.

Taking the necklace, Susannah fastened it around Beth's slender neck. 'A perfect match for your beautiful eyes, my dear.'

William caught Beth up into a silent bear hug, his face crumpled with emotion and quite unable to speak. 'You have saved us all!' he whispered at last. He reached out for Susannah's hand. 'The Princess is to support us financially in our work at Merryfields.'

Susannah gasped and fell into William's arms and her children were delighted and embarrassed when he returned her kisses with particular attention.

Emmanuel and Joseph carried the crates into the kitchen and the guests and servants crowded around as John and Cecily ripped open the first one. Cries of delight greeted the discovery of a haunch of venison.

Peg and Sara set to work opening the remaining crates to reveal a baron of beef, a dozen fine capons, a whole Nottinghamshire ham, a large cask of ale, a smaller one of wine, a great fig pudding and last, but not least, a box of sugar plums for each member of the household.

'Oh my! Merryfields will never see another Christmas such as this!' breathed Peg.

Beth woke early on Christmas morning with her heart as heavy as lead. The excitement of the previous day had waned and she could no longer escape the fact that Noah would be sure to have married his Hannah by now. She imagined him looking at his new wife with love in his eyes, or worse, kissing her with a passion that need not be checked. He was lost to her for ever. Too miserable to cry, she lay staring at the cracks in the ceiling, remembering the way his mouth turned up at the corners when he was trying not to laugh and how he had rocked her in his arms and kissed her with such passion when he found her kneeling amongst the ruins of her paintings. Surely the tenderness he had shown her then had not been false, even if he had afterwards made her false promises? But life had to go on, however painful.

She glanced at Cecily lying beside her, rosy with sleep. Beth stroked the tangled black hair off her brow, thankful that she was no longer so dreadfully thin and waxy pale but restored to her former looks. Shocked out of her tempestuous ways by her disastrous entanglement with Harry de Montford, her little sister was beginning to grow up at last. As she recovered, she had amazed her family by the number of hours she spent amusing the guests and charming them out of the doldrums.

Sighing, Beth rose and dressed in one of the gowns that Princess Anne had given her. Unhappiness had made her thin; she had to lace the sky blue bodice extra tightly. She clasped the exquisite sapphire necklace around her neck, feeling it cool and heavy against her throat.

Hesitating only a moment, she pulled back the froth of exquisite lace at her wrist and slipped on Noah's bracelet. Tears threatened to engulf her again as she ran her fingers over the clasped hands and she had to breathe deeply until the threat had gone. She was determined to put on a smile and not spoil Christmas day for the rest of the family.

Downstairs in the kitchen, preparations for the feast were already under way and Beth was cheered by the comforting aroma of cinnamon and orange peel as the figgy pudding bubbled away on the fire.

Orpheus had stationed himself near the spit, his nose twitching at the mouth-watering scent of roasting venison.

Dr Latymer arrived in time to accompany the family to church where the familiar rituals of hymns and readings soothed Beth's wretchedness enough that she was able to greet old friends and neighbours with a smile.

Home again at Merryfields, Dr Latymer and William went to talk in the study, while Cecily disappeared into the garden to collect greenery to decorate the festive table.

Beth and Susannah folded napkins and set little gifts of lavender-scented hand cream for the ladies, peppermint lozenges for the menfolk and a box of the Princess's sugar plums beside every place setting.

John and Old Silas carried in the yule log with a great deal of huffing and puffing, while Peg fussed around them clearing up the scatterings of earth and twigs that followed in their wake.

At last the festive meal was ready and the guests and family filed into the great hall to take their places.

John linked his arm through Beth's. 'I w-w-wonder what Kit is doing today?' he said. 'Perhaps he's having his Christmas dinner with Noah?'

'And Hannah,' said Beth.

John flushed scarlet. 'I'm sorry, Beth, I didn't mean to upset you.'

William, Susannah and Dr Latymer took their places just as Clarence Smith, his crown, decorated with a sprig of holly, stood up to say grace.

'And may peace be with you all!' he finished. 'Let the feasting begin!'

Chairs scraped and lively conversation broke out as the guests and family fell upon the wondrous dishes set out before them.

'I do hope Poor Joan won't make herself sick with all those sugar plums,' whispered Cecily.

Beth smiled a little at the blissful expression on Poor Joan's face. After everyone had finished their figgy pudding William stood up and tapped his glass with a knife until the chatter ceased. 'Shall we raise our glasses to the Princess of Denmark, who sent us a never-to-be-forgotten Christmas dinner and whose generosity will always be remembered.'

The babble of voices rose up to the rafters until William tapped his knife on the glass again. 'And now I have an announcement to make.' He turned to face Dr Latymer. 'Dr Latymer has become known to you all over the past weeks and in the New Year he will be taking up residence here at Merryfields to assist me in my work.'

A rousing cheer went up from the guests.

Then Old Silas took out his fiddle and Joseph joined in with his penny whistle.

'Edmund is a good man, isn't he?' said Cecily as they watched the others dancing. 'I couldn't see it at first but he's worth ten, no, a hundred, of Harry de Montford. And did you know,' she whispered, 'not only does he have a private income but he's the third son of the Earl of Wimbourne?'

'Cecily?' laughed Beth. 'Have you developed a fondness for him?'

'I'm in no rush,' Cecily said. 'But I could do a lot worse, couldn't I?' Her eyes sparkled. 'Perhaps I'll catch him under the mistletoe kissing bunch and see what he's made of?'

John whirled Poor Joan around the floor and then Clarence Smith stood in front of Beth. He held on to his crown as he bowed and took her hand for the next dance.

Afterwards, retreating to a chair at the back of the hall, Beth sipped a glass of wine, staring contemplatively into its ruby depths. She pictured Johannes's kindly face as he sat beside her last Christmas. She had once thought she would never recover from his loss but her happy memories of him lived on. Of course, he would be deeply disappointed in her now, angry even, that without Noah she was too miserable to paint.

Finishing her second glass of wine her head began to spin as she watched Susannah and William, Sara and Joseph, Cecily and

Edmund, Emmanuel and Peg; all of them laughing with happiness as they danced together. The music became strident and discordant to her ears and misery flooded over her as she tormented herself again with a picture of Hannah enfolded in Noah's arms, under the mistletoe. At last, unable to bear it any longer, she slipped from the room.

She ran upstairs, away from the smoky warmth of the great yule log and the merry voices, heading blindly for the studio. Once inside, she opened her sketchbook to look again at the drawing she had made of Noah. She touched the picture of his sleeping face with a deep longing that pierced her soul. Recalling those happy days sitting under the oak beside the moat, she buried her face in her hands and broke into racking sobs. She wept for the loss of Noah's love and companionship, for the disfigurement of his handsome face and for the artistic gift that she had cherished, that now eluded her. Most of all she wept for the loss of their future together in the house that Noah would build, each allowing the other the time and space for their particular creative talents to flourish.

When all the tears had gone, Beth felt as light and hollow as an empty eggshell. Shivering in the bitter cold of the studio, she faced Johannes's portrait of her. She could hardly bear to look at it. Her painted face was radiant with the expectation of happiness, in cruel contrast to her current condition. And Johannes's tiny portrait reflected in the painted mirror seemed to glower at her in disappointment.

She reached out a finger to touch him. 'I'm sorry, Johannes,' she whispered. 'After all your training, I have failed you. I accomplished my best work when I was secure in Noah's love and the sorrow that has possessed my heart since he left allows no space for my talent.'

Then a sudden draught on the back of her neck made her turn.

A figure stood in the open doorway.

Beth gasped. She became icy cold, with a rushing noise in her ears

like an ocean coming to carry her away. Shadows crowded in on her
vision before a great, whirling vortex snatched hold of her and her
knees buckled.

Strong hands caught her up and she found her face pressed
against his shoulder. His coat carried with it the scent of sea salt and
tar and smoke.

'I thought you were a ghost!' she said.

'Do I feel like a ghost?' He turned his face away so that she could
not see the long red scar on his cheek.

She struggled to release herself but he held her firmly. 'What are
you doing here!' Her voice was sharp but her heart was fluttering
like a song bird trying to escape its cage.

'Is that any kind of a welcome? I've brought you a letter. From
Kit.' He let go of her and reached into his coat. Taking it from him
with shaking hands, she started to read.

My dear Beth
The most important news is to tell you of my great
happiness. I am married now to the sweetest girl you could
imagine.

She glanced at Noah, who looked back at her with anxious eyes. Was
everyone in the world to be happy except herself?

'Read it,' he said, his face pale and his jaw tense.

Overcome with shame at her selfish response to Kit's exciting
news, Beth turned back to the letter.

My happiness is all due to Noah and I thank him from the
bottom of my heart since I did not believe there could be an
honourable outcome. I had resigned myself to never
achieving my heart's desire but when Noah arrived in
October all my dreams came true.

Hannah and I had fallen in love . . .

It felt to Beth as if the ground under her feet had shifted and she reached out to her work table to steady herself.

> Hannah and I had fallen in love and were in the depths of despair since she had been promised to Noah almost since they were children. When he came to beg her to release him, our joy knew no bounds.
>
> My dear Beth, if you and Noah are half as joyful as Hannah and myself, I could not wish for anything better.
>
> My best wishes and love
>
> Your brother, Kit
>
> PS Hannah sends you her love, too.

Beth clutched the letter to her breast, hope erupting like a volcano inside her. She risked a glance at Noah.

His face was still half-turned away from her and his amber eyes were apprehensive as he waited for her to speak.

Gently, Beth ran a finger down the scar on his cheek. 'It makes you look like a pirate,' she said, smiling.

He captured her hand and kissed her palm. 'Have you ever heard of a seasick pirate?'

A quiver of desire ran through her as his lips moved slowly over the delicate skin on the inside of her wrist, leaving a trail of little kisses. 'Was the journey very terrible?'

'The greatest proof of my love for you must be that I undertook that sea voyage twice in three months. The ground is still rolling.'

'So you do love me?' Her pulse echoed in her ears and her mouth was dry.

Noah let out his breath. 'Beth, I loved you from the first day I saw you. I knew you were my soul mate. Of course, since I was betrothed to Hannah, I fought against it and, in any case, I believed you had vowed to shun all men in order to dedicate yourself to Art. It was a torment to love you so and see your sweet face so puzzled and unhappy when I drew away.'

'What about Hannah?'

'She's like a dear sister to me. Our parents always had in mind we'd make a match and there didn't seem to be any reason not to marry her. Until I met you.'

'It tore me apart not knowing if you loved me.'

'I never wanted to hurt you. When I realised that you loved me, I knew then that I had to return to Virginia to throw myself upon Hannah's mercy.' He cupped her chin in his hands and kissed her gently, his mouth soft and warm. 'I've had long hours on a storm-tossed sea to plan a speech but seeing you again has made me forget every word of it. The only thing I want to say is, Beth Ambrose, light of my life and my heart's desire, will you marry me?'

Joy and peace blossomed in her heart and a smile lit up her face. 'On one condition,' she said.

'Anything!'

'I have a fancy to live in a little house on the side of a hill covered in wild flowers somewhere in Virginia.'

With a shout of delight Noah hugged her to his chest, covering her face with kisses.

Over his shoulder, Beth caught sight of Johannes's portrait. She wasn't sure but she would have sworn that he smiled at her.

Historical Note

The Apothecary's Daughter took me nearly four years to write and rewrite. During that time my characters became as familiar to me as those of my own family and it became a wrench to leave them behind. So I didn't. I decided to write about Beth, Susannah's daughter, when she had grown up.

I began to research historical events some twenty or so years after the Great Fire at the end of *The Apothecary's Daughter* and discovered the Glorious Revolution of 1688. This important event had passed me by since it wasn't on my school history curriculum and I had only the vaguest idea of what had happened. In a nutshell, once Parliamentarian Oliver Cromwell died and his son was discovered to be a disappointing successor, Charles II had been brought back to England to resume the monarchy. This was all well and good but Britain was now strongly Anglican and Charles was tainted with Catholicism. He and his brother James had been brought up in France by their French Catholic mother.

The population of Britain was rabidly opposed to a Catholic ruler and feared that Charles's links with his cousin, Louis XIV of France, would lead to a similar despotic reign in Britain and the quashing of the Church of England. Charles, mindful perhaps of his father's execution, chose to keep a low profile as far as religion was concerned. When he died in 1685 he left many children but not one legitimate heir and so, with extreme reluctance, the country accepted his fervently Catholic brother, James, onto the throne.

James had two daughters, Mary and Anne by his first wife, Anne Hyde, who died whilst the sisters were still young. James's second wife was Mary of Modena, a Catholic princess, who appeared to be barren, to the relief of the population and the established church. Charles had insisted his nieces were brought up in the Anglican faith and passed them into the spiritual care of Bishop Henry Compton. Mary was groomed to be James's Anglican heir to the throne and Bishop Compton married her to her Dutch Protestant cousin, William, Prince of Orange. This gave comfort to the country and the church leaders that it was only a matter of time before Mary would come to the throne and all the uncertainties of Catholic interference would disappear.

The cat was set amongst the pigeons when Mary of Modena became pregnant and produced a son, a Catholic heir to the throne. The historical events portrayed in *The Painter's Apprentice* are all based upon fact with Beth's story woven carefully around them. I have allowed my imagination to run away with me with regard to Beth's friendship with Princess Anne but some of the Princess's character traits and comments are taken directly from historical sources. She suffered twelve miscarriages and stillbirths. Of five babies born alive, none survived beyond eleven years of age. It is known that she often went to stay with friends in the country to recover from these sad events and if Merryfields had existed she would certainly have found solace there.

Henry Marshal, painter, horticulturalist and entomologist, lived at Fulham Palace for many years as the guest of Bishop Compton. His *Florilegium* of flower 'portraits' is now lodged in the Royal Library. In my story, Beth slips into Marshal's studio at Fulham Palace after his death. This placed her close to Bishop Compton, who was one of the instigators of The Glorious Revolution.

Bishop Henry Compton's character in the story is as close to the truth as I could make it. He was a soldier before he came to the church but above all, he was a gardener and plant collector. A visitor to Fulham Palace can still detect his influence in the grounds.

The critical turning point in the Revolution was Princess Anne's escape in the night from her apartment at Whitehall. Bishop Compton and George London, the Palace gardener, did take the Princess and her companion, Sarah Churchill, by coach through the night to join the Prince of Orange's troops at Nottingham, *with another servant*. Again, my imagination allowed me to weave Beth's story around the facts and suppose her to be that servant. Once Princess Anne and her sister Mary had demonstrated their allegiance to William of Orange, everything fell apart for James. His pitiful cry of *'God help me, my very children have forsaken me!'* echoes down through the centuries. His only thought then was to flee the country with his wife and baby son since he was convinced he would be executed like his father before him.

Princess Anne became Queen in 1702 following the death of her sister, Mary, and later, William of Orange.

Acknowledgements

I read a great number of books whilst researching *The Painter's Apprentice* but some of the most useful in understanding the Glorious Revolution were:

Monarchy by David Starkey

1688 The First Modern Revolution by Steve Pincus

The Glorious Revolution: 1688: Britain's fight for Liberty by Edward Vallance

The beauty of Alexander Marshal's botanical paintings can be seen in *Mr Marshal's Flower Book*, Royal Collection Publications.

Miranda Poliakof, Curator of the museum at Fulham Palace, answered my queries and sent me photocopies of plans and information relating to Fulham Palace at that time.

My grateful thanks to Lucy Icke, who calmly wielded a red-hot editing pen, Sian Wilson for the gorgeous cover, Madeleine Feeney and Andrew Hally for getting the book out there, my family and friends for listening to me and to WordWatchers for encouragement and cake.

*Turn the page
for a sneak peek at
The Apothecary's Daughter*

Chapter 1

Inside the apothecary shop Susannah stood by the light of the window, daydreaming and grinding flowers of sulphur into a malodorous dust as she watched the world go by. Fleet Street, as always, was as busy as an anthill. The morning's snow was already dusted with soot from the noxious cloud blown in from the kilns at Limehouse and the frost made icebergs of the surging effluent in the central drain. Church bells clanged and dogs barked while a ceaseless stream of people flowed past.

Thwack! A snowball smashed against the window pane. Susannah gasped and dropped the pestle, shocked out of her lazy contemplation. Outside, a street urchin laughed at her through the glass.

'Little demon!' Her heart still hammering, she raised a fist at him. She watched him darting away through the horde until her eye was drawn by the tall figure of a man in a sombre hat and cloak picking his way over the snow.

Something about the way he moved amongst the hubbub of the crowd, like a wolf slipping silently through the forest, captured her curiosity. As he drew closer Susannah recognised him as a physician, one of her father's less frequent customers. Stepping around a steaming heap of horse droppings and a discarded cabbage, it became apparent that he was making his way towards the shop.

Susannah pulled open the door. 'Good morning,' she said, shivering in the icy draught that followed him.

He touched his hat but didn't return her smile. 'Is Mr Leyton here?'

'Not at present. May I help?'

'I hardly think that you ...'

She suppressed her irritation with a sigh. Why did he assume she was incapable, simply because she wore skirts? 'Do, please, tell me what you require, sir.'

'What I require is to discuss my requirements with your father.'

The man's tone tempted Susannah to make a sharp retort but she reined in a flash of temper and merely said, 'He's gone to read the parson's urine.'

The doctor's dark eyebrows drew together in a frown as he took off his gloves and rubbed the warmth back into his hands. 'This is a matter of urgency. Please tell him Dr Ambrose came by and ask him to call on me when he returns.'

'May I tell him what it is you wish to discuss?'

Dr Ambrose hesitated and then shrugged. 'I have a patient who suffers from a stone in the bladder. Leyton mentioned to me that he'd had some success with his own prescription in cases of this kind. The patient's state of health is not so strong that I can recommend cutting for the stone since he has a chronic shortness of breath. Can you remember all that?'

'Oh, I should think so.' Susannah smiled sweetly and vigorously stirred up the ground sulphur with the pestle until it floated in a choking cloud between them. 'Father usually recommends spirits of sweet nitre for a stone, mixed with laudanum and oil of juniper. Your patient should sip a teaspoonful in a cup of linseed tea sweetened with honey.'

Dr Ambrose coughed and pressed a handkerchief to his nose. 'You are sure of this?'

'Of course. And you might try milk of gum ammoniac stirred with syrup of squills for the wheezing in the chest.'

Dr Ambrose raised his eyebrows and Susannah did her best not to look smug. 'Perhaps you would like to warm yourself by the fire while I prepare the medicines for you?' she said.

'Do you know the correct proportions?'

'I am perfectly used to dispensing my father's prescriptions.'

She retired to the dispensary, a curtained-off alcove at the rear of the shop, and peeped through the gap in the curtains while he, apparently thinking he was unobserved, lifted his cloak and warmed his backside by the fire. Stifling a laugh, she turned to the bench and set to work. As she bottled up the last prescription the shop bell jingled. She pulled aside the curtain to see an elegantly dressed lady enter.

'Please, take a seat by the fire and I will help you in just a moment,' Susannah said.

She handed the two bottles of medicine to Dr Ambrose and, in the interests of repeat business, made the effort to be civil. 'I hope you are warmer now?' She wondered whether to tell him he had a sulphurous streak across his nose but decided against it. 'They say this bitter wind comes from Russia, which is why the frost has barely lifted since December.'

'Perhaps that's as well,' the doctor said. 'The cold moderates the severity of the plague.'

'Except in the parish of St Giles, of course. We must pray that the freeze destroys the pestilence.'

'Indeed. Put the prescriptions on my account.' He nodded and left.

Susannah, wondering if he'd been sucking lemons, watched him set off again down Fleet Street. What a shame his darkly handsome face wasn't matched by more pleasing manners!

The other customer was a fair-haired woman of about Susannah's own age and dressed very finely in a fur-tipped cloak with a crimson

skirt just visible beneath. She stood on tiptoe, examining the pre-
served crocodile which hung from one of the ceiling beams. Her
small nose wrinkled with distaste. 'Is it real?'

'Certainly! It came from Africa. My father bought it from a sailor.'
Susannah still remembered her mixed fear and fascination when
he'd brought it home many years before. She had tentatively
touched its hard, scaly body with the tip of her finger, shuddering as
it stared back at her with beady glass eyes. Her younger brother,
Tom, had hidden behind the counter until their mother assured him
the creature wasn't alive.

'This is Mr Leyton's apothecary's shop, at the sign of the Unicorn
and the Dragon?'

'As you see, the sign hangs over the door.'

'Is Mr Leyton here?'

'Not at present. May I help you?'

Pursing her lips, she looked Susannah up and down. 'I would
like ...' She glanced around at the bottles and jars that lined the
walls, frowning a little. 'Yes. A bottle of rosewater will do very well.
Tell me,' she said, running her gloved finger along the counter, 'how
many hearths do you have in this building?'

'Why, we have three bedchambers, the parlour and the dining
room and then there is the shop, dispensary and kitchen,' stammered Susannah, taken aback.

'The house is narrow and crooked with age.'

'But it is also deep.' Susannah stood up very straight, a flare of
temper bringing warmth to her face. 'And the parlour is panelled and
we have a good yard.'

The woman sighed. 'I suppose it is well enough.' She put a handful of coins on the counter, picked up the rosewater and waited until
Susannah snatched open the shop door for her.

Relieved to be rid of the woman with her prying questions,
Susannah stood shivering in the open doorway for a moment, glancing up the snowy street beyond the waiting sedan chair. She saw

Ned, the apprentice, hurtling along towards the shop, returning from delivering a packet of liver pills to the Misses Lane. His head was down against the bitter wind and she realised that he was on course to collide with the departing customer.

'Ned, look out!' she called.

At the last second he swerved, narrowly avoiding barrelling into the lady as she climbed into her sedan chair.

She gave Susannah an accusing look, put her nose in the air and motioned for the chair to leave.

'Take more care, Ned!' snapped Susannah.

He banged the door behind them and hurried to the fire to warm his hands and stamp the feeling back into his feet.

'For goodness' sake!' Susannah's repressed irritation with both her recent customers made her voice sharp. 'Fetch the broom and clear up all that ice from your boots before it turns into puddles.'

'Sorry, miss.'

'And then you can dust the gallypots.'

'Yes, miss.' He blew on his fingers, collected the broom from the dispensary and began to sweep the floor.

Susannah relented. Sometimes Ned put her in mind of her brother, Tom, now living far away in Virginia. She reached a large stone jar down from the shelf, scooped out a spoonful of the sticky substance from inside and smeared it onto a piece of brown paper. 'Here!' she said, handing him the salve. 'Rub this on your chilblains and it will stop the skin from breaking. And don't forget to dust the gallypots!' She retrieved the sulphurous pestle and mortar from the counter and carried it in to the dispensary to mix up an ointment for pimples.

She had lived in the apothecary shop for all of her twenty-six years and it held her most precious memories. As she measured ingredients and mixed the ointment she hummed to herself as she remembered how, when they were children, she and Tom had learned to add up by counting out pills. She recalled experimenting with the weighing beam, fascinated that a huge bunch of dried sage weighed exactly the same as a tiny piece of lead. In the big stone mortar, the same one she was using now, she'd made gloriously sticky mixtures of hog's lard combined with white lead and turpentine as a salve for burns. She'd learned to read by studying the letters, in Latin, painted on the gallypots which lined the walls and then to write by tracing her father's exquisite handwriting on the labels fixed to the banks of wooden storage drawers.

Now she busied herself setting a batch of rosemary and honey linctus to boil, sniffing at its sweet, resinous scent. Cold weather and London's putrid fog was excellent for business since most of the customers had a perpetual winter cough. Licking honey off her thumb, she glanced through the gap between the dispensary curtains to see Ned lying over the counter, teasing the cat with a trailing piece of rag. Suddenly he slid back to the ground and with meticulous care began to dust the majolica jars. Susannah guessed from this that he'd glimpsed his master returning.

Cornelius Leyton struggled through the door with a large box, which he placed on the counter between a cone of sugar and the jar of leeches. The frost had nipped his nose cherry red.

'What have you bought, Father?'

Taking his time, he began to untie the string.

'Let me!' she said, snatching a knife from under the counter and slicing through the knot.

'Always so impatient, Susannah!' Carefully, Cornelius lifted the lid.

Susannah caught a glimpse of dark fur and gasped. Was it a puppy? But then, as her father lifted aside the tissue paper, she realised with disappointment that she was mistaken.

Cornelius gathered up the wig and shook out its long and lustrous black curls. 'What do you think?' he asked.

'It's ... magnificent. Put it on!'

Eyes gleaming with anticipation, he snatched off his usual wig, a modest mid-brown affair that he'd had for a number of years, to expose his own cropped grey hair. Then, reverentially, he placed the new wig over the top.

Susannah stared at him.

'Susannah?'

Speechless, she continued to stare. Her father was fine-looking; tall, with dark eyes and an air of authority, but she had never thought of him as a vain man. In fact, she'd always had to chivvy him into buying a new coat or breeches and his hat was embarrassingly old-fashioned. But this wig was an entirely different affair. It turned him into an elegant stranger and it made her uneasy.

'Well?' His expression was anxious.

'Astonishing,' she said, at last. She lifted up one of the silky curls which fell near enough to his waist. 'It's very handsome.' She fumbled for words. 'I hardly recognise you. It makes you seem so ... young.'

A quickly suppressed smile flitted across his face.

Ned said, 'You look exactly like the King, sir.'

Cornelius threw his apprentice a sharp look. 'You have time for idle chatter, Ned? Shall I find you something to do? The copper still in the yard must be scrubbed. Of course the ice must be scraped off it first ...'

Ned hastily returned to his dusting. 'I was talking to my old friend, Richard Berry,' continued Cornelius, with an amused glance to Susannah, 'and he said a more fashionable appearance will be good for business. Perhaps I should have a new hat, too?'

'I've been suggesting that for months!'

'Have you?'

'Father!'

'I have some visits to make. Did you brush my blue coat?'

'Of course.'

'Then if there's nothing that needs my attention here ...?'

'Oh! I forgot. Dr Ambrose asked you to call on him to discuss a patient of his with a kidney stone. I prepared the prescriptions for him.'

'Good, good.' Cornelius picked up his old wig and went upstairs.

Susannah stared after him. What on earth had inspired him to suddenly start taking an interest in his appearance? Shaking her head, she returned to the dispensary to pot up the sulphur ointment. As always, spooning that particular mixture into jars evoked the familiar recollection of an afternoon eleven years before when she'd helped her mother to do the same thing. Her mother's gentle voice was imprinted on Susannah's memory and she could recall, as if it were yesterday, how her hand had rested tenderly upon the swell of her belly. That was two days before she died and there had been the same sulphurous reek in the air then, mixed with the usual aromas of rosewater and beeswax, liquorice and oil of wormwood, turpentine and drying herbs. Those were the scents of her father's trade and they ran in Susannah's blood.

The shop bell jolted her back to the present and she was pleased to hear Martha's voice. Until her marriage Martha had lived in a neighbouring house and been her closest friend for twenty years, despite her Puritan leanings. Pulling back the curtain, Susannah went to greet her.

Martha, as neat as always in a starched apron and with her dark hair tucked firmly into her cap, recoiled as they kissed. 'Ugh! What is it this time?'

'Nothing dangerous! Merely complexion ointment.'

'It certainly smells dreadful enough to frighten pimples away.' Martha turned bone white and held her slim fingers over her mouth while she swallowed convulsively.

'It's not that dreadful, surely?'

Martha smiled faintly. 'The slightest thing turns my stomach, at the moment,' she said pressing her hands to her apron. 'I came to ask for some of that ginger cordial you made for me last time . . .'

'Last time? Oh Martha! Not another one? Little Alys isn't even weaned.'

'I know.' Martha sighed, the shadows under her hazel eyes dark against her pale face. 'I did warn Robert that if he insisted Alys went to a wet nurse it was likely I'd fall again but you know how stubborn men can be.'

'Stubborn and peculiar,' Susannah added, thinking of her father's latest purchase. She pulled the joint stool from under the counter and stretched up to the top shelf for the ginger cordial, then decanted some of the golden liquid into a bottle and stopped it with a cork.

The narrow door to the staircase creaked open and Cornelius appeared, wearing the new acquisition and his best blue coat. He showed more lace than usual at his throat and new blue ribands on his shoes. The air around him carried the distinct aroma of lavender water and self-conscious pride.

'Martha. Are you keeping well?'

Martha's freckled face turned from white to red as she bobbed a curtsy. 'Mr Leyton. Thank you, I am very well.'

Cornelius's eyes flickered to the bottle of cordial and then to Martha's waist. 'And all your little ones?'

'Well, too.'

'Good, good. I shall not detain you.' He picked up his cane with the silver head. 'Susannah, do not wait up for me; I shall not be home for supper.' He launched himself into the hurly burly of Fleet Street, raising his cane to attract a passing hackney carriage.

Martha stared at her friend with wide eyes. 'Your father looks so different. I never realised before what a handsome man he is.'

After Martha had left, Susannah began to wonder where her father had gone, all dressed up in such finery.